I0677666

Not So Heroes

GERALD C. ANDERSON, SR.

Lyfe Publishing
Publishers Since 2012
Published by Lyfe Publishing LLC
Lyfe Publishing, 10800 Nautica Place, White Plains MD 20695

Library of Congress Cataloging in Publications Data
Anderson, Gerald C. Sr.

    Not So Heroes / Gerald C. Anderson, Sr.
    ISBN: 978-1-957333-31-1
    Thomas Wayne Walker (Fictitious Character)-
Fiction
        1.   Washington DC–Fiction
        2.   Not So Heroes–Fiction
Printed in the United States of America
1 2 3 4 5 6 7 8 9 10
Book design by Olivia Pro Designs and Aionios
Designs

DEDICATION

Also, By Gerald C. Anderson, Sr.

We Come in Peace
27 Hours
Standing Firm
Secrets
The Last Song
The Lawyer
Saved
The Room
Are You Innocent?
Weight Loss
Warlord
The Last Honorable Man
The Dream
The Death Knights
The Ride Along
Twins
Creative Inspirations
Fatal Misperceptions
Love & Lust
Actions Have Consequences
Building Conversations with God
The Compendium (The Complete Series)
Let It Raine
Love & Faith
Let Everything That Hath Breath

ACKNOWLEDGMENTS

THANK YOU FOR YOUR SUPPORT WITH "NOT SO HEROES"

Dr. Vanessa R. Anderson
Beryl A. Brackett
Avis Dillard-Bullock
Danny Sells

Prologue

Before Christ, in the ancient land of Mesopotamia, millions lived their lives interwoven with the worship of mythical gods. These deities, born from stories shared across distant lands, were adopted by the Mesopotamians, their names changed, their forms adapted to fit the local beliefs.

One day, an extraordinary sight disrupted the ordinary rhythm of life: a colossal, cylindrical ship descended from the heavens, landing amidst the towering mountains. Astonished, the people flocked to witness this marvel, never before having seen anything beyond birds soaring through the sky.

As the ship's doors slowly creaked open, several beings emerged, surveying the Mesopotamians with disdain. A man, their leader, stepped forward and declared, "I am Zeus, and this is my son Cain. We are all your gods! From this day forth, you shall bow down and worship us!"

Fear-stricken, the people fell to their knees, offering prayers to Zeus and his companions. Zeus, amused, reveled in the adoration. His head flowed back, and he absorbed the worship.

A century later, a rebellion arose. Not all accepted the rule of these celestial beings. The

Assyrians, a powerful and independent people, were the most vocal dissenters.

The Assyrian Empire flourished, becoming one of the largest in history. Yet, its downfall was attributed to the immense burden of maintaining such a vast domain. Despite its demise, the Assyrians left a lasting legacy: their innovative warfare tactics and advanced technologies were adopted by civilizations across the region.

Legend has it that the Assyrians, in their defiance, engaged in skirmishes with the gods. Possessing technology far surpassing that of their contemporaries, it was believed they acquired it through clandestine means – either stolen from the gods themselves, or gifted by a benevolent deity who later vanished. Some whispered of a god who, in a secret pact, provided the Assyrians with the means to construct ships for interstellar travel. The truth, however, remained shrouded in mystery.

When it became clear that the Assyrians could not defeat the gods, they embarked on a desperate voyage, their ships venturing into the vast expanse of the universe. Recognizing the futility of competing against the god's superior technology, they embarked on a generational journey, seeking a new home where they would no longer be subject to divine tyranny.

A decade later, the people of Earth stopped worshipping the gods. It was believed that their decreased worship caused the gods to lose power. The gods departed Earth aboard their magnificent vessel. The story of the people, the Assyrians, and their struggle against the celestial beings was meticulously recorded and then concealed, hidden from the eyes of the world. The truth, that aliens had

once walked among them, was to remain buried,
awaiting a time when it might be needed once more.

1 – Caught Off Guard

Present Day

The familiar Southwinds community was Thomas Wayne Walker's usual delivery route. He knew many residents by name, even considered some friends. Today's delivery was to Cordell Brown, a frequent customer – always ordering something.

As Thomas Wayne approached the porch, the door swung open, revealing Cordell with a wide grin. "What's up, boy?" Cordell greeted him.

Thomas Wayne chuckled, "Cordell Brown, you order more stuff than anyone I know, man."

"Hey brother, gotta stay busy," Cordell replied. "We're heading to Annapolis tomorrow morning. Let them know black lives still matter. Seems like they might have forgotten."

Thomas Wayne nodded, "Yeah, about that brother who was killed by the police last week. That's why you're going, huh?"

"Absolutely. We need to make our voices heard."

"Well, Cordell, my brother, you're the man for the job."

"Appreciate it. This box here? Supplies for the protest. My team's on their way."

"Stay safe, brother," Thomas Wayne said as he returned to his truck.

An unusual sight drew his attention. Many residents stood outside, gazing upwards. It wasn't the weather; the day was bright and sunny. He approached a woman watching the sky. "Hey, what's everyone looking at?"

"Something in the sky," she replied. "NASA doesn't know what it is. Supposed to be visible soon."

Thomas Wayne watched, a sense of unease creeping in. It reminded him of his Army days, the tense anticipation before the Iranian attack. A familiar dread, the same he felt when his friends and family were deployed, stirred within him. The memory of his brother, lost alone on that battlefield, was a haunting specter.

He was startled by a tap on his shoulder. "Hey brother, you see anything yet?"

"No, man, not yet. Seems like the whole neighborhood's out here now."

"Yeah, most of these folks don't even know me," Cordell remarked. "Think I'm too much of an 'in-your-face' activist. Probably seen me on the news and didn't like what they saw."

"You're fighting for what's right," Thomas Wayne said. "They need to understand that."

Cordell shook his head. "Exactly. We don't want more than anyone else, just equality."

Suddenly, Cordell pointed upwards. "Look!"

Thomas Wayne followed his gaze, his breath catching. Massive objects, blotting out the sun, descended from the heavens. A chilling darkness enveloped the land as the ships positioned themselves ominously over Washington D.C. and the surrounding region, others dispersing across the globe.

"I think your march might be the least of our worries now," Thomas Wayne said gravely. "I need to get to my family."

"Calling my girlfriend," Cordell said, pulling out his phone. "No signal. Those ships must be jamming everything." Thomas Wayne tried his own phone, to no avail. "No signal for me either," he confirmed, his eyes glued to the terrifying spectacle. "I'm out of here, Cordell. Be safe."

"You too, brother."

Thomas Wayne turned to leave, but before he could start his truck, a blinding beam of light erupted from the nearest ship, striking the ground with earth-shattering force. The blast threw him to the ground, along with the rest of the stunned onlookers. He scrambled to his feet, helping those nearest to him. "Cordell, we need to get these people to safety!"

"Roger that," Cordell replied, his face grim.

The ground trembled as more beams of light rained down, unleashing a terrifying barrage upon the helpless populace.

The ground shook violently, throwing Thomas Wayne to the ground again. Dust and debris rained down as the initial shockwave subsided. He scrambled to his feet, a primal fear gripping him. Around him, neighbors lay strewn across the lawns, groaning in pain, some not moving, likely dead. He rushed to help, his mind racing.

Cordell, his face grim, appeared beside him. "We need to get them below ground," he shouted.

Thomas Wayne nodded, his eyes darting around the devastated neighborhood. "Agreed. We need to move fast."

Cordell added, "I know a great place. Follow me."

They began to assist the injured, their fear momentarily overshadowed by the urgency of the situation. As they helped the injured, they exchanged worried glances. The ships remained suspended in the sky, an ominous presence casting long, dark shadows across the terrified community.

The world, as they knew it, had irrevocably changed.

2 - The Onslaught Begins

The attack raged throughout the night, a relentless barrage of fire raining down from the sky. Thomas Wayne and Cordell, working together, managed to guide a terrified group of survivors to an underground shelter – a hidden refuge Cordell previously prepared in case of police raids. Below ground, the air was thick with the stench of fear and the lingering echo of explosions. Thomas Wayne, his ears still ringing, could barely suppress the panic rising within him. He desperately searched for any news of his baby sister, his mind consumed by the terrifying unknown.

He slid against the damp wall, the faces of the huddled survivors mirroring his own despair. Their eyes, wide with terror, spoke volumes about the horror they witnessed. Cordell joined him, their shared look of despair a silent acknowledgment of the grim reality. "I don't think we're going to make it, man," Thomas Wayne confessed, his voice rough with fear.

"I've known you only through deliveries," Cordell replied, "but something tells me you're the one to lead us. Pull yourself together, Thomas Wayne. We need you."

Cordell's words, though blunt, struck a chord. Thomas Wayne knew he was right. His military training, though dormant, offered a glimmer of hope in this desperate situation. These terrified civilians were untrained, unprepared for this apocalyptic scenario. He witnessed the horrors of war firsthand, the chaos, the loss, the sheer brutality of it all. But could he, a delivery driver, truly lead them against an unknown, extraterrestrial threat?

He surveyed the crowd, his gaze drawn to the disproportionate number of women and children. "How can I do this?" he muttered to himself. "But it's not about 'if' anymore, it's about 'how'." Humanity faced impossible odds before and overcame them. They could, no, they *must* do it again.

He forced himself to stand tall, plastering a reassuring smile on his face. These people needed a leader, a beacon of hope in this abyss of despair. He needed to be that beacon. A young woman approached him, her clothes torn, her face streaked with grime. "Are you okay?" Thomas Wayne asked gently.

"I am now," she replied, her voice trembling mixed with toughness. "I escaped the bombing, and then... there was a rape gang."

"A rape gang? We're being attacked by aliens?" Thomas Wayne exclaimed, incredulously.

She nodded, a grim smile playing on her lips. "You wouldn't believe it. You'd think they'd have more important things to worry about."

"You took them out?" Thomas Wayne asked, surprised.

"Yeah, I made them pay for trying to take something that wasn't theirs," she said, her voice hardening. "I was in the Army for four years. After that, I joined the reserves to stay proficient. That rape gang... they won't be coming after me again."

"You were in the Army?" Thomas Wayne asked, a flicker of respect in his eyes. "I was enlisted as well."

"Roger that," she replied, a hint of a salute in her gesture.

Thomas Wayne patted her shoulder. "We can use your skills, soldier."

He moved on, encountering Cordell who was already rallying a small group of men. "Here's the man who will lead us," Cordell announced, a note of genuine respect in his voice.

"Listen up," Thomas Wayne began, his voice firm. "This won't be easy. I'm hearing reports of rape gangs already taking advantage of the chaos. It's a disgrace. We should be united against this alien threat, not turning on each other. This country... no, this world needs men and women dedicated to survival. Are you all with me?"

The men nodded in agreement. Cordell patted Thomas Wayne on the shoulder, his eyes filled with a newfound respect and joy. "You've got this, man," he said, his voice low and reassuring.

Thomas Wayne felt a surge of responsibility. Leadership had been thrust upon him, and he wouldn't let them down. He needed to formulate a plan to organize these disparate individuals into a fighting force. But first, there was another threat to deal with.

A loud crash echoed through the tunnel, followed by the snickers of three men. Thomas Wayne's blood ran cold. This confrontation wouldn't be with aliens; it would be with the very humans he was trying to protect.

"What's going on here?" Thomas Wayne demanded, his voice firm but controlled.

One of the men stepped forward, a sneer playing on his lips. "Are you the boss?"

Gloria, standing beside Thomas Wayne, scoffed. "These are the idiots I told you about. They must have followed me here."

Thomas Wayne sighed. "We have enough to worry about with the alien invasion. We don't need this internal conflict."

The man, seemingly the leader of the group, pulled out a pistol. "All we want is the girl. Give her to us and there won't be any trouble."

"That's not happening," Thomas Wayne stated, his voice unwavering. "Not now, not ever."

The man's eyes narrowed. "I'm asking politely. Give her to us, or I'm going to start shooting people, you first."

"No," Thomas Wayne replied, his voice echoing through the tunnel. If anyone doubted his leadership before, their doubts were surely erased now.

A relentless barrage of fire rained down from above, momentarily blinding the assailants with dust and debris. The would-be assailant, startled by the explosion, hesitated. Seizing the opportunity, Thomas Wayne launched a swift counterattack. With Cordell's assistance, the other two men were quickly subdued.

A fierce struggle ensued as Thomas Wayne grappled with the leader, neither gaining an upper hand. *"I can't let him win this,"* he thought, his adrenaline surging. He wrestled the gun from the man's grasp, then delivered a series of calculated strikes, rendering him defenseless.

"We're in this together," Thomas Wayne declared, his voice firm, "as human beings. No one has time for this. We need to focus on the real threat – the invaders. Are you with me?"

The men, subdued and shaken, exchanged hesitant glances.

"You really think we got a chance against an armada of ships from outer space?" the leader mumbled, still dazed. "You're crazy." He turned to his men. "Let's get out of here. These people are insane." He glared at Gloria. "Don't be alone anywhere. I'll have my revenge."

The men slunk away, disappearing out of the tunnel.

Gloria turned to Thomas Wayne. "Are you alright?" she asked, concern etched on her face.

"I am," he replied, his gaze sweeping across the faces of the terrified survivors. "I guess this makes me... the leader."

An unexpected weight of responsibility settled upon him. He never envisioned himself in this role. "Listen," he began, his voice calm and resolute, "we need to work together. Many of you don't have combat experience. But we need your skills – doctors, nurses, cooks, farmers, everyone has a role to play.

"The bombing won't last forever. They will send ground troops in an effort to eliminate the survivors of the bombing. But we won't go down without a fight. We will defend our home. If you're with me, stay here. If not, you're free to go."

Cordell stepped forward, his voice echoing through the tunnel. "I'm with you, boss."

A wave of relief washed over Thomas Wayne. He knew he could count on Cordell.

He scanned the faces of the survivors, searching for signs of resolve. Slowly, tentatively, nods of agreement began to appear. He smiled, a genuine smile, the first he'd managed since the attack began.

"Good," he said, his voice firm. "Now, let's figure out how to survive this."

The Second Day

Thomas Wayne woke abruptly, glancing at his watch. "Two hours is better than nothing, I guess," he muttered to himself, the distant thud of bombs still reverberating through the underground refuge. The explosions were a constant presence, sometimes sounding far off, other times rattling the very ground beneath them.

Gloria approached him, a determined look on her face. "Good morning, Thomas Wayne."

"Good morning, Gloria. Any updates?"

"Nothing new, except we desperately need food. I've put together a strike team to go topside and see if we can salvage anything. We can't afford to be starving."

"You're right," Thomas conceded, "but I don't want you to lead it. It's too dangerous."

Gloria scoffed, "You can't hold me back because of those idiots. I can hold my own. I did when I was by myself; this time, I'll have a team."

Thomas Wayne met her gaze, a flicker of admiration in his eyes. She must have been formidable in the army. "Okay, Gloria. Take your team and try to find some food. Have you seen Cordell?"

"He's set up guards to ensure no one else gets into the tunnel. At least, no one like the idiots who were after me."

"Great. I'll go chat with him. Thanks, Gloria." Thomas Wayne headed toward the main entrance, hoping to find Cordell there. He spotted him with another man Thomas had come to know as Greg Aiken. Greg was a big man, and Thomas liked having him on the team. Size could be an advantage if they needed to fight the aliens hand-to-hand. Thomas wondered what the aliens even looked like, hidden as they were in their spaceships. *One day, I'll get a chance to see them up close and personal,* he thought, *I just hope they bleed like we do.*

He extended a hand to Cordell and Greg. "What's up, fellas?"

Cordell shrugged. "Nothing new, just waiting for the bombing to end."

Greg added, "You'd think they would have softened us up by now."

"Maybe we're fighting back," Thomas replied. "Who knows what the government is throwing at them in the larger cities."

"You got that right, bro. The government has been hiding stuff for years," Cordell responded.

Thomas Wayne chuckled. "You're a mess, man." It felt good to laugh, even in the midst of such strife. He didn't know how this would all turn out, but most of them were sticking together, and that's what mattered. "Cordell, we need weapons. Any thoughts?"

Cordell exchanged a glance with Greg. "Yeah, I have some thoughts on that."

Thomas Wayne looked from Cordell to Greg and back again, realizing the two knew something he didn't. "So... let me in on the secret."

Cordell clapped a hand on Thomas Wayne's shoulder. "Brother, let's just say we got you covered. People talked about me being an activist and all, but I was prepared for a race riot. I just didn't know the races would be human and alien. We have some weapons, you can bet on that."

"That's great, Cordell!"

"After this bombing, we'll take some guys and go load up."

"Are you sure they haven't been blown up?"

"We prepared for that too, brother. They're safe. If we can survive in this sewer tunnel, those weapons definitely survived."

Thomas Wayne didn't know the details, and at this point, he didn't care to know. As long as they had weapons to defend themselves, it was all good. He nodded to the men and rushed back inside the tunnel to see if he could help anyone else.

As he moved through the crowded tunnel, a woman approached him. She was strikingly pretty. *Wow, where did she come from?* The woman stopped in front of him and sighed.

"What's the problem?" Thomas asked.

"I got in last night, and I want to help the resistance. They said I need to talk to you first."

"Well, who are you and what service are you looking to provide?"

"My name is Elaine Byrd, and I'm a nurse. I can set up a triage area in this tunnel, but I apparently need permission from you."

"These people are looking to me for all the answers. You can understand their shock after this started yesterday. Give them a break."

"I am giving them a break. I just want to get started. I have a feeling we'll need it, and it's not good to wait until then."

"Doctor Byrd, you have my permission."

"I'm a nurse, remember?"

"Yesterday, I was a UPS driver. You're a doctor today. Thanks. Let me know if you need anything." Elaine gave him a thumbs up and headed off. Thomas Wayne continued to wander around, making himself available to anyone who might need him.

A burst of gunfire from the main entrance made Thomas Wayne turn sharply. He raced toward the front, encouraging others to take cover. When he arrived, Gloria and her team were scrambling into the sewer, with Greg providing cover fire. "What happened?" Thomas demanded.

"We were attacked by people who wanted our food."

"I was afraid this would happen," Thomas replied.

"We tried to tell them to come with us, but they didn't want to hear it. The first thing you need to do is unite the people."

"When the bombing stops, we will have several initiatives to start."

Gloria let out a deep breath. "It's slowing down in our area. We could only find one store that was partially hit. We grabbed everything we could. There was a gun store next to it, so we grabbed a few guns too, but it's nowhere near the amount we're going to need."

"I think we have that covered." Thomas noticed one man was injured. "Hey, see Dr. Byrd about that. She's set up in the tunnel about 100 yards from here."

The man nodded, and Gloria's eyebrows rose. "A doctor? When did we get him?"

"Her... she came in last night. She's a nurse, but I promoted her to doctor."

"Wow, you got the juice now."

"Hey, command decision. Can you get this food somewhere and start getting people fed? I think there's a guy setting up that area."

"I got you, boss."

Thomas Wayne chuckled. "Oh yes, that area will need a guard. When people get hungry, they change."

Gloria turned to another man. "Ralph, can you guard the food? I'll get you a relief." Ralph acknowledged her and followed the food to the designated dining area. "So, you need an executive officer to handle these decisions."

"Are you asking for that job?"

"No, heck no. I'm a front-line woman. I came to fight. I'm just saying, someone needs to handle that stuff so you can focus on the fighting."

"Understood. I'll see who's qualified. You've got a good military background; maybe there's someone in the group who's good at administrative things."

Thomas Wayne continued, his thoughts already drifting to the injured man. He wanted to see if the man got the care he needed for his injury. Their camp didn't have many medical supplies, so Elaine would have to make do. He arrived to find Elaine working quickly with the injured man and several others. *I know we're all business now, but in another life, I would be all over her. She's so beautiful.* "How are we doing here, Doc?"

She glanced at him, then continued her work. "I'm doing the best I can." She sighed. "If we make another run, please consider some medical supplies. We have next to nothing here."

"I will make sure it's on the list. Will he make it?"

"Yes, it's not serious. The bullet passed through, so I'm patching him up. He'll need time to recover," Elaine said, continuing her work.

"Good. We don't know how long this bombing will last, so he can use this time to heal," Thomas Wayne agreed. He then headed towards the food setup and storage. Gloria was right. I needed an executive officer to handle these logistical issues. First, I needed to gather information on everyone's skills and determine the best way to utilize them. When we eventually return to the surface, we need to be a well-organized force, not just a ragtag resistance group.

Thomas Wayne settled into his usual spot in the tunnel, lost in memories of his baby sister. "God, I hope she's safe out there," he murmured. "She's a fighter, just like Gloria. I hope that fighting spirit is keeping her safe."

Cordell joined him. "What's on your mind, brother?"

"Just thinking about my sister," Thomas Wayne admitted. "I need to find her."

"Now's not the time, and I doubt she'd want you to risk it," Cordell said. "Focus on surviving here. Then, we'll find her."

"You're right. I need an executive officer to handle all the administrative tasks. Can we get someone to assess everyone's skills to identify potential candidates?"

"Sure, but most people are already filling roles based on their expertise. We even have a short-order cook who's now our head chef," Cordell pointed out.

"I understand, but an executive officer would be a tremendous help."

"I think I know someone who might be a good fit. Melanie worked in government administration. She might be the right person."

"Thanks, Cordell. Introduce me to her in the morning."

"Will do, boss." Cordell then walked away.

Thomas Wayne leaned back, attempting to rest. He felt that the bombing would soon subside, and he needed to conserve his strength for the inevitable ground battles. "Sis, I know you're out there somewhere. I will find you," he vowed.

He could hear the low rumble of conversation and even laughter echoing through the tunnel. The laughter was a welcome sound. Perhaps they were preparing for the next phase of this war.

The Third Day

The morning sun blazed overhead. Above ground, Thomas Wayne and a small group watched the sky with a mixture of hope and trepidation. The enemy ships still hung menacingly, but the bombing ceased in their immediate area. "I hope this means it's stopped everywhere," Thomas muttered, his voice heavy with uncertainty.

Cordell and Gloria joined him. "We need to find other survivors and organize," Thomas Wayne said. "Ground troops will be here soon."

"We can form small search parties," Cordell suggested. "We'll also prioritize gathering food, water, and medical supplies. Here's the list of skilled individuals Melanie and I compiled. She would be a good executive officer."

"Thanks," Thomas Wayne said. "I'll speak with her. You two, be careful."

Cordell and Gloria departed, leaving Thomas Wayne to navigate the growing crowd within the tunnels. People were gathering their belongings, seemingly oblivious to the impending danger. He spotted Melanie and approached her.

"Cordell suggested you for a leadership role," Thomas Wayne began.

"Oh, he did?" Melanie scoffed. "I thought he hated me."

"He believes you'd be an excellent executive officer."

"For what? The bombing's over. We can go home now."

Frustration simmered beneath the surface. "Everyone, stop!" Thomas Wayne yelled, his voice cutting through the chatter. "This is far from over. A ground assault is imminent. We must prepare to defend ourselves."

"You think those ships are here for a picnic?" Thomas Wayne retorted to a man who questioned his assessment. "They're here to finish the job."

"He's right," Elaine chimed in. "We should listen to him. What do we do boss?"

"Call me Thomas Wayne. We have a list of skills. Let's find other survivors, establish a defense perimeter, and continue gathering supplies. Melanie, I've asked you to be our executive officer. What do you say?"

"Well, since you put me on the spot… sure, I can handle it."

"Excellent. Anyone with military or police experience, follow me."

Thomas Wayne led a small group above ground, the weight of impending doom heavy on his shoulders. This was the beginning of a brutal struggle, a fight for survival against an overwhelming enemy.

Above, the enemy ships remained stationary, a chilling display of their power. Reports came in that they were stationed strategically above major cities and outlining areas.

Survivors began to trickle in, sent by the search parties. "Direct them to Melanie for processing," Thomas Wayne instructed one of his men.

Families approached, their faces etched with fear and grief. The bombing took a devastating toll, and the survivors were haunted by the specter of death. "We will not give up," Thomas Wayne vowed silently. "We will fight for every inch of this ground."

Gloria returned, accompanied by a man in uniform. "Thomas Wayne, this is Senior Airman Baker from Andrews Air Force Base. He barely escaped before the base was destroyed."

"Destroyed? That's not good news."

"No, sir," Airman Baker replied.

Gloria chuckled, "He doesn't like sir or boss for that matter."

"Thomas Wayne will suffice. No military survived?" Thomas Wayne asked.

"There may be some survivors scattered but none of our weapons survived. The Assyrians hit us with everything they have. Now they are sending ground troops into DC and the outskirts of Maryland. It won't be long before they are here." The look on Thomas Wayne's face brought more questions for Airman Baker. "You're wondering how we know who they are."

"Pretty much."

Airman Baker continued, "They contacted the base. I work in Communications, so I heard the transmission. They used to be here thousands of years ago. Now they want their planet back."

"Interesting." Thomas Wayne replied. "I know the civilization basically disappeared in the first century, but no one expected they went to another planet."

Airman Baker said, "This group of Assyrians want to annihilate us."

"We won't allow that," Gloria quipped. "Communications expert. Thomas Wayne we can use that skill."

"There's not much left. They destroyed all our satellites and took out our infrastructure. We are so behind right now," Airman Baker added.

"Then we will have to come up with a solution to communicate with others across the country and the world. Can you help with that?" Thomas Wayne asked.

"I can. Just point me in the right direction."

Thomas Wayne turned to Gloria, "Show the man where he can set up."

"Will do—boss," She smirked trying to get under Thomas Wayne's skin. "Come this way Airman."

Suddenly, a loud crackle filled the air. Below the ships, view screens activated. This was it. The ultimatum.

A human face appeared on the screen. "People of Adamina, or what you now call Earth. I am General Ashur, leader of the Assyrian Army. We have come to reclaim what is rightfully ours. Our Empire spans thirty conquered planets. Yours will be next."

Never. Thomas Wayne vowed silently. He glanced around at the faces of the people, fear and despair etched on their features.

General Ashur continued, "We are a reasonable people. Surrender now, and you will be integrated into the Empire. Resist, and we will eradicate you. Those who surrender will be granted positions of power over those who are captured."

Thomas Wayne stepped forward. "We will not surrender. We will fight for our home, for our very existence."

"You are a fool," a voice boomed. "I was with him in Saudi Arabia. Where was this courage then?"

It was Alex Prime; his face twisted with anger. "He was a conscientious objector! He'll lead you to your deaths."

"I was a different man then," Thomas Wayne countered. "This is different. We're fighting for our world."

"He's a coward!" Alex shouted. "Join me, and you will survive. The Assyrians are powerful. Surrender is the only way."

Many in the crowd defected to Alex's side. Gloria, furious, shouted, "You fools! You'll be remembered as traitors! Those who stand with me, follow me!"

The group splintered. Thomas Wayne looked at Gloria, a flicker of gratitude in his eyes. "Thank you."

"Don't let me down," she warned.

Elaine approached. "Don't let his words get to you. He's blinded by fear. You're a different man now."

"I was supposed to kill a 12-year-old boy with a bomb strapped to him. I couldn't do it. My only option was to claim conscientious objector status."

"You made the right choice. Killing that boy would have haunted you forever. Now, lead us."

Elaine's words were a balm to his soul. He felt a surge of renewed determination. The fight had begun.

Decision Day

The scene unfolded before them: hundreds of people, drawn by the allure of promised riches, boarded the Assyrian ship. Thomas Wayne watched, a knot of unease tightening in his stomach. "I fear for their safety, Cordell," he murmured, "I truly do."

Cordell, his face grim, nodded. "This echoes our own dark history, brother. We were shipped away, enslaved in a foreign land. History repeats itself, and I fear their fate may be even worse."

"You may be right, but if history serves me right we didn't have a choice then. We were sold. These people are volunteering to leave," Thomas Wayne replied.

"Look at you brother. You would have been great in my group."

Thomas Wayne smiled. "We must meet, assess the situation. Gloria, what's our headcount?"

"Approximately 150, with fifty-two soldiers, or close to it," Gloria replied.

"Good. And Melanie?"

"She's doing remarkably well, pulling everything together," Elaine chimed in.

Thomas Wayne sighed. "Gloria, gather the platoon leaders. We need a plan."

"On it," Gloria said, hurrying off with Cordell in tow.

Left alone with Elaine, Thomas Wayne felt a surge of courage. "Dr. Byrd..." he began.

"Elaine," she corrected softly.

"Elaine," he repeated, "I need to tell you something." He waited, his heart pounding. "Before this... this conflict begins, I need to say... I like you very much."

Elaine, to his astonishment, kissed him. The world seemed to melt away, but Gloria's voice shattered the moment.

"Wow, didn't expect that!" she exclaimed, a mischievous glint in her eye.

Thomas Wayne, still reeling from the kiss, managed a smile. "Guess we got sidetracked," he chuckled.

"Indeed," Elaine replied, a playful spark in her eyes. "We'll continue this later."

Thomas Wayne joined the other leaders, a newfound lightness in his step. Gloria, ever observant, couldn't help but grin. "Alright, enough daydreaming," she announced. "Let's get down to business. We'll form ten squads, three platoons, each covering a designated section of the county. We anticipate minimal resistance here, so we'll focus on supporting Prince George's County and D.C., where the Assyrians will likely strike hardest."

"Airman Baker, are we in contact with those areas?" Thomas Wayne inquired.

"Messengers are dispatched," Airman Baker answered. "We must be cautious, however. The Assyrians may be infiltrating our own ranks. We'll keep a close watch on everyone."

"Excellent," Thomas Wayne replied, "Security is paramount. Vet everyone, even our own people. We can't afford any internal threats."

"Understood," Gloria confirmed. "Leaders, you have your assignments. Report any anomalies to Airman Baker. Let's move!"

As the leaders dispersed, Thomas Wayne turned to Melanie. "We need a list of those who boarded the Assyrian ship. Anyone returning could be an enemy spy."

Melanie nodded and hurried off. Cordell approached, a grin splitting his face. "Dude, I'm happy for you. She's a keeper."

"Thanks, man. I hope we can build a life together someday. Any news on my sister?"

"Nothing yet. I'm still searching."

"Thanks, Cordell."

"You're welcome, cuz. I'll leave you to it."

Thomas Wayne felt a wave of anxiety. The weight of responsibility pressed down on him. He had to be strong, decisive. The fate of their resistance movement depended on him. He wondered when the attacks would begin. Here in Charles County, they felt relatively safe, but the city would be a different story.

He received a message from Gloria over the radio. "Thomas Wayne, this is urgent. We're near the front lines, near the Woodrow Wilson Bridge. The Assyrians are landing shuttles, taking our people… traitors!"

"Where are you exactly?" Thomas Wayne asked.

"Just off 495. We can see them. They look… human."

"Understood. We need reinforcements in D.C. and Virginia."

"Roger that."

The war began. Thomas Wayne bowed his head, a silent prayer escaping his lips.

3 The Assault Begins

General Ashur, a celebrated warrior who led the Assyrian Empire in conquering twenty planets, surveyed his latest acquisition: Earth. He envisioned it as a crowning jewel, a testament to his military prowess.

"Sambath," he commanded, "report."

"The human collaborators are being gathered, sir," Sambath replied.

"Excellent. Select a few to govern their people. The rest will be sent to the mines of Assyria."

Sambath saluted and departed. Ashur's thoughts turned to his wife, his beloved. "I miss you, my love," he murmured, gazing at the distant stars. "Soon, this campaign will be over. We will conquer these Terrans, and then I will return to you, forever. This will be my last. I will retire to headquarters, never to see another battlefield. I do this for you, for your name means 'a lovely woman,' and I yearn to be with you eternally."

"Sir, the selections are complete. Shall we address those bound for the mines?" Sambath inquired.

General Ashur nodded, his gaze hardening. He entered the great hall, where the human collaborators awaited their fate. "Cowards," he spat under his breath. "To surrender to the enemy… they deserve what's coming."

He mounted the podium, the cameras rolling. "Terrans," he began, his voice booming, "you have chosen to align yourselves with the Assyrian Empire. A wise decision. For those who resist, our wrath will be swift and absolute. To fuel our conquests, we require your labor. You will be transported to Assyria to toil in the mines, providing the resources that power our might."

A murmur of discontent arose from the crowd. Alex stepped forward, his voice defiant. "This is not what was promised! We demand our freedom!"

General Ashur's smile vanished. He reached under the podium and drew a weapon. "Disobedience will not be tolerated." With chilling precision, he executed Alex and two others. The crowd gasped, fear replacing their anger.

"Are there any further objections?" General Ashur demanded, his voice icy.

Silence.

"Take them away," he ordered. "Prepare them for transport."

He left the hall, his resolve unwavering. "Khawa," he instructed, "prepare the communication channels. It's time for my final address."

"Yes, sir," Khawa replied, hurrying away.

General Ashur moved to the operations center. "Are we ready?"

"Ready, sir," Khawa confirmed.

General Ashur addressed the Terrans through the broadcast channels. "Your time is over. Your collaborators will serve the Empire. Resist, and you will face our full fury. Soon, you will beg for mercy." He settled back, a predatory glint in his eyes. "Begin the assault."

Colonel Cheikho

Colonel Cheikho, the most formidable officer in General Ashur's army, was a towering figure, seven feet tall, renowned for his unparalleled battlefield victories. His meteoric rise to colonel was unprecedented. Known for his ruthless tactics, Colonel Cheikho received orders from General Ashur to attack the District of Columbia. He watched with grim satisfaction as his warriors systematically eliminated every Terran they encountered.

Earth, unprepared for the might of the Assyrian Empire, proved to be a weak adversary. "These Terrans are insignificant," Colonel Cheikho declared, "inferior in every way." He anticipated a swift and decisive victory.

A captured Terran, brought before Colonel Cheikho, fell to his knees. "Who is this?" Colonel Cheikho demanded.

"He claims to work for the President," the warrior replied, "offering to guide us to him in exchange for his and his family's lives."

"Where is his family?"

"We have them detained in their residence."

Colonel Cheikho's icy gaze, capable of chilling the bravest soul, pierced the man. "Tell me the President's location," he commanded, "or I will personally torture the information out of you, starting with your family. Do you understand?"

Terror consumed the man. His eyes widened in fear. "Please, not my family! I'll tell you where he is but spare them!"

"Where is he?" Colonel Cheikho repeated, his voice a low growl.

The man, paralyzed by fear, stammered the location: "The PEOC, a bunker beneath the East Wing of the White House."

"What is this PEOC?"

"The Presidential Emergency Operations Center. It's used during war or natural disasters. He'll be there."

"Coward," Colonel Cheikho spat, "lead the way."

The man, escorted by a warrior, guided them towards the White House, where fierce fighting raged. "This place holds significant value for them," Colonel Cheikho observed, "hence the desperate defense."

He ordered a devastating airstrike on the White House, intending to cripple their resistance. However, F-15 Eagles intercepted the Assyrian fighters, swiftly disabling several.

"Destroy them!" Colonel Cheikho roared, but the remaining fighters were no match for the agile F-15s.

"Take me to the building!" Colonel Cheikho barked at the terrified man. "Or your family dies."

"There's a secret tunnel," the man gasped, pointing towards the Treasury Building. "It connects to the White House. No one guards it."

"Lead us there. And resume the attack on the White House," Colonel Cheikho commanded. "It will distract them."

The Assyrians, confident in their invincibility, pressed forward. "Such appalling aesthetics," Colonel Cheikho scoffed, surveying the damaged Treasury Building. "Your people have no sense of style. These drab structures are an insult to the eye."

Reaching the basement, the man indicated a wall. "The tunnel entrance lies behind this wall. It was used by FDR, a former President, during World War II."

"Who is this FDR?"

"A former President, Franklin Delano Roosevelt. He died over a century ago."

"Lucky for him. Who is your current President?"

"President Charleston Hemingway III. Elected a year ago."

"His reign will be short-lived. Lieutenant, breach this wall."

The wall crumbled under the assault, revealing a gated entrance. "We can blow the hinges," the Lieutenant said.

"Do it." Colonel Cheikho anticipated the thrill of capturing the world's most powerful leader. "Behind this gate lies the President of your pathetic world."

"Not the world, just the United States," the man corrected, his voice trembling. "After we conquer, there will be no need for your petty borders. You will all be slaves of the Assyrian Empire."

The man's head hung low. Colonel Cheikho didn't care about his feelings. He envisioned parading the captured President before the world, a chilling spectacle.

The Lieutenant forced open the gate, and they entered the tunnel. As they approached the PEOC, Colonel Cheikho's excitement grew. However, the steel door, five inches thick, presented a formidable obstacle.

"Only authorized personnel have the code," the man explained.

Colonel Cheikho ordered the deployment of an assault cannon. "Can they see or hear us inside?"

"Possibly. Power may have been partially restored after the bombing."

Colonel Cheikho stepped in front of the camera, his imposing figure and steely gaze intended to intimidate the occupants within. He heard approaching footsteps, but they were not Assyrian. "Lieutenant, eliminate them."

"And this man?"

Colonel Cheikho coldly executed the man, silencing his pleas. American soldiers rounded the corner, opening fire. The Assyrians returned fire, a deadly exchange. The Lieutenant, wounded but undeterred, continued fighting.

"Bring the survivors to me," Colonel Cheikho commanded.

The Lieutenant presented the two captured soldiers. Colonel Cheikho forced one to his knees in front of the camera. "Let's see how much your President values you."

"He won't open the door."

"Then you die honoring him." Colonel Cheikho raised his weapon, addressing the camera. "Open the door, or he dies. I will count to ten."

He began the countdown. The man, eyes closed, awaited his fate. Colonel Cheikho, intrigued by the man's unwavering loyalty, reluctantly admired his resolve.

"Ten... nine... eight..." He pulled the trigger, ending the man's life.

A voice boomed from the speakers. "We will not open the door. These soldiers willingly sacrificed their lives for their country. We will fight until the very end. We Terrans are not weak."

"Who is this?" Colonel Cheikho demanded.

"President Hemingway."

"Do you speak for the entire planet?"

"I speak for the United States of America, and we will never surrender to terrorists."

Colonel Cheikho erupted in laughter. "Terrorists? We are the rightful owners of this world. You are the trespassers. You should consider yourselves fortunate if death is your only punishment."

"We are not afraid."

Colonel Cheikho's laughter intensified. The Assyrian soldiers deployed the cannon. "He's no longer of any use." He executed the remaining soldier.

However, more American soldiers and Secret Service agents stormed the corridor, overwhelming the Assyrians. Colonel Cheikho, realizing the Terrans were more formidable than anticipated, ordered a retreat, covering his withdrawal with a hail of gunfire. He heard the sounds of his men falling, one by one.

Defeat, a bitter pill for Colonel Cheikho, fueled his rage. He would have his revenge. He would capture the President and make him pay dearly.

Report to General Ashur

"Sir," Colonel Cheikho reported to General Ashur, "we were unable to retrieve the President. The Terran defense at his location was unexpectedly fierce. I require reinforcements. The Terrans are heavily concentrating their forces to protect their leaders."

"I am disappointed in you, Colonel. You are my heir apparent to this position. I will give you more men. We know the Terrans are protecting that location and a location in a place called Colorado. Many of their leaders, including military leaders, are held up in a place called Cheyanne Mountain. I am sending another regiment of men there to defeat the Terrans."

"Yes, sir."

"I am sending a hundred men. Don't fail again. I only want to see you post victory."

"Yes, sir." Colonel Cheikho turned and walked out of the room. He hated failure, and it was an unfamiliar stench to him. He would get the 100 warriors and capture the White House and the president. Nothing would stop him.

4 - Gloria Davis

Gloria Davis finally found her purpose, though tragically, it emerged amidst Earth's desperate struggle for survival. After her military service ended, she struggled to find fulfilling work, her ambitions consistently unmet. When the invasion began, she was at the recruitment office, eager to rejoin the fight. Now, she led a hardened platoon of resistance fighters, a pivotal figure in a conflict that would forever alter the course of human history.

Known as the "Black Platoon," they distinguished themselves with a black rag tied around their right arms, midway between elbow and shoulder. Gloria's rag bore three red stripes, signifying her command, while her second-in-command, Jason Clowney, wore two strips.

The Black Platoon proved their valor in several skirmishes along the Maryland-D.C. border. Now, a critical mission awaited them: The President dispatched an urgent plea for support. The Assyrians were attempting to extract him from the White House. Gloria's platoon was tasked with rescuing the President, ensuring his safe relocation beyond the reach of the invaders.

Standing on Pennsylvania Avenue, Gloria prepared her troops for the impending battle. "Jason," she briefed, "we have air support—what remains of Bolling Air Force Base managed to scramble a few F-15s, some F-22 Raptors, and even a couple of the experimental F-15EX Eagle IIs. The Eagle IIs are untested in combat, but they're all we have."

"That sounds like a formidable force," Jason remarked.

"Against their armada? Not really. We got lucky during their initial assault on the White House. Those Eagles are incredibly maneuverable, but they can afford to lose a few fighters. We can't."

"You're right. We'll have to neutralize them on the ground," Jason surmised. "Do you have a plan?"

"Yes, we'll coordinate with the Army and the Secret Service."

"Understood. Let's do this."

"Jason," Gloria mused, "you were bagging groceries before all this. I couldn't even hold down a job. And now, here we are, fighting aliens. The world has gone mad, but I can't deny it, I'm exhilarated. Am I going crazy?"

"No. This is a once-in-a-lifetime experience. Even during the World Wars, there were undoubtedly individuals who thrived in the chaos. Our concern will be the aftermath. Can we return to ordinary lives after this?"

Gloria smiled. "Let's not dwell on that now. Let's get our platoon ready."

"Roger that."

Jason disseminated assignments among the troops. As Gloria steeled herself for battle, a profound sense of reflection washed over her. "Lord," she prayed, "I don't know if this will be my last battle, or my last day on Earth. I haven't been a worthy servant in recent years, but I rededicate my life to you. If I fall, remember me. And remember my soldiers too. They have good hearts. Watch over their souls, Lord, and protect them in this battle. We face an uncertain future, but we trust in you. In your son, Jesus' name, Amen."

"Remember," Gloria commanded, "if you can capture enemy weapons, do it!"

The first salvo struck the White House's once-imposing iron gates, now mangled and breached by the enemy bombardment. "My God," Gloria gasped, "their firepower is devastating. We need to acquire their weapons." Gloria paused to catch her breath then shouted, "Fire!"

The night air erupted in a cacophony of gunfire and laser blasts. Gloria knew this would be a protracted, brutal struggle. She prayed for reinforcements from Thomas Wayne but doubted they would arrive in time.

The Assyrian forces converged at the intersection of 15th Street and New York Avenue, fanning out along 15th Street between G and F Streets. The Black Platoon held their ground in front of the White House on Pennsylvania Avenue. Gloria dispatched units to secure the East Gate and the Visitor Center.

The fierce battle illuminated the night. Gloria grabbed two soldiers. "Follow me," she commanded.

They moved north on Madison Place, reaching H Street. Peeking around the corner, she assessed the situation. "The Assyrians have superior weaponry, but they're unfamiliar with the terrain," she observed. "I'm going down H Street to flank them. You, what's your name?"

"Jack," the first soldier replied.

"Jack, I need you to eliminate the sniper on that rooftop. He's a significant threat."

"Understood."

"And you?" she asked the second soldier.

"Tiffani."

"Tiffani, I'm scouting that corner. Stay here and whistle if anyone approaches."

"Yes, ma'am."

"Oh, come now, sister," Gloria chuckled, a rare sound in the midst of chaos. "Stay alert, Tiffani."

"Will do."

As Gloria cautiously moved down H Street, the sounds of battle escalated into a deafening roar. The Assyrians, consumed by their own skirmishes, remained oblivious to her presence. Just five feet from the corner, an Assyrian soldier rounded the bend, his eyes widening in startled recognition. He lunged for the weapon at his hip, but Gloria was a blur of motion. Three swift, brutal kicks hammered into his stomach, doubling him over, before a powerful uppercut snapped his head back, sending him crashing to the ground with a sickening thud. *"I need to neutralize him before he alerts his comrades,"* she thought, her breath coming in sharp, shallow gasps. Without hesitation, she ripped the weapon from his grasp, tossing it clattering into the darkness.

The warrior scrambled to his feet, a chilling grin spreading across his face. "I won't need my weapon to defeat you, little woman."

"Don't underestimate me," Gloria warned.

He lunged at her with a vicious roundhouse punch. Gloria ducked, retaliating with three quick blows to his ribs. *"Stick and move,"* her father's voice echoed in her mind. *"Don't let him grab you."* The

Assyrian pressed the attack, but Gloria remained elusive. He finally managed to grab her shoulder, spinning her around and landing a devastating blow to her jaw. She tumbled to the ground.

"Now I will kill you and display your broken body as a trophy in my camp," he sneered.

He clamped his hands around her throat, cutting off her air supply. Memories flashed before her eyes—her mother, her childhood… *"Mom? I'm not ready to join you."* A desperate plea for divine intervention escaped her lips.

The warrior's head jerked upwards, his eyes widening in shock. His grip loosened, allowing Gloria to break free. "Tiffani! God, thank you!"

"I thought you were trying to be stealthy, so I used my knife. I may not be a sharpshooter, but I can handle a blade."

Gasping for air, Gloria stammered, "Thank you, Tiffani. I thought I was a goner."

"Not yet. You still have a job to do."

"You're right." Gloria picked up the Assyrian's weapon, examining it. "It seems similar to ours."

"Yeah, except it fires proton blasts instead of bullets."

"How do you know that?"

"Just a guess. I'm a bit of a science fiction nerd."

They cautiously moved south on 15th Street, staying behind the Assyrian lines. Several soldiers stood guard, with one man seemingly in command. Gloria turned to Tiffani. "This is our chance. Let's make it count."

Tiffani crossed the street, taking up a position opposite Gloria. As they prepared to strike, the Assyrian leader spotted them and roared in alarm.

"Fire!" Gloria yelled. Tiffani fired her M-16, followed by a blast from Gloria's captured weapon. The leader, in a cowardly act, used a nearby soldier as a human shield. The bullets struck the soldier, allowing the leader to escape. Gloria heard him rallying his troops for a counterattack. "Get out of here, Tiffani!" she shouted.

"Not without you."

A devastating blast from above rained debris down upon Tiffani. Gloria watched in horror as her comrade fell, lifeless. Rage surged through her. She charged towards the source of the attack, only to find Tiffani lifeless.

Looking up, she saw the sniper, a cruel grin etched on his face. He held up Jack's body as a trophy, then callously tossed it to the ground. Jack's scream and the sickening thud accompanying it echoed through the streets. "Jack," she whispered, grief and fury consuming her.

The sniper aimed his weapon at Gloria, but she darted across the street, evading his fire. She retaliated, unleashing a barrage of shots at the building, causing the roof to cave in. The sniper tumbled to the ground, injured but not dead. His weapon teetered precariously on the edge of the roof. Gloria stared at him with chilling indifference. The desire to kill him with her bare hands was strong, but she chose a different form of retribution. She relished in his suffering, watching him writhe in pain, blood gushing from his mouth. "I don't understand your words," she taunted. "I imagine that thing will fall soon. When it does, I know you'll be dead. This is your punishment for killing my friends."

She mirrored his earlier grin and turned away. The sniper's weapon finally toppled from the roof, crashing to the ground below. Gloria took a moment to acknowledge the death of her enemy, a grim satisfaction rolling over her.

Jason and a few other soldiers ran towards her. "Gloria, where were you? The Assyrians breached the White House!"

"I tried to flank them, but I suffered heavy losses. Two good soldiers are gone. We need to get reinforcements to the White House immediately."

On the White House lawn, an Assyrian fighter ascended into the air, carrying the President away. "It's too late," Jason said grimly. "They have the President."

Gloria watched the fighter vanish into the night sky, the image of the cowardly leader and his despicable act seared into her memory. "I won't forget this," she vowed. "I will find him and make him pay."

"What now?" Jason asked.

"We return to camp. Thomas Wayne will provide further instructions."

They retreated to their camp, now relocated to Fort Washington, Maryland, closer to the front lines. *"Thomas Wayne will be furious with me,"* Gloria thought. *"I failed the mission, and I lost many of my people. If we continue to suffer these kinds of losses, the Assyrians will overwhelm us."*

5 - The Reality of War

Thomas Wayne relocated the resistance headquarters to a complex of vacant apartment buildings on Palmer Road, just off Highway 210. This provided them with shelter and a central command center closer to the action in DC. They assumed the Assyrians believed the buildings remained unoccupied, as thorough searches were conducted after previous bombings.

The radio broadcast delivered the devastating news of President Hemingway's capture by the Assyrians. As Thomas Wayne awaited Gloria's return, the recent losses shook the morale of his fighters. Many questioned the continued struggle, but he remained resolute. Hope was crucial. He needed to rekindle their belief in the cause.

The initial allure of war, with its promises of glory, quickly faded. The grim reality of countless casualties set in. Doubts gnawed at him. Was he the right leader? The temptation to abandon the fight, to escape the carnage, was strong. This was precisely the outcome Alex predicted.

But he couldn't surrender. The fight must continue, albeit with a new strategy. Guerrilla tactics were imperative. Direct confrontation was no longer viable.

Gloria and Jason entered the command center. "Where is everyone?" Gloria inquired.

"They've been ordered to rest," Thomas Wayne explained. "The heavy losses have taken a toll. Their resolve is wavering."

"What other choice do they have?" Gloria retorted. "Cower in hiding? Submit to the Assyrians? I've heard the fate of those who surrendered: forced labor on the Assyrian home world."

Jason added, "Slavery, that's their reward. No riches, only servitude."

Gloria added, "The Israelites did the same thing when they fled Egypt. They complained and wanted to go back into slavery because the road to freedom was too hard. We're not giving up."

Thomas Wayne ran a hand through his hair. "I agree," replied Thomas Wayne. "But we need to shift our focus. We'll target key Assyrian staging areas and supply lines. Hit and run tactics are our only hope now."

"I concur," Gloria agreed. "We'll divide into smaller units and hunt for vulnerabilities. I'll present a plan later today."

"Rest, both of you," Thomas Wayne urged. "You've been fighting relentlessly for days."

"We will," Gloria acknowledged, and they departed.

Thomas Wayne sank back into his chair, eyes closed, yearning for respite. The gentle massage on his shoulders was a welcome balm. The sigh of relief rang out around the room. He suspected it was Elaine, the woman he fell for, but any touch felt comforting at that moment.

"Enjoying this, Thomas Wayne?" she whispered.

"Indeed, my dear."

"You should have known it was me," she teased.

"The unique touch of your hands, my good doctor, is unmistakable. A daily pleasure I eagerly anticipate."

Elaine chuckled. "Eloquent as always, sir." She moved to sit on his lap, their lips meeting. "You carry the weight of this resistance alone. You need to release some of that stress."

"Someone must lead," he admitted. "I sometimes question my own ability, but I cannot abandon them. They depend on me. They look to me for guidance."

"I understand, honey, but you need to unwind too. Join me at my apartment later. Eight o'clock." With a playful peck on the lips, she vanished.

Gloria burst in, breathless. "Thomas Wayne, the ships are broadcasting again!"

He rushed outside, joining the others as they awaited the message. Dread settled over him. What new horrors would the Assyrians unleash? He held Elaine's hand, seeking her unwavering support.

General Ashur's face filled the screen. "Terrans," he declared, "we hold your most esteemed leader captive. President Hemingway is our prisoner. Surrender, and his life will be spared. Staging camps are established in every major city. Deliver a sufficient number of captives, and the President will be spared."

The screen went black, leaving the crowd stunned. What could he say? Surrender was unthinkable. The Assyrians were liars, proven by the fate of previous captives. He looked into the anxious faces of his people, desperate for answers he didn't possess.

"We will not surrender," he declared firmly. "They promised a better life to those who surrendered. They were met with slavery or even worst—death. Their word means nothing. We must continue to fight, to make their occupation as difficult as possible. We cannot yield."

A surge of agreement erupted from the crowd. Relief filled his spirit. They still believed in him. Gloria approached. "Thomas Wayne, I have a plan to rescue the President."

"What is it?"

"The execution will likely take place at FedEx Field, their regional headquarters. A small, stealthy team can infiltrate the site, disrupt the execution, and recover the President."

The risk was immense, but it was their only chance. "Take five with you. Stealth is paramount. In and out as quickly as possible."

"We can do this, Thomas Wayne. Trust us."

"I do. But I don't want to lose any more of you."

Gloria pulled him aside. "This is war, Thomas Wayne. Death is a constant threat. We must adapt, but we cannot allow fear to paralyze us. Imagine the sacrifices others are making across the nation. I pray they are not giving up."

"I pray too, Gloria. Go with my blessings."

"Thank you, Thomas Wayne. Roger, Daphne, Craig, and Mark will join me."

"Jason isn't going?"

"No. If I fall, he will lead Black Platoon, if we maintain that structure."

"We'll discuss that later. Now go. Get the President back."

Gloria departed to assemble her team, leaving Thomas Wayne to grapple with the continued weight of his responsibility.

FedEx Field

Gloria and her team arrived outside FedEx Field. A cursory inspection revealed minimal security. "They likely believe we're incapable of mounting an attack on their headquarters," she observed.

"Or perhaps they simply consider us too ignorant to attempt it," Mark countered.

Gloria chuckled. "You might be right. Let's infiltrate through that gate and assess the situation within the stadium. It's almost time for the execution."

As they approached the gate, a hundred feet from their objective, they were intercepted.

"Hold up! Where do you think you're going?"

"Inside that stadium," Gloria replied. "Who are you?"

"Members of Blackstreet," Mark responded.

"The gang? We mean you no harm," Gloria explained. "We're attempting to rescue the President."

"Your weapons. Hand them over, and you can save whoever you please."

Gloria scoffed. "We don't have the time for this. We're trying to save the world! What are you trying to achieve?"

The leader stepped closer. Her team raised their weapons, and Blackstreet mirrored the action. The leader raised his hands in a placating gesture. "No need for bloodshed here. The Assyrians will be upon us all. To answer your question, we're trying to survive. No heroes here, just survivalists. We need your weapons."

"We're not giving up our weapons," Gloria declared. "We have a mission. You can either assist us or step aside and allow us to proceed."

The leader considered her words. "Perhaps we'll let you pass."

"Duce, no!" one of his men protested.

Duce held up his hand. "Suppose we allow you to proceed, and you succeed. What's in it for us?"

Gloria exchanged a glance with Mark. "Any weapons we acquire during this mission will be shared with you. Only those retrieved here."

"Sounds agreeable," Duce acknowledged.

"There's no guarantee we'll acquire any weapons. We may not even return."

Duce chuckled. "True, but we won't perish trying to obtain them either." Gloria nodded. "Consider this a pact. Any attempt to deceive us will have consequences. There are more of us than you realize."

"Then join us. We could use more fighters in this war."

"We're not interested. Just return with our share of the weapons."

Gloria gestured for her team to proceed towards the gate. "I don't trust them," she whispered to Mark. "If we escape, we must be prepared to face them as well."

"Understood."

"It's a shame we're fighting on two fronts: the Assyrians and our own kind. One enemy would suffice."

"Every science fiction film I've ever seen depicts this scenario. Humans inevitably turn on each other.

Now I understand why the writers included it. Self-preservation is ingrained in human nature."

"We witness it daily in ordinary life," Gloria remarked. "Self-interest always prevails. Altruism is a rare commodity."

They approached the gate, finding it unguarded. Gloria signaled her team forward, but Duce halted them again. "What are you doing here?"

Gloria, bewildered, stared at Duce. "There are minefields surrounding all entrances. That's why there's no guards."

"Appreciate the heads-up. Any suggestions for getting inside?"

"Head to Sean Taylor Road. There's a hole in the fence there. No mines have been laid there because they're unaware of the breach. We used to sneak into games through that opening."

"Thanks. We owe you one."

"Don't forget about my weapons."

"Not a chance." Gloria nodded and led her team towards the opposite side of the stadium. They located the hole in the fence near Sean Taylor Road and slipped through, entering the stadium undetected.

Activity was evident within. Through her binoculars, Gloria observed the scene: the President and five others stood on a podium near the 50-yard line, nooses dangling around their necks. The President stood in the center, flanked by the others, including an Army General.

Mark voiced his concern, "There are only five of us. We're outnumbered. This might be a suicide mission."

"You're just realizing that Mark? She asked. "We had to maintain stealth"

"This might be beyond our capabilities," Mark replied.

"Good thing we decided to join you," Duce remarked, appearing behind them with his gang.

"I can't say I'm displeased to see you," Gloria responded with a smile. "How do you propose we proceed?"

Duce suggested, "If your team attacks from one side, we can attack from the other and create a crossfire. It might give us the advantage."

"Sounds like a plan."

Duce said, "We'll signal when we're in position, and then you attack."

"How will we signal?" Asked Gloria.

"You'll know."

Duce and his gang moved towards the opposite side of FedEx Field. Gloria and her team awaited the signal, which arrived in the form of a deafening explosion. "Attack!" she commanded. Her team stormed the field, firing at any moving targets.

Gloria noticed an Assyrian warrior targeting the captives on the podium. Taking aim, she fired, eliminating the threat. Another warrior pulled the lever, sending the remaining captives plummeting to their deaths. "Cover me!" she yelled, rushing towards the podium while dodging enemy fire.

Swiftly, she severed the ropes binding the President and the man beside him. The General and the rest, however, was already lifeless. "Come on, sir. We need to evacuate."

The President followed Gloria as they fought their way out. Her team scavenged weapons from fallen Assyrians. The whereabouts of Duce and his gang remained uncertain, but they managed to escape the field by exiting through the home team's tunnel.

Reaching the tunnel's exit, they paused to assess the situation. "Mark, is everyone accounted for?" Gloria asked.

"Yes, we're all here." He paused to catch his breath, "I can't believe it!"

"I couldn't save the others," Gloria said with a deep sadness in her tone.

"Mr. President, we need to get you out of here," Mark urged.

"Thank you all for risking your lives to save me," President Hemingway acknowledged. "We need to reach Bolling Air Force Base. They have the means to transport me to Cheyenne Mountain."

"We'll do our utmost," Gloria assured him.

Mark moved to the front, leading the group through the tunnel. They emerged from the exit, exercising caution to avoid any remaining mines. An Assyrian warrior emerged, raising his weapon.

Mark instinctively shielded President Hemingway, absorbing the fatal blast. He collapsed, a look of shock frozen on his face.

Two retaliatory shots rang out from the stadium, eliminating the Assyrian. It was Duce and his gang. They rushed out from the fence, seeking safety.

Gloria dropped to her knees, her hands pressing against Mark's still chest, searching for a pulse she knew wouldn't be there. The cold finality of it settled deep within her. Her head bowed, she murmured an apology for his death, followed by a quick prayer for his soul—both a raw sound lost in the chaos. A single, traitorous tear welled, threatening to spill, but Gloria clamped down on it, her jaw tight. She couldn't afford a crack in her armor; she needed to remain the tough soldier, impassive to grief. Yet, the brutal truth was, every loss chipped away at her.

Reluctantly, Gloria followed Duce to their hideout. They needed to lie low until the Assyrian pursuit subsided.

Gloria sat beside President Hemingway in the living room of an apartment building commandeered by Blackstreet as their headquarters. The other survivor, revealed to be Secretary of Defense George Bland, sat beside them.

Duce confirmed that his gang was larger than initially anticipated. "They could be a valuable asset in this fight," President Hemingway acknowledged.

"Sir, with all due respect, I didn't do this for you. I saw an opportunity and seized it. We acquired more weapons for our defense and the chance to eliminate more Assyrians."

President Hemingway replied, "Regardless of your motives, you've rendered a significant service to our nation. Secretary Bland and I can now organize a counteroffensive against the Assyrians. By freeing us, you've served your country and the world admirably."

Duce chuckled. "Sir, before this all began, you signed a bill that could have imprisoned people like me for life. Do you have any idea what prison is like?"

President Hemingway acknowledged, "I do not, but I do know that our nation desperately needs all hands-on deck to repel this alien invasion. Your team could be a formidable force in this struggle."

"That's what she said," Duce retorted. "We're only looking out for ourselves. You fight your war. We're just trying to survive."

President Hemingway nodded in understanding.

Gloria interjected, "Duce, we need your assistance in transporting the President to Bolling. In return, we'll relinquish the Assyrian weapons but retain our own."

Duce appraised her. "Gloria, is it?"

"Yes."

"I've grown to respect you. I won't risk my entire team on this mission, and I won't require your weapons. However, I'll personally assist you. but I may call upon you… for a favor in the future."

"Agreed."

"Vehicles are prime targets. The Assyrians will quickly eliminate them. We do have a car, completely blacked out. If we drive it tonight, we might reach Bolling undetected."

Gloria turned to President Hemingway. "Sir, what do you think?"

"Any method of transportation is acceptable at this point."

Duce added, "We've also established a radio station. We've been monitoring communications to identify potential allies. That's how we knew you were coming here. The Assyrians may be unaware of the lower frequency bands, but we are."

"Excellent," Gloria remarked. "We can contact our leader."

Duce gestured to another man. "Take them to the radio station and attempt to contact Bolling. I'll check on the car."

They dispersed. Gloria, President Hemingway, and Secretary Bland followed the man to another building housing the radio equipment. "They've acquired far more sophisticated equipment than we possess," Gloria observed. "Presumably, as a gang, they've acquired much of it through illicit means. Nonetheless, I admire their technical proficiency."

The man inquired, "What channel are you communicating on?"

President Hemingway responded, "Try channel 25."

The man tuned the radio to channel 25. Static filled the air, followed by a discussion regarding Cheyenne Mountain and the President's location. The man interjected, "This is Bolling communications. Who is speaking?"

President Hemingway took the microphone. "This is President Hemingway."

"Sir, please identify yourself using your voice code."

"Son, my code would be outdated by now. I was captured yesterday, remember?"

"Please provide yesterday's code, sir."

"The code of the day yesterday was 'Rattlesnake.'"

"Thank you, sir." A brief silence ensued. "Sir, your code has been verified. What is your current location?"

"We are secure for now. We require a team to extract Secretary Bland and I from Allentown Road, in front of the Andrews' main gate."

"Roger that, sir."

President Hemingway turned to Gloria. "You've performed admirably in rescuing us. I'd like you to join me at Cheyenne Mountain. Work with my team."

"I can't, sir. I appreciate the offer, but my place is here with my team. We intend to employ guerrilla tactics against the Assyrians and weaken their forces.

Our efforts may contribute to your military's success."

"I understand. I hope there are more fighters like you out there."

Duce returned to the room. "The car is ready when you are."

"Thank you, Duce. I will never forget your role in this. I urge you to reconsider Gloria's offer. We require all the ground support we can muster against the Assyrians."

"I'll give it some thought," Duce replied.

"Excellent. Now, let us proceed. Bolling will meet us at Andrews' main gate at 2000 hours."

"We'll get you there," Duce assured them.

They followed Duce to the designated eating area. "I need to convince him to join the fight," Gloria mused. She never imagined having cursory conversations with the President but here she was. "Duce is a natural leader, and his gang occupies a strategic position near the Assyrian headquarters. They could be a formidable asset. I'll need to persuade Thomas Wayne to meet with Duce. Perhaps that will sway his decision."

"I hope you're successful," President Hemingway replied. "We can use the help."

"Yes sir."

The time for their departure arrived. Duce provided transportation to Andrews Air Force Base. The car, designed to accommodate five, allowed one of Gloria's team to accompany them. Duce navigated, avoiding main roads and opting for backstreets to minimize the risk of detection. The journey, normally a ten-minute drive via the beltway, took thirty minutes.

Reaching their destination, Duce parked discreetly down the street from Andrews. "We need to scout the area to ensure its secure," he instructed.

"I'll do it," Gloria volunteered. "I'll signal if it's safe."

Gloria exited the vehicle and approached the charred remains of a nearby McDonald's. Utilizing the night vision goggles provided by Duce—exceptional devices that they desperately needed for their own operations—she scanned the area. She spotted several men surrounding two vehicles just inside the former main gate of Andrews.

Approaching cautiously, she observed the men. The cold steel of a weapon pressed against her temple, freezing her in place. "Again?" she muttered to herself. "Why do I constantly encounter those who oppose our struggle?"

"Drop the weapon and raise your hands slowly," the man commanded.

Gloria complied. She asked, "What are you doing on this base?"

"None of your concern," he answered, "Now move forward."

Gloria reluctantly complied, approaching the area where the two vehicles and the other men waited. "Captain, I found her in the woods."

The captain responded, "Ma'am, this is a restricted area. Where can we take you?"

"Captain? Are you an Air Force Captain?"

"That's correct. We're from Bolling. Who are you?"

A sigh of relief escaped Gloria's lips. "I'm Gloria Davis, and I have the package you're awaiting."

The captain scrutinized her. "How do I know you're telling the truth?"

"For starters, how would I know you were expecting a package?"

The captain remained expressionless. "Sergeant Bullock, accompany her. Keep a close eye on her."

"Yes, sir."

Gloria stepped out onto the street and signaled to Duce. He cautiously maneuvered the vehicle towards the location where the captain and the other vehicles were stationed.

President Hemingway exited the vehicle and approached the men, who immediately saluted.

"Thank you, gentlemen. Who is in command?"

"I am, sir; Captain Longmeyer."

"Captain, I require immediate transportation to Bolling."

"Yes, sir. We've devised a plan for your safe passage. We'll transport you in separate vehicles, utilizing different routes."

"Thank you, Captain Longmeyer." President Hemingway turned to Gloria and Duce. "Thank you both for your invaluable assistance. We will provide as much support as possible in your fight against the Assyrians, but remember, our focus extends beyond this immediate area."

"Understood, sir. Any support you can provide is greatly appreciated," Gloria acknowledged.

"Duce, I urge you to reconsider joining the fight. We desperately need your support on the ground."

Duce shifted his weight. "I'll give it some thought, sir."

"Excellent. Now, let us proceed."

President Hemingway and Secretary Bland were escorted to their designated vehicles and departed in separate directions. Gloria realized that separating them was a sound tactical decision, maximizing the chances of at least one reaching Bolling safely. "A well-conceived strategy, Captain Longmeyer," she acknowledged. "I doubt I would have thought of that." Captain Longmeyer acknowledged her comment but in a dismissive manner. Gloria knew the military thought their rag tag resistance did more harm than good but she relished in the thought that they saved the President, not the military.

She turned to Duce. "I believe we've accomplished our objective."

"Where are you headed now?" He asked.

"Straight down Allentown. We have a headquarters established there."

"I can give you a ride."

"I'd appreciate that. Can we return and collect the rest of my team?"

"Absolutely."

"I think I'm making progress with him," Gloria mused. *"He'll be a valuable asset. I just hope his men follow his lead. They seem to respect him, but there's always that one dissenting voice."*

Duce in the Fort Washington Camp

Gloria and her team returned to the Palmer apartments just before dawn. She instructed Duce to remain until nightfall, as the black car would be too conspicuous during daylight hours. He readily agreed.

Duce is developing feelings for me, she mused. *I wouldn't object, especially if it solidifies our alliance. And he's certainly not unattractive.*

"Thomas Wayne is currently unavailable, but we have the entire day ahead of us," she announced.

"Sounds good to me," he replied.

"Let's grab some breakfast. The kitchen should be open."

"You guys have regular kitchen hours?"

"We do. It's the only way to ensure adequate food supplies for everyone."

Duce snickered, "My people understand the importance of restraint."

"Different rules apply here. Rationing is essential. Eventually, we need to establish our own food sources and protect those farms from the Assyrians."

"I hadn't considered that."

She chuckled. "A city dweller wouldn't." They proceeded to the dining area for breakfast.

"Tell me," she inquired, "how did you become the head of the Blackstreet gang?"

"Well, back in middle school, they used to harass me after school. They wanted me to join, recognizing my potential to assist them with their illicit operations. One day, they cornered me and issued an ultimatum: join them or face the consequences. They threatened to harm my little sister. What brother could refuse under such duress?"

"I can certainly understand your predicament."

"Once I gained access to their financial records, I devised strategies to significantly expand their operations. Blackstreet isn't just a local gang; it's a national organization. My innovations quickly caught the attention of the national leadership. The Maryland division of Blackstreet tripled its income within two months."

"That must have impressed them."

"It did, but the individual who recruited me felt threatened. He feared the national leaders would replace him with me. He was correct. He attempted to eliminate me, but the national leaders acted first. I assumed leadership thereafter."

"Impressive."

"Yes, but they disapproved of my desire to cease illegal activities. I presented a plan to generate greater profits through legitimate means, but they dismissed it as weakness. Just before the Assyrian invasion, I received word of an impending hit on my life. Thankfully, the attack never materialized. I haven't heard from the national leadership since the arrival of the Assyrians."

"How long have you been in charge?" Gloria inquired.

"Twelve years. I'm 25 now."

"Wow, I'm 26. I thought we were close in age."

"What about you? What's your story?" asked Duce.

"My story? Well, I enlisted in the Army at 18. I aspired to serve in the infantry, and I achieved that goal. Most people shy away from that path."

"You're right about that."

She pepped up more, "I thrived in that environment. After training, I was immediately deployed to Iran. I loved the combat. I served three tours before they were forced to send me home. Medical examinations revealed a minor heart murmur. While not a serious condition, it disqualified me from active duty. I was medically discharged from the

Army, adrift and uncertain of my future. I struggled to find employment, drifting from one dead-end job to another until the Assyrian invasion. Now, I have a purpose again."

"Intriguing," Duce twisted his head.

"So, are you prepared to form an alliance with us?" Gloria pressed.

"If you're a part of that alliance, then absolutely."

Gloria smiled. "I am indeed a key member. You should meet Thomas Wayne. And you'll need to meet Cordell, our second-in-command."

"You're not the second-in-command?" asked Duce.

"No, I lead the fighting forces. That's where I belong. We have other platoon leaders, although I'm uncertain of their current status. I'll need to assess the situation once everyone awakens."

"Sounds good."

This is promising, Gloria thought. *He's far more than just a gang leader. He possesses intelligence and strategic thinking. An alliance with Blackstreet would be invaluable in our fight to reclaim the DMV. The Assyrians better watch out. We're coming back stronger.*

6 – Assyrian Failure

General Ashur slammed his fist on the console, his anger radiating through the mothership. No one dared approach him in this state. Colonel Cheikho arrived minutes after he summoned him.

"What happened? Why wasn't the President executed as I ordered?" Ashur demanded.

"The men you left to guard him failed. They allowed the resistance to infiltrate and extract the President and the Secretary of Defense," Cheikho reported.

Ashur glared at him. "Bring them to me."

"I have already executed them," Cheikho replied.

Ashur, denied the satisfaction of direct retribution, nevertheless approved of the swift justice. He took a deep breath. "Do we know where the President is located?"

"No, we were unable to track him. However, we believe the group known as Blackstreet assisted in the rescue. We have located their base, and I can order troops to eliminate them."

Ashur turned to Cheikho. "No. Pull back all our troops. Unleash the fighters to devastate the entire Washington, D.C. area, including Maryland and Virginia. I want every living creature obliterated."

"Yes, sir," Cheikho acknowledged.

As Cheikho left, a communication appeared on Ashur's monitor. It was King Malka. *He'll want an update,* Ashur thought. *This news won't please him.* "Sire, I welcome your communication."

"General Ashur, why am I hearing that you allowed this president to escape?" Malka's voice was sharp.

"I have already punished those who failed us," Ashur replied.

"They failed *you*, General. What is the status of the other countries?" Malka pressed.

"They are under control. Only China, Japan, Germany, Russia, and the United Kingdom pose a significant threat. After further weakening them, they will concede to the Empire."

"The United States is also fighting back. I expect this engagement to be over within three days, General. Do I need to send reinforcements? General Garima has offered her regiment."

"No, sire. I do not require her assistance."

"I believe you do. I am dispatching her fleet now."

"Yes, sire." The screen went black, leaving Ashur seething.

He pressed the button to contact Cheikho. "Yes, General?" Cheikho answered.

"King Malka is sending General Garima and her fleet. We must complete this operation before she arrives."

"We will handle it," Cheikho assured him.

"Find the President and kill him. He's reportedly heading to Cheyenne Mountain. Intensify our attacks on that facility. It's heavily fortified, but we will breach it."

"Yes, sir," Cheikho replied.

Now it's time to settle a score, Ashur thought. *I can slow down her fleet with a few well-placed acts of sabotage.* He pressed the button to contact his confidential informant and arranged for bombs to be planted on two of General Garima's ships. *This will delay her arrival.*

Unsuspecting Support for the Terrans

Eighteen-year-old Seni, on his first mission, surveyed the apartments near Highway 210 then he would report what he found to his superiors. Hidden in the bushes, he watched the traffic entering and exiting the buildings. He attempted to radio his commander, but a bullet struck his shoulder. Resistance fighters pounced on him, punched him, and dragged him to a holding area. They reported to Thomas Wayne that they caught an Assyrian spy.

Thomas Wayne walked in and paused. He saw the warrior's bloody face and the wounded shoulder. He looked at the fighters. "Why did you beat him?"

"You're kidding, right? How many humans did they kill?"

Thomas Wayne's face tightened. "We are not them." He walked up to Seni and examined his wounds more closely. "Get Elaine in here."

The fighters didn't move. "Get her in here now!" Thomas Wayne demanded. Both fighters left. Thomas Wayne pulled up a chair near Seni. He asked, "What is your name?"

Seni was unsure if he could trust a Terran, but this one appeared to care more about his health than anything else. He wondered if he could trust him?

The answer was no, according to Colonel Cheikho, who told the warriors over and over the Terrans could not be trusted. They were devious and plotted to kill all Assyrians. Now he was a prisoner. He had to find a way out of here or die trying. *These Terrans stank, and this one was trying to trick me.*

"I'm not going to hurt you. I just want to know your name." Continued Thomas Wayne.

"What do we have, Thomas Wayne," asked Elaine?

"He has a gunshot wound to the shoulder." Elaine kneeled down and looked at his shoulder. "Can you help him?" asked Thomas Wayne. She looked at him with a 'are you kidding me' smile. "I'm sorry Elaine, that was a bad question."

"The bullet went through, so he's going to make it. It won't take me long to patch him up," replied Elaine.

Thomas Wayne asked, "Now, how about giving us your name?"

Seni studied them. *Most planets would have killed me on site. They are trying to heal me. What kind of trick is this?* "My name is Seni, fourth regiment, third squad."

"See, that wasn't hard, was it? My name is Thomas Wayne Walker. Most call me Thomas Wayne. This is Elaine. She's our doctor." Seni nodded. Thomas Wayne continued, "So you were in the woods spying on us? I can respect that. We certainly are doing the same, but how can we end this war? What can we do to get your leaders to the table?"

Seni grinned. Inside, he knew there was no way his leaders would ever talk to him. They were there to destroy the Terrans. Those who survived would be slaves to the Assyrians. "There is nothing you can do to make that happen. My commander will never speak to you unless it's to discuss the terms of your surrender."

"That's a shame. We may not have the weapons or technology equal to you, but we have the heart and desire. We will never give up."

"Then you will die."

Thomas Wayne sighed, "Not without taking many of you with us. Is that really what you want? Do you want to see many of your brothers and sisters die in a battle they will never clearly win?"

Seni thought about the questions. He had two brothers that were fighting in his regiment. He didn't want to see them die, but he couldn't fall prey to Thomas Wayne's manipulation.

"Seni," Thomas Wayne began, "this country once embarked on a war, decades ago. We, much like your current mindset, believed it would be a quick and decisive victory. History, however, proved us wrong. The Vietnamese were a formidable adversary; their resilience was absolute. They fought with fierce determination, displaying an evasiveness and cleverness that allowed them to avoid our direct assaults. Their guerrilla tactics, still analyzed by strategists worldwide, are a testament to their resolve. That, my friend, is the caliber of opponent you face. Let there be no doubt: your threats will never sway us, and we are prepared to fight to the very last."

Seni's face tighten, "You won't convince me to tell you anything. Your forces will be annihilated within a few hours."

Thomas Wayne's eyebrow rose. "Within a few hours? They're launching another bombing run? This time to annihilate us?"

Seni realized he said too much. He cursed himself for allowing important information to slip out. Colonel Cheikho would cut his throat if he found out. He refused to answer any further questions.

Thomas Wayne ordered his men, "Get the non-essential personal to the shelters. Spread word to the other camps to get their people to safety. We can expect this to be an all-out attack." The men rushed out of the room.

"Your shoulder should be fine now. Try not to do anything to reopen the wound," said Elaine.

Thomas Wayne extended his hand, "You see, we're not the bad guys you think we are. I'm guessing your commander told you we were bad people. That's not true. We were not bothering anyone in the universe. We had our issues on this planet, but we didn't believe there was other life in the universe, much less hate them." Seni sneered. He would not give in to Thomas Wayne's comments.

Two men brought another Assyrian warrior into the room and tossed him to the ground. One fighter said, "Sir, maybe he'll talk more now."

Thomas Wayne looked at the man. He was in bad shape. "Bring Elaine back in here but take your time. Give us a few minutes." The man nodded his head and left the room. Seni didn't know what was going on, but the man was his brother. He couldn't see him suffer. Thomas Wayne retook his seat by Seni.

Seni looked him in his eyes. The desire to kill him welled up in his spirit. *If he harms my brother, I will kill everyone in his camp. Don't test me, Thomas Wayne.* Seni shouted in his mind.

Thomas Wayne said, "Now you see Elaine fixed you up. We can do the same for your friend here, but only if you tell me something I need to know about how to stop this attack." Seni refused to answer. "I know you understand what I'm saying, so I can only believe you want me to withhold medical treatment for your friend." Still no response. "Okay, I was good with being a reasonable man but when you say you are preparing an all-out attack against us with the intention of wiping us out... well, all bets are off now." Thomas Wayne turned to another of the fighters. "Tell Elaine we don't need her."

"Yes, sir."

Seni's eyes locked in on Thomas Wayne. He wanted to tell him something to help his brother, but Colonel Cheikho would kill him and his brother to send a message to the rest of the regiment. *I can't let my brother die, but I can't tell them what I know either.*

Thomas Wayne said, "Take the injured one in the other room and let him die there. Once he's dead, we can bury him along with the others."

"Yes, sir."

"No! I will tell you what I know, but you must not deliver us back to my people. We will surely be killed."

Seni's brother said, "Do not tell them anything. If you do, I will kill you myself."

Seni replied, "I cannot allow you to die."

Thomas Wayne said, "I sense there is some deep concern for this man. Brother maybe?" Seni cut his eyes at Thomas Wayne. "Ah, I'm right. He is your brother. What can you tell me about this attack? How can we stop it?"

"The only way to stop it is to destroy the mothership at FedEx Field."

"How do we do that?"

"You have explosives?"

"We do."

"I can show you where to place them for maximum effect. It will be difficult for you to get there, and the attack will start at your 4:00 o'clock hour."

Thomas Wayne smiled, "With your help, I'm sure we will get there." He looked at one of the fighters, "Get Elaine in here to treat this man."

The injured warrior said, "Seni, I will kill you myself."

"I could not let you die, my brother." Seni sat and watched Elaine work on his brother. *The Terrans are not what we were told. My people would have killed their prisoners or made them slaves. They are helping us. We have been deceived.* Two times Seni's brother stopped breathing, but Elaine was able to revive him. "Come on brother, you can make it." *She is working hard to save a stranger… her enemy. I do not understand these Terrans. I must tell them about the additional troops coming from Assyria.*

Thomas Wayne returned to the room with several others Seni had not seen before. Thomas Wayne said, "I know you want to see what happens with your brother, but we have to make haste to get to FedEx Field."

Seni didn't want to leave. He didn't care about anything but his brother, but he knew if he failed to help the Terrans, his brother would surely die. Seni rose from his seat with his handcuffs in place. He held them out as a gesture to be released.

"Not yet, my friend. We have to establish some trust and we ain't there yet. Let's go." He grabbed Seni by the arm. He told the fighter who remained with Elaine, "Tell her to radio me with an update when she has a chance."

"Roger that."

Seni followed Thomas Wayne and the other fighters. They headed toward the Assyrian headquarters. Inside, he wanted to escape. The thought of turning against his people didn't sit well with him, but he had to save his brother, Zamar. *Zamar doesn't appreciate what I did, but he will be alive. He can hate me but live to hate me. If he follows through on his threat, so be it. But he will be alive.* They arrived near the stadium on Sean Taylor Road, the same spot that Gloria and her team got inside without detection. Seni said "The gates are all mined but we can get past them. We need to walk a precise pattern. Each gate is different."

Thomas Wayne said, "Lead the way."

Seni led the way through the minefield, and they arrived at the gate. The ship sat at the visitor side of the stadium. Seni pointed, "If you climb to the top of the stadium and place the explosives under the engines, the explosion will cause a chain reaction and blow up the entire ship. For more effect, put explosives at both ends of the ship. However, you may have trouble getting to the end away from the stadium. There are more warriors at that end because the main bridge is located there."

Seni watched Thomas Wayne scout the area he pointed out. Thomas Wayne said, "I agree that there are too many warriors at that end of the ship." He turned to his fighters, "I need two volunteers to go place the C4 on that engine. Who's the best shot?"

"Me, sir; Gabriel."

"Gabriel, take up a position to provide them cover in case any Assyrians show up. I'll stay here out of sight with my new friend." The men hurried off to their assignments.

Seni watched the men follow their orders. Inside, he hoped they would get caught, but he knew if they did, he would be executed with them. "I am now a man with no place in any world. I am no longer Assyrian, nor am I Terran."

"I wouldn't agree with that. What you're doing will save millions of lives. That makes you Terran for sure."

"Really, if my brother lives, he will kill me. He will never agree with what I did to save him."

"Sounds like you're a family man, but he is not."

"Zamar is a devout follower of General Ashur. His every breath is to please him."

"I see. You know we can never let him leave. He will have to be our prisoner."

"I understand." Seni's eyes popped.

"What?"

"Guards are approaching your men. Get them out of there."

Thomas Wayne pulled out his radio. "You have company approaching from your 3:00 o'clock. Get out of there."

Seni said, "What?"

Thomas Wayne asked, "What happened?"

"They went down. Both of the warriors went down."

Thomas Wayne smiled, "Gabriel took them out. I guess he is the best shot."

Seni watched as the fighters finished setting the explosives. He asked, "What is this C4?"

"It's a plastic explosive that can be molded into any shape we need it."

Seni nodded his head in appreciation. "Interesting. Terrans are not what I have been told."

"I'm sure we are not."

The fighters returned and handed Thomas Wayne the trigger for the C4. Thomas Wayne looked at everyone. "Be ready to get the heck out of here fast. They will be coming."

Seni held out his hands to be released from his handcuffs. "It is time that you trust me now."

Thomas Wayne nodded his head. He reached into his pocket. Gabriel said, "Sir, are you sure?"

"I'm sure I want you guys to stop calling me, sir." He laughed. "He's earned it. Besides, if they see him here, they're going to kill him before they kill any of us. He's with us now." Thomas Wayne counted down, "Three… two… one…" He pressed the switch, and the explosives ignited.

Seni watched as the mothership went up in flames. As he said, the chain reaction moved throughout the ship, and it was impossible that anyone on board would have survived. He followed Thomas Wayne and the others as they escaped the way they came. After they got a good distance away, he stopped and turned. The smoke and flames lit up the afternoon sky. *I am no longer an Assyrian.*

7 – The Alliance

Thomas Wayne and the men made it back to the camp. They were met by Gloria, who was visibly upset. "Why did you do this mission without me? I'm in charge of these things?"

"You are correct, Gloria, but there are some things I have to do. This was one of them." He turned to Seni. "This is Seni, an Assyrian who just helped us blow up the mothership at FedEx Field. He gave me his word he would help us, and I didn't want to trust anyone else's life with this mission. As you probably heard, we were successful."

"Yes, but at what cost? This is sure to bring more attacks."

Thomas Wayne asked, "Seni, what were the Assyrians planning?"

"To wipe out every living thing in this area."

"You see, whatever they do, it can't be to that level because we have crippled them."

Gloria sighed, "For now." She walked away.

Seni said, "She is mad."

"Yes, she is. How are the Assyrian women?"

"They used to do whatever we say, but lately they have become leaders in the government and military."

"Interesting. The same happened on Earth, but I guess it took a little longer on Assyria." The two men sat down in the dining area. "Now that you are one of us, we need to decide what to do with you."

"What does that mean?"

"That means we need to discuss our new alliance. We're also discussing an alliance with another human faction."

"I am only one person. There are no other Assyrians that have crossed the line. I only did so to save my brother. To go back would be death for me. I have no choice but to stay here. If I were you, I would lock me up."

Thomas Wayne's eyebrow rose. It was a precarious statement for Seni to make. Thomas Wayne didn't want to lock a man up for nothing. *If Seni can't trust himself, then why should I. I need to run this by Gloria.* "Okay, for now we will place you in a holding area."

"Not with my brother."

"It won't be with your brother. Just so you know, Elaine said he's doing well. She expects him to recover in a few weeks."

"That is great news."

Thomas Wayne motioned for the guards to take Seni to a cell. Gloria joined Thomas Wayne. She said, "We need to sit down with Duce. He can be a real help to us."

"Let's do it." Thomas Wayne followed Gloria to where Duce waited to meet. He walked in and extended his hand to Duce. Duce reciprocated in kind. Thomas Wayne motioned for him to have a seat. "I understand you are willing to align with us to fight our enemy."

Duce reared back, "The Bible says, 'the enemy of my enemy is my friend.'"

"You consider us enemies?"

"I believe in the world before all of this we would not be sitting down having coffee or discussing anything. You would be on one side of the street while I would be on the other. Now that we both have a common enemy, I realized we need to meet in the middle of the street and get rid of these bastards. After that's done, we can go back to our old ways."

Thomas Wayne didn't know what to make of this young man. He seemed wise for a thug, but uneducated to understand the biggest of pictures. "Going back to the way things were is a luxury none of us will ever enjoy." Thomas Wayne waited for a response. Duce sat and listened with a grin on his face. "You see, now that we know we're not alone in the universe, we will never be the same. If we, meaning Earth, get our hands on space travel technology, we will travel the stars just as man traveled the oceans."

Duce replied, "I guess I can't argue with that."

"That's a conversation for another day, though." Thomas Wayne locked in on Duce's eyes. He asked, "What do you envision this alignment looking like?"

Duce answered, "You scratch my back and Blackstreet will scratch yours. We go on missions together, take out the enemy and if there are any spoils, we divide them evenly."

Thomas Wayne nodded in agreement, then looked at Gloria. She wore her stoic face as normal. Thomas Wayne extended his hand again, "I think we can agree to help eradicate our mutual enemy. What happens after that, we'll see. I also want us to share information. Anything we learn, we'll pass to you and vice versa."

Duce popped his lips, "Sounds like a plan to me."

Thomas Wayne said, "How about we grab something to eat and formalize our alliance? Gloria, will you join us?"

"Yes."

"Great, let's do it." The group grabbed some food. During the meal, there was a ruckus outside on the street. Members of Blackstreet and the resistance squared off against each other. "This is not how an alliance should start. Duce, let's squash this." They rushed outside to stop the fracas before it got out of control. Duce's number one, Eddie, lead the members of Blackstreet.

Duce asked, "What's going on, Eddie?"

"Because of them, our home was destroyed. We barely made it out."

Duce replied, "What?"

Thomas Wayne asked, "Why do you feel this is on us?"

Eddie answered, "You blew up the mothership, right?" Thomas Wayne nodded in agreement. "That explosion chain reacted and ended up destroying our territory. We have nothing left but the clothes on our backs." Duce was angered by the report. His breathing increased and Thomas Wayne suspected nothing short of a fight would calm him down.

Duce said, "We have a problem, Thomas Wayne. This alliance can't be now. We need to rebuild our supplies." He stepped over to his people. "Starting with everything you have."

Thomas Wayne smiled, "You're kidding, right?" Members of Blackstreet raised their weapons and pointed them at Thomas Wayne and his people.

Thomas Wayne's people reciprocated. "Everyone, just calm down. We can fight it out here and draw the Assyrians to this location, or we can work something out. We've already agreed to an alliance. So, Duce, let's talk and agree to new terms."

Eddie shouted, "You mean terms that make us refugees? Not happening. You now have two enemies." Eddie turned to walk away. He looked at Duce, "Are you coming, bro?"

Duce looked at Eddie, then at Thomas Wayne. "You have me in a difficult position."

"Let's talk, man. We can work this out."

"No… whether you meant to or not, you destroyed our homes. I can't help you. If I were you, I would watch for the Assyrians—and us."

He turned and joined his people. They headed down Palmer Road toward Andrews Air Base. Thomas Wayne watched until they were out of view. He said to Gloria, "Inform our guards to be on the lookout for Assyrians as well as members of Blackstreet. It seems we have gained another enemy instead of a friend."

"Will do." Gloria sighed, "You should have talked to me before executing this plan." She walked away.

Thomas Wayne realized he made a mistake by not including Gloria in his plan. A mistake he wouldn't make again. For now, they stopped the annihilation of everyone in DC, Maryland, and Virginia. He had to celebrate that victory and not worry about the future.

Thomas Wayne lay in his bed staring at the ceiling. This would not be an easy war to fight. So many people were not aligned and fighting each other while the Assyrians were united. Someone needed to pull everyone together to fight back before no humans were left. Worrying about petty territory was childish.

He didn't know how long he was asleep when she caressed his chin and pecked him on the lips. He held her tightly in his arms. *Ah, this is just what I needed. A few minutes with this beautiful woman away from the world and our problems. Please don't let this stop.* He rolled her over and they removed each other's clothes. The world stopped while the two of them made love to each other.

Thomas Wayne held her in his arms while she slept. Elaine worked for three days straight. She was the only doctor in the camp. *She is so beautiful. If we were in the world that we knew, I would have asked her to marry me by now. Heck, I think I will anyway. Somehow, I have to get a ring and propose. We deserve each other.*

There was a resounding bang at the front door. It startled Thomas Wayne and Elaine. "Sorry, they woke you up, sweetheart."

"No worries."

Thomas Wayne rushed to the front door and opened it. Gloria said, "Seni is demanding to see you now."

"It can't wait." Gloria turned her head in disbelief. Thomas Wayne huffed, "I'll be back, Elaine."

"Okay."

"Lead the way." They walked to the holding area where Seni was being held. Thomas Wayne dared not say anything else, knowing Gloria was not happy. He passed several people in the hallways and nodded his head to each one. He wanted everyone to know he was assessable to them.

They arrived at the holding area, and Seni sat in the corner of the room. He jumped up when Thomas Wayne walked into the room. "I need to speak with you alone."

"My security chief needs to hear what I hear." Sweat rolled down Seni's face, and he paced the room. He looked at Thomas Wayne and Gloria. Thomas Wayne asked, "What is it Seni?"

"Zamar told me something during one of his threats to me. He said General Garima was dispatched to take control of the invasion. She is ruthless, more ruthless than General Ashur. Now that General Ashur is dead, she will want revenge. We are all dead."

Thomas Wayne said, "When is she due to arrive?"

"I'm not sure, but that's why the attacks have stopped. They are waiting for her to arrive."

"Then we will work to get ready." He turned to Gloria, "Get this information to the President. Our band of fighters can only do our part in this area, but the world leaders need to prepare everyone. This war just leveled up."

"Will do. Thanks, Thomas Wayne."

Thomas Wayne said, "Thanks, Seni. We will protect you."

"You cannot."

Thomas Wayne and Gloria left the room. Thomas Wayne said, "Gloria, I am sorry for not including you in the attack on the mothership. That will not happen again. From now on, you'll be in every meeting that involves strikes against the enemy. Okay?"

"Thanks, Thomas Wayne. We're all figuring this out, so I appreciate it. We need to get Blackstreet back on board."

"How?"

"Let me talk to Duce."

"Do you know where they are?"

"Some of our patrols saw them taking up residence at Andrews."

"Go but take some people with you."

"I think it would be best if I go alone."

"Okay, if you feel it's best."

"I do. Have you seen Cordell?"

"To speak of it, no. I'll have to find him."

Gloria nodded her head and walked away. Thomas Wayne headed back to his place to cuddle with his woman.

8 – General Garima

In her lavish home, General Garima finished dressing. Her husband lay across the bed, reluctant to see her go. "This campaign against the Terrans," she explained, "will be the most significant career advancement I can achieve. General Ashur's failure and my subsequent victory will position me to lead all the forces of the Assyrian Empire—a groundbreaking achievement for a woman."

General Garima loathed her husband, but his powerful family within the Empire was a necessary asset for her ambition. She craved a level of success no woman ever attained, and his influence was crucial. Each time he touched her, a wave of nausea rolled over her.

Staring intently into the mirror, she envisioned her coronation ceremony as the First General of the Assyrian Empire. A triumphant smile touched her lips. *"Once I achieve my goal,"* she vowed, *"I will ensure my husband meets with an unfortunate accident."* With that obstacle removed, she would finally be free to be with Ishaia, the man of her dreams.

She imagined herself in his embrace, the warmth of his skin against hers. He would accompany her on this campaign, offering stolen moments of intimacy amidst the chaos of war. These extended expeditions to distant worlds were her solace, providing precious time with the man she yearned for.

Emerging from the bathroom, General Garima sneered at her husband, Baaz, sprawled across the bed. He reached for her, his eyes pleading for intimacy.

Her communicator chimed. *"Thank you, Anu,"* she whispered, the relief palpable. *"I couldn't bear another moment with him."*

"General Garima," she announced.

"Ma'am, King Malka requests your presence in the General Hall."

"I will be there shortly," she replied. *"Anu, I owe you one. Please, end him before I return from this campaign."*

"I am sorry, my love, but I must report to the King."

"But you will be gone for so long."

"I apologize, but upon my return, I will make love to you endlessly," she lied, the thought of it making her stomach churn.

Baaz smiled, a predatory gleam in his eyes. "Then I shall patiently await my wife's return."

She kissed him perfunctorily, the taste of his breath leaving a vile aftertaste. Disgusted, she fled the room. Outside, she spat on the ground, as if to rid herself of the lingering taint of his presence.

General Garima arrived at the palace, a wave of reverence flowing over her as she passed the assembled guards. She entered the grand hall where King Malka awaited.

"General Garima," he greeted her, his voice powerful and confident. "I need you to expedite your departure to Adamina."

"Thank you again, Anu," she silently rejoiced. *"I can escape my husband sooner."* "May I inquire as to the reason for this urgency?"

"Indeed," the King replied, pouring himself a drink. "Your nemesis, General Ashur, has been killed by the Terrans. It seems he was not the formidable warrior we believed him to be." He took a long sip. "You are our best hope to restore the honor of Assyria. Can you handle this mission?"

"I will utterly destroy them, sire," she declared, her voice dripping with icy resolve. "Any survivors will be forced to serve our will. That, I promise you."

"Excellent," the King responded. "Be prepared to depart within the hour."

"Yes, sire." She turned and strode from the hall, a sinister grin spreading across her face. Inside, she reveled in General Ashur's demise. *"I must feign anger at the Terrans for killing our leader,"* she thought, *"but in truth, they have done me a great service. Perhaps I shall even reward the individual responsible with a swift and painless death."* The grin widened as she traversed the palace grounds, preparing for her departure to conquer Adamina.

General Garima stood on the main deck of her flagship, surveying her fleet with pride. King Malka addressed the assembled crew. "General Garima," he proclaimed, "it is an honor to entrust you with the task of rectifying the situation on Adamina. General Ashur gravely underestimated the Terrans, but I have no such doubts about your abilities. Return with the Terran leader's head as a trophy, and you will be appointed supreme commander of all Assyrian forces."

"Thank you, sire," she replied, her voice firm. "We will not disappoint."

"I have no doubt that you will not," the King affirmed.

The screen went dark, and General Garima barked, "Open a channel to the fleet."

"Channel opened, Ma'am," the warrior's voice replied.

"Fleet, this is your General. You have heard the King's orders. Our mission is to reclaim Adamina and avenge General Ashur's failures. We will not falter. Every member of this fleet will be handsomely rewarded for their service. And should you fall in battle, your families will be provided for. Now, let us proceed to Adamina with swift and decisive action, and reclaim what is rightfully ours."

The fleet surged forward, a swarm of warships hurtling towards a planet they abandoned centuries ago, each crew member driven by a thirst for vengeance and the promise of glory.

General Garima headed towards her quarters, eager to rejoin her lover. However, she was intercepted in the corridor by one of her warriors. "Ma'am, your husband has arrived on board. He is currently in your quarters."

The news sent a jolt of icy dread through her. "I see," she replied, her tone carefully neutral. "Thank you for the information." The warrior saluted and departed.

As she approached her quarters, the scene that unfolded before her chilled her to the bone. Baaz and Ishaia stood facing each other, an air of simmering tension between them. *"It seems my plans for his accidental demise will need to be expedited,"* she thought, a cold resolve hardening her features. *"This man is an obstacle. I must eliminate him in a way that his family will be compelled to support me."*

"Baaz," she said, her voice deceptively calm, "I am surprised to see you have joined us on this campaign."

"Equally surprised, I daresay," Baaz retorted, his eyes gleaming with a dangerous light. "Especially considering the company you keep. I can have you stripped of your command, even executed, if I choose. Not even the King can protect you."

"You won't do that," General Garima growled, her eyes narrowed.

"Why not?"

General Garima countered, a chilling amusement in her voice. "Even with your family's influence, you must understand the gravity of this situation. We must reclaim our ancestral home, Adamina. It is the only viable planet for our survival."

"That's not true," Baaz scoffed.

"Evidently, they haven't fully informed you," Garima said, a hint of disdain in her tone. "Allow me to enlighten you. Assyria has less than a year before it faces imminent destruction. A massive asteroid is on a collision course with our planet, an event that will undoubtedly spell our doom. There are no other habitable planets within our reach. We require a new world, a source of labor to exploit the resources we need for survival. Adamina provides both. The Terrans, however, are a tenacious race. They will not surrender easily. My role is to avenge General Ashur and eliminate every last Terran resistance. We have a narrow window of opportunity to complete this campaign and relocate our people to Adamina. If you obstruct my path, the King will have no choice but to eliminate you as a threat."

Baaz stared at her, his voice a low growl, "I've given you everything you've ever asked for, and more. I have been a devoted husband. Why have you betrayed me?"

"You're not a warrior, Baaz," Garima spat, her contempt evident. "You spend your days cooped up, manipulating numbers on your computer. I crave a man of action, a true warrior like me. Ishaia is that man. He and I were destined to be together."

Baaz's lips curled into a sneer. "I see. My influence may be limited during this crucial mission, but it's not entirely insignificant. I can still ensure Ishaia's downfall. He won't escape my wrath." He gestured towards the door with a chillingly casual wave. "Get out," he commanded, his gaze icy.

Ishaia, his face a mask of chilling amusement, exchanged a knowing glance with General Garima before leaving the quarters. *He knows,* she realized with a grim satisfaction. *He understands the lengths I'm willing to go for our love.* By nightfall, Baaz would be gone. She would fabricate a plausible story, her ambition fueled by the promise of victory on Adamina.

Ishaia closed the door behind him, leaving them alone. "So, you know about Ishaia," General Garima said, her voice deceptively calm. "You know the importance of this mission to Assyria. What are your intentions?"

Baaz remained silent for a long moment; his gaze fixed on the swirling stars beyond the window. General Garima tensed, prepared to defend herself. But instead of lashing out, he moved towards her, his expression unexpectedly gentle. "I love you, Brula," he confessed, his voice husky. "I wouldn't want to harm you. But I cannot allow him to continue to exist. I will use my influence to have him removed from his position, exiled to a remote outpost where he will be long forgotten."

"I wish you hadn't said that," General Garima stated, her voice low and dangerous.

"If you believe I would allow you to jeopardize my plans, you are gravely mistaken," Baaz retorted, his eyes narrowing. "I have contingencies in place. Should anything befall me, the knowledge of your affair will be swiftly delivered to my family and the King. You will be permitted to complete this mission, but any aspirations of leading the Assyrian forces will be utterly extinguished."

Hate surged through General Garima, a venomous tide threatening to consume her. She yearned to strangle him with her bare hands, but the chilling reminder of his precautions held her back. Instead, she would play along, a venomous serpent biding its time. "Very well, my love," she conceded, her voice dripping with feigned sincerity. "I will cease this... indiscretion. I ask only that you spare Ishaia any professional repercussions. I should not have involved him in this."

Baaz scrutinized her, his gaze searching for any signs of deception. She met his eyes with a chillingly calm facade, hoping her carefully crafted performance was convincing. Time was of the essence. She needed time to formulate her next move, and this charade was the only way to buy it. In time, she would have her position, her lover, and the sweet satisfaction of revenge against Baaz.

The seven-day journey to Adamina was now underway, the second day already dawning. The abrupt shift in time zones would undoubtedly wreak havoc on the crew, and General Garima would be no exception. She stood at the head of the conference room, dismissing her colonels. Ishaia remained behind, a knowing glint in his eyes. "May I assist you, Colonel?" she inquired, her tone dry.

He smirked, "So, that's where we stand now?"

"You know as well as I do the influence his family wields," General Garima replied, her voice low and dangerous. "If I abandon him now, I lose everything."

"I understand," Ishaia acknowledged, rising to his feet. "I merely assumed you would have dealt with him more... decisively."

"I cannot afford such impulsive actions," she hissed. "He has proof of our affair. If I act now, I will win the campaign but get nothing for my troubles. You... you will become a forgotten man tucked away on some outpost far away from anywhere or worst— dead. I can't have that."

"I see," Ishaia replied, his expression unreadable.

"We must be patient," she cautioned. "I will devise a plan, but for now, discretion is paramount. We must maintain a safe distance."

"I will wait for you," he assured her, his voice low and intense. "A single day away from you feels like an eternity. Let us make this brief separation as bearable as possible."

"You are the only man who can make me forget the horrors of this existence," she admitted, a fleeting smile touching her lips. He turned and left, leaving her alone with her thoughts.

The sudden interruption of a lieutenant shattered her reverie. "Ma'am, we have an incoming communication from Adamina."

"I will take it here," she commanded, her voice regaining its steely edge.

"General Garima," the voice on the screen announced, "we are under attack. The Terrans have launched a surprise assault, believing us to be vulnerable."

"Colonel," she barked, "organize your forces and counterattack with all your might. Hold the line until we arrive. If you fail… I expect you to meet your demise with honor."

"Yes, ma'am." The transmission ended, leaving her with a chilling sense of foreboding. She rose and strode towards the bridge, hoping the urgency of the situation would provide a temporary distraction from the complexities of her personal life.

9 – Blackstreet Discussions

After the Assyrian mothership exploded, many warriors were left leaderless, descending upon the streets of Clinton, Suitland, and Andrews in Maryland. The city, once a haven, became a killing ground. Gloria, desperate to find Duce, made her way towards Andrews' Virginia Gate.

She knew if she could reach the headquarters building, she might find him. The Assyrians, known for their boldness, wouldn't be subtle about their presence, making her infiltration easier. Crossing the street, she slipped through the gate and navigated the golf course, reaching Perimeter Road.

She wished she there were time to scavenge the nearby hospital for supplies but pressed on, staying in the shadows. Approaching the headquarters, she spotted an Assyrian squad entering the building. Panic surged; she needed to warn Duce.

She hurried to a different entrance, fortunate to find one close to where she believed Duce's headquarters was located. As she burst in, guns were leveled at her.

"Lower your weapons," Duce commanded. "Ya'll this is my girl, Gloria."

Gloria said through her panting, "I'd love to chat, but you got company. An Assyrian squad entering the building."

He smiled. "Don't worry, honey. They're not the enemy."

The Assyrians entered the area. "See, when your boss destroyed our supplies and living quarters, I had a choice: war with the resistance or an alliance with the Assyrians. I chose the latter."

"Duce, you can't!" Gloria exclaimed.

"Too late. We can't have you informing Thomas Wayne about this." He gestured to Eddie. "Lock her up with the others. We have resistance fighters to eliminate."

"No, Duce, please!" Gloria pleaded, but Eddie dragged her away, tossing her into a guarded room.

"Make yourself comfortable," Eddie sneered. "You'll be here a minute."

Gloria's rigid expression spoke volumes. "You think I'll stay here and let you traitors kill my friends? I'm getting out of here." She scanned the room, searching for an ally. Most looked timid, but one man in the corner caught her eye—Cordell.

"Cordell? What in the world…" She approached him. "How did you get here? We've been searching for you."

"My team was captured a few days ago," he said, his voice somber. "They were killed, but I was injured and brought here."

"Let me see," Gloria urged, examining his wound. "It's not serious, you'll heal."

"Unfortunately," he muttered.

"Unfortunately? What's wrong, Cordell?"

"I let my team die. I was the leader; I should have been the one to go down."

"We'll face losses in this war, Cordell. We need you focused. We need to escape before they reach our camp."

"These people won't fight," he scoffed.

"That's why I'm counting on you to lead them. Why are they holding them here? I understand why we're here, but them?"

"They know about their dealings with the Assyrians."

Gloria scowled. "I can't stand people who betray their own."

"It's a recurring theme in our history, both as Black people and as humans. The FBI infiltrated the Black Panthers, using Black people."

"Who?" Gloria asked, confused.

"You need to learn more about your Black history, Gloria."

"I wasn't much for history, Black, white, or otherwise," she admitted.

Cordell remained silent. "We need to escape," Gloria continued. "I noticed two guards at the door. Anything else?"

"They feed us twice a day. The next feeding should be soon."

"That might be our chance. Maybe someone fakes being sick or needs to go to the bathroom."

"Girl, it's 2081. You really think that will still work?"

"We have to try something. Besides I didn't know who the Black Panthers were, maybe they don't know this trick."

"Okay. I'll follow your lead."

"Cool." Now, I just needed to devise a plan to save everyone, get to the camp, and warn them. No problem, right? Gloria leaned against the wall, contemplating her situation. Fighting became her daily reality.

I don't know how long this war will last, she thought, *but I'm going to give it my all to survive and keep others alive.*

The guards delivered the food, and Gloria watched for an opportunity. They were clearly untrained, just street thugs with guns. This was her chance.

One guard stood close. *His gun is within reach,* she thought. *I can grab it, neutralize the other guard, and get everyone out.*

She nudged Cordell, signaling her plan. He nodded, but she knew he could offer limited support.

Counting in her head, she exploded into action. In a single fluid motion, she snatched the guard's weapon. The other guard panicked, using a young girl as a shield.

Two shots rang out. The guard crumpled. "Don't do anything stupid," she warned the remaining guard, who raised his hands in surrender.

"Cordell, get these people to safety. I need to reach the camp." She pointed at another man. "Tie him up."

The man quickly secured the guard. "Have they left for my camp yet?" she demanded.

The guard's face hardened. He refused to answer.

"Is this how you want to die?" she asked, cocking the gun.

"They left about ten minutes ago," he finally admitted.

"Good, gag him." The man complied. "I'm going to run ahead to warn Thomas Wayne. If I don't make it, get these people to safety."

"I will, you be safe, Gloria." She nodded at Cordell and headed out. The camp was nine miles away via Allentown Road, but she knew Duce and the Assyrians would likely take that route. To gain an advantage, she decided to cut through several side streets.

They have a ten-minute head start, but I can catch up… I have to catch up.

Fatigue began to weigh on her. *I need to rest. They can't be far ahead, if they are ahead at all.* She scanned the surroundings for a safe place to pause.

In the distance, she heard voices. *I must have passed them on those side roads.* She cautiously peered around a corner and spotted Duce with a group of Assyrian warriors.

She waited until they passed, then veered off course. This would add time to her journey, but a confrontation was too risky right now. *I have to reach the camp before them.*

Suddenly, she heard the sound of an approaching vehicle. She quickly ducked off the road, hoping they hadn't seen her.

A man emerged from the vehicle. "Gloria!" he whispered.

"Here!" She raced towards him. "Where did you get the vehicle?"

"It was abandoned near the hotel. Someone knew it was there, so we took it to reach the camp. Get in!"

Relief fell over her as she saw Cordell and two others. Now she could reach the camp before Duce and the Assyrians. "We need to take Tucker Road and approach from the opposite side of the apartments. If we continue this way, we'll run into them."

"Good, that's the plan," Cordell replied. "You look like you've been running a marathon."

"Very funny." Gloria felt a surge of hope. She could save her friends. *I can't believe Duce betrayed us. I almost...* She shuddered at the thought of what could have been.

They reached the camp, but it was deserted. Gloria and Cordell searched frantically, but everyone was gone. "Where could they have gone?" she wondered.

"I don't know. I expected them to be here too."

"We need to get back in the car and get out of here before Duce arrives. Maybe Thomas Wayne received intelligence and moved everyone."

"Maybe, that's all we can assume right now." Cordell ushered everyone back into the vehicle and they sped off. "We need to warn others and prevent them from coming here."

As they drove, the sound of gunfire and laser blasts erupted from the direction of Palmer Road. Gloria slammed on the brakes. "We need to see what's happening!"

Cordell jumped out beside her. "Pull the car across the street and hide. If we don't return in an hour, get out of here."

The man nodded. "Okay, Gloria, let's go."

"You're injured. You can't do this."

"The heck I can't. I need to help those people. If Duce got to them, it's on me."

The shooting subsided. They cautiously approached the scene and found Thomas Wayne and his fighters standing victorious.

Gloria let out a sigh of relief. "Dude, I'm so glad to see you. We were worried about everyone."

"We received word that the Assyrians allied with Duce. They were planning to attack the camp. We evacuated everyone and set up an ambush."

Gloria smiled. "Good job, bro. Where's Duce?"

Thomas Wayne gestured towards the area where Duce was being treated for a gunshot wound. Gloria approached him, unsure what to say.

Duce sneered. "If you were in my position, you would have done the same."

Gloria leaned closer. "I would never betray my people for anything. You're the lowest. You're lucky we don't have summary executions. Because if we did, I'd shoot you now."

She turned and walked away, ignoring his furious shouts.

Thomas Wayne chuckled. "You really got under his skin."

"Can we institute summary executions?" she asked jokingly.

"No. We will never be like the Assyrians."

10 – Building Human Forces

News of a burgeoning coalition spread through the camp like wildfire. A message from President Hemingway announced that factions across the country were uniting. For the first time since the war began, the United States was rebuilding its forces and strategizing counter-offensives against the Assyrians. President Hemingway specifically credited Thomas Wayne's Northeast region for spearheading this crucial organizational effort.

The impact of destroying the Assyrian mothership was undeniable. With their command and control severely disrupted, Assyrian activity within the United States significantly diminished. No one knew the extent of their reliance on the mothership and their leader, but the loss was clearly a devastating blow.

Thomas Wayne felt a surge of pride. The world was finally fighting back. Borders became irrelevant as nations united against the common enemy. Earth was reclaiming its strength, and it felt good to be human again.

Back at the camp, he found Elaine resting in bed. He was grateful for the influx of medical personnel from across the region, providing much-needed support. The trip to Philadelphia, the new capital of the United States, would be long and arduous, but necessary. The East Coast needed to convene and devise a plan for the impending Assyrian onslaught. Intelligence from Seni painted a grim picture: an all-out blitz designed to leave no survivors.

He gently touched her shoulder. "I have to leave, sweetheart."

A smile graced her lips. "I know, my love. Please be safe." She reached up and gently pulled him down for a kiss. Their lips met, a tender dance of love and longing. To Thomas Wayne, each kiss felt both fleeting and eternal.

"Your kisses aren't helping me leave," he murmured.

"But you have to go, honey. Be safe."

"I'll worry about you every moment."

"There's no need to worry. Cordell will keep us safe."

He rose and pulled her to her feet. They walked towards the door, hand in hand. One last lingering kiss. "Bye, sweetheart."

"Until we meet again."

He smiled and stepped out. Gloria, walking down the hall, couldn't help but snicker. "Lovebirds, oh my God. Will I have to endure stories about how wonderful Elaine is for the entire trip?"

"You might just have to," he replied with a chuckle. "Taking on the responsibility for this region hasn't been easy, but we've achieved a lot. And I couldn't have done it without you and Cordell."

"Thank you. Make sure you tell the President that." She smiled, though he knew she wasn't one for accolades.

"I will certainly remind him of your contributions to the Northeast."

"He doesn't strike me as the forgetful type," she remarked.

"True."

"Oh man, I'm not looking forward to this horse ride."

"Me neither. With gas almost nonexistent, it's either horses or walking." He tried to conceal a grimace. He had limited experience with horses, to put it mildly.

Gloria added, "You can ride right?"

"Yeah, I have a little experience." He laughed inside knowing the extent of his experience was a merry-go-round at the fair. He dared not admit that hoping he could adapt and ride the horse without exposing his non-existent skills.

The horses were waiting on Allentown Road for the group to mount and ride off. Thomas Wayne watched at others mount their horses and tried to do the same. It didn't work. Gloria laughed. *I thought I could get away with it.*

Gloria guided her horse towards him and helped him mount. "Mr. Macho Man. All you had to do was say you were inexperienced. I would have helped."

"Busted. Lead the way, my Chief of Security."

"You got it."

They set off towards Philadelphia, a cavalcade of riders heading towards the future of their nation. The people of Fort Washington waved farewell, offering silent prayers for their safe return.

Just a short time ago, their survival seemed uncertain. Now, they were riding towards a future where they would not just survive but fight back.

The conference in Philadelphia would bring together representatives from the Southeast, Midwest, and Northeast, as well as Canada. A similar conference would be held in Colorado for the West Coast. Soon, a united North America would be ready to face the Assyrian onslaught.

The Coalition of North America Conference

The Northeast delegation arrived at the Philadelphia Convention Center, a stark contrast to the bustling hub it once was. War ravaged the city, leaving its mark on every building, every street. They were ushered to the 200 level, the grand hall where the conference would be held. Finding suitable lodging in this war-torn city was a challenge, but the center made provisions for the delegates.

As Thomas Wayne entered the hall, he was struck by the sight of representatives from across the nation, each wearing a badge identifying their region. A buzz of conversation filled the air.

"Alright, team," he instructed after they registered, "let's mingle and get to know some of these people."

"Friends or not, I'm staying with you," Gloria declared. "You are my responsibility."

"Let me guess, Elaine put you on guard duty?" Thomas Wayne teased, a smile playing on his lips. "I'll be fine, Gloria. You don't need to be attached to my hip."

"I do, and I will. Now, let's meet some people."

They approached a woman from the Midwest. "Hi, I'm Thomas Wayne Walker from the Northeast region. This is my head of security, Gloria Davis."

"Nice to meet you both. I'm Rhonda Similton from the Midwest. We're headquartered at McConnell Air Force Base in Wichita, Kansas. It was hit hard, like most bases, but we've managed to carve out a space and establish a headquarters. Thankfully, we had some resourceful civil engineers who helped."

"That's impressive. We're based near Andrews Air Force Base. Like your base, all the bases in the DC area were severely impacted. Andrews was first occupied by the Assyrians, and then by a local gang that allied with them," Thomas Wayne explained.

"We've faced similar challenges," Gloria added. "Some factions, unfortunately, chose to align with the enemy."

"Exactly. My friend Christopher Robinson is holding down the fort back in Wichita. I just hope these rogue human elements don't cause further trouble. It's the last thing we need right now."

"You're right about that," Gloria agreed.

A man stepped onto the stage, commanding attention. "Representatives from every region and Canada, please take your seats. The conference will now commence."

The room fell silent as everyone found their places.

"My name is Tony Hibler, and I will be facilitating this conference. Please feel free to ask any questions. Now, let's begin. This conference will be brief, as each of you needs to return to your regions and prepare for what lies ahead. Intelligence indicates an imminent and far more devastating Assyrian attack."

A collective gasp rippled through the room.

"Without further ado, please rise for the President of the United States of America."

The room erupted in applause as President Hemingway took the podium. "Good day to each of you. It is an honor to address this gathering. This is a historic moment as we unite in our fight for survival."

Applause filled the hall. "I, for one, would not be standing here today if it were not for the bravery of the Northeast Region. I know several of them sacrificed their very lives to keep me safe. I am forever grateful for them. Will the members of the Northeast please stand?"

Thomas Wayne and his crew stood while others in the room applauded their successful mission to save the President. President Hemingway continued, 'Thomas Wayne Walker, leader of the Northeast Region, please come forward.'

Thomas Wayne, though uncomfortable with the spotlight, couldn't decline the President's request. He approached the podium, joining the President. "Ladies and gentlemen," President Hemingway declared, "The Presidential Medal of Freedom is the nation's highest civilian honor, bestowed upon those who have made extraordinary contributions to the prosperity, values, or security of the United States, world peace, or other significant societal, public, or private endeavors. It is my privilege to award this medal to Thomas Wayne Walker for his leadership in restoring our nation's strength and defending our freedom. Saving my life, the life of the Secretary of Defense, and the destruction of the Assyrian mothership are just a few of the Northeast Region's remarkable achievements on behalf of America."

Thomas Wayne bowed his head as the medal was placed around his neck. President Hemingway shook his hand and offered him the podium.

Addressing such a distinguished audience was a daunting experience for Thomas Wayne. Taking a deep breath, he began, "This medal is a true honor, but it does not belong to me alone. I could not have accomplished anything without the dedication and courage of the men and women of the Northeast Region. Each of them deserves recognition, and I will ensure this medal is displayed in a way that honors their contributions.

One individual in particular deserves exceptional praise. Without her, our mission would have failed. Gloria Davis, please stand."

Gloria rose to her feet. "Ladies and gentlemen," Thomas Wayne said, "This is the most courageous person I know. She single-handedly saved the President and the Secretary of Defense." Applause erupted, and murmurs of admiration filled the room. "I understand the importance of honoring those who have served in this war," Thomas Wayne continued, "but now is the time to focus on the challenges that lie ahead. We must prepare for what is to come. Thank you."

Thomas Wayne received a standing ovation as he returned to his seat.

Gloria whispered, "You didn't have to do that. You know how shy I am."

Thomas Wayne looked at her with a mock exasperation, "Really?"

President Hemingway resumed, "Thomas Wayne is correct. It is time to address the critical issues at hand. As you all know, intelligence indicates an imminent second wave of the Assyrian invasion, and this time, it will be far more devastating. The Assyrians are enraged by our resistance and the destruction of their mothership. They are now determined to eradicate all life on this planet. Again, I might add." A nervous chuckle rippled through the room, but Thomas Wayne remained somber. "They will not be seeking slaves; they will be seeking our annihilation."

A heavy silence descended upon the room. "From what I understand," President Hemingway continued, "the Assyrian Empire is utterly arrogant. Our act of defiance has enraged them, fearing that it will inspire rebellion across the worlds they have conquered. We must be prepared to defend ourselves to the very end. General Roe, please provide us with a briefing."

General Roe began, 'Yes, sir. Ladies and gentlemen, my team has been in close contact with each of your security chiefs and civil engineers. We have provided specifications to aid in withstanding the second wave of attack. Our experience with the first wave highlighted the effectiveness of underground sanctuaries, especially those submerged in water. I have reports for each region outlining potential locations for these sanctuaries, and we have initiated efforts to fortify these structures and stock them with food, water, and medical supplies. Upon your return, it is your duty to verify this information and submit a comprehensive report to command. Are there any questions?'

Silence followed. "Good. General Mace will now address the critical issue of communications."

"Good day, everyone. Communications are paramount in any engagement. The Assyrians gained a significant advantage in the first wave by disrupting our satellite and communication networks. This isolated us, leaving us vulnerable. This time, we have implemented a robust system to ensure inter-regional communication. Each region will be responsible for internal communication within its own boundaries. We have collaborated with a dedicated communications officer within each region, and they are well-versed in the system. Cheyanne Mountain has provided a supply of radios that have been distributed to each region.

As a contingency plan in case of complete communication failure, we have established a chain of riders to deliver messages between regions. This will be a slower process, so patience will be required if necessary. Let us hope our radio network remains intact this time. We have also trained each communications officer in the use of signal flags. We must be prepared for all eventualities. Are there any questions?"

Gloria raised her hand. "Sir, my name is Gloria Davis." General Mace acknowledged her. "With such a heavy reliance on the communications officer, are we training backups to assume this role in case of casualties?"

"Yes, Gloria, each region is responsible for identifying and training backup personnel. This principle applies to all critical roles. Backups are arguably your most valuable asset, along with a well-defined chain of command that everyone understands and adheres to in the event of casualties. Any further questions?"

Seeing no further questions, General Mace concluded, "Mr. President."

President Hemingway resumed, "Gloria, to further emphasize General Mace's point, a robust chain of command is absolutely essential. The Assyrians suffered a significant setback in the first wave due to the absence of such a structure. When their general fell, internal conflict erupted among the colonels, allowing us a crucial window to recover and counterattack.

This is not solely a challenge for the United States. As you can see, Canada is represented here today. Europe, Asia, and the Middle East have all recognized the importance of this unprecedented opportunity. All of Europe is united in its efforts. The Middle East has ceased its internal conflicts. African nations are collaborating. Our collective goal is to defeat this enemy and preserve this newfound global unity.

Regional leaders, I cannot overemphasize the importance of establishing a clear and unambiguous chain of command. Tony?"

Tony stepped forward. "Ladies and gentlemen, the remainder of your day will be dedicated to reviewing the supplies and information available at each table for your respective regions. We recommend departing for your regions at first light tomorrow. We have also prepared handouts detailing fuel acquisition strategies, which are crucial.

I wish you all the best for the remainder of the day."

Thomas Wayne, Gloria, and the rest of the crew made their way to the designated tables. Thomas Wayne ensured that the Northeast Region received all the necessary information and supplies. He understood that the Northeast would likely be the initial target of the second wave, given their role in the destruction of the first wave's mothership.

11 - Back at the Camp

Cordell worked alongside civil engineers to fortify their underground sanctuary in anticipation of the second wave. Instructions from the President's staff arrived, and preparations commenced before Thomas Wayne's return. The sanctuary required thorough sewage removal to ensure the safety and well-being of its future inhabitants. Crews worked tirelessly, battling both the formidable task and intermittent attacks from Assyrian squads.

Cordell was summoned to the medical office, where he encountered Elaine, her face clinched up at the scent. "I know we've been working to clear out the sewage to ensure your survival down there," Cordell said, "No point in surviving the Assyrian bombs only to succumb to disease."

"That's for sure," Elaine replied, pinching her nose before releasing it. "We have a problem."

"What is it?"

"Seni panicked, grabbed a knife, and inflicted a self-inflicted wound. We need blood for his survival, but our supply is dwindling. If we use it all on him and another emergency arises, there could be serious repercussions."

"I understand."

"We can't let him die, Cordell."

"If I let him die, Elaine, Thomas Wayne would hold me accountable. We're not the Assyrians. Use what's left to save him."

"I already have," she said, twisting her head. "I just wanted to inform you. If anyone has objections, they can address them to my future husband."

Cordell chuckled. "And so it begins."

"Indeed, it begins when life and death are at stake," Elaine said with a playful dance. "As a nurse, I don't let people die, regardless of their origin."

"I understand. Is that all?"

"Yes, sir."

Cordell returned to the sewer, a faint scent of air freshener lingering in the air, a reminder of Elaine's efforts to mitigate the unpleasant odors. As he navigated the labyrinthine tunnels, his thoughts drifted back to his childhood in North Carolina. His passion for basketball started when he was young, and he envisioned building a court after the second wave, a place where he and the others could find solace and camaraderie. However, the pressing need for survival overshadowed such aspirations.

A young woman, covered in grime and dirt, approached Cordell. "Do I know you?" she asked.

"I don't think so," Cordell replied. "My name is Aaliyah, and I'm searching for my brother, Thomas Wayne Walker."

Cordell's eyes widened. "You're Thomas Wayne's sister? We've been searching for you!"

"We've been on the run, trying to evade both gangs and the Assyrians. These are my friends. Can we find refuge here?"

"Absolutely. You're welcome here. Thomas Wayne is currently at a conference, but he should be returning within a few days. Follow me."

The group of five, including Thomas Wayne's sister, followed Cordell. "Finally, some good news," he exclaimed. "Thomas Wayne will be ecstatic to know we've found you."

He guided them to the medical office. "Elaine, look who I've found!"

Elaine looked puzzled, then recognition dawned. "Oh my goodness, it's Thomas Wayne's sister!"

"And you are?" Aaliyah inquired.

"I'm Thomas Wayne's fiancée," Elaine replied. "We plan to marry before the second wave begins, hopefully."

"My brother is engaged?" Aaliyah asked, surprised.

"Indeed," Elaine confirmed. "I consider myself incredibly fortunate."

Aaliyah smiled. "Welcome to the family."

"Thank you, Aaliyah," Elaine said. "Cordell, I'll take care of them from here. I'll find them food and a place to clean up."

"I'm honored to meet you all," Cordell said. "We hope you can assist us in defeating these despicable Assyrians." They exchanged smiles and followed Elaine.

Cordell returned to the sewer to complete the work at hand. He encountered Airman Baker, who assured him that all communications were functioning as instructed by Cheyanne Mountain. Everything seemed to be proceeding smoothly. Cordell anticipated returning the camp to Thomas Wayne's command without incident.

Later, while enjoying a rare hot shower due to the electricity rationing, the sounds of gunfire shattered the tranquility. Looking out the window, he witnessed Assyrian warriors and members of the Blackstreet gang launching an attack on the camp.

Cordell grabbed his weapon and rushed to the front lines, shouting instructions to his fighters and returning fire. "They're trying to rescue Duce and the others," he yelled. "Move towards their position!" His men responded, advancing towards the enemy.

Cordell led the charge, but it became clear that they were outmatched. A blast whizzed past him, striking the medical office. "We need to flank them!" he shouted.

"What do you suggest?" asked a soldier beside him.

"Take two men with you," Cordell instructed, "and move behind that dumpster. Then head towards Building 4. You can outflank them if you approach from the rear. Move quickly!"

The soldiers departed. Cordell and the remaining fighters held their ground, desperately awaiting the counterattack. Shots rang out from behind the Assyrian lines, and the tide began to turn. "Hold on!" Cordell yelled. "Our reinforcements are arriving!"

However, the victory was short-lived. A devastating blast struck down the two soldiers beside him. Cordell dropped to the ground, mourning their loss. "I'm sorry, my brothers," he muttered, closing their eyes. "Move to the holding area and assess the situation. Determine if we've thwarted Blackstreet's attempt to rescue Duce."

"Yes, sir."

Cordell rushed towards the medical office, the scene of devastation unfolding before him. Rubble was strewn everywhere, beds overturned, and cries of pain echoed through the air. Seni, despite their best efforts, gave into his injuries.

"We could have saved that blood," Cordell lamented.

He moved on, encountering another casualty. Then, he spotted Elaine, lying motionless on the floor. He carefully navigated the debris to reach her. Blood trickled from a head wound, but she was still breathing.

"Sir, let me assist," a nurse offered.

Cordell stepped back, allowing the nurse to assess Elaine's condition. Another nurse joined her. "Can you help us move her to the table?" the first nurse asked.

Cordell supported Elaine's legs while the nurses gently lifted her head and shoulders. They placed her on the table and began their examination.

"Will she be alright?" Cordell inquired.

"It's uncertain," the nurse replied. "She may have a concussion, but a proper diagnosis is impossible without our equipment.

"What do you require?" Cordell asked, attempting to lighten the mood. "An MRI machine would be ideal, wouldn't it?"

"Indeed," the nurse replied. "However, there are no signs of discoloration around her eyes or behind her ears. She's breathing, and the head wound, while concerning, doesn't appear to be life-threatening. We need to monitor her closely."

"Please do," Cordell said. "I cannot allow Thomas Wayne's fiancée to perish under my watch."

He left the medical office to assess the damage and determine the fate of Duce and his men. Upon reaching the holding area, he found his men dead and discovered that Duce and Zamar escaped.

"I've failed," Cordell thought. "I've let Thomas Wayne and the camp down."

A fighter approached him. "Don't blame yourself for this attack," he said. "We had guards in place, but we were simply outgunned."

"I understand," Cordell acknowledged, "but as the leader, the responsibility ultimately falls on my shoulders."

Trouble on the Return

Thomas Wayne's crew rode their horses back to camp, the familiar terrain signaling their impending arrival. He yearned for Elaine's embrace, the nine days of separation proving to be a difficult trial. He realized how deeply he loved and missed her.

Suddenly, Gloria halted the group. "Something feels wrong," she declared as she dismounted and scrutinized the ground. "I sense a disturbance."

"It's likely nothing unusual," Thomas Wayne replied. "This area is probably heavily traveled as people migrate from city to city."

"That's true," Gloria conceded, "but why are the tracks so fragmented?"

Before he could respond, a volley of bullets erupted. The attackers, clearly human given the use of firearms, ambushed them. Thomas Wayne's crew quickly sought cover and returned fire.

"We cannot engage in this internal conflict!" Thomas Wayne shouted, raising his voice above the din of battle. "My name is Thomas Wayne Walker of the Northeast Region. There's no reason for us to fight. Let's talk."

A voice emerged from the dust, "We want your horses and supplies."

"We're not giving you anything!" Gloria retorted.

Thomas Wayne gently admonished her, "If you please, allow me to negotiate." Gloria rolled her eyes and sighed in exasperation.

"We cannot relinquish our horses and supplies," Thomas Wayne explained. "They are crucial for our survival during the impending second wave. Have you heard of the second wave?" Silence met his inquiry. "Your silence suggests you haven't. The Assyrians are not finished. They intend to eradicate all life on Earth. You are welcome to seek refuge with us. We have ample space."

The attackers remained silent.

Thomas Wayne stood tall, facing the enemy. A group of men emerged, clad in ragged clothing and armed with a motley assortment of rifles and pistols. "You can join us," Thomas Wayne offered. "If you lack a secure haven, you're in grave danger."

A woman stepped forward from behind the group, standing a few feet from Thomas Wayne. She exuded a formidable presence yet possessed an undeniable beauty. She surveyed Thomas Wayne's crew, her gaze assessing each individual. "My name is Hunter Cruz," she announced. "We've been fighting for our survival since the initial attack. We've trusted others, only to be betrayed. We won't be exploited again. Surrender your supplies and horses, or we will eliminate you all."

"Bring it on, lady," Gloria scoffed.

Thomas Wayne sighed, "Gloria." He locked eyes with Hunter. "We're at an impasse. We will not surrender our supplies and horses. However, we offer you a place to stay, access to our food, clothing, medical supplies, and everything else we possess. In return, we ask that you join us in the fight against the Assyrians. No one intends to exploit you."

Hunter looked at her men, her expression betraying a thoughtful contemplation of his proposal. "Let me discuss this with my people," she finally stated, returning to her group.

Gloria leaned towards Thomas Wayne. "Do you think she'll accept your offer?"

"I hope so. We need to proceed. We're losing valuable time. I need to return to Elaine."

Gloria chuckled, "You're smitten."

"Indeed, I am," he admitted.

Hunter returned. "If we accept your offer, but later if we decide to leave, what are the terms?"

"You are free to depart at any time," Thomas Wayne assured her. "However, I believe you won't regret your decision."

"How far is your headquarters?" Hunter inquired.

"Gloria?" Thomas Wayne asked.

"We're approximately 20 miles away," Gloria confirmed, "so we're nearing the end of our journey."

"We will join you," Hunter agreed, "but we cannot guarantee our allegiance indefinitely. We will give it a try."

"How many of you are there?" Thomas Wayne asked.

"Twenty of us remain," she replied, surveying her group. "We were initially fifty, but we've suffered significant losses due to betrayal and conflict."

"You won't be exploited here," Thomas Wayne assured her. "We only have the horses you see. I'm unsure how far we can travel on foot, but we'll find a way."

"We have a few horses as well," Hunter offered. "Perhaps some of your people can travel with us on foot, while some of my people ride with you?"

"That sounds feasible," Thomas Wayne agreed. "Gloria, can you coordinate this?"

"Certainly."

Thomas Wayne turned and smiled, "By the way, it's not my people or your people anymore. We're all one people." Hunter nodded with a smile.

They divided the horses between the two groups, assigning the younger and stronger members to walk while the children and elderly rode. Thomas Wayne enjoyed the conversation with Hunter, but his thoughts constantly drifted back to Elaine. He yearned to see her beautiful face once more.

It Hurts so Bad

The journey back to base camp took an extra day, but finally, Thomas Wayne and his crew, along with their new companions, arrived. They were met by a throng of anxious faces, but Cordell, standing at the center of the group, wore a grim expression that chilled Thomas Wayne. He frantically scanned the crowd for Elaine, but she was nowhere to be seen. She was likely tending to a patient, as usual. Before he could reach Cordell for an update, Aaliyah ran towards him, embracing him tightly.

"Aaliyah! Oh, my goodness. We've been searching for you everywhere."

"I stumbled upon your camp about four days ago," she explained. "You're in charge? I couldn't believe my brother rose to such prominence in this new world."

"Well, it was more like Cordell thrust it upon me," he chuckled, patting Cordell on the shoulder. "Why the long face, man? You found my sister."

"More like she found us," Cordell replied, his voice heavy with sorrow. "But there's some bad news."

A wave of dread consumed Thomas Wayne. Elaine's absence weighed heavily on his mind, but he assumed she was simply preoccupied with her duties. He noticed the fresh damage inflicted upon the camp. "Looks like we had some visitors," he observed, his voice hardening. "What happened?"

Cordell's eyes welled up, revealing the gravity of the situation Aaliyah grip tighten on Thomas Wayne's hand. He knew it was bad news, and it was about Elaine.

Cordell continued, "We were attacked by a combined force of Blackstreet and Assyrian soldiers. They launched a two-pronged assault, their primary objective being free Duce. During the fighting, an Assyrian explosive detonated, devastating the medical building."

Thomas Wayne felt a sickening lurch in his stomach. He staggered towards the wreckage of the medical building, his heart pounding. "Elaine! Elaine!" he cried, his voice raw with anguish.

Aaliyah tried to restrain him, but it was too late. He sank to his knees, his grief overwhelming him. "Elaine!" he screamed, the sound echoing through the camp, sending birds scattering from the trees.

Gloria stood by Cordell, her agony weighed heavy on her face. "What happened?" she asked Cordell, her voice trembling.

Cordell's voice was thick with emotion. "During the attack, Duce, despite his escape, returned to the medical building and… and killed Elaine. I'm so sorry, bro. I failed to protect her."

Thomas Wayne wept uncontrollably; his body wracked with sobs. Aaliyah held him close, offering comfort. Gloria and Cordell stood by helplessly, witnessing their friend's profound grief. The joy of finding his sister was utterly eclipsed by the devastating loss of Elaine.

Finally, Thomas Wayne managed to regain his composure, rising to his feet. "I'm going to kill him," he declared, struggling against the restraining hands of Aaliyah, Gloria, Cordell, and the other men.

Gloria's voice was firm. "As much as you yearn for vengeance, you cannot be the one to kill him. I swear to you; I will be the one to end his life. I give you my word."

The Funeral

The funeral was a somber affair. Mourners gathered around Elaine's gravesite; their faces etched with grief. Countless funerals took place since the war began, but none held the same weight as this one. Elaine, with her unwavering dedication to healing the sick and injured, touched the lives of everyone in the camp. Not a dry eye could be seen among the assembled.

Thomas Wayne stood solemnly beside the grave; a single red rose, an item hard to find with the devastation Earth suffered was clutched in his hand. "Elaine touched each of us deeply," he began, his voice thick with emotion. "Her smile will forever be etched in our memories. For me, the loss is immeasurable. The love we shared was unlike anything I have ever known. She was truly magical from the moment we met. Dr. Elaine Byrd, you will be profoundly missed, but your memory will endure. I vow to avenge your death, even if it means sacrificing my own."

He gently placed the rose atop the casket and blew a soft kiss towards the heavens. Rising to his feet, he accepted a white dove from Gloria. "As I release this dove, let it symbolize the freedom of Elaine's spirit. May she be free from pain, heartbreak, injury, and disease. May she live on eternally." He gently tossed the dove into the air, watching it soar towards the sky, a symbol of freedom and hope.

Following the funeral, Thomas Wayne sat outside the building where Elaine lost her life. Gloria and Cordell joined him.

"Thomas Wayne, I've decided to leave," Cordell announced. "There's a group of fighters in Fairfax who could use my help. I'm heading there to lend my support."

"No," Thomas Wayne replied firmly never raising his head up to make eye contact with Cordell.

"No?" Cordell echoed, surprised.

"No, you're not going anywhere." Thomas Wayne stood and looked Cordell squarely in his eyes,

"You cannot shoulder the blame for this tragedy, Cordell. Elaine wouldn't want you to. We need you here."

"Brother, as the leader, I bear responsibility for everything that happens within this camp. I was in charge; therefore, I'm accountable for this loss."

Thomas Wayne shook his head. "In Philadelphia, the President awarded me the Presidential Medal of Freedom. I stood at the podium and accepted it, but deep down, I knew I didn't deserve it alone. My team worked tirelessly, achieving extraordinary feats. We lead, yes, but unforeseen events are inevitable. You prepared this unit as effectively as possible. If I had been here..."

"Elaine might still be alive," Cordell interjected, his voice choked with emotion.

"There's no way to know for certain," Thomas Wayne acknowledged. "Even if I had been here, the outcome might have been the same. You are my second-in-command, and we cannot afford to lose you. Now, unpack your gear and get back to work."

Thomas Wayne attempted to lighten the mood with a chuckle, though his own grief was profound. "Can you ensure he doesn't leave?" he asked Gloria. "We cannot afford to lose good people."

"I will," she assured him. "That was a powerful speech, by the way. You earned that medal. You made critical decisions in the face of immense pressure. We executed your orders, but you provided the strategic direction. Don't sell yourself short. You're an exceptional leader."

She glanced over her shoulder. "And I think your sister would like to spend some time with you. I believe you should cherish these moments before the second wave arrives."

"Thank you, Gloria," Thomas Wayne replied, his voice filled with gratitude.

Gloria nodded and walked away. Aaliyah joined him, and they spent the rest of the evening together, sharing stories and laughter. Her presence offered a measure of solace, a much-needed distraction from the overwhelming grief. He realized that in the face of such profound loss, the support of his loved ones was the only thing that could sustain him.

12 - The Second Wave

Thomas Wayne watched the skies, a grim anticipation settling over him. Word arrived from Cheyenne Mountain—the alien armada breached the solar system, hurtling towards Earth on a collision course.

Following their previous pattern, they would likely target the United States for their initial strike, the nation they perceived as the most formidable opponent. A devastating blow to the heart of the resistance.

This time, there was no warning from Earth's own satellites. The last of them destroyed at the beginning of the first battle. The only notification came from a lone Russian probe venturing towards Mars.

Aaliyah joined him, her gaze mirroring his own. "Still watching for them?"

"Yeah, gotta be ready."

"We are ready, Thomas Wayne. The shelters are secure, stocked to the brim. We've done everything we can."

"How's the new doctor settling in?"

"He's doing well. Big shoes to fill, replacing Elaine, but he's dedicated."

Thomas Wayne shifted his gaze from the darkening sky to his sister. "Can I ask you something?"

"Of course, big bro."

"I'm still grieving for Elaine, but I can't seem to shake this... feeling for Hunter. She's a good woman, and I think we could have something special."

Aaliyah smiled gently. "Don't rush into anything, Thomas. You've suffered a significant loss. This might be a way to avoid facing your grief. Take your time, let yourself heal. If it's meant to be, it will be."

He sighed. "You're probably right. It's too soon. I'm probably just trying to fill the void. Besides, I think she'd make a wonderful wife for Cordell."

"Cordell? Militant Cordell Brown?" Aaliyah chuckled.

"The very same. He's a good man, Aaliyah. He just believes in what he believes in. This country has wronged us for centuries, and in 2081, nothing has truly changed."

"It will, once this war is over. No one will look at color the same way again."

"I hope you're right, Aaliyah."

"I am. I'm the optimist in the family."

He chuckled. "That you are. Let's head inside and see how things are progressing."

"Yeah, let's go."

They descended into the labyrinthine tunnels, a testament to meticulous preparation. Food, water, medical supplies, weapons—everything was in place. Now, it was a waiting game, a test of their endurance, their unity.

"I'll give my speech soon," Thomas Wayne announced.

Thomas Wayne and Aaliyah encountered Cordell further down the tunnel. "Hey, bro. How's everything looking?"

"Good. Gloria's security detail is tighter than a drum."

They all laughed. "Hunter and her crew have settled in well. One of them is an incredible cook. You have to try his beef and broccoli."

"I will. How do you feel about Hunter?"

"I think she'd make a great partner. Though I suggested she join security, she declined. Said she was tired of fighting and wanted to work with the children. She's surprisingly good with them."

"From leader to daycare provider?"

"Yeah, she mentioned she worked in childcare before the war. Seems to have found her calling."

"Ah, I understand. Look, don't feel pressured, but I think you two might be a good match."

Cordell grinned. "You read my mind. We're having dinner tonight." He paused. "Actually, I should get going."

"Good luck, Cordell."

Thomas Wayne watched him go, a sense of relief settling in. Aaliyah was right; he needed to grieve, to heal. Hunter, with her kind spirit and resilience, was not the answer.

He found his designated spot in the tunnel; a small alcove carved into the rock. He closed his eyes, trying to find some semblance of peace in the face of the impending chaos.

He was startled awake by Gloria. "Hey, Thomas Wayne. Sorry to wake you. Dinner's ready. You know the rule—kitchen closes at eight."

"Thanks, Gloria. I need something to eat. Have you eaten?"

"Just a little. That beef and broccoli was incredible."

"I've heard about it," Thomas Wayne acknowledged, "I guess I'll have to try it."

"Sorry, it's all gone," she smiled. "Hey, it was a big hit."

They moved to the dining area, where Thomas Wayne sat down to eat. Immediately, people began approaching him with requests and concerns. Gloria, ever vigilant, expertly deflected the interruptions, allowing him a few precious moments of peace.

"Being a leader," he muttered to himself, "isn't as glamorous as it seems on television. I can't even eat a meal without someone vying for my attention."

He thought of Melanie, his former right-hand woman. *"I miss Melanie. I wish she were still here. No one could handle the administrative load like she did. This is so much harder without her cheerful presence to keep us all grounded. Rest in peace Melanie."*

His gaze fell upon Hunter, who was assisting a group of children with their meals. *"She's an amazing woman,"* he mused. *"It was hard to see at first, she hadn't had a chance to properly clean up. But underneath that grime, I see strength and resilience."*

He turned to Gloria. "If Cordell knows what's good for him, he'll keep her close. Protect her." He remembered the loss of Elaine, the gaping hole in his life. "I didn't protect mine."

"I feel your pain Thomas Wayne."

The ground trembled violently, the initial wave of bombings finally reaching their shelter. A collective gasp filled the air.

"Everyone, stay calm!" Thomas Wayne's voice boomed through the tunnel. "This is what we expected, and we've prepared for this moment for months. We are safe and secure. Trust in yourselves, trust in the team. We will endure."

He stepped out from the crowd, his presence commanding attention. Cordell and Gloria joined him. "This bunker is designed to withstand this. We have enough supplies to last us months.

"I want to establish a clear chain of command. I am the leader of this region. If I'm incapacitated, Cordell Brown will assume command. If both of us are unavailable, Gloria Davis will take over. We will ensure that leadership remains clear and consistent, unlike the chaotic rule of the Assyrians. Now, hunker down, stay with your families, and support each other. This will be a long journey."

The initial panic subsided, replaced by a more determined resolve. Thomas Wayne felt a surge of pride in his people. They were facing the unknown with a quiet strength that impressed him.

He returned to his alcove, nodding to those he passed, providing them with a reassuring smile that he hoped would keep them calm.

The bombings continued above, a relentless barrage, but the tunnel remained steadfast. They could only hope it would hold.

A few moments later, Gloria joined him. She sat beside him, a reassuring smile on her face. He chuckled thinking he gave the same smile to others in the tunnel.

"We're under attack," he observed, "and you're smiling?"

"Because we're safe, and that's largely thanks to your leadership. Besides," she added with a mischievous glint in her eye, "I'm not going to let you face this alone."

"My bodyguard?" he teased.

"Indeed. As Chief Security Officer, it's my duty to ensure the safety of the Northeast Region's leader."

"You, Gloria? Five feet of fury?" he chuckled.

"Don't underestimate me," she retorted. "I pack a punch, and pulling a trigger doesn't require a lot of muscle."

They both laughed, the shared humor a welcome respite from the tension.

"You know," Thomas Wayne said, "I think about Duce all the time. I know you and he were... close. But if I ever get the chance, I will kill him."

"That's a job for me," Gloria said firmly. "You cannot be the one to kill him. It will taint your leadership." She paused, her smile fading. "And yes, I liked Duce, once. But what he became... siding with the Assyrians... it's unforgivable. Besides, Elaine was my friend too. He will pay for his betrayal."

"I understand," Thomas Wayne said, the pain of his loss returning. "Elaine was... irreplaceable. A once-in-a-lifetime woman."

"She was special to everyone in this camp," Gloria agreed. "The new doctor is competent, but he lacks... Elaine's warmth. Her ability to make everyone feel valued. She had a way of making you feel like you were the most important person in the world."

They fell silent for a moment; each lost in their own memories of Elaine. The bombing continued, a relentless assault on the surface, but within the safety of the tunnel, a quiet strength held them together.

Cordell approached them, his face grim. "We have a collapse at the West end of the tunnel."

Thomas Wayne and Gloria sprang to their feet, following Cordell towards the damaged section. The civil engineers were already working frantically to assess the damage.

"Can we fix it?" Thomas Wayne asked, his voice filled with concern.

"It's difficult to tell with the constant shaking," one of the engineers replied.

Cordell turned to Thomas Wayne. "Was anyone injured?"

The man answered, "There were three people here. One security guard and two others." He turned from his duties, a heavy sigh escaping his lips. "None of them survived."

"We knew there would be losses," Thomas Wayne acknowledged, his voice somber. Sick to his stomach to continue having to make that statement. "It's the inevitable cost of war. But each time it happens, a piece of me dies. These were good people, fighting for our survival. This is senseless."

Gloria placed a comforting hand on his shoulder. "I hate to say it, but we need to accept that not all of us will make it out of this alive. What we must do is honor their memory. Keep a record of their names, of their sacrifices."

"Like the Vietnam Memorial," Cordell added.

"Exactly," Gloria agreed.

"Can you handle compiling that list, Cordell?" Thomas Wayne asked.

"Gladly, brother."

"Also, I need you to find a replacement for Melanie. I heard she didn't survive the initial attack."

"Of course. I think I have someone in mind."

Cordell left to carry out his tasks. Thomas Wayne turned back to the engineer. "How long before we can at least partially stabilize this section?"

"It's difficult to say with the ongoing bombardment. We'll do our best, but it might be necessary to seal off this end of the tunnel until the intensity subsides."

"Do what you need to. Don't risk your lives for a temporary fix."

"Understood, sir."

Thomas Wayne returned to his designated area, a profound sense of melancholy settling over him. Who decides who lives and who dies? Was there a divine plan, or was it all just a cruel twist of fate? Why had Elaine, a beacon of light in their dark world, been taken?

He found himself grappling with existential questions, questions that offered no easy answers. The constant tremor of the ground served as a grim reminder of the precariousness of their existence.

He briefly considered seeking solace from Pastor Henley, but the thought quickly faded. He wasn't in the mood for platitudes or empty promises of divine intervention.

The bombing intensified, casting long, eerie shadows that danced across the tunnel walls. He noticed the children, their faces pale with fear. He knew he had to do something.

"Who wants to play basketball?" he announced, pulling a basketball from his bag.

The children's eyes widened. "You're kidding, right?" one of them asked.

"Not at all," Thomas Wayne grinned. "I want to see if any of you can steal the ball from me."

A young boy, no older than twelve, stepped forward, a mischievous glint in his eye. "Bring it on," he challenged.

Thomas Wayne dribbled the ball, the rhythmic sound a welcome distraction from the constant tremor of the ground. The boy, quick and agile, easily intercepted the ball, a triumphant grin spreading across his face.

Cordell chuckled. "I could have told you not to underestimate these kids, Thomas Wayne."

"Easy for you to say," Thomas Wayne retorted, "This kid's got some serious skills."

The game, a simple act of diversion, seemed to lift the spirits of the children, momentarily easing their fears.

"See?" Gloria observed, patting him on the shoulder. "Sometimes, all it takes is a little distraction."

"You're right," he acknowledged. "Sometimes, the simplest things are the most effective."

"My grandmother always said that," she remarked. "She was a wise woman."

They continued to watch the children play, a fragile bubble of normalcy amidst the chaos.

Later, as the intensity of the bombardment began to subside, Thomas Wayne sought solace in sleep. He dreamt of Elaine, her smile as warm and radiant as ever. He woke with a start, the soft feather tickling his nose.

"You still like to wake me up," he grumbled, opening his eyes to see Aaliyah standing beside him.

"I missed waking you up," she replied, a mischievous glint in her eyes. "Come on, breakfast is ready. You don't want to miss Chef's special."

"I've heard good things," he admitted, sitting up.

"You have no idea," she said with a knowing smile.

As they ate, Aaliyah observed Cordell and Hunter, a tender smile playing on her lips. "They look good together, don't they?"

"They do," Thomas Wayne agreed.

"You think she likes him?"

"I think she does," he replied, a hint of amusement in his voice. "I think you like him too."

Aaliyah suddenly blushed. "I… I don't know what you're talking about."

She quickly gathered her things and hurried out of the mess hall, leaving Thomas Wayne chuckling to himself.

"She definitely likes him," he murmured to himself.

He finished his breakfast and headed towards the communications center, hoping for some good news from Cheyenne Mountain.

Airman Baker looked up from his console, his brow furrowed. "Sir, we're having trouble establishing contact with Cheyenne Mountain and the other regional hubs. The bombing seems to have crippled the limited communication infrastructure we had in place."

"I understand," Thomas Wayne acknowledged, his voice grave. "Have we received any messages at all?"

"Just a brief transmission from Cheyenne Mountain. They confirmed the bombing is proceeding as expected and urged us to hold our ground. They also reported that their forces are preparing for the ground assault. A scout from the Western region sent a message—they're systematically demolishing everything on the surface."

"As expected," Thomas Wayne murmured. "Is there any way to send someone above ground to assess the situation?"

"We could try," Baker replied.

"Only if it's safe," Thomas Wayne cautioned. "I don't want to lose any more people unnecessarily."

A young man stepped forward, his face resolute. "I can go, sir."

Thomas Wayne studied the young man, a stranger to him. "What's your name, soldier?"

"Rance Bell, sir."

"Call me Thomas Wayne," He corrected him. "I don't like formalities in times like these."

"Understood, Thomas Wayne."

"Be careful out there, Rance. I know this is dangerous, but your information is crucial. We can't afford to operate blindly."

Rance nodded, his expression somber. "I understand the risks. I lost my brother and two sisters in the initial wave. But we can't let fear paralyze us. We have to gather intelligence, to make informed decisions. I'll do everything in my power to stay alive and bring back valuable information."

"Thank you, Rance. Get armed. And see Gloria before you go."

Rance saluted and moved towards the exit. Thomas Wayne watched him go, a heavy weight settling in his chest. He remembered the faces of those he lost, the empty chairs at the mess hall.

"Lord," he whispered, his voice barely audible. "I know I'm not the most devout man, but I'm asking for your protection. Guide Rance safely. Keep him from harm. He's a brave young man, fighting for our survival."

He knew his words might be lost in the deafening roar of the bombardment, but he offered them nonetheless, a silent prayer for the young soldier venturing into the unknown.

Reconnaissance Mission

Rance cautiously emerged from the tunnel entrance, his eyes scanning the desolate landscape. The corner of Palmer and Tucker Roads lay before him, a grim testament to the devastation wrought by the alien bombardment. He needed to reach Sean Taylor Road, where the mothership landed during the initial wave.

He navigated the debris-strewn streets, heading towards Andrews Air Force Base. *"Lord knows I'm out of shape,"* he muttered under his breath. *"I used to be able to run for miles without breaking a sweat. My soccer days are far behind me!"* He pulled out his canteen, took a long swig of water, and wiped his mouth with the back of his hand.

Through his binoculars, he surveyed the desolate landscape. Bombed-out buildings and charred remains of vehicles littered the horizon. The base itself was completely obliterated.

Suddenly, he spotted a patrol of soldiers about half a mile away. He quickly ducked behind a burnt-out vehicle for cover. If the ground forces were active, it meant the aerial bombardment ceased. But where did the mothership land? FedEx Field was on the opposite side of the city.

He waited until the patrol moved out of sight, then darted across the street, heading towards the Naylor Road Metro station. As he approached, a chilling sight met his eyes. The massive alien mothership loomed over the station, its hull gleaming ominously in the moonlight. Troops were disembarking, fanning out across the surrounding area.

A cold dread gripped him. *"Oh, my God,"* he whispered, raising his hands in surrender.

"Who are you, and what are you doing out here at this hour?" a gruff voice demanded.

"Rance Bell, sir. I... I was scouting the area."

"Stand up and turn around slowly."

Rance complied, his heart pounding. He was relieved as he recognized the familiar insignia on the soldiers' uniforms. "Thank God," he breathed. "I thought you were Assyrians."

"They don't use our equipment," one of the soldiers observed. "Now, who do you work for?"

"I'm with the Northeast Region. I was sent out to assess the situation and report back."

"Understood. I'm Lieutenant Phelps. Get back to your command and inform them that military forces are engaged. We don't want any friendly fire incidents."

"Sir, we have men and women ready to fight. We can assist."

"No, this is a military operation. We're trained for this. Now go. Deliver the message and stay out of our way."

"Yes, sir."

Rance miffed, turned and sprinted back towards the tunnel, adrenaline fueling his every step. He found an abandoned bicycle and mounted it, the cool night air whipping past him. He could hear the distant rumble of gunfire and the eerie glow of energy weapons in the distance.

"I've got to get word to Thomas Wayne," he muttered to himself. *"Those guys need our support."*

He finally reached the tunnel entrance, gasping for breath. "Thomas Wayne! Gloria! Cordell!" he shouted, his voice hoarse.

Thomas Wayne emerged from the shadows. "Rance! What did you find out?"

"They're fighting," Rance reported breathlessly. "The military has engaged the Assyrian ground forces. They seem to be holding their own, but…"

"But what?" Gloria demanded.

"The lieutenant said to stay out of it," Rance explained.

Gloria scoffed. "That's not going to happen."

Thomas Wayne considered the situation. "Gloria is right. The military might be able to handle this, but we need to be prepared. Let's get our people armed and ready. We'll establish a support position, ready to assist if needed. Gloria, get your teams organized. Rance, I need you to contact Airman Baker immediately. Instruct him to contact resistance fighters in DC. They can deploy their forces north of the mothership, within the DC border. We need to be ready to provide support without interfering with military operations."

"On it," Rance replied, a surge of adrenaline coursing through him. He felt a sense of purpose, a feeling of finally being part of something bigger than himself.

Earth Holds Her Own

Thomas Wayne stepped into the command center where Gloria was issuing orders to her fighters. "I'm going out there too," he declared.

"No... no, you can't," Gloria countered, her voice firm. "We need you here. Your strategic guidance is crucial."

"I can't sit here and watch good people die, Gloria."

She pulled him aside. "Cordell and I are already heading out. That leaves only you in command. We can't afford to lose all of our leadership. This is where you're needed, Thomas. We need you here."

He weighed her words, the weight of responsibility pressing down on him. He remembered the agonizing loss of Elaine, the emptiness that followed. "You're right," he conceded. "I'll stay here. But keep me updated. I need to know what's happening."

"I will. We'll only engage if the military needs our support. We understand your orders and I will make sure we keep them."

"Thanks Gloria," he acknowledged. "But be careful out there."

He watched as his friends, his comrades, prepared for battle. The weight of their potential sacrifices settled heavily upon him. *"Sending good people to die... it's not something I want to be remembered for,"* he murmured.

He turned to Pastor Henley, who observed the scene with a quiet dignity. "Pastor, I haven't spoken to you properly in far too long. I'm not sure what to say."

"It's alright, Thomas Wayne. I understand. These are trying times."

"I... I don't know how to handle this," he confessed. "The loss of Elaine... the constant fear... sending people into battle... it's all weighing heavily on me."

"It's understandable," Pastor Henley said gently. "Losing someone you love is never easy. But you must find a way to cope. Allow yourself to grieve, but don't let it consume you. Remember the good times you shared with Elaine. Focus on the joy you experienced together."

Thomas Wayne closed his eyes, a poignant memory surfacing—Elaine's laughter, the warmth of her hand in his. A small smile touched his lips. "Thank you, Pastor. That... that helps."

"Remember, Thomas Wayne," Pastor Henley continued, "faith can be a powerful source of strength. Lean on it during these difficult times."

"I'll try," Thomas Wayne replied, still processing the pastor's words.

"Now," Pastor Henley said, his voice firm, "let us pray for our warriors."

The fighters gathered, their faces etched with a mixture of fear and determination. Pastor Henley offered a moving prayer, his voice resonating through the cavernous chamber.

"Thank you, Pastor," Thomas Wayne said when the prayer ended. "Everyone, be safe."

The fighters, one by one, moved towards the tunnel entrance, disappearing into the darkness. Gloria gave him a reassuring nod before following her team.

Thomas Wayne watched them go; a wave of apprehension filled his spirit. He knew this was the right decision, but the weight of responsibility felt immense.

Suddenly, Airman Baker rushed towards him. "Sir, we have a message from Cheyenne Mountain. They've developed a new laser weapon. It might be a game-changer."

Hope surged through him, a beacon of light in the face of despair. The weight of the world seemed to lift slightly. Perhaps, just perhaps, they could still win this war.

Back on the Front Line

Gloria and her team arrived on Branch Avenue and established a position on Bonita Street. "We'll set up our base camp here," Gloria announced. "Radio man, stay close and relay any transmissions immediately."

"Roger that," the radio man responded.

"Will, Rod, head to Lassie and Andover. Report back on what you observe," Gloria ordered.

"On our way," they acknowledged.

"Everyone else, maintain position, remain vigilant, and be prepared to move," Gloria instructed. The team nodded their understanding. Positioning herself for a clear view, Gloria reflected, *Mom, I haven't thought of you much lately, but this could be my last day. I know you're watching over me in Heaven. You'd probably even*

*be interceding for me with Jesus. I haven't been to church—
that's the first thing you'd say. I promise, if I survive this, I'll
go. I just want you to know, I always loved you.*

Jason, her second-in-command, approached.
"Everyone's ready. It's frustrating to just sit here
while the war rages. We could be assisting them."

"I agree, but we have orders from above. We
don't have the complete picture. Let's follow
instructions," Gloria replied.

The radioman approached. "Gloria, Thomas
Wayne reports that our military now possesses a laser
weapon. It could be a game-changer."

"Excellent. Keep me informed," Gloria
instructed. The radioman returned to his post. "One
of us should get some sleep while the other maintains
watch, and we should rotate within the ranks. We
need everyone to be alert," Gloria advised Jason.

"I'll spread the word. You can rest. I'm wide
awake," Jason offered.

"So am I," Gloria admitted. She observed Jason
relaying the instructions. The sky crackled with the
intensity of the battle. *Our military is holding its own. If we
intervened, we could push the Assyrians back to their
mothership. However, we must adhere to our orders.*

Gloria approached the radioman. "Any updates
on the DC troops?"

"From what I've gathered, they're in position.
Now it's a waiting game until the military requires our
assistance," the radioman replied.

"Understood. Thanks," Gloria acknowledged.
She returned to her position. She could see some of
the fighting unfolding. Bullets and lasers were now
encroaching on their position.

Jason rushed to her side. "We need to retreat! The military is starting to lose ground. They've issued a retreat order."

"Okay, let's fall back to Wilkinson Drive. That should provide sufficient distance," Gloria instructed. *I detest retreating. We should be actively engaged in the fight.*

The Assyrian forces were overwhelming the military, pushing their advantage across Branch Avenue near the CVS. "Jason," Gloria said, "take some men to Forman Mills, then Iverson. Attack the Assyrians from behind."

"They instructed us not to interfere," Jason reminded her.

"Look at the military forces. They'll be overrun soon if we don't intervene," Gloria insisted.

"Right, I'll go," Jason agreed.

Jason and a small team headed toward Forman Mills. "Everyone, prepare yourselves," Gloria commanded. "This is our opportunity." The military lieutenant fell victim to a blast. The military retreat intensified. Shots rang out from behind the Assyrian lines. Excellent, we caught them off guard. "Attack!" Gloria's team surged forward, flanking the Assyrians. The remaining military joined them, and together they pushed the Assyrians back down Branch Avenue toward their mothership. "Yes!" Gloria exclaimed. Jason and his team rejoined them, and they exchanged high fives.

Gloria checked on the fallen lieutenant. "How is he?" she inquired of the medic.

"He didn't survive," the medic replied.

Another soldier looked at Gloria. "If it weren't for your team, we'd all be dead."

"We're all in this together. We need to prepare. They will return, and they'll be stronger," Gloria cautioned.

"Agreed. We've already radioed headquarters, but the fighting is equally intense in Pennsylvania and New York. They're stretched thin," the soldier informed her.

"That's why we're here. What's your name?" Gloria inquired.

"Staff Sergeant Marquise Gray, U.S. Army. It appears I'm in charge of this unit now. Unlike the lieutenant, I appreciate your assistance," Marquise replied.

"You got it. I suggest we maintain a presence by the beauty store and here to prevent them from flanking us as we did them," Gloria advised.

"Agreed. What should I call you?" Marquise asked.

"Gloria. I'm from the Northeast Region. Thomas Wayne is our leader and sent us to support you despite your lieutenant's reservations. He believed we could be a valuable asset," Gloria explained.

"When this is all over, I'll have to buy him a drink," Marquise offered with a smile.

Gloria laughed. "I'm sure he'd appreciate that." Gloria scanned the area near the mothership with her military-grade binoculars. *They're regrouping. We need to be prepared.* She gathered Jason and Marquise. "They're not taking a break. They're preparing to counterattack. Jason, you're in command of our fighters. Marquise, you're in command of the military forces. We want to draw them down Branch Avenue so we can target them effectively…" A strange sound disrupted the conversation. "Take cover!" Gloria yelled. Everyone scrambled for cover. "They're deploying fighters. Can we radio headquarters? We need air support!"

Marquise responded, "I'll get to the radio and make the call."

Gloria watched Marquise head toward the radioman. He made it ten feet before a laser blast struck him down. Gloria lowered her head. He shouted to Jason, "I'm going to get to the radio. Hold them off!"

"Will do," Jason responded.

Gloria sprang up and darted toward the location of the radio. She halted abruptly as a fighter targeted her position with its fire. Not today! With all her speed, she ran and dove into a ditch. The laser blast just missing her. She rolled over, got up, and ran toward the radio.

She reached the radioman, who was cowering in fear. She placed a hand on his arm. "I need you to focus. I know this isn't what you signed up for, but we need you to radio for air support."

"I can't..." the radioman stammered.

"Private, compose yourself! We need that air strike!" Gloria urged. The man looked at Gloria, grabbed his radio, and made the call. Gloria smiled at him, "Thanks, Private. Thank you."

"I'm scared," the radioman admitted.

"Want to know a secret... so am I," Gloria confessed. She patted him and returned to Jason. "Air support is on the way, but we'll have to hold them off until then." Jason acknowledged and continued to fire at the aircraft and the infiltrating Assyrians. "They believe they can exploit the air support to their advantage. We can't allow that to happen."

"I'll take a couple of people and flank them on the right. We'll push them into the street to create easier targets," Jason suggested.

"Be safe, Jason," Gloria cautioned. Jason and two others departed. Another fighter took Jason's place next to Gloria. They continued to fight, hoping for the imminent arrival of air support.

The man inquired, "Ma'am, how much longer for air support?"

"I don't know, but we must hold this position. There's something on Andrews that they can't allow the Assyrians to acquire," Gloria replied.

"Roger that. It's likely the lasers," the fighter surmised.

Gloria didn't have time to explain the radio message about Andrews. Whatever was located on that base was critical, worthy of their ultimate sacrifice.

Shots continued to ring out. More fighters fell, but an equal number of Assyrians were eliminated. *We can't sustain this line of defense much longer without support. They possess superior numbers.* Gloria looked to the sky. Everyone erupted in cheers as US and Canadian bombers unleashed bombs on the Assyrian forces, escorted by fighters engaging the enemy aircraft. The sky erupted in a fierce aerial battle.

More soldiers joined the ground fight, and Gloria's troops pushed the Assyrians back. The bombers destroyed the Assyrian mothership, and the remaining fighters were eliminated by the allied aircraft. The Assyrian soldiers were overwhelmed. "Bind them," Gloria ordered. "We'll find a location to detain them."

A lieutenant approached Gloria. "Ma'am, who are you?"

"Gloria Davis of the Northeast Region. We were dispatched to support the military. The lieutenant and staff sergeant in charge were lost, so I assumed command," Gloria explained.

"Okay, I'm Lieutenant Bryant. I can assume command from this point," the lieutenant offered.

Gloria stepped closer. "Sir, we've also suffered losses in this battle. We won't be relegated to insignificance again. We were sidelined during the first engagement with the military, and they ultimately required our assistance. Don't repeat the same mistake."

He nodded. "Okay, but your personnel are your responsibility, and you will follow my orders," the lieutenant clarified.

"Understood," Gloria acknowledged.

"Good. We must protect Andrews at all costs. A laser weapon is currently under construction at Andrews, and it has the potential to end this war. We cannot allow the Assyrians to acquire it," the lieutenant emphasized.

"Well, it seems they're currently incapacitated with the destruction of their mothership," Gloria observed.

"That wasn't their only mothership," the lieutenant corrected her.

"Oh," Gloria realized.

13 - Heroes

Abandoned on their home world, devoid of worshipers and love, the gods dwindled. Only a few remained, isolated on an island south of Irkalla, a once-mighty city on Uruk where billions once adored them. Irkalla and Kur, once bustling metropolises, now lay silent, their former inhabitants vanished, their existence extinguished without the sustaining power of devotion.

Cain, one of the last remaining gods, lay on the beach, the vast ocean mirroring the emptiness within him. "With no mortals to observe, to inspire awe, this world has become a desolate wasteland," he mused. "Our purpose, our very existence, was bound to the reverence of others. Why endure this meaningless existence? Cessation seems the only logical resolution."

"My beloved," Serena, his wife, gently stroked his chin, her voice soft, "Surely our love, our companionship, is a reward in itself?"

Cain sighed. "You can always read my mind."

Serena smiled, "After centuries together, how could I not?"

"My love," Cain said, his voice laced with bitterness, "For you, it's always been about love. But your flirtations with Adonis have me questioning that love. Should I not simply cease to exist, allowing the two of you to be together?"

Serena's eyes widened. "My love, I care nothing for Adonis's frivolous advances. I only love you, my husband. If you cease to exist, I will follow."

Cain turned, captivated by the sight of Serena. Her hair whipped in the wind, highlighting the flawless vanilla tone of her skin. Even after millennia, not a single wrinkle marred her face. He stared into her eyes, his heart rekindled. Her words resonated deep within his soul, a stark reminder that his existence was intertwined with hers. "Thousands of times," he confessed, "I've considered ending Adonis. But Zeus's power held me back. Now, with none to rival me, I could crush him like a grape."

Serena shook her head gently. "Why, my love? Is he not an insect to you? Would you crush a Urukite for the amusement of it? No, you wouldn't. They pose no threat. Neither does Adonis. His attempts to provoke you are merely petty games. You know I would never betray our love, a love that has endured for centuries and will never fade."

Cain softened, "Very well. I will spare him for now. But with nothing to entertain me in this desolate world, the temptation to fulfill that threat may yet arise." He searched her eyes, seeking confirmation, finding the unwavering truth he always did.

After the fall of Mesopotamia, the gods relocated to Uruk, rebuilding their heaven and guiding the people. In return, they were showered with love and devotion. It was during this time that their love truly blossomed, a bond that endured through the ages.

Night fell upon Uruk, casting the lovers in shadow as they continued to exchange whispered endearments. Cain gently pulled his wife to the ground, his movements slow and deliberate as he divested her of her clothing. They made love countless times, yet each encounter surpassed the last. Serena's cries echoed across the land, while Cain's moans of pleasure vibrated through Uruk. In the distance, the other five heroes could be seen laughing, their mockery a distant sting. Cain vowed revenge, but Serena, ever perceptive, gently guided his attention back to her eyes.

Morning on Uruk

The morning sun pierced the horizon, illuminating Cain and Serena, still entwined on the beach where they consummated their love the previous night. Cain awoke to find his wife sleeping, her beauty undiminished by the night. He marveled at her timeless allure, her blonde hair cascading down her back like a waterfall.

Cain rose and stretched, then soared into the air, gliding towards Irkalla. He landed on the mountainside where his likeness was carved into the rock. Though he cherished this place, he knew Adonis awaited him, eager to provoke. His patience with the younger god was wearing thin.

Hephaestus stood waiting. "Where are the others?" Cain inquired.

"Adonis and Tutu are inside, enjoying breakfast. Ramos is by the river, watching the fish. Don't ask. And Vayu... well, Vayu is usually nowhere to be found."

"Perhaps if we treated her with more warmth, she'd be more inclined to join us."

"Adonis tried that."

"Adonis tried to seduce her, just as he tried with my wife. If he attempts that again, I will crush him."

Hephaestus sighed. "Adonis delights in pushing your buttons. Don't let him."

Everyone knew Cain's simmering resentment towards Adonis. "We are but seven now," Cain declared. "We need to make Vayu feel welcome among us. We are all the family she has."

"It's been centuries since she arrived," Hephaestus countered. "I doubt she desires a sense of belonging."

"We should try nonetheless," Cain insisted.

Just then, Vayu approached, pausing before reaching them and settling on a large stone. "I will speak with her," Cain said, nodding to Hephaestus.

Cain settled into the sun, the warmth a balm to his soul. He stroked his beard, a comforting ritual. He glanced towards the sky, and there she was: Serena, descending gracefully, her landing as elegant as her movements. She walked towards him with a quiet grace and fell into his embrace.

Adonis and Tutu emerged from the hall. "I trust you weren't planning on entertaining yourselves here, in front of us?" Adonis quipped.

Cain erupted. "You are my closest friend, but I will kill you..."

Serena's voice, a silken thread, cut through his rage. "Cain."

His anger subsided instantly. She was the anchor to his soul, the only voice that could truly command his obedience.

Adonis snickered, "I jest, my friend."

Cain fixed him with a chilling stare, the message clear.

Tutu broke the tense silence. "Remember the days in Mesopotamia, when we ruled over countless mortals? They bowed to our every whim. Now, we squabble amongst ourselves. We need to find a new world, one that will appreciate us."

Hephaestus lamented, "Those were the days. We should never have left Mesopotamia."

"I thrived in Egypt," Tutu countered, "assimilated with their gods. It was a rewarding experience."

Cain, however, remained lost in his own thoughts. He yearned for the adoration of mortals, for the power and reverence that defined his existence. To him, existence without worship felt…incomplete. "One day," he declared, his voice firm, "we will be worshipped again. I feel it in my bones. We will find a world in need of our guidance, a world that will recognize our divine right to rule. We will save them, and in return, they will worship us." Cain knelt at the edge of the patio, lost in his vision, the weight of his loneliness pressing down upon him. The others, unaware of the depth of his despair, continued their conversation, oblivious to the chasm that separated him from them.

14 – Change in War Plans

General Garima's Excelsior-class mothership loomed in space, awaiting updates from the ongoing war. Colonel Sharro entered the conference room where the General sat, her expression grim.

"I have a feeling I won't like this," General Garima stated.

"The Terrans are proving more resilient than anticipated, General," Colonel Sharro reported. "They survived our recent bombings and are effectively countering our ground assaults. They've even managed to acquire laser technology from us and are equipping their fighters. We control two continents, Australia and Antarctica—"

"The two smallest, and Antarctica is sparsely populated," General Garima interjected. "This war cannot continue indefinitely. The Terrans are not our equals."

"Unfortunately, General, they destroyed another mothership, this time near Washington, D.C."

General Garima slammed her tablet on the table. "I'm growing weary of this region. They are responsible for the deaths of General Ashur and the destruction of two of our vessels."

"We believe their command center for North America is located in that region," Colonel Sharro added.

"Then we launch an all-out assault!" General Garima declared.

"Perhaps a different approach might be more effective, General," Colonel Sharro suggested cautiously.

General Garima's eyes narrowed. "Are you questioning my orders?"

Colonel Sharro recoiled. "No, ma'am. But our previous tactics have proven unsuccessful. A change in strategy might surprise them."

"Proceed," General Garima said, intrigued.

"The leader of the Northeast Region is Thomas Wayne Walker. He was deeply in love with a woman named Elaine, who was tragically killed by one of our informants, a man named Duce."

"And how is this relevant?" General Garima inquired.

"Terrans are driven by emotion, General. They grieve differently than we do. Thomas Wayne has been consumed by grief over Elaine's death. We can offer to deliver Duce to him in exchange for intelligence on their command structure. Crippling their leadership would effectively dismantle their resistance."

"What makes you think he'd agree to such a deal?" General Garima questioned.

"He seeks vengeance, General. This is an opportunity for him to exact his revenge while simultaneously we weaken our enemy."

General Garima poured herself a drink. "How do we proceed?"

"I will dispatch Lieutenant Hazail. She will act as our intermediary, facilitating the exchange. Once we acquire their command structure, we can launch precise, devastating strikes."

"See it done, Colonel," General Garima ordered.

General Garima sat in the command chair, a surge of frustration coursing through her. *"This war should have been over by now."* They were struggling against a species she considered inferior. A chilling thought surfaced: this campaign could be the perfect opportunity to eliminate her husband. I can order him to negotiate the exchange, then arrange for his "accidental" demise. I can tell his family he died in battle. No one would question it. I would be free to pursue my true love.

Baaz entered the conference room; his eyes tight and fixed on his wife.

"He must have read my mind," she mused to herself.

"This war is dragging on," Baaz observed. "You've conquered entire planets with greater speed in the past."

General Garima met his eyes, a flicker of icy resolve in her look. *I would love to slit his throat right now,* she thought. But patience would serve her better. "The Terrans are proving more resilient than anticipated," she explained. "We're implementing a new strategy, one that will allow us to gather crucial intelligence on their leadership."

Baaz took a seat, leaning closer to her. The hairs on her arm prickled. "How soon will you obtain this information?" he inquired.

"We'll know soon if the leader of the Northeast Region agrees to our terms," General Garima replied. "If he does, I'd like you to be the one to make the exchange."

"Why me?" Baaz questioned, a hint of suspicion in his voice.

"You're not a military man," General Garima explained, her voice soothing. "Your presence would be less intimidating to their leader. He'll be more likely to open up if he feels less threatened."

"Are you implying I'm weak?" Baaz challenged.

"Of course not, honey," General Garima soothed, placing a hand on his arm, disarming him with her touch. "Your civilian status will be an asset. It will put him at ease, making him more susceptible to our deception."

"Are we winning at least?" Baaz pressed.

"Why all the questions?" General Garima inquired, her tone subtly shifting.

"I'm on this ship, doing nothing," Baaz confessed. "I miss you. I miss being with you."

"Our time will come," General Garima promised, her voice laced with a hint of impatience.

"I know it will," Baaz replied, his suspicions seemingly allayed.

He left the room, leaving General Garima to her thoughts. After a few moments, she rose and headed towards the bridge, her mind consumed by her plan, the image of Baaz's demise a chillingly seductive prospect.

Request for a Meeting

Thomas Wayne returned from his visit with the troops. They were elated over their recent victory against the Assyrians. However, the news that the primary mothership was in space thus evaded their attack on Branch Avenue, dampened their spirits considerably.

Thomas Wayne sat in his living area, contemplating their next move. The troops were in place, their supplies secured, and security was tight. Since the second wave of the Assyrian invasion, there had been no internal disturbances, only the ongoing conflict with the invaders.

"Sir, you have a message," Airman Baker announced.

I hadn't even closed my eyes for ten minutes, Thomas Wayne thought. *I desperately need a vacation.* "What is it, Baker?"

"A message from the Assyrians. For you personally."

"For me directly? Not for the Terran command?"

"No, sir. They specifically requested you."

"How did they even obtain our frequency?" Thomas Wayne rolled his eyes at Baker.

"They didn't sir." Airman Baker stopped, "She's waiting outside?"

"What? She who?"

"She didn't say her name, but they probably intercepted our communications with information from Blackstreet," Airman Baker answered. "We will need a backup system, just in case."

"You're right. Work up some suggestions and let me know," replied Thomas Wayne.

Airman Baker said, "She may be here to destroy us."

"If she intended to harm us, they could have done so already," Thomas Wayne pointed out.

Thomas Wayne looked out the window. The woman standing on the lawn was indeed striking. A goddess, he mused, quickly chastising himself for his momentary lapse in focus. This woman clearly had a purpose. "Any sign of hidden forces?"

"Negative, sir."

Her voice cut through the air. "I know you can see me. You're probably wondering if I'm armed or if I have warriors lurking in the bushes. I do not. I am here to speak with Thomas Wayne Walker. I have a proposal for him. I come in peace."

"Forgive us for our caution," Thomas Wayne responded. "We've heard those words before, and peace has never been an Assyrian hallmark." He stepped out onto the lawn, his initial apprehension giving way to a grudging admiration for her beauty. Was this a deliberate ploy? Was he being lured into a trap, like Samson by Delilah? Get a grip, Thomas Wayne, he admonished himself.

"No need for apologies," she replied, her smile illuminating her face. "We would have done the same."

"What can I do for you?" Thomas Wayne inquired.

She smiled again, closing the distance between them. "We wish to discuss a cease-fire. Is that possible?"

Thomas Wayne chuckled. "I'm not the leader of Earth. We have an organization called the United Nations. That's where such proposals should be directed."

"You are the leader who brought down two of our motherships," she countered. "One of them was commanded by General Ashur, the most celebrated

154

warrior in Assyrian history. He led more campaigns than any other, a legend throughout the galaxy. You ended his career. To us, you are the authority."

"I don't understand," Thomas Wayne said, perplexed. "Why negotiate with me, a former delivery driver, instead of the leaders of our world?"

"We respect those who demonstrate strength on the battlefield," she explained. "Your victories against our forces have earned our respect. When you destroyed our second mothership, we knew you were the one we needed to speak with."

Thomas Wayne was unsure how to proceed. The toll of the war was undeniable; countless lives lost. "I'll have to discuss this with my superiors," he declared.

"One of your 'hours' should suffice?" she inquired.

"Yes, that will work."

"I shall return in an hour, then."

Thomas Wayne nodded as she departed. "What should I call you?" he asked.

"Hazail," she replied before continuing her walk.

He found himself strangely captivated by her. *I need to stop this,* he chided himself. *Elaine hasn't been gone that long, and I certainly don't need to be falling for an alien.* But were they truly aliens? They once called this planet home.

He returned to the radio room. "Get Cheyanne Mountain on the line, Airman Baker," he ordered. Airman Baker quickly established contact with Cheyanne Mountain and, ultimately, with President Hemingway.

"Sir, we have an opportunity with the Assyrians," Thomas Wayne reported.

"What kind of opportunity, Thomas Wayne?" President Hemingway inquired.

"One of them, a woman named Hazail, contacted me. She's proposing a cease-fire."

"Why would they contact you directly instead of our official channels?" the President questioned.

"They have a different philosophy, sir. They respect warriors, those who have proven themselves in battle. They believe the victories by the Northeast region, particularly the destruction of two of their motherships, including the one led by their most revered general, make me the appropriate point of contact."

"I'm hesitant, Thomas Wayne. This could be a trap."

"It's possible, sir, but why target me specifically? Capturing me wouldn't advance their war effort. I believe we should at least hear them out."

"I need to consult with world leaders, Thomas Wayne. Give me some time."

"I have a meeting with Hazail in forty minutes."

"I'll do my best to get back to you before then. Thomas Wayne, do not agree to anything until you hear from me."

"Understood, sir."

"President Hemingway out."

"Thomas Wayne out."

He turned to those observing the exchange. "Airman Baker, alert me immediately if you hear from President Hemingway."

"Will do, sir." Airman Baker paused. "Do you think this cease-fire proposal is genuine?"

"I honestly don't know, Airman Baker. I don't know."

Thomas Wayne walked away, his mind racing. Was his judgment clouded by grief? Was he allowing his fascination with Hazail to cloud his better judgment? He needed advice. Where was Aaliyah?

He found her with Cordell. "Aaliyah, Cordell, I didn't expect to see you here."

"I was back from Andrews on a break, and I ran into Cordell," Aaliyah explained.

They exchanged uneasy glances. "Is it true about the Assyrians wanting a cease-fire?" Cordell asked.

"Yes, it is," Thomas Wayne confirmed. "But I'm not sure if the world leaders will agree to it. The Assyrians value military strength and respect those who demonstrate it. Our system relies on elected officials, which may create a disconnect."

"Makes sense," Cordell said, before excusing himself. "I'm going to grab something to eat. See you guys later."

Thomas Wayne and Aaliyah watched him go. "What's going on with you two?" Thomas Wayne inquired. "I thought Cordell was seeing Hunter."

Aaliyah hesitated. "Things with Cordell are...complicated."

"How about uncomplicating it. Are you seeing him? You shouldn't be one of his harams."

"It's not like that, Thomas Wayne. Hunter broke up with Cordell. She didn't like the militant side of him, something I admire. You know I agree with him and his ideology. We started talking off and on and now we're... dating."

"Not my baby sister."

"Stop!" Her eyes pierced Thomas Wayne's soul. "I'm grown and I can make my own decisions. You're the leader of the entire Northeast Region, but you can't tell me who to date."

Thomas Wayne looked into her eyes. He didn't understand why she would want to date Cordell. He was his boy and somewhere there had to be a man rule that prohibited that. *I guess she's right.* "I guess I don't have any say in it except, I don't like it. He's my boy, and it just doesn't feel right."

Aaliyah laughed and took his arm. "Remember when I was in the 12th grade, and you had a crush on one of my besties?"

"I do."

"How's that any different?"

"I didn't date her."

"Only because she had a boyfriend. If she didn't, you would have been all over her and I had no say so in the relationship."

"Okay, okay. Fine, but I'll be watching him."

"Watch him. There's also another side to all of this." Thomas Wayne knew what she was getting too, but didn't want to answer. "Come on, you know you suddenly have the urge to visit the daycare area, don't you?"

"I need to see if the President reached out to me." He walked away to the sound of his sister laughing. She knew him so well. He wanted to go to the daycare area but couldn't afford the time. Airman Baker met him halfway and motioned for him to come to the radio room.

"The President just got on."

"Thank you, Airman Baker." Thomas Wayne grabbed the mic. "Thomas Wayne here."

"Thomas Wayne, I had a quick call with most of the leaders of the world. We would want you to request that an initial meeting happen with you alone, but long-term negotiations would have to be done with the leaders of the world."

"I understand, sir."

"Thomas Wayne, if this is real, we can't afford any missteps. We have lost too many people in this war. The worst count in the history of Earth. If we can end the hostilities, that would be the best outcome. However, we can't allow them to trick us. Keep us informed of every step in this process."

"I will, sir. Thomas Wayne out." The line went dead. Thomas Wayne looked at Airman Baker. "Well, it's on me to get negotiations off the ground. It's been an hour."

"She's punctual, if nothing else."

Thomas Wayne looked out. Hazail waited for him to join her on the lawn again. "Wish me luck."

"You got it," said Airman Baker.

Thomas Wayne headed outside to resume his conversation with Hazail. Before he left Cordell stopped him. "Bro, I know Aaliyah told you about us. I'm sorry, I should have been the one to tell you."

"Look, I was angry initially, but Aaliyah has that way of making me see things the way they should be. Good luck, Cordell." He turned to walk away. "Oh yes, if you hurt my sister, I'll kick your behind."

Cordell laughed, "I would expect nothing less."

Thomas Wayne arrived where Hazail waited. He said, "I have received permission to open discussions with you, but I can't agree to anything without my world agreeing."

"As I suspected, but I'm sure there are some decisions you can agree to."

"Meaning?"

"Meaning, will you join me for dinner tonight?"

"I guess that's a great way to start negotiations. Where will we meet?"

"I will have a shuttle pick you up here at your 19th hour."

"I'll be ready." Hazail smiled and walked away. Again, Thomas Wayne was stunned by her looks. She was not what he expected of an Assyrian woman. *What if my romance with this woman is the reason these two worlds come to an agreement and end this war? Wow, I can't believe I'm in this position. I really miss delivering those packages.* After rejoining the members of the camp, Thomas Wayne didn't know what to say to them. Everyone waited for him to say something, but he couldn't come up with the words.

Gloria pushed her way through. "What's going on here? Are you seriously going up to their mothership? Have you lost it?"

"Gloria, this has been approved by the President. We have an opportunity to end this war. I can't let that pass."

"They are stalling because of the weapon on Andrews. They probably have intel on it. They will keep you there as their prisoner."

Aaliyah said, "What? Is that possible?"

Thomas Wayne huffed, "Gloria, I understand your sense of security, but you're upsetting people for no reason. They will not keep me as their prisoner. What would they gain from that? I'm not a world leader."

Gloria stormed out. Aaliyah said, "Tell me you will come back. I've lost all my family except you. I can't lose you too."

Thomas Wayne wrapped his arms around his baby sister. "I will return, Aaliyah. Nothing will stop me from returning to my baby sister." He hoped his assurance would help make it easier for her, but the look in her eyes didn't say it. He wiped the tears away and kissed her on the forehead. "Cordell, take care of my baby sister while I'm gone."

"I will, brother."

Thomas Wayne added, "Everyone listen up. While I'm gone, Cordell is in charge. Follow his orders as if they are my own. I know some of you see the danger in this, but I see the potential to end this war. We've lost too many of our brothers and sisters. Now we have a way to end this. If they respect me because this region is responsible for taking down two motherships, then let's use that respect to regain Earth's freedom. I am but one man; my sacrifice is for the many." He didn't wait for a response. Thomas Wayne left the gathering and returned to his space. While alone in his thoughts he hoped he was making the correct decision. It wasn't long before Pastor Henley joined him. "What can I do for you, Pastor?"

"Thomas Wayne Walker, the man selected to represent Earth to the Assyrians. I can't think of a better man for the job."

Thomas Wayne grinned, "Thank you, Pastor."

"Now you have given a moving speech to the group, but I've been doing this for a long time, and I know better."

"What do you mean?"

"You're not only afraid, but you are also worried that you are not making the right choice. I believe you're caught up with the loss of Elaine and that you're praying this war ends now. So much so that you will risk your life to see the end."

"You think I shouldn't go?"

"I think you should go but be careful. Never look a gift horse in the mouth."

"I won't do that, sir," Thomas Wayne replied.

"Good, then we are in agreement."

"Yes, we are. Please keep an eye on Gloria. She's not dealing with this well," Thomas Wayne said with a grin.

Pastor Henley smiled. "She is only concerned for you as a leader. She takes her responsibilities to heart."

"I understand, Pastor."

"Good." Pastor Henley smiled and walked away, leaving Thomas Wayne to his thoughts.

Maybe I can have some time to myself now. I won't let my guard down. I know I am caught up in my emotions. I'm looking to replace Elaine instead of healing from her loss. I have to watch myself carefully. Hazail is a beautiful woman, but she is an Assyrian woman. Hunter is a human and would be good for me. The bottom line is that I should not be focusing on any woman. I need to focus on what this planet needs to end this war. Thomas Wayne looked at his watch. It was time to go meet the shuttle. He walked toward the exit, and people lined the corridors. They patted him on the shoulder and spoke words of encouragement. He reached Hunter, and she smiled at him. It ignited good feelings in his heart.

Hunter stopped him. "Thomas Wayne, I remember the day we met. I didn't trust you, but over time, I have grown, and now I trust you completely. Go and be safe. You are in our prayers. Anu loves you."

"Thank you, Hunter. I appreciate the kind words. Oh, and also, I told you the camp would be good for you." He took two steps and turned, "Anu?"

A look of surprise wore on Hunter's face, "Oh just a word for grace and mercy."

He nodded and walked outside, and the shuttle awaited him. Two Assyrian warriors were at the shuttle entrance. Thomas Wayne nodded at them. One warrior motioned for him to walk inside. He entered. *Wow, this is impressive. I've never seen anything like this before, but I guess I've never been on a spaceship before either.* He laughed to himself. Sometimes he considered himself witty, but most times he was too serious. The shuttle rose. Thomas Wayne watched the ground get farther and farther away. Soon the sky was replaced by the darkness of space. *Wow, this is beautiful. I've never seen stars like this before. Look at the moon. I can see the craters so clearly. We need to figure out space travel.* Soon, the shuttle docked with the mothership. The doors opened, and Hazail stood waiting for him. Thomas Wayne thought, *She's always waiting for me. One of these times, I need to be the one waiting for her.*

"Welcome to the Ishtar," Hazail said.

"Thank you. Is that the name of this ship?"

"Yes, it is." She placed her arm under his and guided him down the hallway. "This is our newest and biggest ship in our fleet. We call it an Excelsior model. Our biggest mothership."

"What does Ishtar mean?"

"Ishtar is a goddess of Mesopotamia. She is the goddess of love, sexuality, justice, and war. Fitting for Assyria's finest warship."

"Yes, very fitting. I didn't know your people knew of Mesopotamia. That was a region on Earth centuries ago."

"My people come from Mesopotamia. We left there centuries ago. I think you refer to it as the first century."

"Yes, if I remember correctly, it was the first century B.C.E."

"What does B.C.E. mean?" asked Hazail

"We refer to it as 'before the common era'. Our dating system was created by a monk in the sixth century. The monk used the birth of Jesus Christ as year one. So, the dates before the birth of Christ are called B.C.E. Those after are called A.D. Don't ask me what that stands for." He laughed. "I'm sorry, I went off on a rant. I do that when I'm nervous."

"You have no reason to be nervous, Thomas Wayne. We are all friends now."

"That's what makes me nervous."

She giggled. "Ah, someone is withholding information." Thomas Wayne didn't want to respond. He wasn't sure how he felt about Hazail. Was he intrigued by her because she was an Assyrian? He didn't know and didn't want to act until he did. "Come inside. We will have dinner here."

Thomas Wayne walked inside. The quarters were nicely designed with the finest décor. Thomas Wayne asked, "You must have a high position on this ship."

"I have done well for myself. If I can bring two worlds together, then I will be rewarded even more." She smiled and offered him a seat. "You see, my goals are sincere. I want this negotiation to succeed, for I will succeed because of it."

"I understand." Thomas Wayne took his seat. The table setup mimicked Earth's setup. They had a dinner plate, a saucer, glass, and silverware. In the center sat the meat. It looked like chicken. Surrounding it were different vegetables. "It all looks delicious."

"Thank you. This is Ktetaa, or what you would call chicken, I believe."

"That was going to be my guess." He laughed, and Hazail smiled. The servant stepped in and fixed the plates for each of them. He tasted the food before he served it. Thomas Wayne said, "Thank you."

Hazail's face was puzzled. "Why did you thank him for doing his job?"

"We are taught to thank those who provide a service to us."

"We do not." Silence befell the setting. Hazail said, "I noticed you mentioned Jesus Christ. Your people worship Him?"

"Yes, many of us do. There are… were about ten million Christians." Hazail nodded, but Thomas Wayne didn't understand where she stood. "You know of Jesus?"

"I do, but we do not worship the Hebrew God."

"I understand. Who do you worship?"

"No one. We once worshiped gods, but we discovered they were not real. In fact, that is why we left this world. The gods were rulers who cared little about the people. They only cared about their desires."

"So, what are the names of these gods?"

"Zeus, Hermes, Cain, Serena, Hathor, Seth… the list can go on and on. There were many of them, some were the same people but known by different names in different countries. Every nation had them."

"I understand. I learned about those gods in history class. You're saying they are real?"

"Yes, they are very real. Some are still alive today. They come from a race of people who lived 2000 light years away from here. They came here and forced the people to worship them as gods."

"Interesting."

Hazail asked, "What would it take to get your world to cease fire?"

"This war is something no one wants. We didn't start this war, so I ask you, what would it take for you to not just cease fire but to leave our world?"

Hazail frowned. "Forgive my look. I forget you don't know."

"Forgiven."

"Our world will not survive another year. There is an asteroid heading toward Assyria. We needed to venture out into the galaxy to find another home. Most of the worlds in the Empire are full, and we want our own world. When our scientists located our home world, what you call Earth, we came back and reclaimed our home."

"I see, so because your world is going to be destroyed, you want to come here and wipe out my people so that you can live. Do I have it right?"

"That was our plan in the beginning. Now that we have seen your people are not the primitive people we thought, we have adjusted our plan. We would like to negotiate a peace. Maybe we can co-exist in this world together."

"That will be difficult. We already have over ten billion people on Earth. Space is not something we have a lot of."

"Forgive my bluntness, but you don't have ten billion any longer." She paused. "We also have technology that can jump your world light years ahead of itself."

Thomas Wayne shifted in his seat. "Speaking of technology, why don't you simply blast the asteroid out of the sky? Problem solved."

"It's not that simple. I'm not a scientist, but the short story is, if we blast it out of the sky, as you put it, the smaller rocks are enough to still cause cataclysmic damage. I'm sure if we all came to the table, we can work this out."

"My leaders are interested in meeting. They want it to be a secure location where everyone will be safe."

"I understand. Let me ask you a personal question."

"Sure."

"I can give you the specifications to our warp drive, laser technology, our ships, whatever you ask. Would you be interested?"

"Are you talking about my world or me personally?"

"You personally."

"I'm not a traitor to my people. I will never trade secrets for personal favors." Thomas Wayne realized why they wanted him. *So it's clear there is something they want from me, and they feel I will give it to them. That will not happen.*

"You would not be a traitor. You would save your people. Our scientists have discovered another planet. It's farther away than this planet, but we are considering it."

"That sounds like a win for all of us. You can simply pack up and leave. No harm done."

"We want this world, but we didn't count on your desire or heart to fight and survive. The writings from this world were that the people here were a submissive people. You could easily be brought to your knees and conquered. Clearly, our information was outdated."

"Clearly."

Thomas Wayne wiped his mouth. "Again, it sounds like you have solved your own problem."

"What I am saying is that we would like to stay here, but as you pointed out, Earth is too crowded. There is not enough land space for us. Therefore, our only options are to wipe out the inhabitants of this world or work with the inhabitants of this world. Trust me, if my leaders find negotiations futile, they will send more forces here than you can imagine. Your underground hideouts will not be enough to withstand it."

Thomas Wayne maintained the best poker face he could. The information Hazail provided did not sound good for Earth. He could not give them information, no matter what the tradeoff would be.

Hazail continued, "I'm sorry if I have caused you to worry. This dinner was supposed to be more of a meet and greet. I wanted to get acquainted with you to help make our discussions going forward easier. Let's retire to the main room."

"Sounds good to me." Thomas Wayne followed Hazail to the main room. "These are your awards?"

"Yes, I competed in many events and training exercises. I am considered a highly decorated officer."

"Impressive."

"Thank you. Have a seat."

"Thanks."

Thomas Wayne took a seat. Hazail curled up next to him. *Is she trying to seduce me? I will not give up any information. Not that I have any.*

"Tell me, Thomas Wayne, is there a woman at home waiting for you?"

That was the question Thomas Wayne hoped to avoid. He hadn't thought of Elaine since he arrived here, but in one question, she now took over his mind. "No, I lost her in the war."

"One of our warriors or the bombing?"

"Neither. It was one of the local gang members who turned on us to support you. If I catch him, I'll kill him."

"Now you sound like an Assyrian warrior."

"I'm just angry he took her from me."

"What are human women like? I hear they are passive, easily bent to their man's will."

"You don't know human women, if that's what you think. Especially my chief of security, Gloria Davis."

"Her name is one that is on our list, too. Seems she's a troublemaker as well."

"Oh, I'm a troublemaker?"

"Thomas Wayne, you destroyed two motherships."

"Okay, I guess I can see your point." Hazail moved closer to him. Her hand rubbed his chest, then down to his stomach. *I think it's clear she's trying to seduce me. Oh man, what do I do? She's so pretty, but I know she doesn't have good intentions. Man, oh man.* When her hand arrived at his groin, Thomas Wayne shot up. "Maybe I should go now. I mean, we discussed a lot, and I need to take this information back to my leaders to see what their response will be."

"Terran men are much different from Assyrian men." She smiled. "Maybe another time when you're feeling more comfortable."

Thomas Wayne sat back down. "You are very attractive. Under different circumstances, I would be excited to be with you. But can we really trust each other?"

"What does trust have to do with sex? We can have sex and conduct business. They are two different things."

"Some of our people feel the same way. I don't. I just lost someone who was the love of my life. I don't think I'm ready for this."

"Why don't you stay the night? We can take you back in the morning." She placed her hands on his chest and glided them up, then wrapped them around his neck. She lightly pecked his lips. "We don't have to go any further. I just would like the company of a good man." Thomas Wayne's excitement could not be hidden. Hazail looked down, then back into his eyes. "It seems one part of you wants me."

"I… I really can't…"

She kissed him again and laid him on the couch. The strength Thomas Wayne thought he had left him quickly. She kissed him all over his body and removed his clothing. He could not resist any longer. *Elaine, forgive me!*

Falling in Love?

The next morning, Thomas Wayne awoke to find Hazail gone. *"I can't believe I fell for her,"* he muttered. *"What are you doing, Thomas Wayne? I was sent here as Earth's representative to start negotiations, and instead, I end up sleeping with my host. I must be crazy. She was so good. I've never been with anyone like her. I need to get it together. Remember, she asked me for information in exchange for 'special treatment.' This could all be a means to get that information."*

Just then, Hazail returned to the bedroom. She lay on top of him and kissed him. *"What am I doing?"* he thought.

Hazail said, "My commander would like to meet you. She's waiting in the conference room."

"Okay, let's go meet her." Thomas Wayne got up and dressed.

Hazail watched him prepare. "Do you have…" She handed him a toothbrush. "Wow, some things evolved in the same way on different planets."

"We take care of ourselves too. The necessities of life don't change much from planet to planet. That's something you'll learn if you join our empire."

Thomas Wayne looked at her. "Join your Empire?"

"My commander will explain more."

Thomas Wayne nodded, finished getting ready, and they headed to the nearby conference room. "What's the protocol for meeting with your commander?"

"You're Terran, just be yourself."

"Okay." Thomas Wayne followed Hazail into the large conference room. The walls were covered with

171

pictures of what he assumed were former generals in the Assyrian Army. Sitting at the end of the table was a woman with a stern face. She looked like she never smiled a day in her life. She quickly proved him wrong.

"Welcome, Thomas Wayne Walker. It is good to meet a skilled warrior."

Thomas Wayne smiled and lowered his head. General Garima's eyebrow rose. "I'm not that much of a warrior general. Before all this started, I was a simple delivery driver. I was thrust into this position out of necessity."

"Never mind the reason. You *became* a warrior. It's what you did after assuming the position that counts. Never in our history has anyone defeated one, let alone two of our motherships. Oh, Thomas Wayne, you are a skilled warrior. You just don't know it yet."

Thomas Wayne couldn't hide the bashful smile on his face. He tried to focus on the room's décor, the pictures, anything to distract him from the compliments. "From what I hear, you're a great warrior yourself. With all this technology at your fingertips, I'm surprised you want to sit down with us." General Garima looked him up and down. *Is she thinking of killing me? Well, I've had a good run if she is.*

"I noticed you looking at the pictures on the wall. This conference room holds the images of our greatest warriors. Every general who rose to the rank of Assyrian Army Leader is here. I hope to one day place my image here. I can do that by negotiating a peace agreement with your people."

"I don't understand. Your people are warriors. You believe in conquering, but now you want to talk? You have all the advantages."

"Be that as it may, we have never fought a battle that lasted longer than seven of your Earth days. Most planets we conquer give up and become members of the Assyrian Empire. But not Earth. Earth continues to fight back with everything you have. We don't have that kind of time. We can't fight a war that lasts years. Therefore, our alternative is to sit down and discuss peace with you."

Something in her tone bothered Thomas Wayne. *She's lying, I can feel it. Hazail is good at it, but this woman isn't used to lying. She's used to carrying out threats and saying what's on her mind. I don't believe a word she says.* "I understand what you're saying about your world, and I will take this information back to my leaders. Hopefully, we can arrange a time and place to hold this meeting."

General Garima replied, "That would be great. Hazail will escort you back to your headquarters. We hope to see you again, Thomas Wayne."

"As I, General Garima." Thomas Wayne walked out, eager to return to his headquarters as quickly as possible. "So, how will I be able to reach you?"

"Here, take this communicator. Use it when you are ready to talk to me. You don't have to wait until you have an answer from your leaders. You can contact me anytime with it."

Thomas Wayne didn't know what to make of her. *Does she like me for real, or is she playing me to get what she wants? I don't know for sure.* "I will certainly keep that in mind." Thomas Wayne smiled and allowed Hazail to enter the shuttle first. "You know I don't know what you expect of me after last night."

"I expect you to continue to be you. What exactly are *you* looking for?"

"On our world, we'd likely be headed for a relationship."

"It was just sex."

"Okay, I guess that's all, then." She didn't respond. Thomas Wayne felt a little down that she didn't want more. He questioned his judgment for even getting involved with her. *She is the enemy,* he reminded himself.

Hazail asked, "If I could hand over Duce to you in return for your continent's command and communications information, would you do it?"

The question shocked Thomas Wayne. It was the real reason they chose him. They knew about Elaine's murder and that Duce was the perpetrator. "So this was the reason you picked me. I'm not a traitor, even if it means passing on revenge against Elaine's murderer."

"I respect that, but I know Terrans suffer emotionally with a loss. Especially when that loss is caused by someone else. I'm giving you an opportunity to kill the man who caused her death. Think about it, and at our next meeting, let me know your decision."

The shuttle landed, and Thomas Wayne got off. "Will do." Without warning, Hazail grabbed him, and her sensuous lips landed on his. For the moment, life stopped, and he wanted nothing else but her. He wondered if he could have all of her and they still be enemies. *I know she's trying to get me to turn on my world, but I can't. She's so sweet, though.*

Back at the Camp

Thomas Wayne walked into the camp, feeling the weight of every gaze. He sensed judgment, though he wasn't sure why. He simply carried out the President's orders. Aaliyah met him at the end of the corridor. "Did you have fun playing house?"

"What are you referring to, baby sister?"

"We saw you kissing her. You've been gone almost an entire day. Did you have fun playing house?"

"It's not like that." He tried to move past her, but she blocked his way. "Aaliyah, please let me by."

"I vouched for you with Hunter, but it looks like you've chosen to sleep with the enemy." She turned away.

Thomas Wayne sighed and headed to the radio room. "Airman Baker, can we raise the President?"

"I don't know, *can* we?"

Thomas Wayne paused and sighed again. "Okay, I am *not* sleeping with the enemy. I didn't even expect her to kiss me like that. I went there to do what the President asked me to do, and I did. We will meet with them to discuss peace. If anyone has a problem with that, then say so now." No one spoke. "Now that's settled, can you raise the President for me?"

"Yes." Airman Baker began working the radio.

Thomas Wayne sat in the radio room, wondering how many people thought less of him because of the kiss. *If they feel that way about the kiss, imagine how they'd feel if they knew for sure we had sex? I can't worry about that now. My focus needs to be on this peace conference. If I can make this happen, then they won't be angry anymore. Most of all, no more people will die. Oh no, here she comes.* The person he least wanted to see sat down next to him. "What can I do for you?"

"Tell me you did it for the mission." She waited for an answer. "I mean, there are many times when someone goes into negotiations, undercover missions, whatever the case may be, and they end up doing something they are not happy about. Tell me this is one of those situations."

"Gloria, I didn't expect her to kiss me. That's all it was, a kiss. I know she's trying to get me to fall in love with her to get information from me. That will *not* happen."

"Okay, I'm going to go with that. I've got your back until I believe there isn't a reason to."

Thomas Wayne studied her. Twice now she supported him when many others turned on him. He couldn't understand her loyalty, but he appreciated it. "Thank you, Gloria." Airman Baker waved Thomas Wayne over to the radio.

"It's the President."

"Good morning, Mr. President."

"Good morning, Thomas Wayne. What do you have for me?"

"They want to sit down and talk peace."

"Really? I'm sending a plane to pick you up and bring you to Cheyenne Mountain. We need an in-person briefing about this."

"Yes, sir."

"Be at Andrews in half an hour. The plane will be waiting."

"Yes, sir."

"Cheyenne Mountain out."

"Thomas Wayne out." Thomas Wayne looked at Airman Baker. "Do we have any vehicles?"

"I think Cordell just returned with one."

"Thanks, Baker." Thomas Wayne left the radio room. Gloria followed. "Where's Cordell?"

"He just returned. He's probably with Aaliyah." Thomas Wayne looked at Gloria. "Don't act like you don't know. They're good together. You should be happy. At least she's human."

Thomas Wayne stopped and rolled his eyes at Gloria. "Look, we can't be doing this."

"Got it, no more Assyrian women jokes." She kept walking toward Cordell's quarters. When they arrived, Cordell stood outside. "Hey, the boss is looking for you."

Thomas Wayne said, "I need your vehicle. Does it have gas?"

Cordell replied, "Happy to see you too, bro."

Thomas Wayne sighed. "Sorry, Cordell. How are you?"

"I'm good. I almost got my butt blasted off, but I'm good."

Thomas Wayne said, "We're under a cease-fire."

"Someone needs to tell all the Assyrians that."

"I see. Can I get the vehicle?" Cordell handed him the keys with his usual big grin. "What, no jokes and condescending words from you?"

"Do what you need to do, bro. I understand what needs to be done where others may not get it."

Hazail's Return to Ishtar

The shuttle ascended, Hazail staring out the window. Deep inside, she wrestled with her unfamiliar emotions, trying to suppress them. *Emotions are for the weak,* her parents always instilled in her since birth. The shuttle docked with the Ishtar, and the doors opened. General Garima awaited Hazail's return. "General—I wasn't expecting you."

"I wanted your final report. Is everything on track?"

"Yes, ma'am. He will meet with the President, and we will have our opportunity, just as you planned."

"I hope you're not feeling any attachment to this human."

"Attachment? No, ma'am. I served at your pleasure. I asked him about Duce." General Garima's head snapped up, waiting for the rest. "He refused."

General Garima raised and then lowered her head. Hazail knew she suspected a lie but lacked the proof to act. Hazail witnessed her question a warrior once, recognizing the deception and executing him instantly without remorse. "Good," General Garima said. "I would hate to learn otherwise. I respected him for his work on the battlefield. If he fell to revenge, he wouldn't have been the warrior we expected. Once the next step is completed, we will bring Earth to their knees." Hazail nodded, continuing to conceal her true feelings. "Return to your quarters and prepare for the next stage."

"Yes, ma'am." Hazail hurried to her quarters, brushing off several people in the corridor. *I wish they would leave me alone! I don't have time for their meaningless conversation.* Reaching her quarters, she locked the door and collapsed onto the couch, burying her face in her hands and crying. *I haven't cried since I was an infant. What has this man done to me? I can't allow him to die. Ishtar, god of love, have you given this man permission to own my heart? If so, why a human? I must stop this assassination!*

Hazail changed out of her uniform, leaving her communicator behind. *If they try to trace my whereabouts, they will think I'm still in my quarters.* She moved through the corridor normally, attracting no suspicion. *I guess they wouldn't notice me doing anything wrong until I get to the shuttle bay.* She stood before the shuttle bay doors. Two warriors were always on duty. She needed to eliminate one quickly before they realized her intentions. The other would be harder, but she believed in herself. *I can't believe I am doing this for the love of a man—a human man.*

The shuttle bay doors opened, and Hazail walked inside. One warrior glanced at her, while the other, the one she thought had a liking for her, approached. *I will need to take him out first, grab his weapon, and kill the other before he can alert the bridge. If I'm caught, I will be executed immediately.* The warrior embraced her. Hazail plunged her knife into his stomach, holding him in place, hoping the other warrior suspected nothing. She was wrong. He sounded the alarm. Hazail acted fast. She grabbed the fallen warrior's weapon and fired two blasts. He returned fire. Hazail kept firing, trying to draw him away from the shuttle. Her next shot hit him in the leg, and he went down. Hazail rushed to the shuttle and started the engines. She overrode the doors and opened them. As she pulled out of the bay, other warriors entered. They were blown out into space.

Hazail did her best to dodge blasts from the mothership. As she neared the ground, one hit her, sending the shuttle spiraling down. Before she crashed, General Garima contacted her. "Hazail, return to the mothership, or we will hunt you down and kill you."

Initially she didn't respond. Then she said, "I can't General. I love him!"

"You do not understand what you are going through."

"I do," Hazail shouted.

"What you feel for this man is not real. You were on a mission, and that is all. Our chemical makeup make us susceptible to these emotions. Return and let the doctors give you a shot."

"I can't!"

"Hazail, return now, and all will be forgiven."

Hazail listened, but she knew in her heart that General Garima would kill her the moment she returned. The shuttle crashed near the camp. Hazail lay dazed on the floor. The crash injured her. She heard fighters breaking into the shuttle. One stood over her. She recognized her as Gloria. "I need to speak with Thomas Wayne."

"Lady, there's no way I'm going to let you talk to Thomas Wayne."

"It's urgent. If I don't speak with him, he will die, and so will your president. Please..." Hazail lost consciousness.

Do I Go to Cheyanne Mountain?

Thomas Wayne sat on the tarmac at Peterson Air Force Base in Colorado. He debated whether to return to Maryland after Hazail's warning against entering Cheyenne Mountain. He contacted President Hemingway. "Sir, I believe it's best if I return and investigate this. She wouldn't risk everything to come back here if it wasn't serious. It's also not worth endangering you."

"I agree, Thomas Wayne. Find out what they're up to and contact me when you do."

"Will do, sir." Thomas Wayne told the pilot, "We're going back to Andrews."

"Yes, sir."

The three-hour flight felt agonizingly long. Thomas Wayne needed to speak with Hazail personally to understand her warning and her sudden change of heart. Yesterday, she wanted sensitive information in exchange for technology and Duce. Now, she risked her life to save him. It made no sense, but he hoped she could explain.

Cordell waited at the terminal. "Hey, buddy. Glad you made it back safe."

"What's going on, Cordell?"

"I can't make heads or tails of it, man. She nearly died trying to reach you before you went to Cheyenne Mountain. They were trying to kill her, too. Since she arrived, we've had to move the camp. No easy task. They came looking for her. Looks like the ceasefire is over."

"I need to talk to Hazail face-to-face. Something's going on that we don't know about."

"Absolutely, bro. She almost died trying to get to you, so that's got to count for something." Cordell glanced at him, then back at the road. "Either that, or you've got some kind of hold on her."

"Dude, please. I get enough of that from my sister and Gloria."

"I think Gloria has a thing for you."

Thomas chuckled. "Gloria? Her only thing is fighting. Take this war away, and she'd be lost."

"You know, cuz, you're probably right."

They made small talk on the way to the new camp location, a welcome distraction for Thomas Wayne. When they arrived, Cordell led him to Hazail's holding place. "Why is she being held here? Do you consider her a prisoner?"

"Heck yeah, cuz. She's Assyrian."

"She also may have saved the President and me. Let me inside." The guard opened the door to the makeshift cell where Hazail sat. Thomas Wayne entered. He said to the guard, "Give us some privacy."

The guard hesitated. "Gloria left explicit instructions not to leave her."

"Who am I?"

"The Leader of the Northeast Region."

"I said leave us alone." The guard nodded and walked away.

"We're as alone as I think we can be, given the situation." She offered a small smile. "What's going on? Why did you come back?"

"You need to get the doctor in here now."

"Why?"

"Please, Thomas Wayne, just do as I ask, or everyone here, including myself, could die."

Thomas Wayne shouted, "Guard!" The guard came running. "Get the doctor in here."

"I'm already here, Thomas Wayne." The doctor walked inside. "I was on my way to check on my patient. What's going on?"

Hazail said, "You need to extract the tracker from his side."

Thomas Wayne said, "Tracker? I don't have a tracker."

"Yes, you do. Doctor, it's on his right side. You can't see the incision because our technology heals the wound without scaring. Feel for it."

Thomas Wayne felt his side but found nothing. Hazail reached for him, but the guards raised their weapons. "Put the weapons down. I doubt she'll kill me while trying to save me." They obeyed Thomas Wayne's command. Hazail found the tracker and placed Thomas Wayne's hand on it. "What the—how did you get that inside me?"

"Last night, I put something in your last drink. It induced a deep sleep. Our doctors came in and placed the tracker inside you. My commander can use it to track your movements. As soon as you got into Cheyenne Mountain, she was going to blow it up, killing your President."

Thomas Wayne asked, "And now?"

"Now she may blow it anyway if she thinks the plan has been compromised." Hazail said, "Doctor, you need to cut it out of him now, or we're all dead."

The doctor pulled out a knife. "I don't have any anesthesia, so this is going to hurt."

"I can take—oh my God!" Thomas Wayne felt brave, but quickly remembered he wasn't. He screamed as the knife cut into his flesh. The doctor reached inside and retrieved the device. "Here we go."

"That was inside me the whole time?"

"Yes. You must take it somewhere and destroy it with your laser. Make sure there's at least a block of clear space. The explosion will be large. Do it quickly before she decides to activate it."

A guard took the device. "I know exactly where to take it."

Thomas Wayne asked, "Are you sure?"

"Yes." He rushed out of the cell and out of sight.

"I hope he knows what he's doing." The doctor stitched Thomas Wayne's side. "Why did you do this? This was your plan from the beginning, but you changed your mind at the last minute." Hazail looked at the doctor. "We'll talk after the doctor leaves."

"I'm almost done." The doctor finished his work on Thomas Wayne's side, then examined Hazail. "You seem in pretty good shape for someone who crash-landed on our planet. How do you feel?"

"I feel fine, doctor."

"Good. Let me know if you feel worse. Otherwise, rest, and you'll be completely healed in a couple of days." The doctor smiled.

Hazail replied, "Thank you, doctor."

"You're quite welcome." The doctor left the room.

"How about that… you thanked someone who was just doing his job."

"You're rubbing off on me."

Thomas Wayne chuckled. "Now, where were we? Oh, you were going to tell me why you suddenly warned me of the Assyrian plan."

"Last night was more than just sex."

"Wow, earlier you were so sure that's all it was."

She stood up. "I have never felt this way about a man, especially a human man. I have never had feelings for a man so quickly. I don't know why I felt compelled to throw away my career and my life to save you, but I did. Now, I have nowhere to go. I am a—I don't know what the human word for it is, but I am a person with no world."

"A nomad?" She looked puzzled. "Someone without a permanent place to live. They move from place to place, but you are not a nomad. You have us."

She snickered. "Your people only see me as the enemy. They locked me up despite me being injured and trying to save your life and the life of your president. They don't see me as you see me."

"That will change. Come with me to the radio room. We welcome any information you can tell us about the Assyrian Army." She stared at him with a look of bewilderment. "If you want to prove yourself, then this is the way to do it. You will need to tell us everything you know if you want to be accepted into this world."

"I only want to be accepted into your heart."

Thomas Wayne couldn't believe his ears. On one hand, he had an opportunity to be with Hunter, a human woman he could trust with all his heart. On the other, he could be with a beautiful Assyrian woman he couldn't trust, but desired more than he would admit. "Take this first step, and everything else will work itself out." He extended his hand to her, and she took it. Thomas Wayne guided her to the radio room. Everyone stared at them with disbelief, but he didn't care. He knew what he was doing was right. In the radio room, he asked, "Baker, get me the President."

"Will do."

He looked at Hazail. "I will tell him first of the attempt on his life, then I will introduce you. You will answer his questions to the best of your ability—is that okay?"

"If you think it is best."

In the distance, Thomas Wayne heard a loud blast. "I hope that was the guard exploding that device and that he's okay." No one responded.

The President was on the line. "Mr. President, I have more information for you."

"Go ahead, Thomas Wayne."

"Apparently, there was an attempt on your life. The Assyrian woman I met with last evening risked her life to come down here to warn us of their plan."

President Hemingway asked, "She turned on her people?"

Thomas Wayne could hear the commotion in the outer room. The guard was telling everyone about the explosion. "Thomas Wayne."

"Just a minute, sir," replied Thomas Wayne. "That was the device that was inside me?"

"Yes, sir. Did you hear it?"

"I did. Thanks for taking care of that."

"No problem."

Thomas Wayne looked at Hazail. "Thank you." She smiled and lightly touched his chest. "Sir, are you there?"

"Yes."

"Apparently last night, while I slept, the Assyrians placed a tracking device inside me. When they tracked me to Cheyenne Mountain, they would activate the device, and it would have exploded, killing everyone within a block radius of me. Their plan was to have me infiltrate Cheyenne Mountain, lead them to you, and kill us both."

"And we have seen this device?"

"Yes, sir. The doctor removed it from me, and one of my people detonated it. Let's say there's a block of land no longer habitable here in Fort Washington."

"That's a lot to digest, Thomas Wayne. Are we sure we can trust this woman?"

"Sir, she risked her life to warn me about this device because she didn't want me to die. She can't go back to her people, and she's willing to tell us what she knows about the Assyrian forces."

"Great. Where is she now?"

"Standing right next to me."

"Ma'am, thank you for saving my life. I can say that I am surprised, given the warring nature of your people, that you would do such a thing."

Hazail responded, "Sir, when an Assyrian woman loves, she loves with all her heart. I couldn't allow Thomas Wayne to die, so I gave up everything to save him."

"Oh—I understand. What can you tell us about your army?"

"I can tell you that in a few hours, your world will come under a massive attack. When General Garima realizes I survived the crash and told Thomas Wayne the plan, she will lift the ceasefire and attack this world with everything they have. She will look to annihilate everything on it, starting with the weapons you are building at Andrews and the one in Cheyenne Mountain."

"She knows about those?"

"You will be surprised at how many humans are betraying your people."

"Actually, I wouldn't be surprised." There was a pause in the transmission. "Thomas Wayne, get down everything she knows and forward it to us as soon as possible. Apparently, we are back at war."

"Yes, sir. Thomas Wayne out."

"Cheyenne Mountain out."

Thomas Wayne looked at Hazail. "That's a great start. We have to debrief you. Gloria will handle that." He looked at Airman Baker. "Do you know where Gloria is?"

"She was with Hunter the last time I saw her."

"Great. Thanks, Airman Baker. Let's go, Hazail." They walked out of the radio room, and Thomas Wayne spotted Gloria and Hunter. He said, "Hey, Gloria!"

Hazail grabbed his arm and stopped him. "What's wrong? Haven't you met Gloria before?"

"She's a traitor to your people. She's the reason we know about the weapons you're building."

Thomas Wayne snickered, "Gloria would never tell that information."

Gloria asked, "Hey, what's going on, Thomas Wayne?"

Thomas Wayne sighed, "She thinks you're a traitor."

Hazail interrupted, "Not her. *This* one." She pointed at Hunter.

Hunter grabbed a gun and yelled, "Get back, or I'll blast all of you!"

Gloria said, "What? You're working for the Assyrians? Why, you're human?"

Hazail said, "She is not Terran. She is Assyrian."

Hunter yelled, "You're the traitor, and General Garima will pay me handsomely after I kill you!"

Hazail said, "Her name is Vibhi, which means fearless. She has worked as a spy for the General many times. The people you found her with are likely spies as well."

Thomas Wayne said, "Vibhi, that's your name, right?"

"Yes, and I am glad you know it before you die."

"No one has to die here. Look around you. There are more weapons pointed at you. You can't take all of them out before they take you out. Put down the weapon."

"That may be so, but I can do one thing before you kill me." Thomas Wayne was confused. "What is that?"

"Kill her!" She pointed the weapon at Hazail, but the fighters killed her before she could fire. "Damn it! Why didn't she just give up?"

Hazail caressed his chest again. The touch was making Thomas Wayne feel a certain way about her. *Is this the Assyrian way of making a man fall in love?*

Hazail said, "You must search her quarters. There, you will find a communicator like the one I gave you. You can use it to hear orders being given to the Assyrian army. Maybe it will help."

Gloria looked Hazail in the eye, then at Thomas Wayne. "Hunter had us all fooled. How can we trust this one?"

"She came to us with the full knowledge of who she is. She saved my life and President Hemingway's life. She also let us know we had a spy in our ranks. I'd say there's a good chance we can trust her, wouldn't you?" Gloria didn't answer. "Go find the communicator. Take it to Airman Baker and see if we can get anything from it."

Hazail chimed in, "I've done nothing but help you." She looked at Thomas Wayne. "The communications will be in Assyrian. I will have to translate the messages."

Gloria said, "We'll meet you there. The language you speak was spoken here on Earth. We actually have a translator, so we won't need you."

"Very well," replied Hazail.

Thomas Wayne asked Gloria, "Can you try to work with her?"

"Only because you ask."

"Round up the others who came with her. We need to investigate them all."

"Roger that." She turned and walked away.

Hazail asked, "Were you once her mate?"

"No. Why would you say that?"

"The look in her eyes. She loves you."

15 – No More Cease Fire

Thomas Wayne sat in his quarters with Hazail. The cease fire ended, and in line with Hazail's warning, the onslaught began. General Garima was merciless in her attacks across Earth. Only North America, Asia and most of Europe remained in human control. Earth was losing the war. Thomas Wayne said, "President Hemingway predicted Earth would succumb to the Assyrians in a month, maybe two. How do I look my fighters in the eye and tell them that information?"

Hazail answered, "The same as you always have. You became a great leader because you didn't sell them lies. You told them from the beginning it was a hopeless battle. They knew from the beginning they could and may very well die. For Assyrians, it is different. We do not expect to die in war. We are expected to wipe our enemy out without loss of death. Therefore, when we lose people, it is more painful for us."

"I don't know if I can agree with that. Losing someone is hard for us as well, even if we expect it. My grandfather was ill for years before he passed, but when he did, it devastated me. Knowing doesn't ease the pain. In fact, it may intensify it."

"We both suffer pain and loss in our own way."

"That is true. Let's head out to the command center and see what's going on."

"I serve at your will."

Thomas Wayne snickered, "This is not the Ishtar and I'm not General Garima. You don't serve me. We are equals in this relationship."

"So, you now agree that we are in a relationship?"

"I do."

"What is a relationship?"

He laughed. "It's when two people agree they will date each other only. They won't date anyone else."

"We do not have this relationship. Our marriages are arranged or negotiated by our parents. General Garima's marriage is one of convenience. His family is powerful in the empire and by her marrying him, she will someday lead all the empire's forces."

"Wow, we did away with that thousands of years ago." They walked into the command center where Airman Baker was showing the communicator to Gloria. "What's going on?"

Airman Baker said, "This thing started blinking a few minutes ago."

"Shut it off," shouted Hazail! "They are tracking us!" She grabbed the communicator and stepped on it, breaking into pieces. "When that light blink, it is in tracking mode. You must get your people out of here."

Thomas Wayne said, "They are your people too now."

Hazail shouted, "Get everyone out of here!"

Gloria shouted down the halls, "Everyone evacuate now! Rendezvous at the backup location in Oxon Hill. Go… go!"

The halls filled with people scrambling to get out, but it was too late. Laser blast ripped into them and the buildings. Thomas Wayne grabbed a weapon and headed out. Hazail stood behind him. He started to tell her to go back but, he knew the warrior in her would prevent it.

The fighting turned to hand-to-hand. Thomas Wayne held his own, but a warrior got the better of him. He knocked Thomas Wayne to the ground, then struck him about the face and chest. Suddenly, the blows stopped, and the warrior's eyes popped open. He fell backwards. Thomas Wayne looked behind him. Hazail winked at him, then turned to take out several more Assyrian warriors.

Thomas Wayne got up and took on another warrior. This one he got the better of by striking him with a left, followed by a right, then an uppercut. Once on the ground, Thomas Wayne kicked him until he was unconscious.

The last of the warriors were down. Hazail joined Thomas Wayne near the unconscious warrior. She fired a blast into his chest, killing him. "Why did you do that?"

"These warriors will fight until death. If you get the better of them, they expect you to kill them. What are you going to do, feed and care for him with food and water you don't have? They will try to escape and kill as many of you as they can." She walked away in disgust.

Thomas Wayne rejoined her. "I'm sorry. I didn't mean to anger you. We just do things differently here."

"You need to change your ways. These warriors will kill you and think nothing of it. More will be coming."

Gloria joined them. "I think we got them all, but we lost ten." Losing more people made Thomas Wayne feel worse. Death was becoming the norm and there was nothing he could do about it. Gloria continued, "I have more respect for you, Hazail. You wouldn't have killed so many of your people if you were not serious about leaving them."

"I am serious about my love for Thomas Wayne. I will fight for humans, and I will die for them because I love him."

Gloria chuckled, "What did you do to this woman?"

"I don't know but it's nice. We have some different opinions, but I guess that can be expected since we're from different worlds. By the way Hazail, thanks for saving my life back there."

"You are my mate. I am expected to do no less."

Thomas Wayne put his arm around Hazail.

Gloria said, "Oh, boy. I think I'm going to see how the rest of the people are doing, then get everyone to Oxon Hill."

Thomas Wayne nodded and walked away with Hazail. He was feeling the same way about her. He never had someone who would risk her life to save his. That was a special feeling, but he reasoned he never dated a warrior before.

Resetting Up Camp... Again

Thomas Wayne, Hazail, and Gloria sat on the
doorstep of an apartment building in Oxon Hill. The
Assyrians pushed them back to the Spark
Apartments. Thomas Wayne's frustration grew more
on his face and in his spirit. "When we first started
this war, I never imagined feeling this way. Now it
seems we are always on the move. A victory one week
only leads to multiple losses the next. So many started
this journey with us but are no longer with us. How
much more can we endure?"

Gloria said, "We keep doing what we started, and
that's fighting for our world. We may not see the end,
but it's what we must do. Every day I wake up, I say a
quick prayer to God because it may be my last chance
to talk to Him."

"God," asked Hazail?

Gloria continued, "Yes, God. Your people don't
know God?"

"If you are referring to the Hebrew God, yes, we
know of Him, but we worship different gods. It has
always been that way. There is a movement in the
shadows of Assyria that is teaching of the Hebrew
God. However, whenever a cell is discovered, they are
killed immediately."

"Wow, there are Christians in some parts of the
world who are killed for their beliefs too. It's a
shame."

"There are stories told about the ancient days,"
said Hazail. "Stories about our gods and how some of
them came to be here. My people were thriving here
until a race of powerful people came and forced us to
worship them. We, being the warrior race we are

fought them but they were too much for us. We used our technology to leave here. That is how we came to be on Assyria. Some gods we continued to worship."

Thomas Wayne asked, "Why would you worship them if you fought them?"

"The old generation believed the reason we lost is because they were gods. The younger generation doesn't believe that. I have followed the traditions of my family, so I continued to worship them, but not as I should. The warrior in me won't allow it."

Thomas Wayne said, "I see. The way this war is going, we may all find out the true answers to the universe soon."

Airman Baker arrived at the stoop. "Thomas Wayne, Gloria... I have bad news."

"What is It?" asked Thomas Wayne.

"Half the camp left. They said being in this camp is too dangerous. They're upset over us harboring one of them—no offense, ma'am."

"No offense."

"The rest just say they believe they will be safer on their own."

Gloria lashed out, "They're fools. Where are they? Don't they know there's strength in numbers?" Gloria followed Airman Baker.

Thomas Wayne and Hazail stayed. Hazail asked, "Shouldn't you go speak to them?"

"Why, they clearly don't respect my decisions. You've killed more of your own people than most of them have together. I'm tired of fighting on multiple fronts."

"Go, Thomas Wayne. Talk to your people."

Thomas Wayne rose and headed in the direction of Airman Baker, and Gloria. Hazail stayed at their new quarters. He wondered what she would do alone. He couldn't worry about that. Approaching the front of the apartment complex, Thomas Wayne heard Gloria speaking to the people. They were calling for her to take over and kill Hazail. They feared she would bring her people to find them, no matter where they went. Gloria told them Hazail was on their side, but they wouldn't believe her. Thomas Wayne stood beside her, "Everyone listen. It is your choice to leave this camp or not. Before you do, you should know that the war is not going well for Earth. North America, Asia and most of Europe is all that is left. The Assyrians have control of all the other continents on Earth. Soon their forces will be fully concentrated here in North America. There will be no place you can hide. As Gloria stated, there is strength in numbers. If you leave, it will diminish this region's ability to defend itself and it will diminish your ability to stay alive." No one responded.

"I know you are concerned about Hazail. When I met this woman, I was skeptical myself. But since that first night, she has done nothing but help defend this camp. She saved President Hemingway and me from assassination. She exposed a traitor in our midst. Hazail warned us that the Assyrians were coming when she saw the communicator blinking. Then she stood with us and fought her own people, killing them to save us. In that fight, she again saved my life. She is an asset, not the enemy. So, if you want to leave—go. You have my blessings and my prayers. If you want to stay, we will continue to work together to save this world." He stepped away and headed back to his apartment.

Gloria ran him down, "Nice job. I think they are going to stay."

"I didn't see Aaliyah and Cordell. Do you know where they are?"

"They left and took the doctor with them."

"What? Why would they do that and not tell us?"

"You know how militant Cordell is. He can't wrap his head around Hazail being here."

Thomas Wayne let out a breath. "Do you know where they may have gone?"

"Come on man, you know me. They headed to Riverside Plaza Apartments across 414. Cordell scouted the area a few weeks back, and it was prime real estate. No one really purged it much."

"Good. I'll go talk to them. Let me go inside and see what Hazail is doing."

"Roger that, boss."

"There you go with that boss stuff again." Thomas Wayne allowed himself the opportunity to laugh again. He walked into the apartment and stood in shock. He yelled, "Hazail! Hazail!" Moving from room to room only to find Hazail laying on the floor in a pool of blood. "No!"

Gloria burst into the room. "Oh, God." She pushed Thomas Wayne out of the way and felt for her pulse. "She's alive." Gloria pulled out her radio. "This is Gloria. Get me a medic to Thomas Wayne's quarters now!" Gloria sat the radio down and continued to work on Hazail. She glanced at Thomas Wayne. "Hey, put your hand here and hold it. We have to stop the bleeding." She continued to work until the medic came and took over. Gloria pulled Thomas Wayne to the side. "Hang in there, boss. She'll be alright."

"I can't keep going through this, Gloria." He flopped down in a chair.

Gloria said, "What was that?"

The sound of a large explosion rattled everything and everyone in the room. Thomas Wayne and Gloria rushed outside to see smoke coming from the direction of Bolling Air Force Base. Thomas Wayne asked, "Do we have any troops over there?"

"I'm not sure. Everyone is scattered now. The regions have broken down; we haven't heard from Cheyanne Mountain. Who knows what was there. "We should send a scout to see."

"Make it happen, please."

"Will do."

Thomas Wayne walked inside to get the status of Hazail. He looked at her as the medics worked on her. She held her hand up to say she's okay. Thomas Wayne asked, "How did they find you? Do you have a tracker on?"

"No, it was your people. Cordell and Aaliyah came to visit, and you were not here. I told them you went to speak to the people. They yelled at me saying I had you under a spell, then they attacked me."

Thomas Wayne's anger rose. He asked, "Is she going to be okay?"

"Yes. She suffered bruises and contusions but for the most part she just needs to rest."

"Stay here until I get someone to guard her."

"Yes, sir."

Thomas Wayne rushed out the door. *They are going to pay for this. I can't believe my friend and sister did this to my girlfriend. I can't believe I just referred to her as my girlfriend.* He returned to the front, where Gloria arranged for the scouts to head to Bolling. He asked,

"Do you have someone who can watch Hazail? I have a mission."

"You have a mission? To do what?"

"Cordell and Aaliyah attacked Hazail. I'm going to find out why."

"Thomas Wayne, you can't do that. Let me send someone to find them and bring them back—"

"I need to do this! This is my sister we're talking about." Gloria froze up. "I need to do this, Gloria."

"Remember the last time you left the camp? When you returned, Elaine was dead. Don't repeat history." Thomas Wayne's anger welled more. "All I'm saying is you need to be by her side right now. She needs you more than you need revenge."

"Send someone." He turned and rushed back to Hazail. He was angry, but Gloria was right. No one could guard Hazail better than he would. He was the only one who believed in her. He arrived back at the apartment. "You can leave now. I'll stay with her."

The medics nodded, gathered their stuff, and left the apartment. Hazail asked, "You didn't go after them?"

"Someone reminded me of Elaine's death. I'm not leaving your side." Hazail smiled. Thomas Wayne took her into his arms and held her tightly. For the first time, it didn't matter where she came from. All that mattered was he was in love with her.

Assyrians Step Up Attacks

Gloria's fighters brought Cordell and Aaliyah back to the apartment complex. They took them into the office until Thomas Wayne arrived. Thomas Wayne looked them both over with disgust. He understood why Cordell would take such action. Cordell was a militant and always looked for an enemy. Before the war and because of racism, Cordell had a legitimate enemy, but he always saw the good in the white people that deserved it. What Thomas Wayne couldn't understand was why he couldn't see the good in Hazail. Why did he hate her so much? Why did he drag Aaliyah into it? Those were questions he wanted answers to. Thomas Wayne ordered, "Take Aaliyah across the hall and hold her there."

Without hesitation, the men did as they were ordered. Once out of the room, Thomas Wayne asked, "Why?" It was a simple question, but he knew Cordell would understand all the complexities of the question.

"She's the enemy, man. That woman is leading you down a path that will cause us all death, brother." Cordell stood shaking his head and grinning, "I know I didn't question it early; maybe I should have but I didn't see it. Neither do you."

"Cordell, she's killed more Assyrian warriors than you or I have in the little time she's been here. She's with us now, more than that, she's with me. You attacked my girlfriend."

"Cuz, she's not your girlfriend. Do you wonder why the Assyrians keep finding you?" Thomas Wayne didn't answer. "It's because she has one of those trackers inside of her like you did."

"The Assyrians are finding us because they are attacking everything in this area. We keep dividing up, and those who get caught tell the Assyrians where we are. That's how, Cordell. People like you leave the group, then you get caught and you dime the rest of us out!"

"She's got you fooled, cuz—"

"Hazail has provided us with so much intelligence you won't…" The explosion burst through the windows. It was followed by laser blast as the Assyrian army marched into the complex.

"I told you, cuz. They found you again."

Thomas Wayne looked through the window. "No, Cordell, you lead them here."

"That's a lie."

"Look out the window."

Cordell looked out the window. "If that don't beat all I've seen."

"Yeah, your boy is fighting with the Assyrians. Instead of fighting Hazail, you should have been cleaning your own house! Now get my sister out of here." Thomas Wayne and Cordell raced across the hall. Thomas Wayne ordered the guard, "Give me some cover. I need to get to Hazail." The guard did as ordered. *I can't lose another woman.* Thomas Wayne raced to his quarters behind the cover fire laid down by the guard. He heard a scream behind him. The guard went down with a wound to the leg. Thomas Wayne went back to help him, but an Assyrian blasted him again, killing him. *Dang it.* Thomas Wayne dodged the blast and struck the warrior in the face. The warrior snapped back and in one move threw his shoulder into Thomas Wayne's stomach. They rolled around on the ground, each trying to gain the advantage. Thomas Wayne saw the warrior's knife tucked into his belt, grabbed it, and thrust it into the warrior's stomach. The warrior was shocked. "Yeah, I killed you!" He held the knife in the warrior's stomach until he was dead.

Thomas Wayne jumped up and continued running to his apartment. *More people dying. This war will wipe us all out. I need to get Hazail to a safe place. There's no need to fight them.* Thomas Wayne arrived at his apartment to find Hazail fighting with Gloria and others against a group of warriors. *Even injured, she's fighting back.* The warrior held his blade and prepared to stab Hazail with it.

"Your traitorous head will adorn the hull of our mothership," shouted the warrior!

Thomas Wayne threw his shoulder into the warrior, knocking him to the ground. He quickly got to his feet and punched the warrior in his stomach and face. The blade fell to the ground. Thomas Wayne grabbed it and slit the warrior's throat. Hazail grabbed Thomas Wayne from behind and startled him. She said, "It's okay, sweetheart."

Thomas Wayne looked at Gloria, still holding her own. "I have to help her."

"Go."

Thomas Wayne went over and help Gloria fight off the remaining two warriors. He grabbed a weapon from the ground and fired blasts at the warriors. They both went down. Gloria was on her knees and out of breath. She said, "Thank you."

"Why are you holding your side?"

"I think I broke a rib."

"We'll have to find someone to help you." Thomas Wayne said the words, but he knew it was likely no one left. The ground held the bodies of humans and Assyrians alike. It flowed with blood.

The battle devastated both sides. Hazail joined him at his side. "We have to get Gloria some help."

"Okay, my love."

Thomas Wayne helped Gloria to her feet. She gasped, "Ughhh!" and fell back down. "I can't do it. Leave me here to die."

"There's no way I'm leaving you here." Thomas Wayne picked her up. She continued to gasp, but he got her inside the apartment. "Wait here. I will go find someone who can help."

"It's useless Thomas Wayne."

"Don't say that. I'm not losing you too!"

"I'm bleeding internally. By the time you find someone, if you find someone, I will be dead. Get out of here, both of you. Get out and get somewhere safe. It's clear we won't win the war, but one day, you may rise again. Go."

"I can't, Gloria." Tears welled up in his eyes. "I can't leave you. You always stayed by my side." He knelt down by her, "I can't lose you."

Gloria looked at Hazail, "I didn't believe you at first, but you have proven yourself time after time. Take care of my friend. He's a good man and he'll make you a good husband." Hazail smiled. "Get her somewhere safe." They heard voices outside. Gloria reached inside her coat pocket. "I've been saving this for a special occasion."

"You can't blow yourself up?"

"I can, and I will take some of them with me. Go Thomas Wayne before we all die." Hazail grabbed him. The tears rolled down his face. Gloria patted him on the cheek and smiled. "I will see you again in Heaven."

Thomas Wayne replied, "Yes, you better." Hazail pulled Thomas Wayne, and they ran out the opposite end of the building. They heard the Assyrians going inside their apartment. Thomas Wayne and Hazail ran into the woods. When the explosion went off, he turned and stared at the building he once called home for a week. He fell to his knees in tears. His friend and confidant was dead. Another in the long list of people who sacrificed their live for the lives of others. Thomas Wayne couldn't stop the tears from rolling down his face. He knew Hazail would lose respect for him. He looked at her as she stood surveying the area for any Assyrians. "I know you think men aren't supposed to cry. I'm sure an Assyrian man would be killed if he did."

"A man who loves with his heart will cry when he loses those close to him. The fact that you shared this moment with me only strengthens my love for you, Thomas Wayne. I will never stop loving you." Thomas Wayne didn't know what to say. This woman fell in love with him quickly and convinced him of his love for her. Now she would stand by him no matter what. He knew in his heart for sure, he loved her too.

The couple walked north toward DC. Thomas Wayne knew there were places they could hide in Southeast DC. He didn't know if they were safe or not, but it was their only option. Hazail said, "Before you saved me from that warrior, he boasted about the war. The Assyrian army has defeated Asia and Europe. This place is the only one left standing."

The news was disheartening for Thomas Wayne. As much as they fought, as many lives that were lost, they faced annihilation anyway. "I don't know what else to do, Hazail. My region is no more. I can't get in touch with Cheyanne Mountain. No one is left but me and you."

"General Garima is a great warrior. When the King sent her, he knew she would do the job."

Thomas Wayne spotted a house off of Highway 210. They darted through the bushes and entered the home. The home looked like a makeshift headquarters. There were plans laid out on tables, half eaten food and a radio. "Hey look, there's a radio. The forces in this area must have used this home as their headquarters before they were taken out." Thomas Wayne sat at the radio. "It must have been used by the Southeast DC faction." Hazail didn't respond. Thomas Wayne attempted to raise someone on the radio.

"This is Cheyanne Mountain. Who am I speaking with?"

Thomas Wayne's head snapped up at Hazail. She returned the look with a smile. "This is Thomas Wayne Walker from the Northeast Region; I'm trying to reach President Hemingway."

The voice replied, "President Hemingway's aircraft was shot down three days ago. He didn't survive."

Thomas Wayne's head dropped. "Who's in charge now?"

"There's not a lot of us left. We tried to move our headquarters to Area 51, but the Assyrians caught wind of it. That's when President Hemingway was shot down. Lieutenant Colonel Kelvin Britton is in charge now."

"I need to speak with him."

"He is attending a meeting with the world leaders at an undisclosed location."

"Ugh, I need to know what's happening in the world. We lost touch with everyone. Our location was overrun by Assyrian warriors. We were told Europe and Asia have been defeated and we are the only continent left."

"Sir, that's not true. Who told you this information?"

"One of the Assyrian soldiers. He thought he would kill us, and this would be the last thing we would hear before he did so."

"He lied, sir. Asia and Europe are still fighting. Even Australia has made a comeback. We're hanging in the fight, sir. No one is giving up."

Thomas Wayne looked at Hazail. "That's inspiring news. What's your name?"

"Airman First Class Leroy Bonner, sir."

"Airman Bonner, can you get me transportation to Cheyanne Mountain?"

"Where are you located, sir?"

"Stop calling me, sir, please. I'm about four blocks outside of DC in Maryland. Near the 495 beltway and 210 Highway."

"Yes, we can pick you up. There's a chopper leaving Andrews headed for Wright Patterson. From there, you can get on a jet to Colorado."

"Great. There's one other person with me."

"Okay. Stay by the radio and I will contact you with instructions."

"Thank you, Airman Bonner." The line went dead.

Hazail asked, "Why are you leaving this area? There could be more people here."

"There's nothing else I can do for anyone here, Hazail. We can do our best at Cheyanne Mountain."

"They will not allow me inside."

"They will. You have valuable intel on that mothership. They have to let you inside." Hazail didn't respond. He knew she worried about her background preventing her from getting into places with him. What she didn't understand was that he would go nowhere without her.

Airman Bonner's voice returned, "Thomas Wayne."

"Thomas Wayne here."

"The chopper will arrive on the beltway near Highway 210 at 1700 hours. It won't wait long, so you and your guest need to be there."

"We will be there."

"Roger that, Cheyanne Mountain out."

"Thomas Wayne out." He said to Hazail, "Why don't you get some rest. We have two hours to be at the pickup location."

"I will rest when you can rest."

"You were injured. I wasn't."

"I am fine, Thomas Wayne."

The couple embraced, and Thomas Wayne felt good about it. He never questioned his love for her again.

Time went by fast. Thomas Wayne and Hazail rushed to the pickup location. They waited where 210 merged into 495 for the chopper. Minutes later, Thomas Wayne saw the chopper coming from Andrews.

Hazail shouted, "Assyrians!"

Thomas Wayne took his laser and fired shots at the Assyrians. Hazail did the same. The chopper avoided the attack from the Assyrian ground forces. Thomas Wayne and Hazail's weapon fire helped the chopper. It landed a hundred yards away from the couple. Soldiers jumped out of the chopper and shouted for them to run over. They laid down fire, helping Thomas Wayne and Hazail get to the chopper. Once inside, the soldiers joined them, and the chopper took to the sky. The soldiers were still firing at the Assyrians. Thomas Wayne said, "Thanks, everyone."

"You're welcome, sir. It's going to be harder getting to Cheyanne Mountain. The Assyrians have shuttles everywhere."

"Can your craft fly above 9,200 meters?" asked Hazail.

The soldier answered, "Yes."

"That will make it difficult for them to find you."

The soldier looked perplexed. Thomas Wayne said, "She's Assyrian, but she switched to our side."

The soldier took a deep breath. "Sir, she can't get on our jet."

"What's your rank and name?"

"Staff Sergeant Clay, United States Army."

"Sergeant Clay, I'm the leader of the Northeast Region. Hazail has been vetted, and she's probably killed more of her people than you have. She goes."

"Roger that, sir."

Thomas Wayne and Hazail arrived at Cheyanne Mountain. They were then taken underground to the main conference room where Lieutenant Colonel Britton waited with others. Thomas Wayne recognized members of all the military branches and a few Canadian military members. "Thomas Wayne Walker, it's an honor to meet the man who took down two motherships."

"It's an honor to be here, sir. This is Hazail. She joined us and has been fighting with us for the last two weeks."

"I know. Sergeant Clay briefed me she was with you. I hope you're sure we can trust her."

"Sir, I've seen this woman fight her own people. We don't fight them with the same tenacity she does. She's all in."

Hazail spoke up, "Sir, I'm not familiar with your customs, but my loyalty has been in question since I stole a shuttle and came down here to save President Hemingway and Thomas Wayne's life. I have killed my people to save your people. I have given information freely, nothing in return. Yet I am still questioned. If you must know the ultimate reason, I am doing all of this it is simply—love."

Lieutenant Colonel Britton inquired, "Love—for what?"

"Who. I am in love with Thomas Wayne and there is nothing I will not do to protect him."

"You barely know him", said Lieutenant Colonel Britton.

"Assyrian women love fast and hard. We are never half in. When we fall in love, we are all in with our love. It happens fast and it last forever. Unfortunately, most of our marriages are arranged, but when a woman like me finds a man that she loves—it is forever, and nothing is spared."

Lieutenant Colonel Britton stood, "I see. Tell us how we can defeat your mothership?"

"It is impossible to defeat that mothership unless you have a craft with equal or superior weapons and can travel to space."

"Then—Hazail that's it?"

"Yes, sir."

"How do we win this war?"

Hazail looked at Thomas Wayne. Thomas Wayne answered, "We don't. We survive it. They outnumber us, and they have superior weapons. Unless the weapon you were building can equal anything they have."

An airman walked into the room. "Sir, you need to come see this."

Lieutenant Colonel Britton rose and followed the Airman into the other room. Thomas Wayne sat and watched as the other members of Lieutenant Colonel Britton's cabinet watched them. He didn't know what they were thinking, but if they knew like he did, Hazail was an asset, not an enemy. Lieutenant Colonel Britton returned. "If you can't help us win this war, then tell us what they are sending at us now." Hazail twisted her head. "Come this way."

Thomas Wayne and Hazail rose and followed him into the room. Thomas Wayne stared at the screen in disbelief. He looked at Hazail, "Tell me you know what that is and how the heck we can stop it."

"I have never seen anything like that before."

Lieutenant Colonel Britton said, "This is what I am talking about, Thomas Wayne. She has been leading you on to get to this point."

Thomas Wayne showed his exasperation, "To what end, sir?" Lieutenant Colonel Britton had no response. "She's standing here with the rest of ready to die along with us. If she had a plan, it sucks."

Hazail added, "Assyrians don't sacrifice themselves in war. We do not believe we will ever die in war. I do not know what this is, but I know it is not Assyrian."

"Okay." Lieutenant Colonel Britton paused. "Airman, find out anything you can about what the heck that is approaching."

"Sir, whatever it is, it's bypassing the mothership and entering our atmosphere. At the rate of speed it's traveling, it will be on Earth in less than a minute."

"Projected impact location", asked Lieutenant Colonel Britton?

"Colorado."

Lieutenant Colonel Britton looked at Thomas Wayne and Hazail. The object appeared cylindrical. It stopped a hundred yards outside of the Cheyanne Mountain complex and hovered in the air. No one could determine what the object was or its purpose.

The Airman said, "Sir, we're getting worldwide reports that the Assyrians have stopped fighting and they are retreating to their ships."

Thomas Wayne asked, "What now?"

Lieutenant Colonel Britton said, "Are you sure you don't know what this object is before we shoot at it?"

"No, I have never seen anything like it before. If my people have something like it, it was above my rank."

Lieutenant Colonel Britton said, "Then we can all say our goodbyes."

16 – The Heroes Arrive

The craft landed, and the door to the cylindrical object opened. A bright light illuminated the doorway. A man walked out, then another and another. Before long, there stood five men, and two women aligned in a row with the man in the middle slightly ahead of the rest. The Airman at the console said, "Sir, we're getting a call from General Garima."

"Probably calling for our surrender."

"Oh, no," said Hazail.

Thomas Wayne asked, "Why do you say that?"

Hazail answered, "Colonel, accept her call."

"Oh, you know what this is now?"

"I have an idea, and she's not calling for your surrender. She's calling to warn you."

"What?"

Hazail continued, "Thomas Wayne, remember the story I told you about the gods in our ancient days?"

"Yes." He looked at Lieutenant Colonel Britton, "They were—are the mythical Egyptian gods with different names and such. You know the myths."

Hazail continued, "They are not a myth. The gods were real—or they professed to be gods but in reality, they were aliens from another world."

Thomas Wayne asked, "What's he doing?"

A soldier approached the people, who continued to stand as if waiting for someone. They exchanged words, and the soldier called into the mountain. The Airman said, "Sir, Sergeant Jeffries said they want to talk to our leaders."

Lieutenant Colonel Britton said, "Tell them I am on my way."

Thomas Wayne said, "I should go with you."

"Why?"

"You shouldn't go alone."

Hazail said, "I am going as well." Lieutenant Colonel Britton and Thomas Wayne both looked at her. "No one knows them like I do."

Lieutenant Colonel Britton replied, "Okay, the three of us will go out. Major Hayes, you will be in charge if I die out there."

Major Hayes responded, "Sir, maybe I should go."

"No, something tells me I should go."

Lieutenant Colonel Britton headed to the exit with Thomas Wayne and Hazail in tow. He asked, "Should I take a weapon?"

Hazail answered, "It would be pointless. If they wanted you dead, you would be dead now. No, they want to tell us something."

After a long walk and elevator ride, the three of them arrived at the exit of Cheyanne Mountain. They were taken to the gate by car. Thomas Wayne watched as the seven people who remained motionless waited. The car pulled up and let the three of them out. They walked over to the man who appeared to be in charge.

"My name is Lieutenant Colonel Britton or Colonel Britton. Who are you, and what can we do for you?"

"It is not what you can do for us; it is what we can do for you."

"Okay, then. What can you do for us?"

"My name is Cain." He looked at Hazail. "You know my name. You are also not like these. Why are you standing with them?"

"I have aligned myself with the people of Earth."

"Against your own people?"

"I have."

"I have never seen an Assyrian traitor before." Cain fixed his attention on Thomas Wayne. "You are Thomas Wayne Walker?"

"I am. How do you know me?"

"Hemes told me you took down two Assyrian motherships."

"I was the leader who ordered those missions."

Cain nodded his head. "Colonel, we will wipe out the Assyrian army for you. In return, we will be allowed to rule on your planet."

Lieutenant Colonel Britton turned to Thomas Wayne, "Why does everyone want to come here to live?"

Cain continued, "The Assyrians will defeat you in a matter of days. We can wait until they defeat you, then we will defeat them and rule this world. Either way, it is the same result. The choice is yours."

"How do I know I can trust you and your 'rule'? We've had rulers before, and they killed and enslaved people. They set our world back thousands of years. Some of them were you. How can I trust that won't happen again?"

Hazail said, "You can't."

Cain smiled, "The Assyrian in you shows. If you listen to her, she will destroy you. The Assyrians are liars, murders, and thieves. They have conquered many worlds in the galaxy. Now she wants you to believe that she fights with you. She does not."

"But you haven't answered my question. You only stated what we already know about the Assyrians."

"We are passionate people. We only want to live in a peaceful world. Being the rulers of such worlds only makes for a peaceful place for all. If you obey our reasonable laws, no harm will come to anyone." Hazail laughed. "Why is she here?"

"She has been valuable to us."

Cain sneered at Hazail. "She will destroy you."

Lieutenant Colonel Britton asked, "There are only seven of you. How do you plan to beat an entire army with only seven people?"

"We are gods, not mere mortal men like yourselves. Watch." Cain ascended into the air. He landed near the vehicle Thomas Wayne and crew arrived in. Cain lifted the vehicle over his head like it was a grapefruit. He sat it back down on the ground and returned to the group. "Each of us have a power." He turned to the group, "Vayu, demonstrate."

Vayu stepped in front of the group. She wore a purple robe that stopped halfway between her thigh and knees. Her gold sandals wove their way to her knees. She brought her hands in the air. The wind swirled until a tornado appeared in front of Cheyanne Mountain. It slowly moved toward the mountain. She lowered her hands before it hit. And the weather returned to normal. Cain grinned, "The Assyrians are no match for us. We are seven, but we are gods."

Lieutenant Colonel Britton said, "I can't make this decision for all of Earth. I will need to meet with the other leaders. However, I see no reason we won't agree to your terms."

"I prefer the word, agreement."

"I see no reason we won't accept your agreement.

Cain returned to the line with the others. "We will wait here for 24 of your hours. If you do not return by then we will allow the Assyrians to destroy you." Cain and his people returned to the object. The door closed behind them.

Hazail said, "You can't trust them."

"Lady, I trust them more than I trust you," said Lieutenant Colonel Britton.

"You were not here when they ruled this world before. Look it up in your history. You do not want them to rule this world."

Lieutenant Colonel Britton replied, "Ma'am, I know my history. I've read about the myths. I have never seen anything that said these people hurt anyone. They just had groups of people worshipping them. That's all. I'd rather institute another belief system into our culture and still have a culture than to be wiped out by your people."

"They are not my people anymore. I am a Terran."

Lieutenant Colonel Britton huffed and re-entered the vehicle.

The United Nations

Lieutenant Colonel Britton gathered everyone in an emergency meeting of the United Nations. He informed them of Cain's proposal. "Leaders of the world, we have an opportunity to get rid of the Assyrians once and for all. The cylindrical object carried seven warriors with god-like powers. They defeated the Assyrians centuries ago, and that is why the Assyrians left. They came back because these gods left Earth."

The leader of Europe asked, "What do they want in return for doing us this favor? No one wants anything for free."

"Good question. They only want to rule again. The same as the Assyrians who want to come home. Except the Assyrians want to conquer us and they have wiped out many of our cities trying to accomplish that goal. They only want to live amongst us; become the leaders of this world to ensure we live peacefully."

Asia's leader spoke out, "That is a deal that sounds as though we would be required to give up leadership of our countries. Is that so?"

"Gentlemen, I believe these people are our heroes, our saviors. They willingly came back here to defend us. However, they can't do it unless we give them our permission to do so. If we don't, the Assyrians will finish the job. We all know they are days from winning this war. We can't sustain it. We will either be conquered and ruled by the Assyrians or allow the heroes to defend us and live in their society of peace."

"Colonel Britton is right. The war is not going well for us," said the African leader. "One of these heroes came to Africa an hour ago and demonstrated her power. Her name is Vayu, and she is the goddess of air, wind, and breath. She used her power to cause a tornado, which eradicated an Assyrian stronghold on my continent. I am in agreement with North America. We should allow them to rid us of the Assyrians once and for all."

Australia added, "Ramos visited us. He did something with time and removed the Assyrians from a stronghold on my continent. This was only a demonstration of their power. Without our permission, they won't go forward. I am also in agreement. Let's make the deal."

"It seems we have no choice but to agree," said Europe's leader. "These heroes are living up to their offer and they clearly have the power to do what they say they can do. Europe is on board."

"So is Asia," the leader said reluctantly.

Lieutenant Colonel Britton said, "As you know, North America is in. South America?"

"Hephaestus visited us and demonstrated his power. He burned down an Assyrian camp." She adjusted her dress, "I guess we are in as well. Since we have no other viable options."

Lieutenant Colonel Britton asked, "Antarctica, it falls on you. What say you?"

"The beautiful Serena visited my continent. In a matter of moments, she had the Assyrian men laying down their weapons and surrendering. Antarctica is not a continent with many people, but those few that we have are in agreement."

Lieutenant Colonel Britton replied, "It is unanimous. We will give permission to the heroes to eradicate the Assyrians from Earth."

Formal Announcement

Thomas Wayne and Hazail left Cheyanne Mountain after Lieutenant Colonel Britton returned from the United Nations. Thomas Wayne wanted no more part in the leadership, the military, or the war. The decision to align with the heroes was against the warnings laid down by Hazail. To Thomas Wayne, Earth was a fool not to listen.

Thomas Wayne and Hazail laid in bed in the morning hours waiting for the announcement from Cheyanne Mountain. He wanted to hear the official end to the world as they knew it. He held Hazail in his arms and smiled at her beauty. *Someday, I hope to wait at the altar for you, sweetheart.*

The loud burst at their front door caused them both to jump up. They grew accustomed to having their weapons next to the bed. They each grabbed one and headed to the living room. General Garima sat on the couch, waiting for them. With her were three Assyrian warriors pointing their weapons at them.

"There is no need for weapons," said General Garima. "Please lower them." Thomas Wayne refused to lower his weapon until the warriors lowered theirs. General Garima turned to her warriors, "I said lower your weapons." They complied. Thomas Wayne and Hazail reciprocated.

"What do you want," asked Thomas Wayne?

"To talk." She smiled; something Thomas Wayne didn't think she could do. "I see that you truly love this man, Hazail. I knew my first instinct was correct. I should have killed you the moment you returned to the Ishtar."

Hazail smiled. "But you didn't. Like my husband said, 'what do you want'."

"Husband, is it? You held the ceremony without me?"

Hazail answered, "We have not had a ceremony but in my heart, he is my husband."

"Interesting. Nahro will not be happy to hear this news. He is waiting for you on the Ishtar. He truly believes you will come to your senses and return."

"Nahro is here."

"Yes. King Malka sent him when he heard of your traitorous ways." Hazail didn't respond. "I started to kill him, but I wanted to see if you cared about him any longer."

Thomas Wayne asked, "Who is Nahro."

General Garima laughed, "She didn't tell you. Interesting." Hazail remained quiet. "Nahro is her husband."

"Husband," shouted Thomas Wayne! "You didn't tell me you were married."

"I am not married. Remember, I said our weddings are arranged? I have been promised to Nahro since birth. We were to get married after the Terran Campaign."

Thomas Wayne said with force, "That's not going to happen."

"It will not, husband. I love you."

"Aww, isn't that touching?" She paused and stood. "I guess I won't have to kill Nahro now. It seems he means nothing to you any longer."

"He doesn't. Only Thomas Wayne matters."

Thomas Wayne said, "You didn't come down here to discuss our relationship situation."

"Relationship? What is that?"

Thomas Wayne sighed, "Our marriage situation. What do you want here?"

"I am sure Hazail warned you about these gods or heroes, as you call them. They will not be your heroes. Our history is filled with stories of them. They are aliens from another world who thrived on being worshipped. When my people realized who they really were, we fought them—and lost. Something we are not proud of. We will fight them again, but with your world's support, we can rid the galaxy of them forever."

"So, the enemy of my enemy is my friend."

General Garima smiled, "You know that proverb as well."

"You've heard it?" asked Thomas Wayne.

"The radicals in the empire have a book that has meaningless stories and such sayings in it. I believe these Christians call it the Bible."

Thomas Wayne was shocked. *Christianity has spread throughout the universe.* "You've heard of Christianity?"

"I have. We will eliminate them as well."

"For centuries people have tried and failed. But back on point. After we team up to defeat these heroes, we will then find ourselves back fighting you. is that right?"

"You will need our help to defeat them."

"That may be true, but what benefit do we have fighting with you to eliminate them when and if… that's a big if, we win, you will turn on us again."

"I give you my word. We will not attack you after the gods are defeated."

Thomas Wayne huffed, "Forgive me if your word is meaningless at this point. You told me you wanted to talk with our leadership but planted a bomb inside me. If it wasn't for my wife, I would be dead right now."

General Garima replied, "When you are down to nothing, you will come to me for support. My mothership is leaving. The rest of the troops will stay and fight the gods with everything they have. If they defeat the gods, we will come back and take this world."

"If I had a dime for every time, you have said that to us."

General Garima turned to walk out. "Good luck. You're going to need it."

General Garima and her warriors left the house. Thomas Wayne hated they blew open the front door and dreaded having to fix it. He looked at Hazail. "Husband? You never mentioned that you were getting married."

"Because it meant nothing to me. I have renounced Assyria and everything they stand for. I am no longer pledged to marry any man except you. Therefore, in my heart… I am getting married—to you."

The radio went live, and Thomas Wayne realized it was time for the announcement. A voice announced that the event would be broadcasted to the entire world. Lieutenant Colonel Britton's voice flowed next through the radio. "To the people of Earth, we have been in a raging war with the Assyrians for months. The war has gone well at times, but not so well at other times. The Assyrians are a warlike society, and they will not stop waring with us until they are defeated, or they have demolished us." He paused to regain his thoughts. "Now we have an opportunity at our doorstep. The gods we thought were mythical have returned to fight for us. Cain, Serena, Adonis, Tutu, Hephaestus, Vayu, and Ramos. Together they will expunge the plague of the Assyrians Empire from our world. In return, these heroes only ask that they lead us into a world of peace. We only have to agree to their laws. A small price to pay for peace. The loss of life has impacted this world like never before. The three world wars that came before this time compare to nothing like the death toll inflicted on us today. I ask you to open your hearts and minds. Welcome the heroes and step back while they defeat our enemy. Afterwards, obey their laws and allow them to lead us. The world leaders and I have agreed this is the best decision for us. I pray you agree."

Thomas Wayne looked at Hazail. "I guess we will step back and see what happens next."

"The gods will wipe out anyone that stands in their way of being worshipped. It won't end with the Assyrians. It will include anyone who doesn't worship them. Your people... our people don't realize what they have done."

17 – The Heroes vs The Assyrians

Australia

Hephaestus, known as the god of time, landed in Canberra, the capital of Australia. The only continent that is a country welcomed Hephaestus to their land. They were ready to get rid of the Assyrians who were left by their leader, General Garima. The crowd yelled and screamed their approval of their new hero. They praised him for coming to save them.

Hephaestus enjoyed the love and admiration they were giving him. His power increased dramatically with the cheers and praise as he hovered over them. He aligned his body and sped off into the horizon. At the edge of Canberra were the Assyrians. Waiting for a battle they would never receive. The god of time envelope them in a time bubble, freezing their movements. One by one, he killed every Assyrian warrior, then released time. The warriors fell to the ground. A pool of blood flowed into Canberra. The Assyrians lost the battle before they ever knew it was fought.

Hephaestus flew to other populated areas in Australia, eliminating the Assyrian warriors each time until there were no more. He returned to Canberra.

Hephaestus landed in the center of town where the leader of Australia knelt before him. "We are honored to have you as our hero, Hephaestus. Nothing will ever harm Australia again!" The crowd shouted their praise for their hero.

Hephaestus said, "I am your god; as long as you worship and praise me, I will protect you!"

The crowd continued to scream their acceptance of Hephaestus.

Antarctica

Serena dropped to the icy ground of Antarctica, causing ice and snow to shift throughout the continent. She was not happy at her assignment to a land with few people, but trusted her husband, Cain, with all her heart.

She could feel the increased power as the others were winning the support, love and admiration of the inhabitants of the continents they were assigned. Now it was her turn to win such approval from the people of Antarctica. *They will all love me and worship me as no one before them. I will be their goddess, and they will abide by my every commandment.*

She arrived at McMurdo Station on Ross Island, south of New Zealand. Before the war started with the Assyrians, there were only a few thousand people living on the continent. Since the war, many migrated there to get away from the Assyrians, but they could not hide there. The Assyrians followed them and quickly overpowered Antarctica. They held total control until Serena arrived.

She released her powerful pheromone into the air and commanded, "Bow to me, Assyrian men!" The

Assyrian warriors bowed to her without question. "Now, pull out your knives and slit your throats!" The men again followed her orders without question. Blood ran red at McMurdo Station. The humans left behind loved and admired the power and beauty that was Serena. They bowed to her and gave her all the honor and praise. Serena said, "I am your god. Worship me and I will forever protect this continent from all harm and danger!"

The people yelled and screamed louder than they ever have. The people fell to their knees in worship to Serena and it felt good to her.

Africa

The loud, thunderous sound cracked throughout Africa. Everyone looked to the sky, but there was not a cloud present. The Assyrian army took control of South Africa. Vayu removed them from Tanzania. She flew across the continent to Angola by the Atlantic Ocean. Many onlookers watched her. She turned to them. "Terrans, go seek shelter. This hurricane will be powerful. It will go to the Assyrian headquarters on the border of Angola and Namibia and wipe them away. Once its job is done, it will go away, and the Assyrians will never harm you again!" The crowd yelled and praised Vayu. They heard of her powers from the people of Tanzania and welcomed her to their homes to free them of the Assyrians.

Once the humans were gone, Vayu commanded the clouds, rain, and wind to combine into a massive hurricane. She whirled it toward the border of Angola and Namibia. The Assyrians were unprepared for the massive storm. Many of them were swept up into the funnel, instantly killing them. Others were thrown miles away and came crushing to the ground. After every Assyrian warrior was dead, the massive storm stopped immediately, and the skies returned to crystal clear. Vayu blew a powerful wind across the land drying it out.

The people of Africa praise her for saving them. They were free of the Assyrians; not a one was left.

Vayu landed in Southern Africa, and the people ran to praise her. They bowed at her feet. "I am your god. Worship me and I will always protect you!" The crowd yelled their approval. She walked among them sashaying, catching the eye of every man among them. "You, come to me." The African man rose and rushed to Vayu. She caressed his chin, took him by the arm, and flew away with him.

18 - General Garima's Anger

General Garima pulled the Ishtar away from the Earth's orbit. She continued to receive reports that her warriors were dying by the hundreds. Soon her forces would be depleted, and Earth would no longer be a viable solution for Assyria. She returned to her quarters where her husband waited. "I guess you have been receiving the same reports from the grounds I have received."

Baaz replied, "I have. Not only does it look bad for your career, but Assyria is doomed as well. These mythical gods must be stopped."

"I tried to get the Terrans to realize they were being deceived, but it didn't work. They were so focused on us they didn't look deeper into what these so-called gods were asking. They will be fooled, just like our ancestors."

Baaz said, "It is us who are the fools. Now we will have nowhere to go. Our ships can only hold so many people. Millions of Assyrians will die unless we defeat the gods, then the Terrans."

"I understand the cost. You don't have to remind me."

"As for us, what have you decided?"

"We are doomed, and that is all you can think of?"

"I think we will be among those who live to see another day. What is your decision?"

"Why would I stay with a man I don't love?"

Baaz nodded his head. "Then you leave me no choice." He rang the buzzer in the quarters and two warriors joined them. "Take General Garima into custody."

"You have no authority to do this."

"But I do. I have authority from the King himself. Would you like to see it?"

"No."

"Good, now take the General into custody." The warriors didn't move. "I said take her into custody, now!" The warriors still refused to move.

General Garima laughed, "These warriors have sworn an oath to live or die at my word. They won't follow you. You are nothing but a politician running

Assyria, thinking you have power. The real power is in the military. We are the leaders of Assyria." She grabbed the gun from one warrior and pointed it at Baaz.

Baaz plead for his life, "No, please. I wasn't going to have you killed. I promise."

She fired two blasts into his chest, frowning each time. General Garima took pride and joy at killing a man she never loved. She handed the weapon back to the warrior. "Get him out of my quarters and send Ishaia to me." The warriors followed her orders without question. She would soon report to the King that Baaz was killed in battle.

General Garima pressed the button to contact her communications officer. "Yes, General."

"Can you see if we can dig up any text from the ancient days on Terra Prime?"

"Yes, ma'am. It may take some digging. Those books were archived and categorized as useless by the archaeological department years ago."

"Put a rush on it. They may come in handy when trying to defeat these gods."

"Yes, General."

The doorbell to her quarters sounded. She hoped it was Ishaia. She answered, "Come." The door slid open and Ishaia stood outside. "Welcome my love. Baaz is dead. Now we can be together forever."

"That may not be long, I imagine."

"In this life or next, it would not matter to me." They embraced. General Garima led him to her bed.

19 – The Heroes Continue

South America

Ramos landed in an isolated part of South America. The Assyrians conquered most of the fourth largest continent on Earth, therefore he had his work cut out for him, but he didn't mind. Since Isis' death, Ramos spent a lot of time alone. Most of his time was spent admiring the world and the creations that sat in it. *This forest is beautiful. If we were true gods, we could create something like this for the enjoyment of those who worship us. But we are not. We only pretend to be something we can never achieve. A true god is all knowing, all seeing. We are not. I will complete my assignment as instructed, but we… we are not gods.*

Ramos rose into the air and headed to the Assyrian headquarters in Columbia, where most of the Assyrians camped. As he got closer, he realized they were waiting for him and fired their laser blasts at him. *Fools they cannot kill me. I may not be a god, but I am immortal.* He dodged their blasts and released fire from his eyes. The explosion took out several of the Assyrians. The rest continued to fire their lasers at him.

Ramos landed on the ground and wheeled his mighty fire wave over and over at the Assyrians. Two warriors got behind him and struck him about the head and neck. Ramos turned and struck one in the face. He then grabbed the neck of the other and held him in the air. He felt the power growing in him from the worshipping of the humans. It brought joy to him. Ramos pulled his fist back, then plunged it into the face of the warrior. The warrior landed 20 yards away into a tree. He slid down. Blood gushed from his body.

More warriors grabbed Ramos and tried to hold him. Ramos went to the ground, then raised quickly back up, flinging the warriors in different directions. He then whirled around, firing blasts of fire from his eyes. The warriors were burned to a crisp. Those remaining ran hoping to stay alive, but he hunted them down one-by-one until they were all dead.

With his work done, Ramos rose in the air and headed to Brazil, the largest country on the continent of South America. He landed in Porto Velho, an Assyrian stronghold. Again, Ramos realized the Assyrians were waiting for him. They attacked him as soon as he was in range. This time they had a shuttle appear from behind a burned-out building. It fired multiple blasts at him. Two of the blasts caught him and knocked him to the ground. The Assyrians pounced on Ramos trying to subdue him, but he was too powerful for them. He yelled while flinging them off him.

Ramos was a skilled hand-to-hand fighter. He struck blow after blow at the warriors, knocking them off their feet as fast as they attacked him. The shuttle landed, and a large Assyrian warrior stepped out with a larger laser. Ramos watched him fire the blasts him. He stood poised, believing the blast could not hurt him. It didn't kill him, but it knocked him off his feet.

The warrior fired several more blasts. Dust and smoke rose. The Assyrian warriors celebrated, thinking Ramos was dead.

Ramos walked out of the dark smoke. His eyes released fire at each Assyrian warrior, burning them. He then motioned to the large Assyrian warrior to come to him. The warrior cast the weapon to the ground and ran toward Ramos. The two locked arms in a battle of wills, but Ramos was too strong for the warrior. Ramos slowly pushed him to his knees, then he quickly jumped around the warrior and wrapped his powerful arms around his neck. "I will make this slow so you and others like you know you cannot kill a god!"

Ramos kept his word, and the life drained slowly out of the warrior until he was dead. Ramos released him, and his body fell limp to the ground. He looked around and there were no more warriors in sight. The inhabitants of Porto Velho knelt to the ground and praised Ramos. He felt their worship inside of him and his power grew more. He loved it. "I am your god, and I will always protect you!" The crowd celebrated their delight of his words.

Ramos' next stop would be São Paulo in the Southern part of Brazil. Suspecting the Assyrians would be waiting for him again, Ramos set down a few hundred yards outside the city. He walked the rest of the way, keeping his eyes peeled for warriors. *I grow tired of eliminating these worthless warriors. They are no match for us. We may not be gods, but we are superior to them.* Ramos watched as the warriors attempted to set a trap for him. He walked up behind them. "Is that trap for me?" The warriors were surprised. Ramos grinned. His eyes turned bright red, and he spewed fire in every direction, burning all the warriors, leaving nothing but ashes and burnt ground behind.

Ramos turned and headed into the main part of the city. He ran into Assyrian patrols along the way, but they were no match for him. He wiped them away without working up a sweat. Ramos arrived at the heart of the São Paulo. An Assyrian warrior stood with a human woman in front of him. "You are their god, then protect them!" He pointed his weapon at her head. Ramos leapt toward the warrior before he could pull the trigger. He grabbed him by the neck, lifted him off the ground and slammed him back into the street. The move left an indentation in the ground around the warrior. He was dead. More warriors attempted to fire at him. Ramos stood in front of the woman, protecting her from the blasts. His eyes redden and fire spewed out, burning the warriors. The remaining warriors fled the city.

Ramos turned to the woman, "You are safe now."

She fell to her knees, "Thank you."

Ramos rose in the air and spoke, "I am your god. As long as you worship me, I will protect you from any harm." The people of São Paulo fell to the knees and praised him.

Asia

The Pacific Ocean opened up. Raising up from the rushing waters was Tutu, the god of dreams and nightmares. The armies of Asia joined to fight the Assyrians. They could hold their own, but they could not defeat the Assyrians. The army waited at the border of China and North Korea. There were thousands of them representing all the nations of Asia. Tutu set down in front of them. "I am your god.

Together, we will march into the Assyrian strongholds and destroy them. March forward, kill any Assyrian who challenges us." They yelled their support, then marched across China. Most of the Assyrian forces were camped in Northern China near the border of Mongolia. The Asia army, led by Tutu, arrived outside their camp. "Wait while I eliminate the sleeping." Tutu raised his hands. The Assyrians who were sleeping began having nightmares. They grabbed their heads and screamed. Many of them pulled their blades out and killed themselves. The Assyrians who were awake were confused. Tutu shouted, "Attack them!"

The army rushed toward the Assyrians. Tutu stood in the middle. He snapped the necks of two Assyrians warriors while grabbing others and pummeled them to death. The ground flowed with Assyrian blood. The Asian army raised their weapons and yelled their appreciation. Tutu said, "I am your god. As long as you worship me, you will never be defeated!"

Europe and North America

The continents of Europe and North America were the biggest and most widely spread of the Assyrian armies. All the heroes converged on Europe and spread out to eliminate the Assyrians. Adonis arrived in Italy. The Assyrian army took control of Naples and ran their operations from there. Adonis landed near the headquarters and warriors attacked him. The increased worshippers in the world gave great strength to Adonis. He fired punch after punch at the attacking warriors, knocking them down with no effort. He stepped through the group, snapping a neck, punching another in the heart, causing a heart attack, yet another was punched in the throat, breaking his trachea. The warrior grabbed his neck, trying to catch his breath, but to no avail. His face turned blue with significant respiratory compromise, followed by death.

Adonis spun around, causing the sun to be hidden and darkness to prevail. It was too dark for the Assyrians to see anything. He rolled through each of them, killing them one-by-one until they were all dead.

The remaining heroes joined Adonis. Cain said, "Now to finish it with North America." They rose into the air and headed toward the last continent, North America.

Thomas Wayne Frowns on the Onslaught

Thomas Wayne watched from his quarters in Southeast DC as the heroes wiped out the Assyrian warriors. Since the heroes were now ridding the Earth of the Assyrians, television broadcast was returning in limited fashion. He frowned at the blatant death caused by the heroes. "This is not the way we are as humans. We don't kill for the sake of killing."

"But they are removing our enemy from the planet," said Hazail.

"At what cost? You said yourself they want us to give up our rights to choose who we worship. The original deal was for them to lead us and obey their laws. Now they are saying for us to worship them." Thomas Wayne and Hazail suddenly jumped from their seats. "What are you doing here?"

"I come in peace," said General Garima. "As you can see, I have no weapon, nor do I have any warriors with me."

Thomas Wayne asked, "What do you want?"

General Garima said, "I have asked my people to research our records to find something to defeat the gods… heroes, as you call them. We have found nothing in our archives. What we know is that we never defeated them. Instead, we left this planet and headed out to the stars. We found a habitable planet and built our empire there."

Thomas Wayne replied, "That's information we already learned. What's your point?"

"My point, Thomas Wayne, is that not all Assyrians left. Some stayed here. It is believed that those Assyrians may know the secret to defeating the heroes. Find them and we both win."

Thomas Wayne laughed. "Are we back on that again?" He looked at Hazail, who was not laughing. "We know that if—and that's a big if—if the heroes are defeated, your army will return, and we will be at war again."

General Garima sat on the couch. "You are right. I had conversations with the King. I am going to be tried and hanged upon my return to Assyria."

Hazail asked, "Why? No one can beat the heroes."

"I executed my husband. He was going to turn me and my lover Ishaia into the King. I told him I would no longer be married to him."

"Let me guess, this was an arranged marriage," said Thomas Wayne.

"Correct. His family is powerful and could do a great deal for my career, so I married him, but I didn't love him. I love Ishaia. Now, none of that matters. I will either die here at the hands of the gods, or I will die on my home world at the hands of our king." She paused. Thomas Wayne didn't know if she expected a response or not. "Unless you work with me to find a way to kill the gods."

"We have that one annoying problem."

"I will give you my mothership in return for your support in this mission. I know my people lived near the area you call Iran. There may be some still there. We can go there and see if we can find any of the ancient text. Using that text, we may discover the weakness of the gods."

Thomas Wayne asked, "How can I be sure you will give me your mothership? I don't even know how to fly it."

"You have Hazail." She looked at Hazail. "Hazail, I will give you the codes to the ship to do with them what you wish. You love this man, so I can be sure you will use the Ishtar to defend this planet. Am I correct?"

"You are correct," answered Hazail. "Thomas Wayne, if she provides me with the codes, I will be in control of the ship."

Thomas Wayne asked, "What about the warriors on it?"

"I have executed those that are not loyal to me. The others will come down to the planet with me. Part of the deal is that we are allowed to live here peacefully. We will not bother you and you will not bother us."

"How many warriors are you talking about?"

"Only 50, including me and Ishaia."

Thomas Wayne thought the offer over. Earth could learn a lot from the technology contained in the mothership. Most of all, they could defend themselves from any other worlds coming to attack them. *Can I trust this woman? Maybe she pinned herself into a corner that she can't see any other way out.* "Hazail, may I speak with you in private?" She nodded, and they proceeded into the bedroom. "Can we trust her?"

"If she was having an affair with Ishaia, then we can trust her. Adultery is against our highest law. She will be summarily tried and then executed. I think we can believe her."

"What about the codes?"

"If she gives me the codes, I will have control of the ship."

"I want the codes first."

"Yes, get them first, but I believe she will work with us. What she says is true that some Assyrians stayed here. If we can find them, we may find the ancient text."

Thomas Wayne responded, "I know there are Assyrians still here. When the war broke out, they were persecuted and placed in camps. I don't know what happened to many of them, but we can find out." Thomas Wayne paused. "Let's make the deal. What do we have to lose? The heroes will have us all bowing to them soon." They returned to the living room where General Garima waited on the couch.

Thomas Wayne spoke, "If we make this deal, I want the codes first." General Garima tossed a packet to Hazail. "Are those the codes?"

"I anticipated you would request that, so I brought them with me. We can use my communications system in the shuttle to change the codes."

Thomas Wayne grinned, "I can say, I didn't expect that from you."

General Garima stood, "By now you must know when an Assyrian woman loves, she loves hard and will do anything for her lover. I sacrificed my career for Ishaia just as Hazail did for you." She looked at each of them. "Let us go to the shuttle."

Thomas Wayne was still skeptical of General Garima's intentions. A man's limp body laid on the ground next to the shuttle. Blood flowed from it like a river. His neck was snapped like a twig. General Garima fell to the ground in tears. Thomas Wayne suspected the man was her lover. He looked at Hazail. Hazail answered, "When we love, we love hard."

General Garima gathered herself, "If you think I am trying to deceive you now, you are a fool. I want to see them dead for killing my mate!"

"Excuse me for my ignorance, but how do you know the heroes did this?"

She pointed to the indentation on the ground, "Only a god can make an impression like that. He must have landed here when he spotted the shuttle and killed Ishaia. I will use all my days left alive to see that they pay."

Thomas Wayne replied, "I guess you're right. No human man could have made those footprints. Let's do this. I don't want to worship a false god and I'm sure the world doesn't either. They are just happy the war is over."

Hazail said, "Until they realize their freedoms are no more."

They moved inside the shuttle, where Hazail used the codes to take control of the mothership. General Garima contacted the ship, "Warriors of Assyria, this is General Garima. You are hereby ordered to stand down and stay out of Earth's orbit until you receive further orders from Hazail. She is now in command of the Ishtar. Our forces on the ground have been eliminated by the gods. We are taking actions to get our retribution." General Garima handed the communicator to Hazail.

"Warriors of Assyria, this is Hazail. As your commander, it is imperative that you stay where you are. If you approach Earth, the gods will destroy you. I will contact you when our mission is completed. That is all."

General Garima said, "There, you have what I said you would. Now it is your turn to help me get my revenge."

"I know there were several Assyrians living in the United States. Most of them lived in Detroit. Some live in Chicago, California, and Arizona. If we can use this shuttle, we can get to Detroit and see what we can find."

Hazail said, "If we use this shuttle, it will attract the gods."

"Then we use it at night or during the world celebration day in two days."

"I will wait in here," said General Garima.

Thomas Wayne replied, "That's not a good idea. Come into our quarters. You will be safe there." General Garima thought about it, then rose. Thomas Wayne motioned for her to follow him.

The World's Celebration

For two days Thomas Wayne, Hazail and General Garima watched the heroes take back the world. They eradicated every Assyrian stronghold and wiped out any Assyrian warriors they found. The day the world would come together and praise the heroes for saving them arrived. It sickened Thomas Wayne to his stomach. He said, "The world will be focused on the heroes and the heroes will be focused on all the love and worshipping they will receive. For us, it's time to seek those Assyrians in Detroit." He looked at the two ladies. With their tears, and love he forgot they were Assyrian warriors. "I forgot for a moment that you ladies were warriors. You don't need a pep talk. You are already ready to go. Let's do it."

They headed to the shuttle in the twilight hours, hoping no one would notice the ship taking off. Hazail guided the shuttle to Detroit. The shuttle landed in a now secluded area of Detroit. The bombings left their mark in one of America's major cities. *Wow, it's been a while since I've been here but Detroit you didn't look like this last time I was here. All the towering buildings are gone. Nothing but mostly burnt-out buildings and streets.* "This city was one of the best before you came."

General Garima looked at him, "Do you want me to apologize?"

"I guess that's not part of your nature, is it?"

General Garima stopped. "It is not in our nature to submit to any world. We are warriors, conquerors. We do not apologize for our actions. You will never understand us."

"What I don't understand is how the Assyrians of this world are so different from you. The Assyrians here are peaceful, God loving people. They wouldn't go to war with anyone. What happened?"

General Garima refused to answer. Hazail answered, "The group that stayed behind already believed in the Hebrew God Jehovah. My ancestors thought they were weak because they did not want to fight the gods, so we left them behind to suffer their fate with the gods. The gods were defeated."

General Garima said, "Why does it matter? We need to find them and get the answers we need to kill the gods."

Thomas Wayne huffed, "I have no idea where to look for them." He looked around the empty streets, but no one was around. They continued to walk the streets, hoping to find someone.

General Garima said, "Stop!" Everyone stopped in their tracks. "We are being followed."

Thomas Wayne asked, "You can tell that?"

She looked around, then focused on one area. A few men stepped from around a building in front of them. More came from behind them. "They are not Assyrian."

"I am Thomas Wayne, leader of the Northeast Region. Who is in charge here?"

"There aren't any more regions," said the young woman who stepped between the men. "There are only pockets of people who haven't drunk the Kool-aid."

"Aaliyah? Is that you?"

"It is my brother."

"What are you doing up here?" She came closer to Thomas Wayne and hugged him. "I'm so happy to see you."

"I'm happy to see you as well." She sneered, "You're still with her, though."

"She is not a traitor."

Aaliyah replied, "But I know she is." She pulled out her Glock and pointed it at General Garima. General Garima held her head back and took a deep breath. She was not afraid. "She's their leader."

Thomas Wayne grabbed the gun from Aaliyah. "We have made a deal to find a way to defeat the heroes."

"You don't believe them either?"

"Come on, momma took us to church every Sunday. These guys may have powers, but they are not gods."

Aaliyah smiled, "Okay, but if I suspect anything from either of them, they will be killed."

"Agreed."

"Follow me." Thomas Wayne and the others followed Aaliyah. Thomas Wayne noticed some faces of the men in the group. They appeared not to agree with Aaliyah's decision to bring them to their camp. *I need to keep my eyes open for trouble. These guys are ready to kill my woman, and we won't have that.* "Where's Cordell?"

"After that incident with your girl, we split ways." She stopped and looked at Thomas Wayne. "I never wanted to harm her. I just wanted her to admit she was a spy. Clearly, I was wrong… and so was Cordell. Last I saw him, he was putting his militant skills to work in North Carolina. That was about two months ago."

"What brought you here?"

"I hooked up with some new friends who said they were taking the war to a new level. That turned out to be a lie. Then I ended up meeting with Carmichael."

"Who is Carmichael?"

"Carmichael ran a faction of the Crips back in the day. Now, he organizes us all and keeps us from starving. We fight off any Assyrians, although that's not been a problem lately, and we survive. A simple life. But I'm guessing that's about to change with you here."

"We just want to defeat the heroes. They're not what people think."

"That we agree on, and so does Carmichael." They walked into what used to be a hotel. In the lobby were people milling about. Some appeared to be guarding the building while others sat around. Aaliyah led them around the lobby to a conference area. "Hey, Lilly. Is Carmichael in?"

"Yes, go ahead."

"Thanks." They entered the office and behind the desk sat an older man in his 40s. He stood and looked Thomas Wayne up and down. "Carmichael, this is my brother, Thomas Wayne Walker."

"It is good to meet you."

Thomas Wayne nodded, "It's good to meet you as well." He smiled, "This is my girlfriend, Hazail, and this is General Garima."

"I know who she is, but what I don't know is why she is here now. Afraid the heroes will kill you?"

"I'm not afraid to die." General Garima's face never flinched.

"She's here to help us find a way to defeat the heroes," said Thomas Wayne. "Believe me, you don't want them to hang around. Things will not be so happy."

Carmichael motioned to one man. The man cut the television on, and the world celebration day blared into the room. "Let's just see what our heroes will have to say." Thomas Wayne nodded. Carmichael said, "Everyone… take a seat."

Thomas Wayne watched intently as the celebration carried on. The people of Earth worshipped the gods as they did in the ancient days. The leader everyone came to know as Cain stood before the crowd. "We have eliminated the Assyrian plague from your planet as only gods can do. This world is now ours and you will worship us as your gods. You will pray to us two times a day; once in the morning and once in the evening hours. Anyone caught not praying to us will be executed on the spot. As your saviors, you should be thankful that we have freed you from the Assyrians! Each one of us will be responsible for a continent on Aaru. Yes, we have renamed this planet. You will no longer call it Earth; you will call it Aaru." Cain turned away from the podium. Each hero followed him off the stage and they reentered their ship. The ship rose into the sky and headed to space.

Hazail's communicator went off. She said, "May I take this in private?"

Carmichael replied, "Yes. Take her to the room next door and allow her to speak in private." Hazail left with the guard.

Carmichael asked, "Now the world knows the truth about our saviors. They are not saviors at all, but rulers. First the Assyrians, your people, now these false gods. Everyone wants a piece of Earth and its people. Oh, I said Earth, and nothing struck me down." He laughed.

Thomas Wayne grinned, "I think we all knew that nothing would strike you down, but we need to fix this and finding the Assyrian people who lived here could be the key. Do you know where they went? There was a great deal of them living here until the war started."

"There were many Assyrians here. They owned grocery stories, shops, liquor stores, you name it. They were peaceful, nothing like you, General Garima." She continued to stay silent. "The ones who escaped the gangs and soldiers went into hiding. The others were killed."

"You have no clue where one of them might be?"

"My guess, and this would be strictly a guess, would be a church. One that isn't completely burned out by the warriors." He pondered. "There's one on Monroe Street that may be still mostly together. I would try that one first. I can send some men with you."

"No need. The smaller the group, the better."

Carmichael nodded. Hazail reentered the room. "I understand the tactic of smaller groups. We have used it well since the war started. I wish you well, Thomas Wayne."

"Thank you, Carmichael." Thomas Wayne, Hazail, and General Garima left the room and the hotel. Once outside Hazail stopped them.

"Did you know," Hazail asked General Garima?
"Know what?"

"The gods are not here by chance. They came here because they made a deal with King Malka. The gods found us in Assyria and were going to destroy us. King Malka offered them Earth instead of Assyria. The gods refused because they knew Earth to be stubborn and that many of them followed Jehovah, the one true God. He told them he could attack Earth, make them suffer and the gods would come save them, making them ripe to worship the gods again." The look on General Garima's face told Hazail what she needed to know. "You didn't know, did you?"

"I did not." She dropped her head. "But our world will be destroyed in a year."

"That is a lie. King Malka made it up."

"I need to get back to that mothership and go to Assyria. I will kill him myself."

Hazail sighed, "It is too late for that. The heroes destroyed the mothership minutes ago. That message was the last message they could get out. That and something about the hero's ship. I didn't get it all because they were destroyed."

General Garima leaned against the wall, "This has all been a lie. My Ishaia died for nothing, and countless number of warriors all died for nothing."

"Don't forget the humans that died," added Thomas Wayne.

"We must find the human Assyrians and defeat the gods. Then we must find a way back to Assyria and deal with King Malka. Where is this Monroe Street?"

"I believe it's this way." *Countless people died to spare one world from destruction. This is the craziest thing I have ever been involved with in my life. I have a story to tell my grandkids if I live long enough to have grandkids.* Monroe Street was a short walk for the group. When they arrived on the street, Thomas Wayne was amazed. The obliteration surrounding the church was astonishing. However, the church itself was almost undamaged. "God protected the church."

A voice behind them said, "Because of our prayers."

They turned around and three people stood on the street with them. Thomas Wayne said, "We are not here to fight anyone."

"That is good because we don't fight. We believe God is in control of our lives."

"Are you Assyrian?"

"We are, and this church has been our home since the war. God watches over it and protects us."

Hazail stepped forward, "We are kindred. I am also Assyrian."

"But you are one of the people who came to destroy this world. So is General Garima. Everyone recognizes your face, General."

General Garima said, "I realize that, but my mission was a lie. It was a lie that my King told me and thousands of other Assyrians. I am not a threat to you any longer."

"Do you still believe in the ways of those who left us centuries ago?"

"I… I am struggling to believe in anything at this time."

Hazail chimed in, "I do not believe in their ways." She stepped closer to the Assyrians. "I believe we are the chosen people. The people who are to free this world of the so-called heroes. In order to do that, we need your help."

"How can we help you? We are not an aggressive people."

General Garima asked, "Do you have any of the ancient text from when the gods ruled this world before?"

"We do not have that here, but there is one person, a guardian, who protects our history. It would be difficult to find her."

Thomas Wayne asked, "Why is that?"

"She lives in the Zagros Mountain range of Iran. No one knows the exact location."

Thomas Wayne sighed. "Iran? This is going to be more difficult than anyone imagined."

The man said, "Come, let us go inside. You can talk more to Father David."

The group followed the man into the church. There were many Assyrians housed in the church. Thomas Wayne was amazed the church withstood attacks from both sides and now the heroes as well. *The more we get into this, the more I believe there is a God.*

The man introduced Father Bento the group. Thomas Wayne introduced Hazail and General Garima. "We are here, Father, to find the ancient text. We hope there might be some clue in there to help defeat the heroes."

Father Ben nodded his head. "The heroes, gods, whatever you would call them, are nothing more than aliens from another world. You see, the science fiction shows that featured beings with superpowers are an adoration of those times. Man has always been fascinated with increased abilities, but in the ancient days, they were real. Beings with unheralded power and abilities walked this earth. Most of our Assyrian brothers and sisters fought them. My tribe did not.

We believed, as we do today, that there is but one God and He would fight our battle."

General Garima asked, "How has that worked for you?"

"Very well General. Look at this building, then look at the others surrounding it. Our faith is what is protecting us." General Garima snickered and turned away. "The powers these beings have grown stronger with worshippers. That is why they command you to worship them twice a day."

Thomas Wayne asked, "You know this for sure?"

"Yes, I do. I am one of a handful of people who have read parts of the ancient text. None of us read the entire text, for we would be susceptible to people like the good General here. They would have to capture all of us to learn it."

"I understand, but it would be impossible to make the entire world stop worshipping them. There has to be another way."

"If there is, I don't know it." Father Bensighed, "The only person who may know lives in the Zagros Mountains. On Mount Dena, there is a cave just past the 10,000-foot elevation point. The entrance is tricky. You will have to feel the sides of the mountain for a slight crease. It is there that you can open the door. Her name is Isabel. If you find her, you will find your answer. May God be with you."

General Garima replied, "Then He isn't."

Father Benasked, "Why do you say that?"

"I was given explicit orders to target that mountain range and that mountain. We destroyed it. If she was living there, she's dead now."

"Then, so is your solution."

All hope left Thomas Wayne. The one chance they had to find the way to defeat the heroes may be dead. "So, King Malka must have known she lived there as well?"

Hazail asked, "So, if God protected you in this church, why not her in the mountain?"

Father Benanswered, "I have not been to the mountain in decades. Therefore, I can't answer your question. I can only go by what your general here said. Maybe she survived. I don't know."

Hazail said, "Thomas Wayne, it's worth going to see for ourselves. If this church survived, she may also have survived."

"You're right, my love."

"You're both crazy," laughed General Garima. "We destroyed that mountain."

Thomas Wayne asked, "Were you given orders to destroy Detroit too?"

General Garima thought about the question. "I was."

Thomas Wayne replied, "Look at this church. You didn't do a complete job."

Father Benadded, "God hid this church from you. You could not have targeted it."

General Garima replied with a hint of sarcasm, "Any of you know that for sure? You talked to Him?"

"We talk to God every day. You don't realize it because you don't have a relationship with Him."

"The two of you can go to these mountains. I will handle this on my own."

Hazail asked, "What are you going to do?"

"I don't have a plan, but I will do something. I just know it is pointless to go to Iran."

Thomas Wayne said, "Suit yourself. Father David, may we stay through the night and leave in the morning?"

"You may."

Thomas Wayne and Hazail made themselves comfortable in a quiet part of the church. He watched her sleep and relished in her beauty. Through all the tragedies he experienced since the war, she was the best thing that happened to him. He thought Elaine was the one, but Hazail was special. She had something that no one woman he ever knew had. Hazail was strong yet loving. She cared about him more than anything else in the world and she would not hide that fact from anyone. Thomas Wayne chuckled at the thought of the mantra 'Assyrian women love hard'. *God, if you're up there, it would be nice to get through all of this with this woman by my side. She's awesome.*

20 – Iran

Cain sat on his makeshift throne in Washington, DC, with his wife, Serena. "They call this place the capital of the United States. Since there are no more countries, we will name Philadelphia the new capital of North America."

"My love, why do you give me Antarctica? It is such a small place with few inhabitants."

"Because I want you by my side. With a small continent, you can be here more than you need to be there. You can go there occasionally and oversee the people of Antarctica but most of your time can be spent here with me, ruling North America."

"Yes, my love." They both looked to the sky and watched his landing. "Hephaestus, my brother, what brings you here?"

"Serena, my sister. It is good to see you again. Cain, I have news from one of my worshippers."

"What is it, Hephaestus?"

"He says the humans have teamed up with General Garima and another Assyrian woman. They are searching for the Ra's tablets from the ancient days."

"Who are these sinners?"

"I only know of General Garima and Thomas Wayne Walker. I do not have the name of the third person, but she is Assyrian."

"King Malka warned us that General Garima was going to be a problem. Find them and bring them to me. Their execution will be publicized on this television, so the world will see it is not good to defy their gods."

"I will find them." Hephaestus soared the sky in search of the group.

Cain stepped down from his throne and gazed into his wife's eyes. She smiled back at him. "I grow tired of your flirtation with Adonis. It will end or I will end him."

"Adonis means nothing to me, my love. He is a boy trapped in a god's body. Let him play in Europe. He will have all the women he desires there."

Cain took her by the arm. "Let us fly over the land and ensure they are praying to us."

The Long Trip to Iran

Thomas Wayne and Hazail arrived at the shuttle. Thomas Wayne said, "I guess you changed your mind."

"I realized I can't do anything without your support, so I joined this futile trip," answered General Garima.

Hazail responded, "I am glad you have joined us, General. Your wisdom is much needed."

Thomas Wayne smirked at Hazail. He wondered why Hazail would buttering her former commander up. It wasn't necessary at this point. They could complete the trip without her help. "Are we sure flying low will not set off any bells for the heroes?"

General Garima answered, "We are not sure. We can only hope for the best. They are spread out over the world. We will keep to routes where the population is low."

"I guess the Atlantic Ocean will help. Not many people are out there." He grinned, but no one else responded. "Oh well, I guess you have to be human."

Hazail replied, "You know we are human, same as you."

"I do, but it was just easier for us to differentiate between your race and ours." Hazail nodded. *Is she growing tired of me? Hazail has never acted so distant towards me.* Thomas Wayne took her hand and rubbed it. She smiled and mouthed the words 'I love you'. Her smile and words encouraged him.

The shuttle rose and headed east. General Garima said, "We will pass over New York and Massachusetts before we hit the ocean. We will stay away from the normal ship routes to Europe."

"How do you know all of this?" asked Thomas Wayne.

"We studied your world before we attacked. We know more than you think we know."

"I see, and I'm learning every day." Thomas Wayne settled into his seat. "How long do you think it will take? These seats aren't exactly comfortable."

"It should take us nine hours," answered General Garima.

Thomas Wayne's eyes popped. "Nine hours? It took me 14 hours when I went."

"You are forgetting our technology is more advanced. The engines on this shuttle are more advanced than anything you have on Earth." Thomas Wayne listened to General Garima, but he didn't care to hear what she said. He leaned over to kiss Hazail, and she responded to his move. Her lips made his blood boil each time he kissed her. His uncontrollable desire for her was something he never experienced before, and he loved it. General Garima continued, "Time will pass quick with you being in love with my lieutenant."

"I certainly hope so." Hazail took Thomas Wayne's hand and smiled at him. He pointed, "That's the Statue of Liberty. It was given to the United States by France. Of course, the bombing takes away from its beauty."

"I have seen images of it. We have them stored in our computer Bell. Well, we had them stored."

They continued to make small talk on the trip. The shuttle's early warning system went off, startling Thomas Wayne. "What's going on?"

"Missiles are headed this way. Someone is trying to shoot us down."

"Can we avoid them?"

"Hazail, I need your help up front." Hazail rushed to the navigation chair. "I'll guide the ship. You fire the countermeasures."

"Yes, ma'am."

The two women worked together to avoid the missiles. General Garima said, "We need to get to the ground."

"What's going on?"

"Adonis is headed this way."

"Adonis? How did he find us?"

"His people probably warned him." The shuttle made a quick turn and headed to the ground. General Garima avoided Adonis using smokescreen countermeasures. She set down in Egypt near the red sea. "This shuttle is one of our experimental shuttles."

"Meaning," asked Thomas Wayne.

"Meaning, it has a translucent mode."

"It's invisible? Why didn't we fly that way so they couldn't see us?"

"It can't be in translucent mode while in flight." Thomas Wayne's face frowned. "I know. It's a quirk we were working out," General Garima added.

They exited the shuttle. Thomas Wayne said, "That's the Red Sea. We need to cross it then cross Saudi Arabia. It won't be easy because these Middle Eastern countries don't get along with everyone. Keep your eyes open."

The group headed out. They got to the Red Sea and bought passage on a ship to cross over into Saudi Arabia. Thomas Wayne noticed one of the crew pull out a radio. "Wait here for me," he said without making eye contact with either of them.

He followed the man down the boat and overheard him reporting them to someone. Thomas Wayne grabbed the man from behind. He placed his arm around his neck. The man dropped the radio and tried to grab his gun, but Thomas Wayne knocked it into the water. "Who did you talk to?" The man refused to speak. "Tell me or I'll choke the life out of you."

"The Saudi Armed Forces. They wanted information on the two women you are with." He pulled out a piece of paper from his pocket. It was a bounty on General Garima and Hazail.

"Saudi, put this out?"

"No, the gods put it out to every military organization in the world."

Thomas Wayne released the man. "Do you want to worship these false gods for the rest of your life? Your children?"

"I just wanted the money."

"You disgust me." Thomas Wayne struck the man, knocking him out cold. He grabbed the radio and tucked it inside his pants, then rejoined General Garima and Hazail. Whispering, he said, "We have a problem." He showed them the bounty. "One of the crew radioed ahead. The Saudi military might be waiting on us to land."

Hazail asked, "What do we do, my love?"

Thomas Wayne started to answer when he noticed General Garima move toward the captain. She was quick and precise. She grabbed his weapon, wrapped her arm around his throat, and pointed the weapon at the crew. "If you want your captain to live, throw your weapons into the sea." They all complied. "Now, all of you jump in as well." The men hesitated. "I said jump in... now!" They jumped into the Red Sea, leaving the ship empty. General Garima threw the captain overboard with the rest of his men. "Now we change direction and enter the country without being noticed."

"I must say, I'm impressed. You also didn't kill anyone. Maybe my way is rubbing off on you, but there is one more crewman on board. The one I punched."

"Wake him up and toss him overboard, else we risk coming face-to-face with a god."

Thomas Wayne went back to where he left the crewman. He was still unconscious on the deck. Thomas Wayne woke him and told him the others jumped overboard. Thomas Wayne said, "Sorry man." He tossed the man overboard and watched him as he struggled to get himself under control. He returned to the front of the ship. Hazail drove the ship while General Garima plotted a course on the map.

"Instead of going ashore on the Southern part of Saudi Arabia where the captain was taking us, we will go ashore on the Northern shore. We will then need to make our way through Iraq to get to Iran."

"That won't be easy."

General Garima replied, "Anywhere we go, it will not be easy."

Coming Ashore

Hazail navigated the ship and dropped anchor 20 yards from the shore. The eight-hour time difference worked in their favor. The darkness covered their arrival. Each of them disembarked and swam ashore. Once on the shore, they made their way to a covered area and tried to dry themselves the best they could. Thomas Wayne said, "Hopefully we can find new clothes somewhere." Neither of the women responded. "Let's head out." It didn't take them long to reach the Iraq border. From their advantage point, they could see the guards. "I can't believe they're still protecting the border. I thought those things were over now."

General Garima responded, "Because of the gods, they have gone back to their petty little territory disputes. I'm surprised the gods allow this to continue, since they govern the entire world."

"Probably a deal they made with the local leadership to keep their people in line." Thomas Wayne paused. "We have to get through that gate."

Hazail asked, "How far does the wall extend?"

"From Kuwait to Jordan, if I remember correctly. We could head to Jordan, which will be easier for us to get across, then travel to Iraq from there. It will take us longer, but we shouldn't confront anyone."

General Garima replied, "Lead the way."

Thomas Wayne pulled away from their lookout location and led the way. He walked ten feet and stopped in his tracks. Hazail said, "What's wrong, honey?"

"I see red eyes in the dark."

General Garima shouted, "Move!" She pushed them to the side, and fire landed on the trees and bushes behind them. Thomas Wayne shouted, "What was that?"

Ramos answered, "I am your god, and you have sinned." He stepped from the woods and stared at the ladies. "Assyrians, you will pay dearly for your sins."

Thomas Wayne asked, "All these guys talk like that?"

"Terran, you will pay for your impudence."

General Garima shouted, "Run!" Thomas Wayne and Hazail followed her. Thomas Wayne could hear Ramos shout at them. He gained ground on them, but they kept running. General Garima pointed, "This way." Thomas Wayne and Hazail ran the way she pointed, but General Garima ran in the opposite direction.

Ramos ran after her. Thomas Wayne said, "We have to go after her."

Hazail responded, "She sacrificed herself so that we can complete the mission."

Thomas Wayne pushed past her, "I'm so tired of this sacrifice thing." He headed toward Ramos and

General Garima. It wasn't long before he caught up with them. Ramos held General Garima in his hand and readied himself to kill her. "Let her go!"

He looked at Thomas Wayne with disgust. "How dare you challenge a god?"

Thomas Wayne spotted something that he noticed about Cain as well. He pulled out his gun and Ramos laughed.

"Your weapons are puny and won't harm me."

"Really? I think I want to test that theory." Thomas Wayne fired the gun at Ramos and the bullet fell to the ground.

"Fool."

"I just need to aim a little better." He fired again, hitting Ramos' wrist. The object on his wrist came loose and fell to the ground. Ramos' face held shock. He reached for the object, but Thomas Wayne fired again and again, backing him away. "I'm guessing my gun will kill you now. Go, tell the others we know how to kill you now." Ramos ran away at a considerably slower speed.

Hazail said, "How did you know?"

Thomas Wayne picked up the object and bounced it around in his hands. "I noticed on the broadcast that all of them wore this on their wrist when they were fighting the Assyrians and when they talked to us in front of Cheyanne Mountain. I wondered if it was a decoration or something else. No better time than now to test that theory."

"It was a hunch?" asked Hazail.

"Yes." He looked at General Garima, "Are you okay?"

"You are stupid? You could have died and then no one would be alive to kill them."

"You're welcome."

"Ugh." She walked away.

Hazail said, "She's not used to someone coming back to save her. She owes you a debt."

"Not really. I played a hunch. It could have cost us our lives. We don't know the full extent of these things. Can they survive without them?"

"I'm sure the text will tell us all we need to know."

"I'm sure you're right, but the problem now is they know we know about the device. They will guard it next time." Thomas Wayne started to put the device on.

"What are you doing?" Hazail shouted.

"I want to see what it does."

"That could kill you! We don't need you to play a hunch right now, Thomas Wayne!" Hazail's anger was apparent. Thomas Wayne was shocked by it.

"Okay, I'll put it in my bag. Hopefully, I can get it to one of our scientists." They walked away, catching up with General Garima along the way. The darkness covered their movements, but without speaking, they all knew the next encounter with a god would be different... much different.

The trip through Jordan in the night was uneventful. They came to a house. It appeared no one lived there since the war started. They made themselves comfortable hoping to get some rest, then continue the journey to Iran the next morning. Thomas Wayne took the first shift while the ladies slept. He thought of all the people who died since the war began; all because of one King's weakness and fear of the heroes. *The enemy of my enemy is my friend. I'm believing that one for sure now. My grandmother probably turned over in her grave at all of this. She wanted me to know God for myself. Well, grandma, I realize He is real because we got some fake ones now.* He thought about the devices on the hero's wrist and what it could grant the wearer. Maybe the message that the warriors were trying to transmit would have given them more information. At least his hunch turned out to be right, but at what cost? *They know we know and that means they will come at us with a vengeance.*

Hazail touched him on his shoulder. "My love, it is my hour to watch. Get some rest."

Thomas Wayne wanted to argue with her, but decided it was better to get some sleep. They all needed to be fresh when they started their journey. He laid down a few feet from her, wanting to be near in case something happened.

Hazail woke Thomas Wayne. The sun was over the Jordan. Thomas Wayne rubbed the sleep out of his eyes. Hazail handed him a glass of water. "My love, we must leave. The soldiers are likely coming this way; looking for us."

"I'm up." General Garima watched as he rose to his feet. They hurried out of the home. On the way out, Thomas Wayne spotted a soldier in the mirror. "Wait!" He pulled General Garima back. The solider didn't see them. They stayed pressed against the inside walls of the home as he peeked inside. Thomas Wayne noticed General Garima put her hand on her blade. He whispered, "Don't do it. More will be behind him." She eased it off. The soldier yelled some words in Arabic and headed out of the village. "Whew, that was close, but they must be on to us."

They left the home, ensuring they scanned the area for more soldiers. Some people of the village watched them. *I surely hope they don't dime us out.*

A Jordanian woman approached them. "Don't go to the East," she told them. "They are waiting for you there with one of the gods. If you are heading to Iran, you must go north into Syria, then east into Iraq and Iran. Otherwise, they will catch you."

Thomas Wayne said, "You speak good English."

"I am married to an American soldier—was married. He died in the war with the Assyrians." She looked at General Garima and frowned.

"I'm sorry," General Garima replied with a sadness on her face that Thomas Wayne never witnessed before.

Thomas Wayne's mouth dropped. *Wow, did I just hear what I think I heard? She said she was sorry. Maybe she can be trusted.* "Thank you for helping us."

"There's no one in this village that believe in the heroes. We go through the motions, so they don't kill us. Please, stop them."

Hazail said, "We will."

Following the village woman's directions, the group headed north toward Syria. Thomas Wayne said, "Syria became a deadly place during the war. I heard stories of gangs taking over the area and forcing people to do their will. Keep your eyes open."

General Garima replied, "We know how to protect ourselves. We were raised as warriors."

"Yeah, I don't doubt that, but I just want to be sure that my beautiful woman and my friend are safe."

General Garima's neck snapped. "Friend?"

"Hey, you've grown on me. I also see a change in you. Please don't deny it."

She stopped and looked him in the eye. "I have changed. Terrans are not what we were told." She took a deep breath, "You came back for me despite your mistrust of me. That is something I would never have suspected. Together, we will defeat the gods. Then I will find a way back to Assyria and get my revenge."

"Sounds like a plan to me."

The walk to Syria was short because a good Samaritan gave the group a ride. Thomas Wayne didn't trust anyone, but his feet hurt, and he gave into the temptation of the ride. It turned out the man was a devout Christian who was moving his family into hiding from the heroes. He vowed to never pray to a false god. The man dropped them off near the Syrian border. "Now the fun begins."

"What does that mean?" asked Hazail.

"It's sarcasm for we're in danger now." Thomas Wayne started to take a step, but General Garima stopped him.

"Move back slowly." Thomas Wayne didn't know why, but he suspected she saw something he didn't. He moved backwards. "There is a mine here. If there's one, there could be others."

Thomas Wayne looked down, "I see. I guess now we're even again."

General Garima said, "If we blow these mines, they will know that we are here."

"Yes, but if we blow them and hide in the brushes, we can catch them off guard. It's safe to say they will not walk through their own minefield.

Whatever direction they come will give us a hint of where the minefield ends."

General Garima replied, "I have a growing respect for you as a military man, Thomas Wayne. I see why Hazail loves you."

Thomas Wayne waited on one side of the road while General Garima waited on the other. Hazail climbed a tree and prepared to throw rocks on the road to see where the mines were. She tossed the first one, but nothing happened. She threw another with the same result. The third landed near the place where Thomas Wayne nearly stepped on the mine, and it exploded with a loud bang. Thomas Wayne scanned the horizon to see if anyone would come running. No one came. He motioned to Hazail to toss another rock. She did near the first but out of the range. A second mine exploded. Three men came rushing towards the area from behind General Garima. Thomas Wayne pointed behind her and to the left. He let her know they were coming, and she moved to make sure she stayed hidden.

General Garima signaled to Thomas Wayne to take on the man closest to him. She counted down. At one, they attacked the men. Hazail came out of the tree and pounced on the third man. They subdued the men.

General Garima said to her man, "We need to get to Iraq, and you're going to show us the safest route." The man was afraid but didn't answer. "Do you understand me?"

Thomas Wayne said, "He understands." He stood next to the man and said, "Maybe we should kill him and ask one of the others."

The man said, "If you stick to the Eastern part of Syria, you will have no problems. We are manned in Central and West Syria protecting Syria from Turkish intruders."

General Garima said, "Find something to tie them up."

"There's nothing out here for that."

"Then we only have one choice."

Thomas Wayne shouted, "No…" General Garima struck the man in his temple, knocking him out cold. "Oh, I thought you were…" He shook his head, "Never mind."

She did the same with the other two men. "We will stick to the central route through Syria."

"General, wait—he said stick to the east," replied Hazail.

"He lied. I can tell by his eyes he was lying. In my former life, I would have killed him for lying to me."

Thomas Wayne added, "Also, the Turkish have so few people left, I doubt they are attacking another country. General Garima is right. Let's stick to the central part of the country."

The group headed in the direction the men came from, then veered to the central part of the country. General Garima said, "They will probably be unconscious for an hour. They will think we're headed East so that should give us about two hours."

"Agreed." He watched Hazail. "Are you okay, honey?" Hazail looked at him, then down at the ground. She continued to walk but didn't answer Thomas Wayne's question. Thomas Wayne took her by the arm and stopped her. She continued to look down. "Honey, what's wrong?"

General Garima showed her frustration, "We need to keep moving."

Thomas Wayne was firm with Hazail, "Tell me what's wrong? Are you injured?"

"No, my love."

General Garima stepped between them. She pulled Hazail's chin up and looked into her eyes. "You should tell him so we can continue. We don't have time to waste. You are a warrior; you can handle it."

Thomas Wayne asked, "Honey?"

Hazail looked up. The water rolled down her face. Thomas Wayne wiped it away but more replaced it. "I am sorry my love, but I allowed myself to get pregnant."

Thomas Wayne couldn't believe his ears. He was happy but worried about bringing a child into the world under these circumstances. "You have no reason to be sorry!" He sighed, "Honey, how long have you known?"

"As a warrior, I should know better. I should have taken steps to ensure this didn't happen to me."

Thomas Wayne shook his head. "Warriors get pregnant, too. When did you find out?"

"I realized it early this morning while you were sleeping. I should not have climbed the tree or fought the soldiers."

"Are you okay? Is the baby, okay?"

"Oh, quit whining. She's a warrior," shouted General Garima. "We need to move."

"General Garima is correct. We need to keep going," Hazail added with a hint of a grin.

"We're not going anywhere until I know you're okay." He rolled his eyes at her, expecting an answer. "Well?"

"I am okay, my love."

Thomas Wayne took her hand, and they started the long journey. *I can't believe this. I'm going to be a father. This is unreal. If someone asked me a year ago what I expected my life to be like today, I would never have said this.* The group came to a point on the road where a man and his family were on the side of the road. The man was trying to fix his car while the children played, and the mother watched. Hazail took Thomas Wayne's arm and smiled. *She must be thinking the same thing I'm thinking. That could be us one day. This makes a man want to smile.* Thomas Wayne stopped the group and asked the man, "What's the problem?"

The man motioned to the engine. "No English?" He nodded 'no' and continued to work on the vehicle. Thomas Wayne touched the man's hand and motioned to let him try. The man understood and stepped back, allowing Thomas Wayne to look at the engine.

The mother brought the older child over to Thomas Wayne. The boy said, "My parents don't speak American, but I do."

"How did you learn?"

"In school. My Papa is saying the car is smoking, but he doesn't know why. Mama says he's useless when it comes to cars."

Thomas Wayne laughed. "Thanks. Tell him I will look at it and see if I can find out why." Thomas Wayne looked for the reason the car was smoking. He found motor oil leaking from a seal onto the engine. He turned to the boy, "Tell Papa that oil is leaking from a seal onto the engine." Thomas Wayne waited for the boy to translate, then he continued, "The seal is probably bad." He waited again. "We can use something to fix it temporarily until you get somewhere."

The man nodded. Thomas Wayne looked through their car and found something he could use to fill the seal. He looked at General Garima, "Good old duct tape. Works for everything." General Garima half smiled. Thomas Wayne shook his head, "You've got to loosen up a bit."

"I don't have time to loosen up a bit."

Thomas Wayne smiled, "This should hold for a while."

"Why are you wasting time helping them?"

Thomas Wayne laughed, then turned to the boy. "Tell your Papa, I've fixed it, but it won't hold." When the boy translated, he said, "Can we get a ride to the next town?"

The boy translated then said, "Papa says you can ride in the back with us, but only to the next town. He knows you're wanted, and they are looking for you."

"Tell him thank you." The boy went to his Papa and Thomas Wayne turned to General Garima, "That answer your question?"

She shrugged her shoulders. "There was a time I would have simply taken the vehicle; quicker and easier."

"That time has passed." Hazail was sitting on a stone along the road. Thomas Wayne made his way to her and caressed her chin. "We have a ride to the next town. That will have you off your feet for a while."

"I am fine, my love. I just want this to all be over."

"So do I. Come on, let's get in the vehicle." Everyone got inside the vehicle, and they made it to the next town without incident. As they got out, Thomas Wayne checked his work to see if it was still holding. He told the young boy that the seal was holding, but his Papa should have it repaired soon. The group grabbed some water, then headed on their journey. Before they got out of town, the man stopped them. He was with the boy to translate his message.

The boy said, "Papa said you can use that car to take you to the border. The owner of the car was killed during the war, and no one has claimed it."

"Really? Tell him I said thank you so much." Thomas Wayne shook hands with the man and the boy. The group got inside the vehicle and started it. Thomas Wayne looked at the dashboard. "Well, it has a little over half a tank of gas, but that's better than nothing."

General Garima asked, "How far is it to the border?"

"It's about 500 miles across Syria, but the route we took probably cut that down by 100. The ride we got was another 100 miles. So by my estimate, we have about 250 to 300 more miles to go. We should have just enough gas to get there." Thomas Wayne looked in the rearview mirror. Hazail was lying on the back seat. He worried more about her than about saving the world.

Thomas Wayne pulled off, praying nothing else would challenge them on their journey. "By the way, this is another reason for helping others rather than taking. People help you back."

"Your way worked—this time."

21 - Ramos' Return

Ramos arrived in the DC area. He stormed to the makeshift throne, where Cain and Serena relished the gifts given to them by the citizens. Ramos pushed through the people, his eyes red as fire, and climbed the steps to the throne, which was at the top of the Lincoln Memorial. Cain removed the statue of President Lincoln and placed his throne in its place. He made the people come to him and worship him and told them their prayers were answered. Serena sat on a smaller throne next to him, relishing her role as wife.

Ramos stood in front of the throne. He glanced at Serena then back at Cain, his eyes returned to normal, "Send these peasants away!"

Cain's face frowned. He stood to his feet. "How dare you talk to me this way!"

"You will want to hear my words, Cain, and not in front of them."

Cain ordered, "Leave me!" His voice echoed through the land. It felt like the air itself fractured, a raw, brutal *crack* that wasn't just heard, but felt as a physical blow. It was the sound of the world's spine snapping, a ground-shattering roar that made the soles of the people's feet vibrate, many falling to the ground screaming in fear and pain. Cain said, "Now, what do you want, Ramos, and why do you not have Thomas Wayne and the Assyrian women's heads with you?"

"Thomas Wayne figured out what the bracelets are. He destroyed mine."

Cain shot up from his seat, "What? Who gave him this information?"

"I don't know. I don't have my bracelet, so I had to get here the best way I could. I need a new one."

"You have failed your god."

Ramos snickered, "Don't throw that garbage at me. We both know we are not gods."

"Do you wish to feel my wrath, Ramos?"

Serena intervened, "My love, please don't strike down Ramos. He is only angry at Thomas Wayne. If Thomas Wayne knows the source of our power, we must work together to end the threat. You remember what happened the last time the people rose up against us?"

Ramos added, "I do not wish to fight you, Cain. I only want a new bracelet, so I can destroy Thomas Wayne and anyone else that has learned our secret."

"I will grant your wish, Ramos. Let's go to the ship." Cain and Serena grabbed Ramos' arms and flew toward the ship in Colorado.

22 - Crossing Into Iraq

The car ran out of gas two miles from the border. The group left the vehicle and walked the rest of the way. When they arrived, there were Iraqi guards everywhere. Thomas Wayne said, "Not sure if these guards are friends or foes."

General Garima replied, "We must assume they are the enemy."

"You're right again, General. Got a plan?"

"I do not, my friend."

"Hey, you called me friend." He smiled, and she smirked back at him. Their friendship increased and Thomas Wayne appreciated it. *For this mission to succeed, we will need to be friends. I'm glad she's seeing it that way.*

Two men approached the Iraqi guards. Their discussion appeared to be heated. Thomas Wayne whispered, "Hey, this might be our opportunity to sneak past them." General Garima nodded. Thomas Wayne looked back at Hazail. She smiled at him, but Thomas Wayne figured she was faking it. The argument continued to heat up. The Iraqi guards drew their weapons, but the men grabbed them, and the fight ensured. Thomas Wayne said, "Let's go."

The group stayed in the shadows and ran across the border. Once in the clear, Thomas Wayne stopped and asked, "Are you okay, honey?" He grabbed her arms.

"I am fine, my love. I am only pregnant."

General Garima said, "The further we get away, the better."

The group followed General Garima's advice and headed away from the border. Thomas Wayne realized she was correct. If any surprises or attacks would happen, it would be at points such as the border and major cities. *Even though she is correct about getting away from the border, my main concern is Hazail and my child she is carrying. I know my thoughts could cost us our lives, but I can't help but protect the woman I love. God, there must be a way to keep us all safe.*

After two miles of walking, General Garima stopped. A burnt-out town lay ahead. "We may find a place to sleep in that town. It doesn't look like anyone is there."

"I agree. Hopefully, we can find something to eat as well," replied Thomas Wayne with a tired grin.

"Agreed."

General Garima lead the way while Thomas Wayne walked with Hazail. "Have you thought about a name?"

"No, I just found out this morning. What do you think?"

"I only found out hours ago so that would be a no, baby. I would like for him, if it's him, to be named after me. Thomas Wayne Walker Jr. Sounds good to me."

"Then it sounds good to me too, my love."

"What about a girl?" asked Thomas Wayne.

"Alexandra. I was reading through your history before this mission. I read about Alexander the Great. He was known as a great military general who created a great empire. So, my daughter would be named the feminine version of a great general, Alexandra."

"I can go with that."

"He never lost a battle in 15 years of conquest. I was very impressed by him."

"So, I see." They chuckled. It was nice to spend a few moments laughing and talking about the baby. He only met Hazail two months ago, and their relationship went from suspicious of each other to love in a matter of hours. Now, they have a baby on the way. It was fast, but he enjoyed every second. "I can't wait to tell Aaliyah she's going to be an aunt."

"I have no siblings left to tell. Nor do I have any parents."

"Aaliyah is all I have. Our parents died in a car crash, and we were the only two children. We had aunts and uncles, but I haven't seen or heard from anyone since the war started; not that I heard from them before that. Don't worry, we will build our own family."

"My only worry is that you worry over me. Like the General said, I am a warrior; stronger than you may know. I will be fine."

"I'm your man and I will always worry. No matter what." He pecked her on the cheek. "I love you, Hazail."

"I love you, Thomas Wayne."

They arrived at the burnt-out town. General Garima was correct, there was no one there. The town appeared to have been deserted for some time. They stopped at a home that suffered less damage than the others and went inside. Hazail took a seat to rest while Thomas Wayne and General Garima searched the house. Thomas Wayne said, "It's clear on my end."

"Nothing over here either."

"Then you two rest. I will search the town for food and water."

General Garima said, "There is bread, and something called grape jelly on the counter in the kitchen."

Thomas Wayne laughed, "Jelly is a preserve made from sugar and grapes. It's spread on bread, and we eat it for lunch or a snack."

General Garima replied, "You waste grapes with this jelly? We use grapes to make wine."

"Don't knock it until you try it." Thomas Wayne smiled at her. "I'm going to search for some water; maybe something else other than jelly to eat as well." Thomas Wayne left the house and searched the town. Most of the buildings were completely destroyed. Nothing was left in them. He came across what looked like a market. There was some fruit, but it was spoiled. Behind one of the buildings were fig trees. *Bingo! This should at least put something in our bellies. If only we had water to go with it.* Thomas Wayne gathered some figs and carried them back. Along the route, he discovered a well. He made a mental note to return and see if it had water.

Back at the house, the ladies were sitting and resting. Thomas Wayne gave them some figs. "They are good to eat. Iraqi and the Middle East are known for their fig trees."

"This we know," said General Garima. "You know my ancestors lived here."

"Good, I saw a well about 100 yards from here. I'm going to check it out. Hopefully, we can get some fresh water as well." General Garima nodded. Hazail was drifting off to sleep. Thomas Wayne was thankful she was getting some rest. He headed back to the well when he heard troops coming through the town. Thomas Wayne rushed back to the house, but General Garima already noticed the men. They took cover and watched, hoping the men would move on.

Thomas Wayne counted seven. The two of them couldn't take on all the soldiers, so they could only hope they would not stay. After 30 minutes, the soldiers gathered their things and continued in the direction Thomas Wayne's group would travel. "They must be looking for us."

General Garima replied, "You think?"

Thomas Wayne laughed inside, but he was really enjoying General Garima now. She was fast becoming Americanized in her language. "Yeah, you stay on Earth a while longer and you will talk exactly like us." General Garima continued to follow the men with her eyes. "Always the warrior, though."

"I heard you, but I am cautious. Taking chances can cost you your life." Thomas Wayne did not respond. "They are gone now."

The group came out of hiding. "I can go to the well now. We need that water."

"I would wait at least an hour. You can't be too safe," replied General Garima.

"Okay." Thomas Wayne sat down on the couch with Hazail. She laid her head on his shoulder.

"Tell me where this well is and I will go retrieve the water."

"No, I can do it."

"Your place is with Hazail. She needs your comfort."

"It's dark out there." She rolled her eyes at him. "I know you're a warrior and all, but like you said, there's no sense in taking risks. I will go. Just give me a few minutes."

General Garima sat down. "You know, I have been thinking about this journey."

"And…"

"We have overcome some obstacles that frankly, I don't understand why we did. We should be dead now, but we are not."

"Why do you think that is?"

"Someone is looking out for us." Thomas Wayne didn't know where she was going with this but wanted to hear more. "Your God—I have heard He is real. I have heard that He speaks to you in different ways, such as your dreams. Is it possible that He is clearing a path for us?"

"More than possible, it's likely He is. God is not someone you see. I mean, Jesus came to Earth and lived amongst us but that was only to die for our sins." General Garima twisted her face. "It's long and complicated, but hopefully one day I can tell you what I know about Him."

"I have read your Bible."

"Seriously?"

"We study everything about a world before we conquer it. I've read the Bible, the Holy Qur'an, the Torah, just to name a few. I probably know more about Jesus than you do."

"I wouldn't doubt that. I went to church when I was a kid because I was forced to go. I haven't been much since I became an adult. After all of this, I'm going back to church, and I will never stop." Thomas Wayne slapped his knees and popped up. "I guess it's time to find the well."

General Garima pushed for him to change his mind, "I need to be the one to go. Your place is with Hazail."

"Please stay with me, my love," added Hazail.

"Is there something you two aren't telling me?"

"There is nothing. You need to be with Hazail. I don't have anyone. It makes sense for me to go. Stay here with your wife."

"We haven't had that ceremony yet."

General Garima froze. She turned around, "What does a ceremony need to do with love? If you love Hazail and forsake all others, then you are her husband. Traditions, formalities, ceremonies are all meaningless without the love. If you have the love, you are her husband."

"That's—you know you're right. She is my wife. Thank you for pointing that out." General Garima nodded and walked out the door. Thomas Wayne retook his seat. He didn't know what to say to Hazail. General Garima put it in a way no one else put it to him before. *She's right. Man created ceremonies, traditions, and formalized marriage. In the eyes of God, we are married. My grandmother used to say no man needs to intercede for us to go to Jesus in prayer, so why do we have to stand in a church and say our vows to prove we are one? We don't. This is my wife, and I will love her always.* He smiled at Hazail as her eyes slowly closed. He loved watching her sleep.

23 - Dissension in the Ranks

Vayu landed in Madrid, Spain. She waited along the street for Adonis to arrive. The people bowed to her as they passed by. She relished the worship and love they exhibited to her. She took in a deep breath, enjoying the aroma of worship and love for her. One man fell to his knees and prayed at her feet, "Please god, save my young son. He has leukemia, and the doctors don't know what to do. Please heal him."

"Your son has been healed according to your faith." The man thanked her and ran off. *Pitiful human. If I had the power to heal your son, I would not.* Adonis landed 10 feet from Vayu. "You had me waiting here for you. These pitiful humans got on my nerves. One even asked me to heal his child."

"Forgive my lateness. I had to punish some humans who got out of hand."

Vayu frowned, "What is it you want?"

"Are you tired of ruling these humans only to be ruled by Cain and Serena? I am. It is time we stand up to them."

"You know that is impossible. Cain's device is stronger than anyone else's. Zeus gave it to him when he ceased to exist."

"I've been thinking about that myself. No one ever challenged Zeus. Instead, we all believe he was the mightiest of all of us, but what power does Cain have? Strength, that's it. You… you control the air and wind. I control the night. He is nothing but muscles. Together, we can eliminate him. You could remove the air around him, and he would die."

Vayu popped her lips, "Why would I help you do this?"

"One of us can rule this world and the other can rule Assyria."

"Cain made a deal with them."

Adonis smiled, "You're right. Cain made the deal. We don't have to honor it once Cain is dead."

"What of Serena?"

"As beautiful as she is, she must die with her lover."

"I see. And what about the others? Ramos is loyal to Cain and Hephaestus would not allow you to kill his sister. He will stop you."

"Ramos lost his powers. Because of him, the humans now know about our bracelets. Hephaestus will not be an issue."

The statement shocked Vayu, "What? When did this happen?"

Adonis replied, "A few days ago. However, they don't know the true source of our power. It is believed they are on a journey somewhere in the Middle East to find the ancient text to discover the truth. We should kill Cain and Serena before the humans discover the truth."

"No, Adonis. We should wait until they discover the truth. In the battle to stop them, we can kill Cain and Serena. The humans will be dead, and so will Cain and Serena."

"I like your thinking." Adonis took her hand. Vayu had not felt the touch of a man in centuries. It felt good. "There's a place in this country I love to relax. Let us go there and relax together."

"Lead the way."

24 - The Journey Continues

Thomas Wayne jumped at hearing the crash from the kitchen area. He ran to check it out.

"I dropped the pail of water. I apologized for disturbing you and Hazail."

"No worries. Glad I didn't have to fight again."

General Garima stretched her back. "How is my lieutenant?"

"She's fine. Still sleeping, which is unusual for her. She usually wakes at the smallest sound."

"She's probably exhausted." General Garima placed her hands on the counter and sighed. "I am getting too old for this. Being a warrior is a young person's game." She shook her head. "Anyway, there's plenty of water in the well. I got as much as I could carry."

"We will manage. Maybe we should stay here another day. You both are tired, and I could use a little sleep myself."

"For once, I will not argue with you. A little rest for all of us will be good. Maybe your God will bless us with peace and another vehicle."

"The faith of a mustard seed." Thomas Wayne snickered and returned to the couch with Hazail. She was still sleeping. Thomas Wayne wanted to caress her face, but he didn't want to wake her. Instead, he fantasized about their life in a beautiful home with their children playing in the backyard. *One day… one day, I will get to see that dream come to reality.*

The morning sun rose over them. It struck Thomas Wayne in eyes, causing him to wake up. He looked at Hazail. Her eyes were open as well. General Garima was nowhere to be seen. Thomas Wayne got up. "Where's General Garima?"

"I don't know, my love." Hazail got up and stretched. "I feel much better today."

"Good. Let's see if we can find General Garima." The couple walked outside. The town was still vacant. "Where could she be?" They heard footsteps approaching from behind them. Thomas Wayne led Hazail to a hiding spot inside the house.

"You can come out now," said General Garima. "I easily tracked you a while ago."

"Where have you been and what is that?"

"It is what you call protein. We have not eaten in days. I went out and tracked this animal down, made a fire in a spot where the smoke would blow away from this town. We must eat."

Hazail said, "It is a kirvish."

"It looks like a rabbit," Thomas Wayne replied. "What exactly is a kirvish?"

Hazail took a bite and visibly enjoyed it. "Yes, your word is rabbit, I believe. Some translations are not easy for me."

"Ah, my grandmother used to cook rabbit. I never ate it."

General Garima said, "You need to eat it now. It is the only protein that I could find. You may need your strength. Either that or you can continue to have the faith of a mustard seed."

"Are you mocking my God?"

"I am not. If He has protected us this far, I would not mock Him. However, my beliefs cannot be changed overnight. Now eat."

Thomas Wayne forced himself to take a bite while the ladies laughed at him. He shook his head in disbelief that he was entertaining them, but in his mind, some creatures were not made to be eaten. "Wow, this is actually pretty good. I missed all the meals my grandmother made with rabbit. Dang, they must have been good, too."

After eating, the group headed toward Iran. General Garima said, "The soldiers should be confused by now and have no clue where we are. Hopefully, we will be free of any more turmoil."

Thomas Wayne stopped, "You spoke too soon." Soldiers stood poised to kill them. "They were likely waiting for us all night."

"You're probably right. There's too many of them for us to take out."

One man walked to the front of them, "I am General Masih of the Iraqi Republican Guard. You are my prisoners. Our god will handsomely reward me."

General Garima replied, "You are a fool if you believe they are gods."

General Masih slapped her with the back of his hand, knocking her to the ground. "Your blasphemy will lead to your death if you say it again!" Thomas Wayne helped General Garima to her feet. "Tie them up and take them to our headquarters. We will await Adonis' arrival."

The soldiers tied each of their hands behind their back and walked them to their headquarters. Once on the compound, they were placed in a locked room to wait. They made small talk, hoping to pass the time until their fate was decided. General Garima said, "So much for your God."

Thomas Wayne didn't have a reply for her. He wasn't an astute believer in Christ, so having a comeback wasn't something he specialized in. His eyes focused on Hazail. He would give his life for her, and this was one of those times that he may need to do that.

Two hours passed before General Masih walked into the room. He huffed, "You are very blessed people." He turned to the guards, "Free them, give them food, water and a vehicle to get to Iran."

Thomas Wayne looked at General Garima and Hazail. They were just as confused as he was. He asked, "To what do we owe this honor?"

"It seems you have favor with Adonis. He has given you a free pass to Iran."

The group didn't want to waste time asking questions. They grabbed the food, water and jumped in the vehicle. Thomas Wayne drove off. He looked at General Garima, "That work for you? I mean, I can honestly say I didn't expect God to come through like that, but hey… I'll take it."

"That was not your God. We need to keep our eyes open. There may be a trap waiting."

"Why? They had us in custody, tied up and at their beck and call. There's no reason to free us just to catch us again and kill us."

General Garima sighed, "You are probably right."

Hazail added, "Either way, we should take advantage of this and get to Iran as fast as possible.

We can be sure Adonis has a reason to release us, and it's not in our favor. That we can be sure of."

Thomas Wayne replied, "That's for sure. We need to keep our eyes open for that."

"He wants us to lead him to the ancient text," said General Garima. "That is the most likely reason he let us go."

Thomas Wayne laughed, "I know this is rhetorical but, isn't he all seeing, all knowing?" They each chuckled as they rode to Iran.

After a hundred miles, the group stopped to rest and eat. Hazail went into the brush to relief herself. "So, if we find the text, what do you think the heroes will do?"

"You call them heroes; I call them gods. We need to agree on a term."

"I will never call them gods."

General Garima nodded her head, "Then I will call them heroes, too. They have never been my god." She smiled. Thomas Wayne recognized she was trying to be more personable, but other times, that military general came out in her. "I think we will have to play it by ear. Not knowing—what's wrong?"

"Let her go!" Thomas Wayne pulled his weapon out, "Let her go now or I'll blow your head off!"

"I have the hostage; you drop your weapon, or I'll kill her."

"I'm sorry Thomas Wayne," cried Hazail.

"It's not your fault, sweetheart."

The man laughed, "Sweetheart. How nice. You're in love with an Assyrian warrior. You must be Thomas Wayne. People are saying a lot about you."

Thomas Wayne wanted to smack that giggle off his face. "What might that be?"

The man let Hazail go and put his weapon away, "Some say you're a traitor while others are hailing you as the real hero. Either way, I'm looking for what you're looking for, so maybe we can team up." Thomas Wayne studied the man to get an idea if he was telling the truth or not. "My name is Paul Waiters. I'm from Dallas, Texas and I'm searching for the ancient text too. I mean, who isn't? Word gets around quick that this book is filled with information on the location of gold and silver. That's why you want it, right? We can split the loot."

Hazail joined him in his arms, "The book is the key to saving this world. We're not looking for it to discover any loot."

"Whatever you say, my friend. I just want my share if I help you find it."

Thomas Wayne asked, "How did you come to know about this book… and don't give me that rumor crap?"

Paul answered, "When these heroes showed up and 'saved' us from the Assyrians, I suspected more. I did some research and talked to some of the American Assyrians. I gather you did too. So, I'm looking for that text to figure out how to beat these SOBs too, but my main goal is to get the loot that is hidden away." Thomas Wayne continued to study him. Paul continued, "I know you don't believe me, but trust me. Like I said, my reasons are not the same as yours; I'm in it for the money. If you figure out how to get rid of these jokers from our planet, I imagine the world will owe us a debt. Preferably an eight or nine figure debt. Add that to the treasure that the book talks about and we're into a large haul, if you know what I mean."

Thomas Wayne shook his head in disbelief, "You're in it for the money."

Paul reared back and patted his chest. "Absolutely. I make my intentions known up front, so we have an understanding. Our goal is somewhat the same, rid the planet of the false gods. It's just I'm looking for a payday at the backend and I gather you're not."

"No, I'm not. After this is over, I just want to live happily with my wife."

"Whatever suits your fancy. Let's go find this text."

General Garima asked, "Where is it?" Paul looked at her. "You said you did your research, so where is it located?"

He grinned and pointed at her, "She's good. No wonder you're a general. Mount Dena, I believe it's called. The Zagros Mountain range of Iran. There's a lady that lives somewhere in those mountains. Find her and we'll find the ancient text."

Thomas Wayne replied, "We'll talk for a minute. You don't move."

"I won't move an inch, partner."

Thomas Wayne and the ladies moved away to discuss Paul. "What do you think, General?"

"He's a lying, conniving, jerk of a man. Not a good example of a human being. However, he knows a lot, so he may be telling the truth."

"I say we let him come but keep an eye on him. I got a feeling he's up to something."

General Garima nodded, "Agreed."

The group returned to Paul. "You're in, but if we see one thing out of the ordinary, you'll be out. You won't like the way General Garima kicks you out."

"You got it, buddy."

Thomas Wayne said, "Let's load up and head out. The Iranian border isn't too much farther." The group headed out. Thomas Wayne asked Hazail to sit up front with him. He hated Paul for having his hands all over her. That was only reserved for him. If he needed to kill Paul, he might enjoy it, but he felt he would have to beat General Garima to the punch.

25 - Gods Recruiting Gods

Adonis and Vayu landed on Okinawa Island. Tutu made his palace there because the water on three sides made him feel protected from attacks by any of the gods. "Welcome, my friends. I see you have found my palace."

Adonis said, "We have, and it is a wonderous feet of construction in such a short amount of time."

"The Asians are masters at building things. Vayu, how are you today?"

"I am fine, Tutu. It is good to see you again."

Tutu nodded, "May I interest you both in the pleasures of the Asian life? These two beautiful women are but a taste of what this culture offers. Vayu, there are some men for you as well."

Adonis answered, "We are mates."

"Really? When did that happen?"

"Recently."

"Congratulations. I for one, will continue to enjoy these beauties." Tutu kissed both women and smiled. "What may I do for you today?"

Adonis answered, "We know you dislike Cain. You know I do not care for him as well. We arrived on this planet, and he commands us to do his bidding again. We do not want the same thing to happen in this world that happened in the last one."

Tutu pondered his statement. "You're saying he needs to be replaced? He will not go quietly."

Vayu added, "We're saying he needs to be killed."

Tutu's eyebrow rose. "That is a mighty task. He is the strongest of us all."

Adonis laughed, "That has never been tested, my friend. Zeus said the same thing, and he passed it on to Cain when he left us. But in a thousand centuries, no one has tested that statement."

Tutu asked, "You do not believe it to be true?"

"I do not."

No one responded. Tutu continued, "When you challenge Cain, Serena will be by his side. That also means her brother will stand with them, too."

"That is why I am here. Join us my friend, then we will have a fighting chance. Right now, you rule Asia. If we are victorious, your territory will expand even more. We will also go to Assyria and conquer that world. Their worthless king will beg us not to destroy them."

"Cain made a deal with them."

"A deal we will not honor. Are you in, my friend?"

Tutu gave it more thought. "What about Ramos?"

"We will visit him next. He is currently on the ship. The Terrans figured out our power source."

"I heard that. Ramos should have been killed."

Vayu said, "If Cain would have killed him, the Terrans would have believed they killed a god. We could not allow them to become arrogant again."

Tutu acknowledged her comment, "You are correct. I am in, but what if Ramos refuses? He will tell Cain of your plan."

Adonis stood tall, "If Ramos refuses, he will die."

Recruiting Ramos

Adonis arrived in the South American country of Brazil. Ramos made his palace near the Xingu River. Adonis moved back the worshippers who were outside the palace that once was the home of a major drug dealer. The gates flew open when Adonis got nearby. The guards recognized him; he needed no introduction. Ramos met him in the yard in front of the house. Adonis stopped ten feet away from him. "We need to talk, my friend."

Ramos studied him, then replied, "Why do we need to talk?"

"Somewhere private, without humans around." Adonis' face was stone cold. He expected no resistance to his request. He was the second in charge of the gods, and no one should question him.

"Adonis, we can go into my home. I will dismiss everyone inside." They headed inside and Ramos commanded, "Everyone out, now!" Everyone ran out of the home. "Now what is it you want, Adonis? I do not have time for games. If this is about the bracelet, I have a new one, so don't threaten me."

"I am not here to threaten you, my friend. I am here to offer you a deal. One that is beneficial for both of us."

"What offer might that be?"

"As you know, the Terrans know about the bracelets. Soon they will discover the ancient text and learn our secrets. When that happens, we can take them out along with Cain, Serena, and Hephaestus. That will leave this world for us."

"That is a mighty undertaking. Cain is the strongest of us all."

"Each time we say that, I cringe, knowing everyone is afraid to challenge him because of it. We keep the Terrans in line because we show them our power and they live in fear of us. If they knew our secret, do you really think they would fear us?"

"They would not, but I don't believe the two of us can take Cain, Serena, and Hephaestus."

Adonis raved, "With you, there would be four of us."

"You have gained the support of Vayu and Tutu?"

"I have. All I need now is to know that you're on my side." Ramos pondered the offer, but Adonis was sure he would not take it. He planned to kill him without him suspecting it.

"Adonis, reconsider what you are saying. We have survived all these years because we have been united. We cannot fight each other now."

"We have been fools, Ramos. Zeus did not cease to exist like the others. He did not give his power to Cain. Cain took it. He killed Zeus."

"That is a lie, Adonis—a lie to get me to be on your side."

"I only have my word, my friend, but I know Cain killed your father. Why else would your father not give you, his power? You were his only living son."

Ramos' lips popped, "I never understood why, but still, I cannot sign off on this. We will not fight each other. We have a second chance to rule this planet as we did centuries ago. I will not allow your ego to ruin it."

"Then you leave me no choice." Adonis pounced on Ramos before he could make a move. The look of shock and fear in Ramos' eyes was something Adonis would remember forever. He squeezed tighter and tighter with his massive arms around Ramos' neck. He squeezed until Ramos' eyes popped. Red lines stretched their way from Ramos' pupils, leaving no doubt. He was gone.

Adonis released his hold on Ramos, and his limp body fell to the ground. Adonis closed his eyes. "I am sorry, my dear friend, but I can't allow you to ruin this for me and the others." Ramos' body changed from its human form to his true existence. Adonis picked Ramos' fallen body up and walked outside through the rear sliding glass window. He bent down then shot up into the sky carrying Ramos' body back to Greece, where he made his home with Vayu.

Adonis arrived and laid Ramos' fallen body in a room where no could enter. He removed Ramos' bracelet and placed it in a drawer. Vayu walked into the room. "He did not join us?"

"No. I will command that no one enters this room. If Cain or the others ask where he is, we do not know."

"I understand, my love. I am prepared to take what is ours."

26 - Zagros Mountain Range

The group stood at the basin of the Zagros Mountain range. Thomas Wayne took in the enormity of the site, wondering how they would find this needle in the haystack. "They said the woman lives on Mount Dena, but still, that's a large mountain to climb and try to find one woman living there."

General Garima snickered, "Time for your God to help us out."

"Oh, one of these days He will become your God, too."

"God talk," asked Paul? "I thought you guys didn't believe in that stuff."

Thomas Wayne replied, "We don't believe these guys are anymore of a god than you or I. There is, however, one true God and his name is Jehovah."

"Oh, you're one of them. My bad."

Thomas Wayne shook his head in disbelief. "Everyone is entitled to their beliefs."

Hazail said, "It doesn't matter who believes what. We need a way to go. We can't search this entire area by ourselves."

Thomas Wayne added, "Hazail is correct. We need a clue. Maybe there are Assyrians living in the area that may help."

General Garima stared hard at the mountains. "I remember seeing some text from the church. I think

Father Ben knew where the woman lives, but maybe he didn't trust us enough to tell us."

"What did you see?"

"I thought it was strange, but it said, 'from the north, between Yasuj and Semirom you will see me'."

"What does that have to do with anything," asked Paul? "Did I hook up with the wrong people or something?"

Thomas Wayne rolled his eyes, "Why does that come back to your remembrance?" She guided his eyes to the sign that pointed toward Yasuj and another that pointed toward Semirom. "We are standing between Yasuj and Semirom. Maybe we should go straight to the mountain peak in front of us."

Hazail started to walk. Thomas Wayne shouted, "Hey where are you going?"

"There's no better place to start!"

27 - Cain's Anger Rises

Cain stood in the Oval Office of the burnt-out White House. He slung anything he could get his hands on. Serena watched as he vented his anger. She understood Cain more than anyone else. When Cain stopped, she stepped in to calm him. "Cain, my love, I know you are angry, but please do not let Adonis get to you so much."

"Are you saying that because you love him?"

She snickered, "You know I do not. I love only you." She pecked him on the cheek, then slowly moved to his lips. "Adonis is on his way here. I'm sure he has an explanation."

"I know Adonis is trying to make a play to be the leader. I will kill him. Do you understand that, Serena?"

"I do, and if it comes to that, then so be it."

He studied her face, but she could easily convince him of anything. However, her love for him was something she didn't have to fake. She truly loved him and only toyed with Adonis. She would stand by Cain forever, but sometimes he questioned that love. It was then she had to reinforce it to him. "Why do you believe Adonis is trying to kill you?"

"I have a feeling. He's been traveling to visit the others. He hasn't visited your brother or you—or has he visited you?"

"You know he hasn't, my love."

"I don't know anything anymore, Serena, except whenever you're around him, you seem to forget you are my love."

"That is not true, Cain." She was stern with her voice. When she called him by his name, she meant for seriousness to come forth. Her face formed that familiar frown, letting him know she hated it when he questioned her love for him. He knew she loved him with everything she had, but he always found reason to question her love. Serena spoke in a soft, melodic tone, "I do not have any feelings for Adonis or anyone except you. That has been forever, and it will always be forever."

Cain rolled his eyes at her, the doubt clear on his face. "Why is he not here yet? Does he think he can make me wait for him?"

"Give it some time, my love." The ground shook as only it did when one of them landed nearby. "That is likely him now."

A few moments later, Adonis entered the room. "You asked to see me?"

"I commanded you to come see me." Adonis' face turned with anger. The room was tensed.

"Commanded? Why do you continue to live in this place? You made the capital Philadelphia, but you stay here. Why?"

"This place has grown on me." Cain folded his massive arms and gave a cold stare at his nemesis, "Why did you order the Iranians to let Thomas Wayne and the others go?"

"Because I see the bigger picture. You don't?"

"Enlighten me?"

Adonis rolled his eyes, "If we kill Thomas Wayne then, we would not learn the location of the ancient text. Those books contain information that the Terrans can use to kill us. Let them find the text, then kill them and burn the text."

Cain's head shifted back, enlighten by the strategic move put in place by Adonis. Serena watched carefully. Cain replied, "Why have you been visiting the others?"

"As your number one, is it not my responsibility to ensure they are keeping their people in line? I, as you, have felt a drop in worshippers. I visited each one to ensure they are doing what they need to keep the people in line."

"You seem to have an answer for everything," replied Cain.

"Because I have nothing to hide. Is there anything else?"

"There is one thing."

Serena interrupted, "Cain?"

He held his hand up to quiet her, "Where is Ramos?"

"I don't know. Am I his keeper?"

"You were the last one to see him. No one has seen him in a day now."

"He's probably with one of his concubines. Give him time. He will return."

"If you have done something to Ramos, you will feel my wrath."

Adonis grinned, "Your threats don't bother me. I am the one who doesn't believe in your power."

"Is that so?"

Serena said, "Stop it. We are gods over this world. We do not need to fight with each other. If the people saw us bickering like them, what would they

think of us? The two of you need to end this feud."
Serena looked back and forth at each of them.

Cain said, "If I find out you have been with
Serena, I will strike you down."

"Like you did Zeus?"

Cain's head snapped around. The two men rolled
their eyes at each other. They each took a step toward
one another. Serena stepped between them. She said,
"Adonis, you have angered my husband. It is time for
you to leave."

Adonis looked at her, then at Cain. "I will leave,
but only at the bequest of Serena. For the record,
Vayu is my mate." He turned and walked out of the
office.

Cain said, "If you step between me and someone
else again, I will kill you both."

Serena's Thoughts

Serena nodded her understanding and returned
to the window. She stared out at the vast waste of
what used to be Washington, DC. *My longing for this
world and this life is coming to an end. The desire to play god to
people who only allow us to play god out of fear has drained
away. Finally, my love for a man who doesn't trust me hurts
intensely. Maybe it is time for me to cease to exist.*

28 - Mount Dena

The group drove as far as they could up Mount Dena before they had to stop. The vehicle couldn't go any further. They got out of the vehicle to rest and assess the situation. At the base of Mount Dena was climbing equipment. Thomas Wayne was amazed at every break they got in trying to find the text. "This is convenient. Climbing equipment left behind just for us."

Hazail replied, "It wasn't for us." She pointed with her eyes. "These unfortunate souls probably planned to go climbing when the war started."

Thomas Wayne looked at the bodies. It was a man and a woman. "Judging by the decay, it looks like they had been dead for a while. Well, there's nothing we can do for them now."

Paul said, "There's only two sets of equipment, so who's going up?"

"Thomas Wayne and I," answered General Garima. "Certainly not you."

Paul laughed. "Still don't trust me. I made my intentions known from the beginning, but you still don't trust me."

"I do not."

Thomas Wayne added, "He certainly isn't staying here alone with Hazail."

"I will be fine, my love. Remember, I am still a warrior."

General Garima asked, "Who do you recommend, Thomas Wayne? I do not think he should go up there."

"I agree. I guess I have no choice but to leave you with him, Hazail."

General Garima huddled Thomas Wayne, Hazail and herself together away from Paul. "Hazail can take care of herself. She is one of my best warriors. Trust her."

"I trust her. I don't trust him."

General Garima emphasized, "That… is why he can't go up."

Thomas Wayne announced, "General Garima and I will head up the mountain. Hazail and Paul will stay behind." He looked at Paul, "If you harm her in any way, there's no place on Earth you will be able to hide."

"Aaru. You mean Aaru. They renamed the planet, bro. If you don't follow the laws, you will be struck down." Paul burst out in laughter, then walked away.

"Whatever." Thomas Wayne and General Garima gathered the climbing gear. "Sweetheart, whatever happens to me up there, remember, I love you more than you can ever know."

"I love you too, Thomas Wayne. You will be fine."

"Thank you, sweetheart." Hazail and General Garima gave that knowing nod of best wishes to each other. "General, I hope you know how to use this stuff."

"Your military didn't teach you how to climb?"

"Nope."

"Then you need a new military. It is required by all warriors. Follow my lead, Thomas Wayne."

Thomas Wayne kissed Hazail. He followed General Garima up the mountain, expecting an interesting journey. He couldn't tell how many miles they had to travel before they needed to climb, but he hoped he wouldn't need to do much climbing.

Thomas Wayne couldn't get his mind off Hazail. The walk up the mountain was killing his legs, but he dared not say anything to the General. She appeared to be handling it with ease. *How can she be in such good shape? Dang, I'm about to die here.*

General Garima said, "Do you need a rest?"

"Oh me, no, I'm good." *I'm dying for real, General.*

"You don't look good. Let's rest a minute."

"If you need to rest, go ahead." She shifted her eyes to him. "Looks like this is a trail used by tourists. How much farther do you think we will have to go before we need to climb?"

"I don't know. We have no idea where this woman is. All we can do is keep going straight and hope to get a sign." She paused, staring at the road ahead. Thomas Wayne continued to think about Hazail. "Why is it Terran men have to feel superior to women?"

"I guess men are typically bigger and stronger, so we feel like we should outdo women in everything. It's a mental complex."

"It's stupid."

"I can't argue with you."

"If you are tired, then you should not feel less of a man to admit it. You are not in the same shape as I am. I have trained all my life. You, I'm guessing, have not."

"You got that right." Thomas Wayne realized she was right. "Most men feel physically superior to women, but that's a myth. There are women who can outdo men in almost everything." General Garima nodded. "Let's hit the road. The longer we leave Hazail with Paul, the worse I feel about it." They started their journey again. The mountain climb lay ahead, and Thomas Wayne wasn't looking forward to it.

Into the twilight hours, they reached Kohgol Lake. Thomas Wayne placed his empty water bottle in the lake and got water. He drank it. General Garima did the same. On the ground was a half-burned sign. Thomas Wayne picked it up. He was curious about the symbol on the sign but didn't know what it meant. He looked at General Garima, but she was looking at the nearby mountains. Thomas Wayne asked, "What are you thinking about?"

"We are being followed."

"How do you know these things?"

"I have been in training all my life. They are smart. They laid back long enough for me not to pick them up, but now that we are in the open, it's difficult for them to stay back."

"What do you want to do?"

"Continue like we don't know they are following us. When we get a chance, we will catch them."

"Can you tell how many it is?"

"At least two."

"Okay, I'll follow your lead." They continued their journey up the mountain. "I wish we had a radio to contact Hazail. I'm worried about her."

"She's a warrior."

"I knew you would say that, but what I mean is, I just miss her."

"I understand. When this is all over, I'm sure you and Hazail will have a great life."

He smiled. "Thank you, General."

"My name is Brula. It means pearl. I am no longer a general."

"Brula. I can't believe you shared that bit of information with me. We are truly friends now."

"We are. When we get around that mountain, we can hide and wait for them."

"You still sense them?"

"I do." They got around the edge of the mountain. "Now!" They took up a hiding place and waited for the individuals to come around the edge of the mountain.

A man and a woman turned the corner in a hurry to see which direction Thomas Wayne and General Garima went. Thomas Wayne jumped out and stopped them. He held his hand toward them, hoping there would be no trouble. However, they pointed a gun at him. It was an old .38. Thomas Wayne believed they did have any experience with weapons. "We're not here for any trouble."

The man said, "Where's the woman that was with you?"

"Why don't you put your weapon down so we can talk?"

"Where is she?"

"I'm behind you. Drop your weapon like Thomas Wayne said."

The man did as ask. "So, you are Thomas Wayne." He turned around. "You must be General Garima."

Thomas Wayne answered, "We are. Who are you?"

"This is Diyana, and I am Naram. We are friends of Carmichael. He sent us to follow you."

General Garima asked, "Why would he have you follow us? He's not Assyrian."

Naram answered, "But he is. He keeps his roots a secret in order to get information for us. He doesn't trust you. Does anyone trust these days?"

General Garima replied, "I guess not." She huffed. "We are not here to steal anything. Our only desire is to free this world from the false gods. That's it."

"I believe you," said Naram. "We can lead you to Shamura. She is the person you will need to talk to."

Thomas Wayne said, "Great. Thank you." The team headed through the mountains on the way to the woman who could give them the information they needed.

Waiting Patiently

Hazail waited inside the vehicle. To stay hydrated she drank water. She kept a warrior's eye on Paul. She didn't trust him. There was something about him that told her he was shady. She looked down at her stomach and smiled. The thought of carrying a child never came to her. She didn't think she would ever be married and if she did, her arranged marriage would not occur for years. Now she carried Thomas Wayne's baby and looked forward to the ceremony to make them officially married.

"Hey!" Hazail pulled out her blade and held it at Paul. "What are you doing? I'm a friend, remember?"

"You better be careful. In another life, I would have killed you."

"I just want to talk. Boredom is driving me mad."

"I don't want to talk to you. Leave me."

"You Assyrian woman are bossy." He walked off, continuing to curse at Hazail.

I hate him. There is nothing good about him. I just don't know what his angle is right now. She wanted to close her eyes and get some sleep, but she couldn't trust Paul. If he attempted anything, she would kill him. *I know my love is against killing, but if he touches me, I will kill him.* She held her eyes open for as long as she could before she drifted off to sleep.

The sound of voices woke her. It was dark outside, but she saw Paul talking to two soldiers. He appeared to be friends with them. That struck her as odd, since they have avoided soldiers at all costs. The men walked away, and Paul noticed she was watching. He walked over to her, and she placed her hand on her blade.

"Hey that was close. They need to hurry because the soldiers are getting suspicious."

"They looked like friends of yours."

"Honey, they are not friends of mine." He laughed. "I have a way of making people be at ease. That's all it was."

She didn't believe a word he said. "Okay." She moved out of the vehicle and walked across the street.

Paul shouted, "Where are you going?"

She didn't respond. She needed to relieve herself and didn't want him near her. When she was finished, she made her way back. Paul stood on the corner by a building. *Is he on a radio?* She crept closer to see if Paul was talking to someone. She got to the corner, and he was not on a radio. *He looks guilty of something.* "What are you up to, Paul?"

"You guys think I am up to something, but I'm not. I only want the money from taking these gods out. That's all."

"Do you have a radio?"

"A radio?" He half heartily laughed. "Look lady, I don't have a radio." He walked away, visibly upset.

I know he's up to something. When my love returns, we will find out what it is and make him pay.

Shamura

Thomas Wayne and General Garima followed the guide to a cabin tucked away in a secluded area of Mount Dena. The cabin was well kept up and the grass around it was a beautiful green. Naram knocked on the door and a petite old woman answered the door.

"Naram, Diyana, it is nice to see your both again."

Diyana replied, "Thank you, Shamura. It is good to see you as well." Naram hugged her. "This is Thomas Wayne and General Garima. They were sent by Father Ben to retrieve the ancient text."

Shamura's face shifted. Thomas Wayne said, "I know this is something you're not happy with, but we need those texts to get rid of the false gods."

"I understand your purpose, but there are men out there who want these texts for selfish reasons. Not to mention our brothers and sisters who left us centuries ago." She cut her eyes at General Garima.

"They would love to get their hands on it to conquer other worlds."

Thomas Wayne looked at General Garima. "Are you referring to my friend, General Garima?"

"If she is your friend, then you are my enemy."

Thomas Wayne was exasperated. "Shamura, this woman has saved my life on several occasions. She has fought the false gods with me. There is no one I would trust in battle right now than her. Well, except Hazail. She is not your enemy any longer. She was my enemy, but we both have a common enemy; therefore, we are friends."

General Garima added, "I am not your enemy. My family once lived here centuries ago. We came back under false pretenses to conquer this world. I now know the truth. That truth will be dealt with when this is over."

"I don't know if I can believe you. Especially when it comes to the ancient texts." She motioned for them to sit. "You see, the texts have come to light to the world now, but for years, there have been people searching for them. The Assyrians have kept them hidden since the days the gods rule the Earth. We kept them hidden because they not only tell about the gods and their secrets but they tell about hidden treasures around the world. The United States was not discovered by Columbus or the Vikings. It was discovered long ago by these gods, and they hid their gold there. You say you want to destroy the gods, but the Assyrians want what is contained in these texts to improve their ships to conquer more worlds." She cut her eyes at General Garima again.

Thomas Wayne sat in front of her. "Ma'am, I only want to end the terror around the world. The heroes or gods, whatever, are here because the king of Assyria made a deal with them. To avoid the destruction of their world, he told them they would attack ours. Once we were on the brink of destruction, the heroes would come in and save us, thus enduring people to love and worship them. You see, most of the Assyrians, like General Garima, were deceived. We need the text to find out what we need to do to destroy them and end the terror."

"I believe you, Thomas Wayne. It seems Carmichael believes you, too. He wants me to give you the texts with the promise that you will turn them over to him once you have used them to destroy our enemy."

"You have my word."

Shamura sighed, "The texts are buried eight kilometers to the West. We can go there in the morning. For now, get some food, water, and rest."

General Garima said, "There are people waiting for us at the bottom of the mountain. Can we retrieve the texts now so we can go to our friends?"

"No, it will be difficult to find in the dark. Your friends will be okay."

Thomas Wayne hoped she was right. He didn't like the idea of leaving Hazail alone with Paul any longer than necessary, but to get the texts, he needed to do what Shamura wanted. "Okay, then let's get some rest."

General Garima rolled her eyes at him. "You're okay with this?"

"I don't think we have a choice, do we?"

"No, you do not." Shamura smiled.

The morning sun woke Thomas Wayne. He noticed Shamura was outside gathering wood for the fire. He went out to join her. "You're always up this early?"

"I am. I gather wood for the stove, then cook my morning meal. I'm guessing you want to skip the morning meal."

"Let me take that for you." He took the wood and carried it. "Yes, I would. My wife is waiting at the bottom with a man I don't trust. I would like to get back to her as soon as possible."

"Then we shall start our journey. Where is the General?"

"I don't know. You haven't seen her?"

"Hmm… I have not."

Thomas Wayne brought the wood inside and set it down near the fireplace. He looked out back and there was General Garima performing something akin to martial arts. He went outside. "Well, don't we have an early start?"

"I am always training and preparing. Something Terrans apparently do not do. I do not know how I am going to survive in your world."

"The first thing you can do is stop saying my world. It's your world too now."

"I guess it is." She wiped the sweat off her brow. "Are you ready to leave now?"

"Yes, we are." Thomas Wayne and General Garima caught up with Shamura and the others. They set out to retrieve the texts.

Halfway into their journey, General Garima stops the group. "Someone is behind us."

Thomas Wayne said, "Again?"

Shamura added, "Yes, I can sense them too."

"Really," said Thomas Wayne.

General Garima replied, "You must train better." She pulled out her weapon, but it was too late. The bullets flew at the group. "Take cover!"

Thomas Wayne grabbed Diyana and dove to the ground. They hid behind a rock and Thomas Wayne returned fire. He could see General Garima and Shamura firing their weapons. A voice from the tree line shouted, "Put down your weapons or we'll have to kill you!"

General Garima shouted, "Try it."

Thomas Wayne knew she loved this. The action was what she lived for. He saw a way to get behind them while they were engaged in conversation with General Garima. He motioned to Shamura his plan and she acknowledge it. Thomas Wayne said to Diyana, "Stay here. I'm going to get behind them." She nodded. *She's certainly not cut out for this, bless her soul.*

He made his way around and counted six men. He recognized the leader and couldn't believe his eyes. The man speaking and the other four were not familiar to him. "Everyone freeze! Put your hands up." The men did as they were told. "General, Shamura, come out."

The ladies came out, and Thomas Wayne forced the men to leave the tree line. General Garima said, "Who do we have here?"

Shamura said, "This is why I told you the texts should remain hidden."

Thomas Wayne shouted, "Cordell, what are you doing here?"

"The same reason you're here, except I'm not colluding with the enemy to do it."

"General Garima is not our enemy."

"How did you learn about the texts?" General Garmia asked.

"I learned that years ago. This is the best opportunity to find it and all the gold that goes with it. America is sitting on a gold mine and don't know it, cuz."

"We're certainly not family anymore." He looked at General Garima, "We can't let them slow us down. What are we going to do with them?" General Garima smirked, "Not kill them."

"Then we can only…" shots rang out, striking one man and everyone hit the ground. Thomas Wayne shouted, "Diyana, what are you doing?"

"They killed Naram. He was my mate." She fired two more shots, killing two more of the men.

General Garima said, "Honey, put the gun down." She looked at General Garima. Her eyes were frozen in a bug-eyed position. "I feel what you're feeling. Personally, I would kill them all too, but Thomas Wayne has taught me a better way. You have killed three of them. One of them was likely responsible for your mate's death. Let that be the end."

Diyana lowered her weapon and wept on General Garima's shoulder.

Thomas Wayne rushed to Cordell. After touching his neck, he nodded his head. "He's dead." He placed his hands on his thighs and sighed. "That leaves us with three to tie up. Fortunately, it looks like they brought zip ties. I guess you guys were planning to tie us up." Thomas Wayne tied the men up and they left them at the tree line.

Shamura and Diyana walked ahead of Thomas Wayne and General Garima. "She's really shook up about Naram. I remember how I felt when Elaine was killed. I could have done the same thing to the men that killed her."

"You should have."

"I'm not that type of person. It just doesn't come easy for me to kill another person. I got out of the military because I was a conscientious objector."

"What is a conscientious objector?"

"Let's see, the book's answer is someone who is opposed to serving in the military and carrying weapons because of religious principles." General Garima cut her eyes at him. "I knew you would look at me like that."

"You don't strike me as this conscientious objector."

"I changed for this war." He nodded. "Since ships from outer space came over my home and started firing laser blasts at us, everyone had to bear arms or be killed. A war like the one your people brought changed us as a people. It got rid of racism too. I hope that part is permanent."

"Racism?"

"Oh, yeah. America was built on the suppression of people, mainly black people. But they also came to America and took the land from the Native Americans."

"If the Native Americans could not fight back, then they didn't deserve to keep the land."

"We are really going to need to change that thinking if you want to live here."

She stopped. "I am a warrior, a fighter from birth. I was born before the time I was due."

"Premature?"

"Yes. No one thought I would live. My father... he wanted to kill me at birth, but my mother would not let him. Since I came into the world, I had to fight to gain everything. Don't lecture me. I may not be sympathetic to these Native Americans you speak of, but it's not because I don't like them. It's because I fought for everything I gained. If everyone had my spirit, maybe those Native Americans would not have lost their land."

"Wow, I learn a little about you every day." She cut her eyes at him. "It just wasn't as simple as you put it, but I respect your opinion. Maybe you can read about the Native Americans and learn to understand their plight." General Garima didn't respond. Thomas Wayne left the subject alone. "Or not."

"Thomas Wayne, I will learn all that I can about this world, but your world, your people, will also need to understand our world and what we have lived through. People see us as conquerors, but we are more than that. We have a rich culture and heritage that only someone from Assyria can understand. You cannot expect me to learn about your world, and you do not do the same."

"You are correct, and I will make it my point to learn everything about you and Assyria. But this your world/my world, your people/my people thing has kept this country divided for centuries. Assyria and Earth can be one people."

"I will agree with that."

The noon hour approached, and they finally reached the spot where the ancient texts were buried. Thomas Wayne asked, "Does your Spidey senses tell you anyone is near?"

General Garima answered, "I don't know what you mean?"

"Got to live here to understand the reference. Are you picking up any signs that anyone is nearby? We don't want anyone else to get the jump on us."

"No, my Spidey senses are not picking anyone up."

"Was that a joke? A joke and a smile? Oh my, I'm rubbing off on you."

"Do not get ahead of yourself, Thomas Wayne."

"Hey, Brula, one more thing. Stop talking without contractions. You sound like a robot."

"Really?"

"Yes. You said, 'Do not get ahead...' When you should say, 'Don't get ahead...' Hear the difference?"

"It's the same thing."

"Yes, but it sounds better."

"It's the same thing, Thomas Wayne."

"It's cooler." He laughed.

Shamura said, "Okay, this is the stone. This stone has sat in this spot for years. It is too big for anyone to move by themselves, so we have used it as a marker. We are to take three paces north." She walked three paces. "Now seven paces west." She walked the seven paces again. "Finally, three paces north again." Again, she walked the three paces. "Here."

Thomas Wayne asked, "Here? I expected there to be more here. There's nothing but grass."

"Yes, beautiful green grass." Shamura smiled. "Come stand with me." Everyone in the group stood next to her. "Come a little closer." They again moved closer. "Good." She placed her hands on Thomas Wayne's and General Garima's shoulders. "Now, oh

Lord, bless me!" In a matter of seconds, a light shined down on them. They were transported to another location. As soon as they arrived, the lights turned on. On a pedestal sat a book with a light shining down on it. "Here is the book of the ancient texts."

Thomas Wayne asked, "Where are we?"

Shamura answered, "It is a secret location. I'm not even sure where we are. I just know the only way to get here is the way we came." Shamura walked over to the pedestal and ran her hand across the book. "I have only come here once when my mother taught me how to get here. She said one day this book would save our world. Now maybe it will." Thomas Wayne reached for the book. "No, only my DNA can retrieve the book from its place. If you touch it, a trap will go off and we will be here forever left to die."

"We don't want that."

Shamura retrieved the book. "Now we may leave."

General Garima said, "There is so much more here." She smiled looking around the endless tunnels. "I have never seen this much gold, silver and jewels before."

"We are only here for the book. We must leave now." General Garima nodded in agreement. Everyone took their place in the spot they arrived and Shamura uttered the spiritual words again. They were transported back to the original transport spot. "I am trusting you with this book Thomas Wayne, according to your word."

"I could care less about any gold or riches. I want my world free of these people. If this book will unlock the key to defeating them, then that's all I want it for."

General Garima said, "We could easily go back to that place and take whatever we want."

Shamura replied, "Stand in the spot and utter the words."

General Garima twisted her head but complied. After uttering the words nothing happened. Shamura smiled, "You see, only the one who has access to the book may utter the spiritual words to gain access to it the treasure." She looked at Thomas Wayne, "Another thing that I am trusting you. Not to go back to that place except to return the book."

General Garima laughed, "I guess Paul will not get his riches."

Thomas Waynes joined her. He then looked at Shamura, "You have my word."

Shamura touched Thomas Wayne's shoulder, "Lord, bless the man who's carrying your book to save this world. I grant him and only him the permission that you have given my family for centuries." She rose her head and looked at General Garima. "I cannot pray the same prayer for you. Even if you have changed your ways, they are not changed enough. Only Thomas Wayne can touch this book. If anyone else touches it, they will die." Shamura handed the book to Thomas Wayne.

"Wow, no pressure."

General Garima said, "I understand. I am beginning to understand a great deal now."

She smiled. "You will understand more as time goes on." She patted General Garima on the shoulder. "Go now, save the world."

Thomas Wayne nodded, "Thank you, Shamura. Thank you, Diyana."

Shamura and Diyana smiled. They headed back down the mountain. Thomas Wayne wondered about the book, the place they were transported to, and the woman who led them there. It all seemed angelic to him. General Garima was quiet for the trip back. Thomas Wayne realized she was touched by the experience, too. He said, "You have a swatch of grey hair."

"So do you."

"I think we were in some place that was close to God. The one and only true God."

"I think you might be right, Thomas Wayne."

29 – Ambushed

Thomas Wayne and General Garima walked the last long stretch of dirt road that led to where they left Hazail and Paul. He spotted her from a distance and ran toward her with the book held tight in his hands. She did the same and immediately his male protective instinct kicked in. Thomas Wayne worried that his pregnant wife would hurt herself or the baby. "Sweetheart, what are you doing? You shouldn't be running."

"My love, I am only pregnant. It is good to see you both again."

General Garima said, "It is good to see you again. Anything happened with Paul."

Hazail's face changed, "He cannot be trusted. There is something going on with him. He was very friendly with the Republican Guard."

Thomas Wayne replied, "We will keep an eye on him to make sure he stays away from the book."

"You have it," said Hazail!

"Yes, we do. The woman who gave it to us said that anyone else who touches this book will die." Paul joined the group. "Paul."

"Thomas Wayne. I took good care of your lovely woman." Hazail and Thomas Wayne rolled their eyes at him. "May I see the book?"

"You may not. The woman who gave us this book spoke over it. She was the only one who could touch the book, and now I am the only one who can touch it."

Paul laughed, "That's bull. You're trying to hold on to it for yourself."

"I wouldn't lie about something like this. Even General Garima has not touched the book."

"You're not shutting me out of this. I came all this way and agreed to sit here and babysit your woman. I'm getting my cut!"

Hazail huffed, "I don't require babysitting!"

Thomas Wayne added, "You were not left here to babysit my woman. We don't trust you, but we would never lie to…" The pounding sound of the heroes striking the ground cause everyone to scatter and hide. Everyone except Paul. Thomas Wayne and Hazail hid in the brush out of the sight of the heroes. Thomas Wayne said, "That traitor!" Paul talked to Cain. He pointed in the direction where Thomas Wayne hid.

Cain turned to the area. "If you don't come out with the book, we will kill her."

Hazail asked, "Who is he talking about?"

Cain held out his hand. From an area hidden from Thomas Wayne's view General Garima was pushed into Cain's arms. Cain grabbed her saying, "I will snap her neck if you don't come out with the book."

Thomas Wayne moved. Hazail said "Thomas Wayne, no. General Garima is prepared to die for the cause."

"I am not prepared to let her." He stood. Here I am. Hazail joined him. "No, you stay there."

"If you die, so do I. There is no purpose in living without the man I love."

The sentiment touched Thomas Wayne's heart, but he didn't want her to join him. At the moment, he couldn't argue with her either. Thomas Wayne walked toward Cain. General Garima said, "You should have let him kill me."

"That time will still come, General. You should have followed the King's orders and returned to Assyria. Now you will die with these worthless Terrans." Cain motioned for Paul to take the book.

Paul walked over to him and held out his hand. Thomas Wayne laughed. Paul said, "Now I will prove to you what the old woman said was bull."

"Why do you think he's telling you to take it?" Thomas Wayne rose one eyebrow.

Paul paused. Cain said with a strict voice. "Get the book Paul, President of Africa."

"Yes, that's what I'm talking about." He looked at Thomas Wayne, "Hand it to me or Cain will snap the old bag's neck. Personally, I would love to see that."

General Garima said, "No, Thomas Wayne."

"I can't see you die." He handed the book to Paul. "But, I don't mind seeing him die."

Paul took it in his hands and smiled. He ran his hands across the book, loving every centimeter he covered. "See, what did I..." In seconds, he gagged. Paul fell to his knees. He wobbled more and more until he disintegrated in front of them, dropping the book on the ground where ashes of his former self once stood. Thomas Wayne picked the book up. It was undamaged.

He looked at Cain with a smirk on his face. "You want to try?"

Cain answered, "It seems we need you, after all. Lucky for you. But there will come a day when I will burn you at a stake in front of the world as a message to never challenge us."

Serena said, "Cain, why don't we kill them? No one can touch the book."

Adonis replied, "We don't know how many Terrans can hold the book. Cain is right. We must keep him alive, but we don't need the others."

Thomas Wayne said, "If you kill either of them, I will never do what you want. But I will tell the world how to destroy you."

Cain said, "We will take them to Colorado, then decide what to do with them." He pushed General Garima toward Thomas Wayne and Hazail. "He has a fondness for these two. It will be his downfall."

Adonis walked over to Vayu and Tutu. Thomas Wayne suspected something was about to happen. He grabbed Hazail by the hand. Thomas Wayne said to Cain, "Hey, I thought there were seven of you? Did you lose someone?" He smirked, causing Cain's ire to rise.

Cain yelled, "Don't think for one—" Adonis' group seized the moment and attacked. Thomas Wayne grabbed both ladies and they rushed to get away from the battle.

Battle of the Gods

Tutu vs. Hephaestus

Tutu unleashed a crushing blow that slammed into Hephaestus's temple, sending him reeling. Before

Hephaestus could recover, Tutu was on him, straddling his chest. "It is time for you to die, Hephaestus," Tutu snarled.

"What are you doing? We're friends!" Hephaestus cried, disbelief etched on his face.

"Not anymore." Tutu's fists became a blur, raining down blows on Hephaestus's face. Each impact resonated like an earthquake across the surrounding landscape. Hephaestus managed to catch one of Tutu's punches and, with a powerful heave, flipped Tutu off him. Tutu landed hard in the brush several yards away.

"If this is how you want it, Tutu, then so be it," Hephaestus declared, rising to his feet. He lunged, delivering a powerful blow to Tutu's face, but Tutu spun, countering with a swift kick to Hephaestus' jaw.

Hephaestus attempted to freeze time, but Tutu scoffed. "You know that doesn't work with another god. Did you forget our bracelets cancel each other out?" Tutu seized Hephaestus by the throat, his grip tightening. "Now you will die, and I will gain your strength." Tutu didn't see the incoming blow until it was too late. Serena's foot connected with the side of his mouth, drawing blood. Tutu staggered backward, releasing his hold.

"How dare you attack my brother!" Serena roared.

"Get her!" Tutu bellowed, and Vayu charged at Serena.

Tutu lunged back toward Hephaestus, but Hephaestus met him with a devastating punch to the stomach. Tutu gasped, doubling over and dropping to one knee. He looked up, meeting Hephaestus's gaze. "Now I will end your existence, my friend."

"You should have stayed in line. Cain is the strongest of us all. Following Adonis is a fool's move," Hephaestus admonished, winding up for his finishing blow. But Hephaestus never saw the blade. In a flash, Tutu produced it, plunging it deep into Hephaestus's stomach. Green blood splattered outward for yards. "It is you who are the fool, my friend. Tell Zeus we said hello!"

Hephaestus's blood gushed onto the ground like a river. He crumpled to his knees, then to his side, his hand still clutching his wounded stomach.

"Noooo!" Serena screamed, her voice raw with anguish. "You will pay for killing my brother!"

Serena vs. Vayu

Capitalizing on Serena's raw grief, Vayu moved in for the kill. "Don't worry, beautiful Serena," Vayu purred, "I'll send you to see your brother again."

Serena's rage exploded. She lunged, tackling Vayu in the stomach and sending them both tumbling backward. They rolled over and over, each god clawing for dominance until Serena managed to kick Vayu off her. Vayu slammed against a tree ten feet away.

Both gods charged, locking arms in a brutal test of strength. Serena's power didn't surprise Vayu as she forced her to her knees. Vayu strained, desperate to regain her footing, but couldn't. With a desperate surge, she twisted her arms, breaking Serena's hold.

Serena stumbled back. Vayu saw an opportunity to weaponize Serena's anger. She glanced sideways, confirming Adonis still held Cain. Vayu shot up, spun, and landed a powerful blow on Serena.

Tutu seized Serena from behind, trapping her as Vayu unleashed a barrage of punches. Vayu laughed as Serena's struggles grew weaker. "No, my wife!" Cain roared.

Vayu looked at Cain, then delivered a finishing blow to Serena. Life drained from Serena's eyes, and she slumped out of Tutu's grasp, collapsing to the ground. Enraged, Cain struck Adonis in the face, then sprinted to his fallen wife. He slammed into Vayu, sending her reeling, then unleashed a blow that sent Tutu flying ten feet away. Cain scooped up Serena's body and launched himself into the air, escaping Adonis, Tutu, and Vayu.

"Let's go after him!" Vayu urged.

"No," Adonis replied. "We've crippled him enough for now. We need to find the Terrans and retrieve that book. Get Hephaestus's body. We can't leave it for the Terrans to examine."

Tutu grabbed Hephaestus's body, and they flew off to regroup. Vayu looked at Adonis, a flicker of doubt in her eyes. The pain of Serena's death, an emotion she never felt before, settled deep within her: regret.

30 - Bereavement

Cain landed on a beach in Hawaii. He laid the body of his fallen love to the ground. Tears rolled down his face as he cried in the bosom of Serena. "I love you, Serena, and I will join you in the afterlife. But before I do, I will hunt down each of the traitors and kill them with my bare hands. Your death will be avenged."

Cain looked to his left. There were people watching him mourn the loss of his wife. He no longer cared they knew the gods were vulnerable. He only wanted to kill those responsible. Cain asked, "Does anyone have matches?"

A man approached him and handed him a book of matches. Cain struck one match and lit Serena's body on fire. He stared into the fire. Cain's tears continued to roll down his face and drop into the fire. With each second that passed, his anger grew more. The man who handed him the matches said, "I'm sorry for your loss."

"Why? We are evil and ruthless towards your people. Why do you care about my loss?"

"It doesn't matter who you are or where you're from; a loss is a loss. Anyone suffering a loss deserves to know there are others who feel for their loss. Matthew 5:44 says, '…to love your enemies and pray for those who persecute you.' That is the kind of people we are."

"This is from the Hebrew Bible?"

"Yes, it is."

Cain realized the pretense of being gods to people who would love him even though he treated them evil was wrong. "I have learned that what we were doing was wrong. We are not gods. We do not deserve your kindness."

The man said, "Everyone deserves kindness."

Cain watched as the last of Serena's body burned away. She was gone. Cain looked to the sky. "I will get my revenge, then I will set your people free." He launched himself into the air, knowing Adonis' camp would try to find Thomas Wayne and his team.

31 – Unsuspecting Support

Thomas Wayne drove through the Iranian cities and towns, avoiding any traffic along the way. Most people were taking shelter because of the battle taking place between the heroes. "I can't believe they are fighting each other."

General Garima said, "There were rumors from the old days of jealously between the gods. I guess those rumors were true."

"It worked for us. Now we need to get to a safe place and learn the secret of destroying them."

Hazail said, "My great grandmother once said Adonis and Cain always had a feud between them. Most of it was over Serena. This seemed more like a power play by Adonis. I don't know how he convinced the others to join him, but he did."

"In the Bible, the devil convinced a legion of angels to follow him to war against God, so why would Adonis be any different," added Thomas Wayne. Hazail and General Garima looked at him. "What? At least my comment are about a real God." He shrugged his shoulder.

General Garima said, "None of it matters. What matters is their fight with each other allowed us to get away."

Thomas Wayne replied, "You noticed Cain couldn't touch the book? He knew it would kill him, or at least he thought it might. That's why he had Paul touch it first."

General Garima replied, "I noticed that. In order to destroy the book, they need you to do it. The question is, would you destroy the book to save one of us? This is where your Terran morals will hurt you and the world."

"I am who I am. I believe God chose me for this and He would not put me in that position. If He did, then He would want me to save you." Neither of them replied. Their Assyrian beliefs would kick in and they would allow him to die to save the book. That's not his way and he wouldn't change. "I know you both disagree, but I'm not allowing either of you to die if I can help it. Hazail is carrying my child. I would never allow her to die."

"That is where your Terran morals will cause the world to be destroyed."

"I heard you the first time." Thomas Wayne checked the dashboard. "We need gas."

"There appears to be a city ahead."

"I hope there's some gas there." Thomas Wayne pulled up to a gas station outside of the city. Everyone was looking up, so Thomas Wayne did the same. Three of the heroes flew across them, carrying the body of a fourth one. He ducked under a canvas, hoping they didn't see him. "They kept flying, so they probably didn't see us."

Hazail replied, "Let's hope they didn't."

Thomas Wayne pumped the gas. He filled up the tank and grabbed a couple of gas cans. He filled those up, as well. People were coming back outside. A man approached Thomas Wayne. "I saw you on TV. You were there when the gods were fighting?"

"I was, and they are not gods." He nodded his head. "Who won the battle?"

"Adonis, Vayu, and Tutu won. Serena and Hephaestus were killed. Cain survived but left before they could kill him. I believe they will hunt down Cain."

"So, there's only four of them left now."

"No, no… Ramos too."

"No, my friend. If Ramos were alive, he would have been there too. I suspect he is dead as well. Anyway, we need to get out of here."

"Did you see their true form?"

"No, I did not."

"Hideous creatures. The Bible says we were made in God's imagine. These creatures are not like us. They are green and look like serpents. When Serena was killed, she lost her human form, and we got to see what they really look like. I agree with you Thomas Wayne; they are not gods."

"Thank you. That is good information to know. Be safe, my friend." Thomas Wayne was amazed at how many people knew him now.

The man waved at Thomas Wayne. He reentered the vehicle, and they continued their journey back to the shuttle. "Did you hear what the man said?" They both nodded that they didn't. "He said the heroes are not human. They are in human form to fool us. They look like serpents in their real form."

General Garima replied, "I am not surprised."

Hazail added, "Nothing surprises me anymore."

They rode in silence for the next hundred miles. Thomas Wayne was deep in thought. Now more than ever, Earth was close to being free. No Assyrian army to be at war with and no false gods ruling over them. All he needed to do was get somewhere and read this book to figure out the secret.

By nightfall, the team returned to Iraq. They found a place to hide the vehicle and get some rest for the night. The man running the hotel recognized them and thanked them for trying to end the reign of the false gods on Earth. He told the story of how Adonis killed his sister for not worshipping him.

His television was replaying the battle of the gods. Thomas Wayne watched as the gods fought among each other. He saw what the man at the gas station told him about Serena and Hephaestus returning to their true form after death.

The next morning, the group returned to the vehicle and headed to Syria. Thomas Wayne said, "The return trip will be easier now since the heroes have been exposed for who they truly are."

General Garima said, "You are correct for now. When Adonis' group settles in, they will be worse than you can expect. Adonis has been known throughout our history as being more ruthless than any of the other gods."

"Thanks… that's something to look forward to."

"Is that more of your sarcasm?" asked Hazail.

Thomas Wayne giggled, "Yes, sweetheart. It is. We've been through so much since this war started that looking forward to a more ruthless leader seems par for the course."

"My love, you speak funny sometimes."

General Garima said, "We should just be ready for more death with Adonis in charge."

Thomas Wayne drove to Syria and back into Saudi Arabia, only stopping for gas. They arrived back at the shuttle in the early morning hours. Thomas Wayne said, "That was a long trip."

General Garima replied, "I could have driven the vehicle."

"No worries. You got your chance now. Drive the shuttle back to Detroit." She didn't respond. "Sweetheart, are you okay?"

"Yes, my love. I'm going to navigate for General Garima."

"Good. I'm going to grab some sleep." Thomas Wayne cuddled in the back of the shuttle. Anytime he could grab a few hours of sleep, it was meaningful to him. *I promise when this is all over, I'm going on a long vacation somewhere where there's no fighting. Nothing but clear blue water and white sand.* He drifted off to sleep.

The shuttle landing woke Thomas Wayne from his sleep. *Wow, it's been nine hours already.* He looked up front and the ladies were getting out of their seats.

Hazail came to him and caressed his chin. "Hello, my love. How was your sleep?"

"It was good, sweetheart."

"We could tell." She placed her hand over her mouth and giggled.

"I take it I was snoring."

"Very loudly at that," said General Garima. "I have sat us down near the church. We should only be a few blocks away."

"Good. But since it's so early in the morning, maybe we should stay here until the sun is up. No telling what's going on in this town and how many of the church people are probably sleeping."

General Garima flopped down in the seat. "Then I will sleep."

"Is the transparency on?"

"Yes, and as you Terrans say, good night."

"Good night, General."

Thomas Wayne put his arm around Hazail. "You should get some sleep too."

"I will, in your arms."

"Hmm, sounds like a good plan to me. We haven't had much cuddle time lately." Thomas Wayne stayed awake while the ladies slept. He couldn't take his eyes off the book and wondered about the secrets it must hold. He took his mind off of it and tried to think about a life without a war or heroes flying around. A life where he could raise his child in peace. He smiled and kept watch for the rest of the night.

"Ladies, ladies, ladies… the morning is upon us. Let's head out to the church and see what we need to do to end this reign of terror on our planet."

Hazail woke and kissed Thomas Wayne on the lips. "Anything you wish, my love."

"Before this is all over, I think I'm going to puke," chuckled General Garima.

"No, wait. Hazail, did she just make another joke? The military stern woman, take no mess leader, made a second joke? Wow, the world must be changing."

"Thomas Wayne, you are having an effect on me. I need to get back to my warrior training."

They laughed and exited the shuttle. Thomas Wayne said, "That is so weird getting out of something and no one can see it."

Hazail took Thomas Wayne's arm, "You get accustomed to it." They walked along the road. You could see the church from where they parked the shuttle. When they arrived, no one was there. "Where is everyone?" asked Hazail.

Thomas Wayne answered, "I don't know. The building looks the same as we left it, but everyone is gone." A young African American boy rode by on a bike. "Hey, do you know the people that lived here?"

The boy looked at him, "You're that guy that has a bounty out on you." He looked at the ladies, "You're the women too."

"Bounty? That's still in effect?"

"If I were you, I wouldn't be seen out in the open like this. There're people looking to make money off all of you."

A woman ran up to the boy. "Jalen, what are doing?"

"Mom, it's them, from the broadcast last night."

Jalen's mom studied their faces. She said, "You need to get out of here before someone comes to cash in that bounty."

"We know about the bounty. Do you know where the people from the church are?" asked Thomas Wayne.

"Adonis ordered the capture and execution of all Assyrians and Christians. He placed a bounty on each of your heads. You're worth two million dollars each."

Thomas Wayne asked, "Wow, it went up. We must be doing something right." No one laughed. "Okay, tough crowd. Did they round up the people from this church?"

"Yes, shortly after the broadcast, soldiers came here and arrested everyone here. A few escaped and scattered around, but most were rounded up. They are scheduled to be executed at noon."

"Here?"

"Yes." She looked at each of them. "Now, go because the gangs will see you."

Thomas Wayne and the ladies hurried back to the shuttle. They needed a new plan. Now there was no one to read the ancient text, and returning to Iran was not an option. Everyone was on the lookout for them.

Hazail said, "Every time we seem to get close to the end, another obstacle is placed in our path. Why does your God make it so hard?"

"This isn't just about us. This is about the entire world, and every knee will bow. My guess is God has a reason, and we just need to slow the pace down for a minute. We will find a way to end this."

"I have something on the radio," announced General Garima.

"This is Tony Cochran from WXLJ News here in Detroit. Soldiers have rounded up hundreds of Christians and Assyrians. They will be executed in front of City Hall at noon today in accordance with the edict issued by Adonis last evening. Here's a replay of that speech.

"Citizens of Aaru, this is your new supreme god, Adonis. There has been a change in the leadership of the gods. The former supreme god was weak. I am not. I will not tolerate any disobedience to my word. My word is the only law in this land. Follow it or die. Those are your only choices!" He paused. "From this day forward, anyone found to be a Christian, an Assyrian, or both will be arrested and executed the next day at noon." He paused again. "I am increasing the bounty placed on the heads of Thomas Wayne Walker, General Garmia and Lieutenant Hazail. Whoever captures and turns them in to me will receive two million dollars for each of them. I want them alive to be executed formally by me. That is all!"

Tony Cochran continued, "Wow, two million dollars now!" He stopped to gather himself. "Okay, today will be the first day of executions and from the reports we have received around the world, there could be hundreds of thousands of people executed. This is Tony Cochran reporting live from Detroit, Michigan."

Thomas Wayne was solemn. "I don't know what to do. We've got to stop this from happening, but what can we do in four hours?"

Hazail answered, "Find Cain."

"What?"

General Garima added, "You've lost your mind."

"Cain isn't dead, and Adonis killed his wife. The enemy of my enemy is my friend, remember?"

General Garima replied, "She's got a point."

"Even if I thought that was a good idea, we don't know where to look for him," added Thomas Wayne.

"Washington DC. That's where he made his home. Remember, he was going to move the capital to Philadelphia but stayed in DC. That's the first place we should look."

General Garima responded, "I agree, but flying this shuttle during the day will attract attention. Getting from here to DC in four hours is not possible either."

"Maybe we have another solution," added Thomas Wayne. He smiled, seeing that glowing face he always loved. "Aaliyah, my sister."

Hazail grabbed his arm, "Is it possible she wants to collect the bounty?"

"That's the first thing you've said to me to anger me, sweetheart." He turned and exited the shuttle. Thomas Wayne ran to his little sister and hugged her. "I thought you were captured."

"I barely escaped. The woman you met in front of the church, she told me she ran into you. You have the book?"

"I do, but if Carmichael got captured, there's no one to read it and tell us what to do."

"He's not captured. He's with me." She looked at the shuttle. "Where are the others?"

"I had to leave them behind. Why are you shaking?"

"I just feel a little cold." She glanced at Thomas Wayne. "Let's go while we can. We can't be out in the open like this."

"I need to get something out of the shuttle. Hold on a minute."

"Okay."

Thomas Wayne ran back inside the shuttle. "She's lying to me. It's a trap."

"How do you know?"

"General, do you have siblings?"

"I do."

"Then you should know that growing up you spend so much time with each other that you learn all of their traits, their habits, their tells. I know my sister and she's lying. She's being forced to lie by someone. I just don't know who that someone is right now."

"You're right, Thomas Wayne. What's the plan?"

"I told her the two of you left. I will leave the book here and go with her. You follow behind me out of sight. When she leads me to the trap, you can save me. I hope you're a good shot."

Hazail said, "I don't like this plan."

"It's the only way, sweetheart. We need to see what's going on."

"This is probably some low-level gang trying to collect the bounty."

"If it is, then kill them all."

"Thomas Wayne," shouted Hazail!

Thomas Wayne's frustration was apparent. His morals met head on with his anger. He wondered inside which one would truly win out. "I'm tired of bouncing from wall to wall. We don't need money hungry humans getting in the way. We need to end this reign and return this world to the state it was in before all of this started. General Garima stay close. Don't let me down."

"I won't."

"Hey you used a contraction…nice." He smiled then exited the shuttle and jogged back to his sister. As far as he could see, there was no one around. Thomas Wayne felt less secure as they walked away from the ship. He asked, "Apart from Adonis placing a bounty on my head, why all the secrecy?"

"That's enough of a reason, don't you think?"

"I do. You're not acting like yourself, Aaliyah." He placed a hand on her shoulder. "Stop." He looked her in her eyes. "Are you leading your big brother into a trap? If you are, why? It can't be money—not you, Aaliyah."

Tears formed in her eyes. "We have to go, Thomas Wayne. We have to. Where are the others?"

"I don't know." Which wasn't a lie by now. He didn't know where they were, but he hoped they would stay back long enough for him to find out what was going on with his sister."

She took him by the arm, "Let's go, please."

Thomas Wayne jerked his arm away. "Not until you tell me what's going on." Aaliyah shifted her weight. "I know you, Aaliyah, and you are not making eye contact… that's not you. You don't want to—"

"She's going to kill everyone if I don't bring you and the others to her."

"She who?"

"Vayu. They captured all of us last night. This morning, they caught Janice, the lady and little boy you saw this morning. She found out that I was your sister and said if I didn't bring you, they would kill us all."

"Vayu is going to do that anyway, Aaliyah. You can't negotiate with them."

"Thomas Wayne, I love you. You're my big brother. You know I wouldn't do this unless I felt I had no other choice. I believe with all my heart; you would have done the same. It's how we were raised."

Thomas Wayne knew she was right. He would have done the same. Their parents instilled in them a moral compass that placed a high value on life. They never understood his decision to go into the military. He thought he would never go on the battlefield. Now he faced the question, does the needs of the one outweigh the many? "You're right, Aaliyah, I would make the same choice, but we've got to figure out how to beat this woman without anyone losing their life."

"How do we do that?"

"I don't know, but I know the bracelet on her arm weakens her if we remove it."

"She's too strong. We would never get that close."

"I know, but I'm hoping we get a break somehow. Take me to her."

"I won't be able to live with myself if she kills you, Thomas Wayne."

"Well, God seems to have a purpose for my life and, hey, Daniel went into the lion's den… maybe this is my time to go."

"You always have a way to see the good in any situation. I was setting you up, but you still love me."

"Are you kidding me? You're my baby sister. That will never change. Oh, by the way, Cordell is dead. He tried to get rich off the book in the Middle East."

"I heard he went further off the deep end. Unimaginable, that I once loved him."

Thomas Wayne and Aaliyah entered a parking garage down the street from the shuttle. He didn't know where General Garima and Hazail were, but he knew they were close. The two were skilled warriors, and he prayed they would get him out of this situation.

When Thomas Wayne walked inside, he noticed people were being held inside the garage. One of them was Carmichael. Thomas Wayne didn't want it known that he knew him. From out of the shadows stepped Vayu. "I should have known one of you would be behind this. New outfit?" Vayu didn't laugh at Thomas Wayne's humor. "You know in another life a woman in a black leather short pants set with high boots would work for me, but I'm not into the false god thing."

"Your insolence will be the death of you, Thomas Wayne Walker. If it were not for my love, I would kill you now."

"Your love?" Thomas Wayne snickered at her words.

"Adonis is my mate, and he wants you alive. Please give me a reason to kill you."

"Not today."

Vayu rose her head with arrogance, "Where are the Assyrian women?"

Aaliyah answered, "He says he didn't know where they were. They left him at the shuttle."

"He's lying."

Thomas Wayne shrugged his shoulders, "I'm standing right here."

"You will tell me where they are, or I will start killing people."

Thomas Wayne snickered, "Wait, aren't you a god? What happened to the all-seeing, all-knowing stuff?"

Vayu stepped closer to him. Thomas Wayne thought, *just a little closer and I will grab that bracelet.*

"Where… are… they?"

"I can't tell you what I don't know. So, I guess you're going to have to do your god thing and kill everyone here. Strange though, I didn't think gods killed people like you do. Where's Ramos?"

"Shut up! I grow tired of your insolence! Tell me what I want to know!"

Aaliyah twisted her head, "Why are you pissing her off?"

"Hey, I thought you wanted to make an example of me. You know, the old kill me in front of the world threat you gods make?"

Vayu turned to the soldiers. "Bring them all to the place you call City Hall. We will kill them all there. Keep a lookout for the Assyrians. They are here; I know it. Do not kill Thomas Wayne. He will be mine." Vayu sprung into the air while the soldiers rounded everyone up and herded them to City Hall.

Aaliyah asked, "Any ideas, big brother?"

"It's coming."

City Hall, Detroit Michigan

The crowd of people to be executed arrived at City Hall. Thomas Wayne was in awe of the number of people who were there to watch. *Our people never cease to amaze me. We are here to be executed, and they want to support the execution by watching. Reminds me of the many fights passed along on the internet. We have truly got to do better.* He looked around, wondering where his friends were. Vayu landed on the ground. Her impact caused many to fall and others to run in fear. Thomas Wayne suspected she and the others enjoyed striking fear in the people.

She walked down the road confidently, rolling her eyes at those she despised. She ate up the worshippers as they increased her strength. Thomas Wayne made his way to Carmichael. He whispered, "Any hints on what might be in that book?"

"None. I wish you had it. We could use it now."

"Amen."

Vayu ordered her soldiers to stand in front of the group to be executed. She ordered, "Bring Thomas Wayne to me…now!" The soldiers brought Thomas Wayne to her. "Kneel before your god."

"I would if Christ were here."

She slapped him with a power blow to the face, knocking him several feet away. Thomas Wayne looked around, cursing the people who held cameras to witness his demise. The soldiers stood him up and dragged him back over to Vayu. She grabbed him by the collar. "You will kneel before me, or I will slaughter not only the ones marked for execution, but everyone else here."

"You made a mistake." She looked perplexed. Thomas Wayne quickly grabbed the bracelet off her wrist. Vayu knocked him down and took two steps back. *This can't hurt.* He placed the bracelet on his wrist. The rush of power pushed the air out of him. Vayu rushed him, but he quickly regained his feet and threw a powerful right hook at Vayu. She flew 20 feet through a building to the adjacent street. The crowd roared. Thomas Wayne shouted, "Get out of here!" Everyone ran as fast as they could. He looked at several of the guards. I don't know why you were working for her, but you better leave now. The guards joined the crowd and ran.

Aaliyah shouted, "Thomas Wayne, lookout!"

Vayu threw her shoulder into him, knocking him to the ground. She tried to retrieve her bracelet, but Thomas Wayne jerked it away and punched her in the face. Green blood poured down Vayu's face. She turned and sprung into the air. Thomas Wayne tried to fly, but it did not work. *Anyway, I got you now, fake god.*

Back at the Shuttle

Thomas Wayne, Hazail, General Garima, Aaliyah and Carmichael were inside the shuttle. Thomas

Wayne said, "Carmichael, now is the time for you to read this book and tell us how to defeat the false gods."

"Yes, of course, but you will need to open it and flip the pages for me. No human can touch it without the anointment of God."

General Garima asked, "Then how did Shamura touch it?"

"I said no human." He smiled.

Thomas Wayne asked, "So, you're saying she wasn't a human?"

"Shamura has been living in that place for at least a thousand years. Do you think she is human?"

Thomas Wayne said, "So she's God?"

"No, an angel is more likely. But enough—let's look at the book."

Thomas Wayne opened the book. He held it so Carmichael could read each page. Thomas Wayne read his face. It looked as though the news was not good for the world. After a half an hour Carmichael motioned for Thomas Wayne to close the book. Carmichael held his head down, then sighed. Thomas Wayne asked, "What is it?"

"There is nothing in this book that tells us specifically how to defeat the gods."

Thomas Wayne couldn't believe his ears. "What do you mean, nothing?"

"I mean just that; nothing."

Aaliyah asked, "What did it say?"

Carmichael sighed again. "It tells the story of the Assyrians and their life in the ancient days. It, like most books, tells of their creation and then their struggle under the reign of false gods. How some of us divided off and followed the ways of the Hebrew

God. The others fought the gods, then they left for another world. After they left, many of the Assyrians and people of other nations followed the one true God. A decade later, the number of Christians grew, and the gods left. We were free to worship whomever we wanted. It doesn't tell how the false gods were defeated. They left on their own accord."

Thomas Wayne said, "You're telling me we went all the way to Iran, walked up that mountain, fought people who wanted to steal the book, and fought a god for nothing! We almost died a few times!" Thomas Wayne slammed the book down. "I can't believe this. Every time we think we're going to end this thing, something stops us."

General Garima added, "For centuries, everyone thought this book held treasures and it doesn't hold anything of that nature. Rumors are spread and expanded on until they become more and more believable when the truth is; it just tells a story of a people."

Hazail replied, "But why have a book hidden away with an angel guarding it and it only tells a story? There has to be more to it."

Thomas Wayne asked, "Carmichael, are you sure you're translating it correctly?"

"I'm sure."

Thomas Wayne pounded his fist against the shuttle. "What are we missing?"

General Garima said, "We need to take the fight to the gods. We know their bracelets are the key. If we get those bracelets away from them, we will defeat them."

Thomas Wayne responded, "Yes, but they still have powers without the bracelets."

Hazail added, "There's something different, though."

Thomas Wayne said, "What's that, sweetheart?"

"When we fought Ramos in the Middle East, he could not fly back to America. When you fought Vayu, she could fly away. Why?"

Thomas Wayne snapped his fingers. "I need to think. There has to be a reason." He paced the floor of the small craft. "Why would one be able to fly but the other could not fly? They both had their bracelets. Ramos was clearly weaker without his bracelet than Vayu."

Carmichael stated, "Maybe it's because without their bracelets, they are normal, and Vayu may simply be stronger than Ramos."

"You may be right," replied Thomas Wayne. "Carmichael, could there be a code in the book? A clue about what would defeat them?"

"Why would they hide a code in a book that no one can get to and if they did, it would kill them? No, it's simply a story of a people from the ancient days."

"I guess you're right. General Garima, you're probably right too. The rumor mill is responsible for us thinking this book held the answer."

Aaliyah asked, "Carmichael, does the book talk about how the false gods got here and how they left?"

"Um, they arrived in a ship similar to the one they arrived in here. It's what made the people believe they were gods. With our level of technology and seeing the Assyrians arrive in ships, it was not impressive to us. Imagine living in 1000 B.C.E. and seeing a ship land in your backyard."

Aaliyah asked, "How did they leave, the same way?"

"Yes, it says they boarded the ship and left."

"So, if they can fly, why didn't they fly away? Why did they need a ship?"

General Garima answered, "Because they can't fly in space. They need to breathe."

"That was my initial thought, but let's add stuff up. Ramos couldn't fly without his bracelet. Vayu could. When they destroyed the Assyrian mothership, they had to get into their ship to do it. Each night, they return to the ship for a few hours."

Thomas Wayne asked, "What are you getting at Aaliyah?"

"I'm thinking the ship is the key. Ramos couldn't fly because he was far from the ship. Vayu could because she was closer. The bracelets are not the key to their power; it's only the conduit that allows them to be farther from the ship and use their powers."

"You might be on to something," Carmichael snapped his fingers.

"Thank you."

Aaliyah continued, "Think about how we relayed our radios after the Assyrians knocked the communication systems out. Those bracelets work the same way. When the false god is far away from the ship, the bracelets act like a relay."

"The book does talk about them returning to their ship each night. It also told the story about one god, Shamash. He battled Ra and lost. That evening he couldn't make it back to the ship and began to die. However, Hermes arrived picked him up and rushed him back to the ship. Without the ship he would have died."

General Garima added, "So, there is information in the book to help. It just needs to be interpreted."

"You're right," Thomas Wayne said."

General Garima continued, "There must be something else to get the signal to. If we find that object, we can destroy it, and their bracelets will be ineffective away from the ship."

"Right," said Aaliyah.

Carmichael jumped up, "Thomas Wayne, open the book again." Thomas Wayne opened the book. "Keep flipping. I'll tell you when to stop." Thomas Wayne continued to flip the pages. "Stop!" Thomas Wayne froze. "There, it talks about the gods and how they established posts in the different lands and ordered no one to go near them." Carmichael snapped his fingers, "This has to be the relay system they put in place. It also talks about the nightly ritual held at the ship. One individual was there when they held the ritual, and he was killed for what he saw that night. General Garima is right, the book holds the key; it's the ship. Destroy the ship and they can be defeated."

Thomas Wayne said, "Awesome! When they arrived here, they did the same thing here. We didn't pay it any attention. We need to map out those locations, then take out the relays. That will equal the playing field."

General Garima chimed in, "I think we need to forget about the relays and take out the ship. That's where we gain a complete advantage."

Thomas Wayne agreed, "General Garima is right. Let's aim to take out the ship, but how?"

"Explosives," replied General Garima.

Aaliyah said, "One more thing I think we're missing."

"What's that, Aaliyah?"

"Listening to the story," Carmichael said, "the world switched to worshipping God, the real God, and it led to the gods leaving. Remember, the ancient people didn't destroy the ship or the relay posts. Something else made the gods leave. I think that something else was worshipping Christ."

Hazail said, "That is why they wanted to kill the Christians."

"Exactly, Hazail."

Thomas Wayne sighed, "There's no way we can convince the world to worship Christ that fast. They've had two thousand years, and many haven't been saved."

Aaliyah replied, "I realize that. What I was thinking is that when we fight them, if our focus is on Christ, we may stand a better chance of winning. If God is with us, then who can be against us?" Aailyah danced, Momma said that." She smiled and high fived Thomas Wayne.

Thomas Wayne smiled but then his focus moved to Hazail. He pondered Aailyah's words. It made sense to the humans, but he feared for Hazail and General Garima, who didn't grow up in church learning about Christ. "I understand and for all we know, that could have been the reason I was successful against Vayu. My issue is we have two Assyrians on our team who didn't grow up the way we did. What about them?"

Aaliyah looked at General Garima and Hazail. "We can convert them."

General Garima replied, "That's not going to happen. I know I was impressed with the place where we found the book, but I am not ready to believe in a God I can't see."

GERALD C. ANDERSON, SR.

Aaliyah touched her shoulder, "We will pray for you."

Hazail responded, "I am ready." Thomas Wayne looked at her. "I have been thinking of nothing else while you were gone. I read your Bible, and I believe in Christ."

Carmichael moved closer to her, "Do you believe Christ died for your sins?"

"Yes."

"Do you believe He is the son of God?"

"Yes."

"Do you accept him as your Lord and Savior?"

"Yes."

"Then your belief has saved your soul! Welcome to the body of Christ."

Aaliyah hugged her, "Welcome, my sister."

"Thank you."

Thomas Wayne hugged her. "I am so happy for you, sweetheart. May we be together for all eternity."

"Yes, my love."

General Garima said, "Now can we go take out that ship?" She moved to the front of the shuttle and sat in the pilot's seat.

"I'd better join her." Hazail moved to the navigator's seat.

Carmichael said, "I need to get back to the people. I believe you and your crew can handle this. Aaliyah, will you be coming with me or going with them?"

Aaliyah looked at Thomas Wayne. He suspected by the look what the answer would be. "Thomas Wayne, my place is here. We nearly lost everyone. I need to be here to help the people."

"I understand." Carmichael and Aaliyah left the shuttle. General Garima guided the shuttle in the air and headed toward the ship in Colorado. "What kind of weaponry does this shuttle have?"

General Garima answered, "Standard lasers and bombs, why do you ask?"

"Just in case we need them to destroy the ship." Thomas Wayne sat in the back of the shuttle for the quick trip to Colorado. "Do we have anyway to tap into the radio system to see what's going on in the world?"

Hazail answered, "Let me try."

Static piped into the shuttle while Hazail tried to find a station to tune to. Finally, she reached one. "This is Albert Jimerson from KZTA Radio. We're receiving reports from around the world of uprisings against the heroes. Footage of the battle between Thomas Wayne and Vayu inspired others to fight back. The heroes are killing people, but most will not give in to them. There are churches who are leading thousands in prayer for the world." Thomas Wayne heard some papers shuffling. "We just received a report that the heroes are headed back to Colorado, where their ship is located. It is believed they are leaving our planet."

Thomas Wayne said, "Did you hear that?" They nodded. "We may not need to destroy the ship now."

General Garima replied, "What about the people out there in the universe that they will deceive? Should we just be selfish and not stop them here?"

"You have a point. Let's take it out." The shuttle made its approach toward the ship. The heroes made it there just before them. They were embarking on the ship. General Garima halted the shuttle.

General Garima asked, "What should we do?"

"Fire!" General Garima fired the laser at the ship. The heroes jumped in the lasers path, preventing it from hitting the ship. "Well, it looks like we have the right idea."

"What can we do?"

"Well General, I guess this is where I don the bracelet again."

"No, my love! There are three of them this time."

"I have to move them away from the ship. Pray for me." The look on her face hurt Thomas Wayne, but he needed to do this, and he was the only one who could. *God be with me.* The shuttle moved closer to the ground and Thomas Wayne placed the bracelet on his wrist. He got out of the shuttle and the shuttle returned to the air. "Okay, who wants to die first?"

Adonis said, "You are brave for a Terran, but today the only one who dies is you."

Vayu yelled, "Adonis!"

Cain came down from the sky like a bullet, plummeting Adonis to the ground. The battle ensued between them. Tutu and Vayu stood poised to fight Thomas Wayne. Tutu pushed Vayu back. Thomas Wayne noticed Vayu was without a bracelet. *I guess they don't have replacements. Good for me.*

Tutu placed his hand on his temple and stepped forward, sending a dream toward Thomas Wayne. However, Thomas Wayne was unaffected by it. Vayu said, "Fool, he has my bracelet. That won't work on him."

"Then I will kill him with my bare hands."

Thomas Wayne locked arms with Tutu, their muscles coiling and straining. With a surge of newfound strength, Thomas Wayne forced Tutu to the ground, then unleashed a thunderous blow to Tutu's face. Tutu's eyes widened in shock. A grim smile touched Thomas Wayne's lips; the bracelet pulsed on his wrist, giving him the decisive advantage he needed.

Thomas Wayne aimed another right, but Tutu, recovering quickly, blocked it. Tutu countered with a gut-wrenching blow to the stomach, followed by a vicious uppercut to the chin. The impact sent Thomas Wayne soaring ten feet into the air. He landed twenty yards away, skidding across the dirt, but scrambled to his feet just as Tutu charged. They collided again, locking arms. This time, Tutu overpowered him, flinging Thomas Wayne face-first into the ground.

"Now I will kill you, Terran. You have no place among the gods," Tutu snarled, wrapping his stone-like arms around Thomas Wayne's neck. Air escaped Thomas Wayne's lungs, and he felt the cold tendrils of death reaching for him. "Father, I accept my fate, but do not let those who worship you suffer any longer under these false gods!"

Tutu threw his head back and laughed, a booming, cruel sound. He glanced at Vayu. "He cries for his daddy!"

Suddenly, a blinding lightning bolt from the Heavens struck the ground between them, throwing Thomas Wayne in one direction and Tutu in another. Thomas Wayne scrambled to his feet, shaken but unharmed. Tutu, however, remained sprawled on the ground, his body flickering, then transforming back into his original, less imposing form. Vayu rushed to Tutu's side and desperately tried to remove the bracelet from his wrist. She screamed, a sound of frustration and pain, and flung the bracelet to the ground.

With a snarl, Vayu charged at Thomas Wayne. She aimed a strike, but he blocked it with a newfound confidence, a certainty in his movements he hadn't realized he possessed. Again and again, she attacked, but each blow was parried with surprising ease. Finally, Thomas Wayne seized her, lifted her effortlessly, and slammed her to the ground. She lay unconscious at his feet. Thomas Wayne looked up to see Cain and Adonis still locked in their brutal struggle.

The blows between Adonis and Cain were thunderous, each god vying for dominance. In the background, military vehicles arrived, but they remained static, seemingly under orders to stand down while the false gods battled. Hazail joined Thomas Wayne, a troubled expression on her face. "I don't know who to root for, sweetheart."

"Cain must have had a change of heart, my love," Thomas replied, his gaze fixed on the brutal fight. "Why else would he be fighting his own kind?"

Hazail shook her head. "That's true, but once Adonis is dead, Cain will turn on us."

"Then I must be prepared to fight him, too."

Hazail's eyes scanned the clear sky. "Where did that lightning bolt come from earlier? The sky's so blue, no clouds at all."

"I can only believe it came from God," Thomas Wayne answered, a tremor in his voice. "I thought I was dead for sure."

Adonis, meanwhile, had Cain by the throat, his grip tight. Cain struggled, pushing at Adonis's hand, a difficult battle for both powerful figures. Finally, Cain slipped behind Adonis, attempting to lock in a choke hold. But Adonis dropped to the ground, fluidly escaping the hold. Both gods sprang back to their feet, circling each other, their eyes never breaking contact. They locked arms again, but Cain swiftly kneed Adonis in the stomach, then jumped behind him once more. In one quick, brutal move, he snapped Adonis' neck.

Adonis' body went limp, collapsing to the ground. Cain looked down at his fallen adversary. "That was for my love, Serena. May your soul stay in the underworld forever."

Cain slowly raised his eyes, sweeping them over the army waiting on the sideline. Then, his gaze settled on Thomas Wayne. Thomas Wayne stood firm, poised and ready for what would be his third confrontation with a god. He felt no fear of Cain. "Go back to the ship, sweetheart," he told Hazail, his voice low but resolute.

"Thomas Wayne…"

"Go, sweetheart."

"No. If you die, so do I."

Cain stopped short of Thomas Wayne and Hazail. "I am no longer your enemy, Thomas Wayne Walker. You have impressed me. I never believed a Terran would equal us, but you have taught me well. Terrans are no longer a race of people who want to be ruled by false gods. You have your one true God." Thomas Wayne nodded. "I am the last of my people. We have either died on the battlefield or we have ceased to exist. Now, it is time for me to cease to exist."

"What does that mean?"

"We are immortals and can only be killed by another immortal or we can choose to cease to exist, meaning we evolve into another realm of existence. Some say that the realm doesn't exist; others say it is a better place for us. We have our own mythology that we have struggled with. Now, I will see which one was right."

"I see. Is there no other way?"

"No, I am alone now. We were once a race of billions spread out over the young universe. Now most planets have evolved and no longer want to be ruled by a race pretending to be something it is not. My time has come to end my existence."

"Vayu is still alive."

"I will take her with me. She cannot be allowed to stay here." He looked at the ship. "I cannot allow the ship to stay here either. I must destroy it and the bracelets."

"Why is that?"

"Your race may be one that loves your one true God, but not all of you are there. Some of you will attempt to recreate the technology behind the ship, the bracelets, and the relays. I have destroyed all of the relays. Now, the ship and the bracelets must be destroyed." He reached out his hand for Thomas Wayne's bracelet. Thomas Wayne removed the bracelet and handed it to Cain.

"The military will try to stop you from destroying the ship."

"I will keep them at bay. You have the General fire a laser blast at the ship. That will destroy it and the bracelets. When I cease to exist, everything I am touching, including my bracelet and Vayu, will come with me."

"I understand."

Cain reached out his hand. Thomas Wayne shook hands with him. "It has been an honor learning about you and this planet, Thomas Wayne Walker. You are a true leader; make this world a better place."

"I will."

Cain turned and headed toward the military. Thomas Wayne and Hazail returned to the ship. "General, Cain will distract the military. Fire at the ship."

"Roger that."

"Tell me you're not like us now." He laughed. General Garima waited until Cain held the military's attention, then she fired. The ship went up in flames. She fired two more blasts to ensure it was completely destroyed. The military moved away, and Cain returned. He destroyed the bodies of Tutu and Adonis. He lifted Vayu off the ground. She woke and Cain spoke to her. The two of them held hands. Thomas Wayne watched as their physical form changed from human to the serpent like creature they truly were. Then the physical form dissipated into the air until they were no longer. "That's the end of everything."

General Garima said, "Not everything."

"What do you mean?"

"I need to get rid of this ship."

Hazail asked, "How will you do that, General?"

"This ship can fly long distances. I will return to Assyria in it." Hazail and Thomas Wayne looked at her. "The two of you can disembark, and I will head to Assyria."

"You planned this all along."

"I did. King Malka must pay for his part in all of this."

Hazail asked, "Will you return?"

"Unfortunately, it will be a one-way trip. I don't believe the King will go quietly. Therefore, I doubt I will return." Hazail hugged her. "We are warriors. Why are you hugging me?"

"You are a warrior. I am a Terran woman who has learned that God is real, and this world is now my home. Go well and go with the real God."

Thomas Wayne nodded at General Garima. "Be safe, General—Brula."

"I will Thomas Wayne."

Thomas Wayne and Hazail left the shuttle, and they watched it head to the sky. The shuttle got smaller and smaller until it could not be seen any longer.

An Air Force General stood in front of Thomas Wayne. "I'm General Huffington."

"General."

"You destroyed the ship and let that shuttle get away. I should arrest you for that."

"General, we both know that if that ship or any of the technology would have fallen into the hands of any country, we would destroy ourselves. Arrest me if you will, but remember, I am the man the world knows fought gods and won. You wouldn't be a very popular man." The General popped his lips, turned, and walked away. Thomas Wayne took Hazail's hand. and they walked away. "I'm so tired of walking, baby." She laughed.

32 – Assyria Prime

After the long trip to Assyria Prime, General Garima laid down in the back of the shuttle. The speed of the shuttle was considerably slower than their mothership, so the trip took her weeks. When night came, she planned to get up and enter the palace. As soon as she laid down, sleep overtook her mind and body.

General Garima didn't know how long she was asleep, but it was night outside. She parked the shuttle on the North side of the capital city so the hike to the palace would not be far. Most of the people who lived in that area were asleep.

She made her way down the side street, knowing the main street would be patrolled by the King's guard. General Garima suspected they would not expect her to return to the planet since the motherships were destroyed. She hoped the King didn't realize the experimental shuttle survived. As she approached the street, she eased onto the location of the secret entrance to the palace. She stepped through the fence and moved to the door. Only a few knew of the secret entrance. Most used it to slip their concubines into and out of the palace.

Once inside, she heard voices nearby. She suspected they were the guards on duty. The break room was near the secret entrance. She eased by their location and headed down the hall. She needed to go two floors up to the main floor, where the throne room and bed chambers were located. At this time, the King would sit on his throne reviewing the business that occurred the previous day. In a few moments, he would head to his bed chamber, which was located down the hall from the throne room.

The guards were very few at this hour. She easily got past them and slipped inside the bed chamber. She would wait for him to come inside and settle her debt.

General Garima felt something speak to her. She didn't know what it was, but the voice comforted her. It made her feel at ease about her mission. *Are you Thomas Wayne's God speaking to me?* She brushed the thought off. *It would not be Christ. I am not worthy of a true God to speak to me.*

It wasn't long before the doors to the bed chamber opened, and King Malka walked in. "I know you're here, sweetheart. You might as well come out."

Is he talking to me? Was someone else in here when I came in?

My dear Brula, come out and let's have a talk. It was wonderful to hear from the guards that you returned. I must say, I was amazed that you survived the onslaught by the gods. I was even happier to hear that the Terrans killed the gods, and we no longer have to worry about them. Now we can conquer the universe and there's no one to stand in our way. Rule with me, Brula.

Never! I am a child of Christ now. General Garima stepped out of her hiding spot. The guards approached her, but King Malka stopped them. "You are a coward, and I will have my revenge."

"What about Baaz's family and their revenge? We know you killed him."

"You killed Ishaia, and you will pay. If I am to pay for Baaz, so be it."

King Malka laughed, "Forever the hero." He motioned to the guards. "Arrest her!" General Garima had one chance for her revenge. She needed to spring forth and cut his throat, but the laser may cut her down before she tried. She looked at the guards, and they were not moving. King Malka ordered again, "I said arrest her and throw her in the jail for execution!"

The guards still did not move. Instead, they looked at her for orders. *Christ does exist.* "Well, it seems your treachery hasn't gone unnoticed by the warriors here." She looked at the guards, "Are you with me?"

Both guards kneeled and said, "Yes, Queen Garima."

Queen Garima felt emotions inside. She came back seeking revenge, but she's getting a kingdom. "Arrest him and throw him in prison. Bring Baaz's family representatives to me."

"Yes, my Queen."

The guards removed King Malka screaming and left Queen Garima in the bed chamber snickering at the sudden change. A young maiden joined her. Queen Garima asked, "What happened here while I was gone?"

The maiden said, "There was a quiet uprising. Many of us found out about the deal King Malka made with the gods. We said we would rather fight and die than to kill for others. That is not the way of the warrior. We hoped you would return to take your place on the throne."

"But I am not of the royal bloodline."

"That was done away with. Some ways of the Terrans have traveled here. After losing many of our brothers and sisters in a senseless war, we realized a better way. The way of the Terrans. It may not be great, but it is better to follow Jesus Christ."

Queen Garima didn't know what to say. She resisted Christ's way, but He followed her back to Assyria, protected her and gave her the entire kingdom of Assyria. She said, "There will be an installation ceremony tomorrow. In that ceremony, I will proclaim the way of Christ is our way. But, if there are those who do not choose Christ, they are not to be harmed. Coming to Christ must be a choice."

"Yes, my Queen."

"Also, are there any other ships left in the fleet?"

"Yes, there are several ships waiting. Shall I tell them to prepare one?"

"Yes, I'm traveling back to Earth… Terra Prime. There are some friends back there that must know what has happened here."

"Yes, my Queen. I will make the arrangements."

The maiden left. Queen Garima looked out the large window. She smiled. *After I have resisted You so much, You have given me all of this. How can I repay You?* She felt that same voice again saying, 'your debt has already been paid.'

33 – Terra Prime – The Return

Thomas Wayne played with Hazail in the garden of their new home. They settled in Wiamuma, Florida, a small town that suffered minor damage during the war. Thomas Wayne grew tired of the cold weather and wanted to spend his days in the warmth of Florida. The house was abandoned and required little repair. He fixed up the room that would eventually be the room for his child when she arrived. "Who would have thought you would be the gardener in the family? Amazing job, sweetheart."

"It was actually one of my hobbies on Assyria. When I got a break from training, I would spend hours in the garden. I love the smell of the flowers. Some of them are the same as the ones here on Earth."

Aaliyah walked from the front of the house with Carmichael. "Hey, Walker family! How are you guys?"

Thomas Wayne laughed, "Well let's see, we're not being bombed, lasered, don't have false gods fighting us and we're through searching for a book that no one but me can touch. I think we're doing just fine. You?"

Everyone laughed. Aaliyah responded, "Well, me and my hubby are doing great as well."

Carmichael added, "Yeah, the best decision I ever made was to marry this young woman."

Aaliyah squeezed his shoulder, "You better know it."

The all too familiar sound of a ship interrupted their conversation. Thomas Wayne said, "It can't be. Not again!"

Aaliyah shouted, "Carmichael, grab the weapons out of the car! Thomas Wayne, where are your weapons?"

"They're in the garage."

"I'll grab them. You look out for Hazail."

"I can take care of myself, my love."

"Sweetheart, you are five months pregnant. I need to get you to a safe place." Everyone in the neighborhood was running for shelter.

The voice came over the sound system, "It is good to see you again, Thomas Wayne Walker and Hazail. Hazail your belly is growing. I am so proud of you both."

Thomas Wayne smiled and looked at Hazail. Aaliyah and Carmichael rounded the corner with the weapons. "Aaliyah, we won't be needing those." He looked up toward the ship, "General, come on down."

"I am on my way, Thomas Wayne."

A small shuttle left the ship and landed in Thomas Wayne's backyard. Before long, Queen Garima exited with a big smile. Thomas Wayne said, "Would you look at that? A big smile on your face. I knew you could do it!" Queen Garima hugged Thomas Wayne and the others. "A hug too. Oh my goodness, she's changed y'all."

Hazail said, "General, that is a royal robe you are wearing."

"That is true Hazail. When I returned to Assyria, I made my way into the palace to get my revenge on King Malka, but what I didn't know was that there had been a quiet uprising on Assyria. He caught me laying a trap for him in his bed chamber and ordered the guards to arrest me. They refused. Instead, they followed my orders to arrest him." She smiled, "No Thomas Wayne, I did not kill him. They anointed me Queen of Assyria and I installed the religion of Jesus Christ as the way for our world."

Thomas Wayne shouted, "Hallelujah! You're a saved woman."

"Not yet. I need Carmichael to ask me the questions he asked Hazail."

"It would be my pleasure." Carmichael stepped to Queen Garima. "Do you believe in Jesus Christ?"

"I do."

"Do you accept him as your Lord and Savior?"

"I do."

"And do you believe Jesus is the son of God?"

"I do."

"Like Thomas Wayne said, 'Hallelujah!' You are a saved woman!"

"Thank you, Carmichael. I offer you and any Assyrian the opportunity to join your people on Assyrian Prime. We are now people of Christ, but we need teachers to help us. What do you say?"

"Well, I would have to ask my…"

"Yes! We'll go."

Everyone laughed but Thomas Wayne. "Aaliyah, you can't go there. I… I'll miss you."

"Thomas Wayne, this new life of ours requires a lot of change and spreading the word of God to a new world, well I can't pass on that. Besides, I want to ride the mothership!"

Thomas Wayne and the group laughed. After all he went through over the last year, everything worked out. Many people lost their lives in the struggle, but today millions more on two worlds are free and worshipping Jesus. *Father, I know you will protect and watch over my baby sister as she travels to another world to spread Your word. We thank you for all that you have done, are doing, and will do in the future. In your amazing son Jesus' name… Amen.*

Author Bio

Gerald C. Anderson, Sr., a native of Florida, draws upon a rich tapestry of life experiences in his writing. His formative years in the Belmont Heights neighborhood, coupled with a graduation from King high school, laid the foundation for a life of service and exploration.

Following his graduation, Anderson embarked on a distinguished career in the United States Air Force, a journey that took him across continents, from California to Korea. These diverse postings instilled in him a profound understanding of the human condition, a theme that resonates throughout his work.

After retiring from the Air Force, Anderson began his pursuit of knowledge. He earned a Bachelor of Science in Computer Information Systems followed by a Master of Administration in Criminal Justice Administration.

A pivotal moment in Anderson's life came in 1992 when he embraced his faith, dedicating his life to Jesus Christ. This spiritual journey informs his perspective and imbues his writing with a sense of purpose.

Anderson is a devoted husband and father. He is married to Vanessa Anderson and continues to craft stories that reflect the complexities of life, faith, and the enduring power of the human spirit.

Thank You!

I would like to take this opportunity to thank you for reading my novel. "Not So Heroes" was written to entertain my fanbase. I hope I carried out this goal, and you have enjoyed the story and maybe learned something from it.

Please consider reading my earlier novels, novellas and short stories listed at the front of this novel and in my bio.

Your opinion matters! If you enjoyed this novel, please go to Amazon and write a review. Reviews help move novels, novellas, and short stories on Amazon so that other potential readers can find it.

Thank you so much and always have a blessed day!

Gerald C. Anderson, Sr.
Christian Fiction Author
www.geraldcandersonsr.com
Facebook: @geraldcandersonsr
Twitter: @geraldcanderson
Instagram: @geraldcandersonsr
Associate Member, The Authors Guild
Member, Maryland Writers Association

www.ingramcontent.com/pod-product-compliance
Lightning Source LLC
Chambersburg PA
CBHW032142010726
47494CB00002B/326